"Trail of Murder a provocative Sierra Nevada Tale of Fiction."

—*Tahoe World*

"Locals will dig into *Sierra Nevada Trail of Murder,* as will dog lovers and anybody who enjoys a solid whodunit tale."

—*Tahoe Daily Tribune*

"In her sophomore outing, Quashnick ups the ante by nailing another good storyline while adding depth to her main characters."

—*Tahoe Mountain News*

"Quashnick gives us a sweet second date in *River of Lies.*"

—*Tahoe Daily Tribune*

"[*Dangerous Developments*] is an action-packed story . . . filled with suspense and non-stop surprises."

—*Tahoe Daily Tribune*

"[Quashnick's] sense of timing and clever plotting keep one reading, hungry to know what happens next."

—*Tahoe Mountain News*

Also by Jennifer Quashnick:

Sierra Nevada Trail of Murder

Sierra Nevada River of Lies

Sierra Nevada Dangerous Developments

Sierra Nevada Burning Revenge

JENNIFER QUASHNICK

South Lake Tahoe, CA
mountaingirlmysteries.com

ISBN: 978-0-9906750-7-5

Library of Congress Control Number: 2019917351
Cover: Jennifer Quashnick
Copy Editor: Mary Cook

Orders, inquiries, and correspondence should be addressed to:

Mountaingirl Mysteries
PO Box 550145
South Lake Tahoe, CA 96155
mountaingirl@mountaingirlmysteries.com
mountaingirlmysteries.com

Don't miss the first three adventures of the series!

Sierra Nevada Trail of Murder:

When Rachel Winters looked into the man's lifeless eyes, little did she know that her dog's discovery would change their lives forever.

On the run from a killer, Rachel, Bella, and Private Investigator Luke Reed must unravel a deep-rooted environmental conspiracy stretching from Lake Tahoe, California, to Denver, Colorado.

Sierra Nevada River of Lies:

A gruesome murder, a missing professor, and an attempted carjacking. Or was it?

An offer to help a friend leaves Rachel Winters in the killer's sights. As Luke Reed's family ties threaten them both, Rachel, Bella, and Luke become entangled in a dangerous scheme spanning across Northern California, from Susanville to Mammoth Lakes.

Sierra Nevada Dangerous Developments:

Kristina and Derek have disappeared, and the only clue left behind is a message written in blood.

Could their fates be tied to political maneuvering for major development projects in the West and North Shore areas of Lake Tahoe, or something else equally as sinister?

Still recovering from a skiing accident, Rachel must race against the clock to save her loved ones.

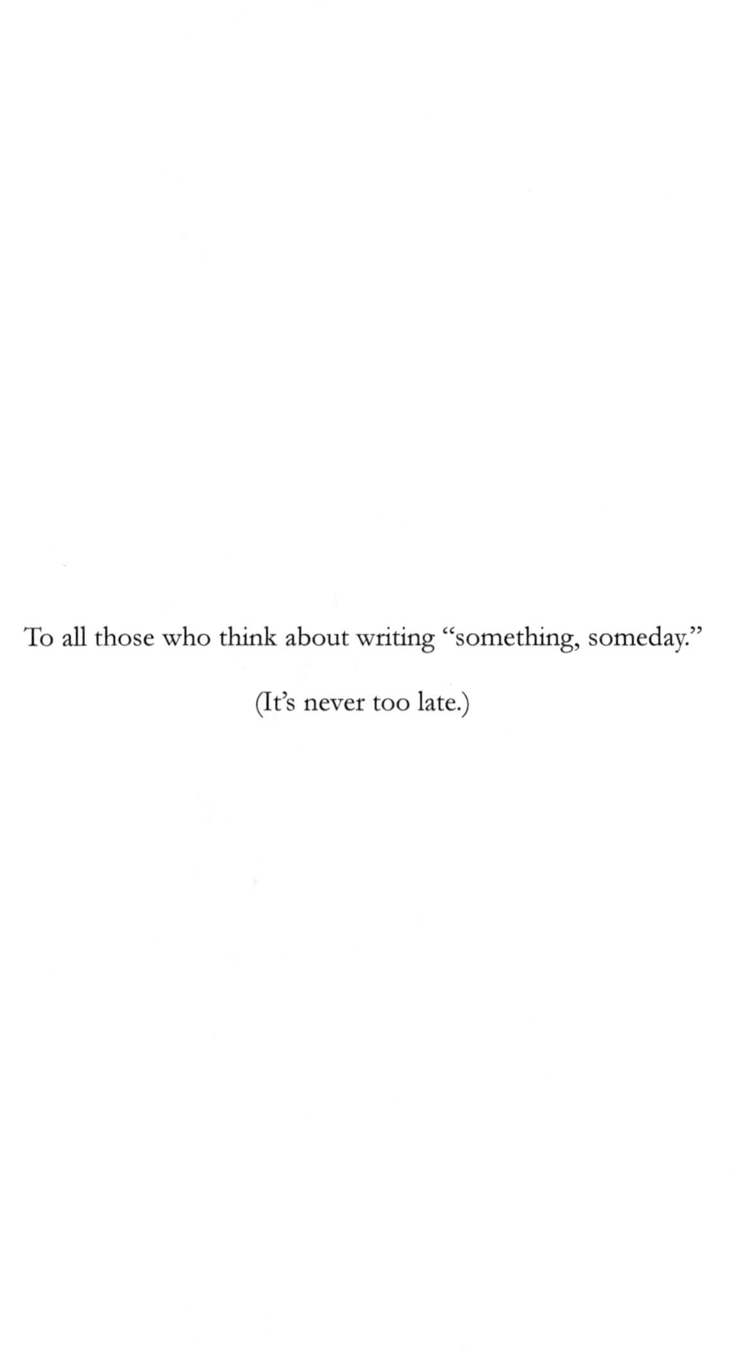

To all those who think about writing "something, someday."

(It's never too late.)

*When one tugs at a single thing in nature, he finds it attached
to the rest of the world.*

—John Muir

Prologue

The smoke alarm screamed overhead. Raging flames danced in front of Lacey's eyes. She swiped at the tears running down her cheeks as she stared out the window, horrified at the embers raining down around the cabin.

"Oh my God. Oh my God."

Who was talking?

She heard it again.

"Oh my God." Only then did she realize the words were coming from her own lips.

Calm down, she told herself. *You're fifteen years old; you can get yourself out of a burning house.* Lacey nodded, as if confirming her own thought.

Another quick glance through the window revealed the growing fire outside, consuming the pine trees in its path. Her grandfather's cabin was the next thing in that very same path. Embers were already igniting the front porch below her and probably the house's walls. The old Tahoe-style woodsy architecture that gave it a warm, rustic feel now turned it into a dangerous tinderbox.

Move!

Lacey looked back at the bed she'd been napping in. She longed for this all to be nothing more than a very bad dream. But it wasn't. She grabbed the robe lying at the foot of the bed and tossed it over her T-shirt and shorts as she ran out of the bedroom. The stone floor felt cool on her bare feet, even as sweat dripped from her brow. Time slowed as she dashed down the stairs, almost slipping twice in her haste. Finally, there it was; the stained glass image of perfectly shaped green pine trees and the aquamarine color of Cascade Lake. She always thought the stained glass window was odd; the actual Cascade Lake wasn't far from the front door itself. *Why not just have regular glass so you could look outside at the real thing?*

Something heavy crashed near the front windows, jolting her. Lacey forced herself not to look. She reached for the doorknob instead and paused. They'd watched several fire safety videos in school. Sometimes doorknobs could be hot. Would it heat up this quickly? Ominous orange-red flames as tall as the century-old pine trees danced outside. She couldn't tell how far away the fire was. Three feet or thirty feet—she didn't know. Either way, she had to get out.

Lacey's gaze moved to the side of the door where she'd left her slip-on shoes. She jammed her feet inside, bunched her robe up in her hand, and turned toward the front door, grabbing the knob with the material and twisting. She whipped the door open and burst outside, halting herself when she saw the flames seemingly all around her, devouring the old shed at the edge of the property. She looked to her right; fire had not yet ignited everything on that side. Lacey jumped off the porch and dashed toward it, her arms barely registering the painful sensation of the heat on her skin as she ran for her life.

"Lacey!" a man called out to her. Following the voice, she saw the outline of a car at the end of the driveway. The door was flung open, and someone jumped out and ran toward her. Lacey almost collapsed in relief.

Chapter One

Three months later

Rachel couldn't believe she'd let her friends talk her into doing this as she looked across the table at her dinner date—"Richard, but my friends call me Rick"—her first date since her breakup with Luke over a year ago. Well, that was not entirely true. Last week had been the actual first date since Luke, but when she'd shown up to meet the man, there was a full dinner plate already waiting on her side of the table. When she asked about it, he replied matter-of-factly, "A man should always determine what a woman eats." When she realized it wasn't a joke, she'd immediately bowed out.

"I'm embarrassed to admit this, but it's my first date since the divorce," Rick said and then sipped from the strange green concoction he'd asked the bartender to tailor blend for him.

"Well, it's my first date since my last breakup over a year ago, so there you have it." She lifted her wineglass and made as if to clink it against his for a toast. "To newbies on the thirty-somethings dating scene."

He finally picked up his own glass and tapped it against hers, an unreadable look in his eyes.

Rachel tipped her glass to her lips as she admired his Native American features and chocolate eyes. The mixture of sweet and tart merlot felt smooth as it went down.

"You don't have kids though, right?" he asked in what sounded to Rachel like an accusation more than a question. *You're overanalyzing,* she thought to herself as she watched him set down his drink.

"Only the canine variet—"

"Mine, it's just . . . they're teenage boys," he interjected as though she hadn't responded. "They're going through so much because their mother cheated on me. They've really needed me. I guess it's why I waited so long to get back out there." He looked down at his plate and carefully avoided eye contact. "Because I wanted to be available for them. Especially my oldest. He started acting out last summer. It was freaking me out, I tell you. I didn't know what to do."

Rachel sympathized. "I'm sorry to hear it. Were you able to—"

"I mean, how can a mother do that? Break up her family like that?" He fisted his drink and took another deep swallow.

"It sounds like you're doing what you can for your—"

"I'm so tired. It's exhausting being a parent, let alone when the other parent does something like that." He rubbed his hands down his face. "I thought she loved me."

She waited, unsure whether he would continue and getting tired of being talked over. Sounds of muted conservation and music in the background flooded her senses as the silence stretched at their table. Rachel took it as a cue that she was indeed supposed to respond.

"I'm sorry to hear it. How old are your—"

"I've been working so hard to put food on our table with just one income now. I could really use a break, I tell ya."

"I'm sure you have. Do you have any vacation pl—"

"And my job is hard. My muscles are so tight." He moved his head from side to side, stretching his neck as if to accentuate his point. "I could really use a massage, but I need to pay for the kids' sports uniforms next week."

Rachel's empathy waned with each interruption. *Try not to judge; this is his first date since it happened after all.* "What sport?"

He paused like he was caught off guard by her question. "Oh, uh, basketball." Then he reached behind his neck, rubbing as he tilted his head back. "This time of year is even more difficult. High point of the fire season and all. I'm so worn down."

Rachel had the impression his solo conversation could go on for a while. It was a heavy subject for the beginning of their first date— presuming it was the truth. She'd started to get the feeling that he was trying to garner her sympathy, and perhaps more. *Time to attempt a subject change.*

"Were you on shift when that fire near Cascade Lake burned a few months ago?" Rachel hoped for a more stimulating and less emotional conversation, preferably one where she could complete a full sentence. Asking a firefighter about a recent fire seemed to be a safe bet. Plus, she recently contracted with a new client to assist with the planning for a forestry project in that area and was mildly curious. Rick's initial silence made Rachel start to wonder if he was going to answer. She had the sense he was upset that she hadn't allowed him to continue his own story and was debating whether to steer back to it. Finally, he answered.

"I sure was. Man, that was heartbreaking, although it could have been worse." He shook his head.

"Crazy the senator's granddaughter almost died."

"Yep, poor girl. Lacey, if I recall her name correctly. They sure have done a good job of keeping her out of the media."

"Did they ever determine how it started?" Rachel hadn't seen the official cause listed in any of the reports. "Was it an old campfire or cigarette or something?" She remembered it had been a windy and dry day, with meteorologists spreading the word of a "Red Flag Warning" when weather was hot and windy with very low humidity—conditions ripe for a fire to spread large, fast, and wide. The day had been reminiscent of the infamous day in June 2007 when the well-known Angora Fire, ignited by an abandoned campfire, spread rapidly, burning hundreds of homes on the outskirts of South Lake Tahoe. However, Mother Nature minimized the damage by bringing in rain showers overnight, helping firefighters get control of the fire early on.

"You know," he said as he leaned in conspiratorially, his cologne overpowering her senses, "the official cause is listed as a suspected abandoned campfire. But personally, I think it was arson."

Cologne or no, Rachel's interest piqued. She urged him on. "What makes you say that?"

"I was part of the postfire crew, and I know the area very well; I've spent my whole life playing around out there. Of all the spots people have set up camps over the years, I've never seen anyone camping or even hiking in the area where it started. The location and wind direction couldn't have been set up any better to head straight for the senator's place. I'm not an arson investigator, but it all seemed staged to me. Like someone wanted to make it look like an abandoned campfire. Just my own two cents." He reclined back with both hands raised in front of his chest as if he were surrendering to her.

"That's interesting. I'm surprised no one else reported anything suspicious."

"I have no idea if anyone else feels the way I do. When I mentioned it to one of my superiors, I was told it wasn't true and to never suggest it to anyone. In fact, not sure why I'm telling you," he mumbled, then reached for his beverage.

Rachel wasn't sure how to take his last comment. A slight pang of guilt coursed through her for not mentioning her contract for work in the area, even if her part of the project had nothing to do with the investigation into how the fire started. Realizing he wasn't going to continue, she decided to break the silence. "No worries. I'll be discreet. But it's curious that arson investigators wouldn't have noticed something out of the ordinary."

"Maybe they didn't because they didn't grow up around here. Or maybe they did but were advised to keep their mouths shut. Like me." He took another sip. Rachel noticed his glass—the second drink of the night—was almost empty. Maybe that's why he was telling her things he probably wouldn't otherwise share with a stranger.

As though he read her mind, he said, "I need to shut up now." This time he slurred; it was so subtle she may not have noticed had she not been expecting it. His drinks must have been extremely strong.

Rachel didn't know what to say next but was saved from having to worry about it when the waiter arrived with their dinner plates. She already knew there would be no date number two. But her stomach rumbled when the wonderful scent of the spicy barbecue sauce invaded her senses, and she decided even if he resumed his self-focused lamenting, it was a worthy sacrifice because these ribs were too good to reheat later.

~

Luke, glad to be free of his office, jumped on his bicycle to head home. He loved his work as a private investigator. Most of the time. But he also looked forward to these warm autumn Tahoe nights. Once the snow had melted last spring, filling up his evenings with long rides on the mountain trails around Fallen Leaf Lake or through the burn area below Angora Ridge had been the only way he could tire out his body in hopes of sleeping and escape the turmoil he was feeling inside. For a little while. As soon as he got home, which was as late as possible, he'd shower, eat, and attempt to watch something on Netflix but would find himself still thinking about Rachel. Another night of tossing and turning would ensue, and the whole cycle would repeat the next day. Enduring that routine for far too long, he decided he needed some new hobbies.

Luke signed up for a woodworking class at the local community college and found he really enjoyed it. His garage was now filled with everything but his Subaru: a large circular saw and table, numerous sheets of plywood, cans of stain, an array of new tools, and, in one corner, three cabinets he'd constructed on his own. The condition of each progressively improved over the one before it; those first few were clearly just "practice," so much so that he was embarrassed to even consider donating them to a thrift store. So there they sat, collecting dust. Cabinet number four had been donation-worthy, number five was good enough to use in his spare room, and number six sat next to his sofa. He recently embarked on his next mission: a dresser of drawers.

"If Rachel could see me now . . . ," he said to himself as he carefully positioned the drawer track before screwing it into place. Of course, he wouldn't want her to. Not yet. Because he was a coward when it came to that other little problem he'd planned to work on during their separation. Back when he'd hoped the breakup was temporary and his resolve to stop taking prescription painkillers would be enough for him to, well, stop taking them. He'd tried twice, both times failing within a day, which only made him feel worse about himself. *She's better off without me.* Yet what did it mean when after being apart for more time than they were together, his feelings for her remained so strong?

Luke shook his head as if the physical act could toss out his thoughts of Rachel. Finishing his installation of the rollers, he turned the drawer back over and positioned it to slide inside the middle slot on the dresser. It slid smoothly until it was about halfway in before it began to tighten as though the dimensions weren't lined up properly on the front half of the drawer.

"Great," Luke said as he pulled it back out and began examining the construction. It took a few view angles before he could identify the problem: the wood was warped. How had he not seen it before? Now he'd have to disassemble several edges to fit a new piece. He looked up at the clock: 8:42 p.m. He'd been at this for hours and forgot to eat dinner. *Again.* Luke set his tools down and looked around the room. Everything else could wait until tomorrow, so he opened the door and switched off the light as he stepped outside into the crisp air. Someday, maybe he could build a walkway to connect his garage directly to his house. He thought of the crooked drawer and smirked. Such a project may have to wait awhile; best to stick to furniture for now, he thought.

As he turned to close the door, a rustling sound cut through the otherwise quiet night. Luke turned back around, peering in the direction he thought it had come from. The only light came from a sliver of a moon overhead. Was there a movement at the base of those two old Jeffrey pines across the street? Luke stared, waiting for his eyes to adjust to the darkness. He waited for what felt like a few long minutes, but still nothing stirred.

"Stop being paranoid," he reminded himself under his breath. Tahoe neighborhoods were filled with wildlife. He shook his head as he walked toward his house.

Chapter Two

"You owe me," Mike stated matter-of-factly, his gruff voice so loud in her ear she had to hit the volume button. She did owe him, but that didn't mean Monica was happy about it.

"I'm very aware of that fact," she grudgingly admitted. The screeching sound of sliding metal doors echoed in the background of the phone line like it was timed perfectly to emphasize his point. Mike had been sent to prison about two years ago; he knew enough to send Monica there too, but he had kept his mouth shut. She doubted it was out of any kind of loyalty; it was more likely that he simply saw an opportunity to have her own him a favor, and he'd sure called in a big one. Monica pulled her glasses off her nose and let them fall. A beaded neck strap kept them suspended on her chest.

"Good to hear you remember," Mike grunted.

Monica hadn't seen him since around the time he was arrested two years ago, but she could still recall how he looked. His dark hair barely sprinkled with grays and hazel-colored eyes inspired immediate ease in strangers—something he'd used to his own advantage on many occasions. She had almost forgotten just how much she disliked dealing with this man. "So now what?"

"You do what I asked, and I'll call you next week."

Monica heard more background noise, this time, the distant voices of other prisoners. He must be using the phone for inmates instead of one of the disposables he seemed to have no trouble obtaining, she thought. At least if the prison tried to trace his call, she, too, was using a burner phone. "All right, but after this one favor, we're square. Got it?" she declared.

"Next week." He hung up, failing to answer her question.

Asshole! Well, it was definitely as she'd expected; no surprises there. She leaned back and exhaled a deep breath. Things were getting serious now; she had to be careful and rely only on people she could trust. Monica, lacking any remorse over what she had planned, pulled up the digital image on her computer screen. Her only guilt would be over lying to her lover. Except he'd understand if he knew all of the details, wouldn't he?

Monica's gaze shifted to the two people displayed on her monitor: an athletic-looking woman with long brown hair braided down her back and a handsome thirty-something man with captive blue eyes and a sexy grin. *Yeah, maybe if I were twenty years younger.*

The smiling faces of Rachel Winters and Luke Reed stared back at her.

~

Leo couldn't believe he'd been assigned patrol duty. At any rate, that's what the guys called it; yet those were the same "friends" who'd started calling him Leo years ago because of his striking resemblance to Leonardo DiCaprio, at least when he wasn't in disguise. He wasn't fond of the nickname. But eventually he learned two things: one, his friends weren't going to stop using the name, and it only got worse when he resisted, and two, women loved the real Leonardo, so when they learned it was his namesake, they'd sometimes move a little closer to him. It happened more often back when his political career was on the rise and he didn't have to lie about his job. It was a far cry from the line of work he was in now, but he was damn good at his current job. Even so, he couldn't wait to see the person responsible for his reluctant career change get what was coming, but he had to be patient—bide his time, finish his current assignment, and then he could focus on carrying out his revenge. It would be even sweeter because no one would see it coming.

For now, Leo had done exactly what he had been instructed to do: leave his post in Tahoe and drive down to the site. Someone else had called in sick—in this business, *dead* was more like it—and there was no one else to cover his job for the next few days. Now Leo was hot, and bugs swarmed his face as though he were lathered in sugar. It was amazing how different the environment could be just a few thousand feet lower in elevation. Mother Nature was one amazing bitch.

With absolutely no disturbances, wildlife or human, his temporary assignment had been about as exciting as watching paint dry. His stomach grumbled, reminding him it was lunch time. Looking around the dense forest of pine and manzanita bushes, he spotted a narrow boulder he could sit on for a few minutes. Once relaxed on the granite seat, Leo opened his backpack and removed his lunch bag. Just as he'd taken the second bite, a voice penetrated the otherwise quiet setting.

"I think it went this way." The male voice contained a slight accent. Leo set his sandwich down and quietly removed his gun from its holster. What the hell was this guy doing way out here?

"Shhh!" The whisper was about as loud as the first guy's voice but clearly came from someone else in a different direction. How many were there?

"Like anyone's going to hear us! The damn thing already knows we're after it. Now git on over here and help me find its trail again!" Crunching branches indicated nearing footsteps.

Annoyed, Leo glanced longingly at his food before stuffing it in his pack. Then, he carefully stood up, grabbed his backpack, and hid behind a thick copse of trees. He watched as two men came into the clearing about fifteen feet to his right. One boasted a bright red flannel shirt covered by a hunter's vest, with graying hair sticking out from underneath a dirty cowboy hat and a rifle gripped in his hand. The other was younger and shorter, with similar attire but no hair or hat. He had to be the whisperer.

"There's a trail here. Not just footprints from the bears. I mean a real trail." The whisperer had abandoned all attempts to be quiet. Leo gritted his teeth as he considered the repercussions of someone discovering the path. If those two dumbasses followed it, he'd have to take action. No one could discover the secrets Leo had been brought here to guard.

"Unless you see paw prints, I don't give a flying fuck about no trail," Flannel swore and spat to his side.

"Fine. I've gotta piss anyway. Give me a minute." Whisperer headed down the trail as he called out, "Dale, we already got the mom. I say let's just go back, bag her up, and get the hell out of here."

Leo fumed; he did not need this. In about twenty steps the man would get his first glimpse. Leo couldn't let that happen.

"Oh, don't get your panties in a bunch!" Flannel spit again as if to reinforce his point. "Hurry up before we lose any chance of catching it."

Whisperer swore under his breath as he continued on the path.

There was no choice; they both had to be silenced. These idiots were obviously illegal hunters since California didn't allow mother bears or their cubs to be hunted, a law they had clearly ignored. Heck, he'd be doing the world a favor. The planet was already overpopulated. Strategically placing each step to intercept the younger man, Leo crept sideways and positioned himself so he could emerge onto the trail just behind him. He considered his gun but knew it would be better to make it look accidental. He watched as the man's eyes reacted to what he saw in the distance.

"Well, would you look at that!" Whisperer exclaimed. This was Leo's chance. He jumped out and closed the gap between them with two long strides. The hunter started to turn in his direction, but Leo was fast, grabbing the man's head and neck from behind before he could get a full view. "What the—" Leo twisted with all his force and snapped Whisperer's neck. The man, lifeless, fell to the ground.

"What is takin' ya so long? Hurry up!" Flannel called out. Leo jerked around, happy to see the intruder wasn't coming in his direction. It would be much easier if the other man never saw him approaching. Retracing part of his route, Leo made his way closer to the remaining man. Even better, Flannel had his back to Leo. He could subdue the guy and take him out easily; no muss, no fuss. Both bodies could be dropped off a tall cliff like they'd fallen. If he hid them well enough, the coming winter's snow would help erase any evidence by the time they were discovered, not that he planned to leave any evidence. There were several drop-off options if he drove back up State Route 88 toward Kirkwood. He was just feet away when his foot landed on a dried branch. *Crack.* Flannel turned.

"About time—" His eyes widened as he saw Leo. Dale instinctively raised his gun, but Leo launched at the man, knocking the weapon to the side as they both tumbled to the ground with Leo on top. The man was more solid than Leo had anticipated. A blow to Leo's jaw knocked him backward. He quickly recovered, slamming his knuckles into the man's gut. It knocked air out of his belly, giving Leo the extra second needed to pull back and land another punch. The man swung at him again, but it was a weak attempt as he gasped for air. Leo noticed the flat, hard surface underneath them.

He grabbed the sides of the man's head, pulled up, and slammed it back into the flat slab of granite. The man held both hands in front of him as if he could push Leo away, but Leo was stronger. He slammed the man's skull down again and again. Blood smeared onto the rock. Leo felt the welcome rush of adrenaline through his veins as he dealt several more blows, almost unable to stop himself. Eventually, his brain prevailed, and he let go and leaned back. The man's eyes stared lifelessly at the sky. He checked for a pulse, but there was no need. While a spine injury and head injury may still raise the eyebrows of the most anal detectives, without any other evidence to the contrary, they'd have to conclude the two hunters had met an unfortunate end courtesy of Mother Nature. Perhaps they'd been too distracted chasing their prey to realize they'd come upon a drop-off.

Leo sighed. Now the hard part involved getting them to his vehicle and transporting them to the location of their unfortunate accident. Should he risk leaving his post to take care of it, or should he contact his boss to send someone else during his absence? He decided the risk of not saying anything, and then his boss finding out later, was too great. Better to just lay it all out now. Plus, while it was rare that anyone would come out this far, he'd best not leave the location unattended. Obviously the two men had ended up here.

There was no way around it. He pulled his phone from his

pocket to dial his boss as he looked down at the crumpled figure in front of him.

I don't give much of a shit about humans, but hunting down mama bears and their babies? Not cool. Leo had a conscience after all.

Chapter Three

"I'll tell you what, Kris, I don't think I have the patience for this whole dating scene. Not really sure I'm ready yet anyway," Rachel sighed into the phone. She was comfortable in the soft pajamas she'd changed into after returning from the unfortunate date with the firefighter.

"Rach, it's been, what, over a year since you and Luke called it quits?" While Kris had been supportive, she also admitted not understanding why Rachel still had feelings for Luke, even if the breakup had been a mutual decision. At the time, Rachel hadn't thought it would be forever. But here they were, over a year gone by, actively avoiding each other except for the rare get-togethers among mutual friends. She did her best to hide her feelings and act like she'd moved on, but damned if she didn't still think of him far too often. Wonder what he was doing. And if they would ever have another chance at being together.

"I get it. But it's not just my feelings for Luke. This is my second date from this website stuff, and I'm already feeling hopeless and exhausted. Frankly, it's not like I need a man right now—or ever, really," she chuckled, reaching her hand out to pet the two furry black and white heads now rubbing against her as though it were some kind of competition. And with her two border collies, Bella and Avi, it sometimes was.

"It's not that bad," Kris chided.

"Um, let me see. The first guy ordered my dinner for me before I even arrived, because 'a man should always determine what a woman eats.' I thought it was a joke. After all, my profile explicitly says I believe in equality in a relationship. I mean, who does that?"

"Friend, this is the world of Tinder. I told you—a lot of people don't even read the profiles. They just look at pictures. You'll learn to weed them out."

"But *I* read them. His description claimed he was looking for an independent woman. Why have a profile if no one reads them?"

"He lied. It happens." Kris's curt reply revealed she had grown tired of Rachel's complaints on the subject. "Give it another shot or two. If they end up being duds, I'll promise to let it go."

"Still don't get why you're so intent on my love life; yours isn't exactly running in high gear. How many dates have you had in the past year?" Rachel teased, wanting to lighten the mood. Kris wasn't into relationships, plus she was probably pickier than Rachel when it came to would-be suitors. Well, *most* of the time. Rachel had been surprised at the attraction between her older brother, Derek, and Kris the previous year. Talk about an unlikely pair. Sure, Kris had forged ahead as if nothing happened when the two had locked lips after being rescued while fleeing from their kidnapper.

"Subject change," Kris interjected. "How's that forestry project going out by Cascade?"

Rachel would let her get away with steering the conversation to a new topic—this time. "Fine. I haven't done much yet. But get this: the firefighter was on the crew called out to that fire and let it slip tonight he didn't think it was accidental." Rachel pulled her hand away to reach for her water bottle. Two sets of eyes followed her hand's every move until it returned to its rightful place rubbing them again. "By the way, mum's the word on that." Rachel wasn't worried; Kris was not one to gossip or reveal secrets.

"That's interesting. Every report out there has indicated it was an abandoned campfire."

"Exactly. Think there's just a crazy arsonist running around Tahoe? Or maybe someone wanted to make some kind of political statement? It was very coincidental how it burned straight toward the senator's house." Rachel leaned back and stretched her arms to her side. "Amazing luck it rained," she added under her breath.

"Regardless, Rachel, it's not your job to investigate it. Your job is to help develop a good forest management strategy for that area, *right?*" The last word was spoken with special emphasis.

"You've made your point." Rachel sunk down further into her sofa and extended her legs out.

"Then my job is done for tonight. Gotta go." As often happened, Kris abruptly ended the call. Rachel laughed as she set her phone down and decided to catch up on the most recent episode of *Supernatural.* The storylines could be entertaining; even better, the actors who played the famous brothers, Sam and Dean Winchester, were well-known eye candy among countless female viewers.

Chapter Four

Luke smiled at his creation. It had required two long weeks of coming home after evening bike rides, grabbing a quick dinner, and heading straight to his garage to get to work, cutting the materials and staining the wood. And now, the mahogany dresser actually looked good in his bedroom. It was his first dresser and had involved a lot of building, tearing apart, and rebuilding. But he'd done it. The sense of accomplishment reminded him of how he used to feel when he'd solved a new case. Either the excitement of his job had completely worn off, or he had become bored with his bread-and-butter clients, now largely comprised of cheating spouses.

He heard a loud chime coming from the living room. It was his cell phone alarm reminding him to head out for his class in ten minutes. Throughout summer he'd been riding his bike to the Lake Tahoe Community College campus. He gathered his backpack, put on his helmet, climbed on his bike, and rode out. As he turned left to the main street that would take him to Highway 50, South Lake Tahoe's main thoroughfare, a loud screech sounded from behind him. He turned in time to see a large beige SUV, seemingly aimed straight at him, come bellowing around the corner. Luke looked around and considered his options within the few seconds he had.

Luke wrenched his front wheel to the right. His bike slid across the road's shoulder, straight into the storm drainage ditch. The SUV rushed by, clipping the tail end of his back tire and whipping his bike around so fast that Luke flew off. His body slammed against the rocks lining the ditch, knocking the air out of his lungs. He lay there, focusing on taking a breath while listening for the sounds of a vehicle backing up. There was nothing. Luke wasn't sure how much time had passed before a small Audi stopped in the lane above him. A few seconds later he heard a strained female voice call out.

"Oh my gosh. Sir? Sir, you okay?" the woman asked as she peered down at him. "Wait, Luke, is that you?"

Luke recognized his neighbor from a few houses down the street; with her bright blonde hair and small frame, she was a dead match to Chrissy from *Three's Company.* "Hi, Shannon. Yep, just me." He started to push himself up, wincing as the adrenaline slowed and he began to feel the scuffs and aches throughout his body.

"What happened? Do you need an ambulance? I could take you to the ER—"

"I'll be okay." He stopped her, recalling the night Shannon and her husband had invited Rachel and him over for dinner. The woman dominated the entire evening's conversation. "No need for the emergency room." Luke sat up and dusted off his chest.

"Are you sure?" She tilted her head.

"Yeah, no worries. I just need another minute and I'll take myself home."

"How did you end up in the ditch?" she asked, reminding Luke of the unanswered question.

"Some idiot almost ran into me."

"Probably a drunk driver!" she spouted, her gaze looking down the road as though she could see the accident happening like a recorded video. Luke just wanted to get back to his house and take a hot shower. So much for tonight's class.

"Thanks for checking on me." Luke slowly stood up, bending to stretch his aching back. "I'm going to walk my bike home. Appreciate you stopping."

"Well, call if you need anything," she sighed dramatically as if he were inconveniencing her by not letting her take him to the emergency room.

"Will do, thanks." As Luke carefully walked alongside his bike, he tried to recall details that his eyes may have captured but his brain had failed to process. Had it been a random hit-and-run? He thought the driver seemed to have been aiming for him. Yet that didn't mean it wasn't a drunk driver as Shannon assumed. Perhaps the driver was tipsy and accidently hit the accelerator instead of the brake. Considering the sense of being watched the other night, Luke decided it was worth talking to his friend Ted, at least off the record for now, even if he knew his buddy took his job as a police detective seriously and wouldn't be happy to forgo an official report. Regardless, first things first: a cold, frosty beer and strategically placed ice packs were calling his name.

~

"Rick did what?" Monica shouted the words into the phone before entering into another coughing fit. She should quit the smokes, but it was the only way she could deal with stress. And this was stressful. The line remained silent as large gulps of water helped ease her raw throat before she continued, "I thought you said he could be trusted, Cassandra!"

"Nothing indicated that Rick couldn't be trusted. I was told by other firefighters that he has a reputation for following orders to a tee."

"And you're sure it's not a coincidence? I'd hate to potentially draw any attention if there's no need." Monica tipped her glass again for another sip but banged her teeth against the rim. She almost slammed the beverage on the table but thought better of it.

"As I said, I'm not sure of anything. All I know is he was spotted having dinner with Miss Winters last night."

"All right." Monica took a deep, calming breath. "Give me a moment to think." She reclined in her chair and gazed out the expansive windows at the deep blue water of Lake Tahoe in the distance. While her life had been in chaos for the last few years, at least she still had her family's old cabin. She'd lost most of everything else and had depleted her stores of political favors just to keep what little was left. If she blew this current situation, not only would she lose the man she loved, she'd also have no hope of getting her life back. "I say let's ask him what he told her, see if he fesses up." Monica struggled to remain composed. Of all the people he could have revealed something to!

"You want me to do the asking?" Cassandra queried with obvious excitement. The woman was good at her job, albeit alarmingly enthusiastic about some of the less desirable activities it required.

"Yes, feel free to get creative. I know how you like a challenge." Monica began to spin the beads on the strap holding her glasses.

"I'll get right on it."

"I'm sure you will," Monica remarked before ending the call. She'd hoped to avoid having to take such extreme measures. It had all been going as planned this whole time, and now one minor hiccup could threaten it all. She should have just dealt with the firefighter right away, but she didn't want to risk anyone looking into his activities too closely. Plus, he seemed to go about his life after his supervisor told him to leave it alone; he didn't ask any more questions. But that was *before* Rachel Winters had come into the picture. Now she had no choice. Rachel was not going to screw her over again.

Chapter Five

Luke sat propped up on his sofa as he iced the spots where his body had been pounded into the ground during his fall. He slowly sipped a cold beer and stared, unfocused, while his mind continued to replay the bike incident. The more he thought about it, the more convinced he was that it was no simple wrong-place, wrong-time situation. Luke stood and stretched his aching muscles as he carried the cold packs back to his freezer. He retrieved his laptop from his bedroom, plopped back down on the couch, and began exploring his files.

Could he have been targeted because of a case he was working on? He reviewed his list of recent cases. There were a few cheating spouses; Luke supposed providing evidence of an affair to a significant other could upset the offending cheater enough to come after him, but it had never been an issue before. His other cases involved typically benign activities, like helping locate long-lost family members or running background checks on prospective employees and, in one case, a prospective wife. Nothing indicated fallout from any current projects. He reached for his phone and dialed Ted. An overreaction, maybe, but considering the last few years of his life, nothing could be discounted.

"Yo," Ted answered, sounding out of breath.

"Hey, it's Luke."

"What's up?"

"Bad time?"

"Uh, no." A hushed whisper followed some shuffling sounds.

Luke grinned. "If you have company, I—"

"Just hold on." Luke waited as he heard a low female voice in the background followed by Ted's heavy footsteps. A door closed, and Ted came back on the line. "Okay, what's up?"

Luke knew better than to ask any questions about Ted's guest. It certainly wasn't rare for his friend to enjoy the company of a woman. In his midforties, Ted remained perfectly content living a bachelor's life. Luke focused on the reason he'd called and decided to get straight to the point.

"I was run down by a car today while biking. I'm fine," Luke added before Ted could ask. "Just banged up. It was probably nothing, but I don't know. I've also felt like I'm being watched."

"Do you need to go to the hospital?" As usual, Ted easily switched into cop mode, his tone conveying all seriousness.

"No, nothing's broken. I wanted to bounce the situation off you, see what you think." Luke recounted the details as Ted silently listened.

As soon as he was done, Ted spoke. "First, you need to file an official report. We can do that tomorrow. Second, keep an eye out. Want me to send someone by tonight?"

"I'm good." Luke didn't think a police drive-by was warranted. Plus, he was trained to defend himself. He'd been an officer years ago before switching to private work. "Tomorrow is fine. I'll come over around ten."

"I should be there, but if not, someone else can take your report." Then, as if it were an afterthought, Ted added, "You still up for checking out that old place off Highway 4 next week?"

Luke had almost forgotten. Ted had been compelled to follow some kind of historic kick lately; he had become fascinated with early settlements in the Sierra Nevada. His current interest included the remnants of Silver City along the West Fork of the Carson River south of Markleeville.

"Should be fine. It's not like it's one of Rachel's twenty-mile hikes, right?" The words left Luke's mouth before his brain could process what he was saying. After all this time, it didn't take much for memories of her to cross his mind. Ted paused, unsure of how to respond. Ted knew the breakup had been difficult for Luke, but deep down Luke suspected Rachel had Ted's sympathy more than he did. And that's how it should be.

"Yeah, just a little walking. Though if the weather's good, we could bike up to the summit afterward. But if you're not up to it, just let me know. You're getting older now, and it may hit you hard tomorrow. Or even the day after."

"Hey now, none of that age crap. Plus, you've got a few extra years on me, my friend," Luke joked, even though Ted was not sensitive about his age. Perhaps because he looked ten years younger—closer to Luke's midthirties—and was as fit as a twenty-year-old.

"And that's how I know. Respect your elders," Ted chuckled.

Luke heard the woman calling Ted's name. "I'll let you get back to your company. Talk to you tomorrow."

"All right, take it easy tonight." Luke was about to thank him when Ted added, "And keep your weapon nearby."

~

Rick sat at the bar nursing a beer with the look of a man who had lost his best friend. He'd learned over the years that women were more apt to engage with him if he looked sad or heartbroken. It was as though they couldn't handle seeing a man with the blues and felt compelled to try to cheer him up. *Not that it worked every time*, he thought as he recalled his recent date with Rachel Winters. But it worked enough. He'd been sitting in the same spot for twenty minutes with no approaches, but it looked like that was about to change. A tall red-haired woman with a low-cut blouse and a matching scarf appeared to be heading in his direction. She grasped a small purse, and a light coat was tossed over her arm. He glanced her way, gave a partial smile, and looked down at his beer. Too much eye contact wouldn't be right for a guy here to drown his sorrows alone.

"Excuse me," she drawled. "Is this seat taken?" Her smile was bright, her teeth among the whitest he'd ever seen.

"Um, no," he responded as he lifted his mug with a strategically shaky hand and took a long sip. She sank onto the barstool before signaling the bartender.

"You look like you could use some company." She started to laugh. "Wow, if I'm not just full of clichés tonight!" She reached out her hand. "My name's Cassandra."

Rick let a few seconds go by before extending his hand and taking hers. "Rick."

He allowed himself to become more talkative as they discussed inane things like the weather, sports, and the personalities of the announcers airing on the TV set propped above the counter. It was his way of letting her think she was slowly drawing him out of his shell until he finally fessed up about his bad argument with his "emotionally unstable" teenage son. It was working, and before he knew it, she'd placed her hand on his leg, leaned in, and said with a seductive tone, "Is there somewhere else we can go?"

"My condo is a few blocks away."

Cassandra smirked, withdrew her hand, and extended off the stool. "Sounds good."

Worked like a charm. Barely ten minutes later his hands trembled as he tried to insert the key into his door lock. Only this time his unsteady hands weren't an act; the woman's magical fingers were making it impossible to focus. Her close breath triggered goose bumps on his neck.

"Hurry, Rick."

"I'm trying." Finally, the key slipped inside and the knob and turned. As the door opened, her body pushed against his, nudging him inside. This was going better than planned. It didn't always work out the way he wanted on the first night.

Rick stumbled inside and turned around to face her. She nudged the door closed as her lips pressed against his. He kissed her back, hard, as he ripped off his coat and tossed it to the side. He reached over and locked his front door. He didn't want any distractions tonight.

"Bed?" she whispered in between deep, strained breaths.

"Follow me." He grabbed her hand and led her toward his bedroom. Once inside, he turned to face her. Before he could do anything, she pushed him onto the bed and climbed on top of him until she straddled his waist. This night was going well. Very well, indeed. He grinned. "I like your style."

"I figured you would. How do you feel about ratcheting this up a notch?" She bent down and licked the crevice between his neck and shoulder. His pants became far too restrictive.

"I like the sound of that. What do you have in mind?"

"Hmm, I'm feeling a little frisky tonight." She slowly peeled away her scarf, then reached for his hand and raised it above his head. She left it resting there and slowly wrapped the scarf around his eyes. "I'll make you forget all about your bad day, Rick." He felt her mouth touch his, and she began sucking on his lower lip. He really needed his pants to come off; he was bursting at the seams. And why was she still wearing that damn coat?

"You're killing me, woman," he moaned, both pleased and frustrated with the torture.

"Not just yet, Rick." Something sharp pricked his neck.

"What the hell?" He reached around to feel his skin like he needed to scratch at a mosquito bite and noticed his arm felt heavy. His body was quickly becoming uncoordinated. A realization dawned on him: he'd been drugged! "Why?" he asked, the word coming out in one long slur before everything went dark.

~

Relieved of his sentry duty, Leo had been pleased to return to Tahoe. Better yet, today's assignment had been simple. His instructions had been to injure Luke Reed, not kill him. For some reason his boss wanted the guy scared and on guard. Everything had gone smoothly, from the moment he'd procured a vehicle in the Raley's parking lot to the timing of his attack; a small amount of reconnaissance in previous weeks had revealed a pattern in the man's schedule. Once in Luke's neighborhood, he hadn't needed to wait long for there to be no other vehicles around his target. As was his customary procedure, Leo had been heavily disguised, this time wearing a wig, large sunglasses, and a few other feature-distorting items that could fool any identity scanner. Sometimes he missed the days when he could simply go about his business as himself. But those days were gone. Very few people he associated with knew his real name and face.

Now, sitting in the Italian restaurant, thoughts raced through his head like bees buzzing around a disturbed hive, yet his body language would reveal nothing to onlookers. Nor would his facade that, combined with the shaded atmosphere, guaranteed he would not stand out to anyone. He was simply another customer enjoying a drink and appetizers while reading the local newspaper and occasionally stealing glances at the two beautiful women across the room, as any man with a pair of eyes would be apt to do. Leo wasn't sure which woman he considered more attractive. While Rachel had an athletic build and the kind of soft skin a man would love to feel rubbing against his own, her friend's combination of feminine features and tough-girl smile was also compelling. Leo tore off another piece of the small loaf of bread, stuffed it in his mouth, and flagged down a nearby waiter.

~

Rachel stared at her friend Jill and disguised her shock with another sip of red wine before responding. "When did this happen?"

"Last week." Jill smirked, the perfect image of the cat who ate the canary.

"I still can't believe it. He just called you out of the blue, all these years later?"

"Yep. Hadn't seen him since our last tour in Afghanistan. We kind of danced around the attraction at the time because we were serving together, and romantic entanglements create distractions that can get soldiers killed." Jill finger-brushed her dark brown hair—recently sprinkled with grays—and tucked it behind her ear. "Plus, at that time I hadn't dated anyone since discovering 'the asshole' in bed with his coworker. Even though our marriage was clearly over, I was still waiting for the final papers, and it felt wrong to consider starting a relationship with someone else before it was official. Not that it didn't stop Jake." She spat out the last word.

Although it happened before she'd met Jill, Rachel was aware of Jill's ex-husband's infidelity. She also heard the ongoing tales of how Jake continued to be a jerk when it came to their two children, making life difficult for Jill, who attempted to shield her kids from his negative behavior. Of course, doing so meant she often went out of her way to "accommodate" his antics. Like being late for a meetup with the kids or changing plans on her at the last minute. After a recent horseback ride with Jill's fourteen-year-old son, Tanner, Rachel was certain Jill's oldest had started to see what was really going on.

"You won't even kiss on the first date. Hell, do you even date? I'm surprised . . . and impressed," Rachel grinned with an overdramatic wink.

"Very funny, Rach." Jill let out a laugh.

"So . . . when will you see him again?"

"Tomorrow night. We're going to head into Carson for dinner."

"Got your mom set up to watch the kids? Hmm . . . does she know about Lorenzo?" Rachel pronounced his name with a lame attempt at a sexy Spanish accent.

"She knows we met up last week and that we set a second date. Otherwise, well, she's *my mom*. Of course I didn't elaborate on the details of our first 'date.'" Jill stated the last word with air quotes. "Enough about me. How's your dating life going?"

Rachel laughed as she thought about the two first dates she'd had. "Well, it's been entertaining, to say the least. But," she sighed, "my heart isn't in it."

"Then why are you doing it?"

"That's a question I keep asking myself. Kris and CiCi have had so much fun setting up the online profile and 'talking shop' with me. I suppose part of me just wants to go along to see them excited. On some level, maybe I thought it would help me get over Luke faster. To stop thinking about him so often." Her friends meant well, she knew, but part of her wished they'd lay off. Then again, she *was* an adult fully capable of saying no.

The waiter appeared and gently placed a basket containing cloth-wrapped bread on the table. Jill called out a quick thank you before unwrapping it and ripping a partially cut piece of warm bread from the loaf. Rachel winced as her friend lathered thick butter on both sides.

"Some bread with your butter?" she teased. "Seems a medical examiner would know what that much butter could do to your insides."

Jill smirked and held the butter knife toward Rachel. "I don't want to hear it!" Continuing with her task, Jill said, "I'm the last person to give romantic advice, but, my two cents: first, has it helped you think of him less? Even for a little while?"

"I suppose it has provided a distraction, temporary as it may be," Rachel conceded.

"Then so long as you don't lead anyone into thinking you want more than you are willing to give at this point, I suppose I don't see the harm." Jill bit off a corner of her artery-clogging appetizer. "But don't feel like you need to date if you aren't up for it either."

"Thanks, I appreciate being able to bounce this off you." With her mouth watering from the scent of the freshly baked french loaf, Rachel gave in and tore off her own piece.

"How's work going these days? Any word on that atrocious housing project off Brockway? Tahoe–Truckee Pines, was it?"

"The conservation groups filed the opening court briefs, so it's going to be in the litigation process for a while. I sure hope the courts will reverse Placer County's approval, but too often they just side with the government agency." Rachel enjoyed another sip of wine before speaking. "Otherwise, I just started working on the planning documents for a forest rehab project over by Cascade Lake." Damn her for starting with that first slice of the restaurant's homemade bread. Rachel took another slice from the basket.

"Where the fire was? The one that almost killed the teenage girl?" Jill set the half-eaten bread and butter on her plate and reached for her wine.

Rachel nodded, still chewing as she thought about the firefighter's supposition. Suspected arson was a juicy piece of gossip, but she had agreed to keep Rick's confidence. She already felt a pang of guilt for mentioning it to Kris, even though she knew Kris wouldn't say anything. Why make it worse? Before she could swallow and respond, a petite waitress approached their table.

"Hi, ladies," she greeted with enthusiasm while placing two more glasses of wine on the table.

"We didn't—"

"These are courtesy of that gentleman over there." The woman nodded to the side. Rachel looked around the room until her gaze fell on a man sitting in the corner. The room's dim light made it difficult to see him. The man appeared to be in his forties and sported thick black hair and a goatee.

"That's sweet, but we're here for some girl chat tonight," Jill said.

"That's between you two and him. I just deliver the drinks," she said. "Might as well enjoy the *vino*. It's our best red."

Rachel looked toward the solo man for another few seconds. Deep brown eyes stared directly at her; something about his look sent chills up her spine. Not the good kind. He nodded, so subtly that she almost missed it. She turned back to Jill, who was also eyeing the stranger. As she dipped another slice of bread in rosemary-flavored olive oil, she muttered, "I hope he doesn't come over here."

"Actually, he just put a hat on and left." Jill tilted her head to the side in his direction. Rachel looked; the table was empty.

"That's odd—" Rachel's phone vibrated in her pocket. "Let me just check who this is," she stated apologetically to Jill as she retrieved it.

"No problem." Jill reached into her purse. "I should check for messages from the kids anyway."

Rachel nodded, then examined the display. The numbers looked familiar, but she couldn't place who it was. All that mattered was who it was not—friends or family—so she let it go to voice mail.

Chapter Six

Rick woke up and opened his eyes. Complete blackness surrounded him. His muscles ached. Awareness of what happened began to return as he noticed his hands were positioned above his head, his fingers numb. Instinctively he tried pull them down, but his wrists were tied to something: the bed frame? His ankles were also bound. Cool air touched his skin, and it took a second to realize he wore no clothes.

"What the——?" he whispered into the darkness. Suddenly, the small lamp on his bedside table clicked on, revealing Cassandra sitting in a chair next to the bed.

She inched toward him and said, "About time you came to; I was starting to worry." She smiled so innocently he almost expected her to whisper, "There, there," while patting his leg.

"What's going on?"

"I just need to get some information from you, that's all." She leaned back. He noticed the surgical gloves she wore and began to squirm, testing the tightness of his bonds. There was no give. His eyes darted around the room, looking for any inspiration to help him get out of this situation. He saw nothing helpful and returned his attention back to the crazy woman in front of him.

"Look, yes, I fibbed a little to get you here. But if I offended you, then I'm sorry." He wasn't, but what else could he say? He was at this woman's mercy.

"Oh, please. Don't pretend you weren't calculating every word you spoke tonight," she chuckled, "but that's not why I'm here."

The cold look in her eyes told him she wasn't messing with him; his friends weren't going to jump out of hidden corners and yell, "Gotcha, sucka!" Fear began to build inside. "I'll tell you whatever you need to know," he pleaded.

"Glad to hear it." Cassandra stood up, turned around, and reached into the pocket of the coat he'd been so anxious to take off her earlier. It now hung down from the back of the chair. When she faced him again, he saw the object she'd retrieved. A knife. Was she going to cut him? As his mind raced, she casually slid the chair closer to the bed, its legs generating a sound against the floor reminiscent of Freddy Krueger's blades scraping along pipes in the *A Nightmare on Elm Street* movies. "Tell me the truth and you'll be fine. Lie to me and, well, it won't be good for you. Got it?"

He nodded, feeling sweat bead on his forehead.

"Good. Now, you had dinner last night with Rachel Winters, correct?"

What the hell did this have to do with that? Was she jealous or something? "Why are you asking about—"

"Yes or no?"

"Yes, but—"

"Why?" she asked as she slowly ran her finger along the blade.

"It was a date."

"And how did you two meet?"

"Online."

"Really?" She smirked like she didn't believe him.

"Yes, I can show you my profile and our messages if that will make you feel better."

"Oh, I'm sure you can. Who asked who?"

Rich had to think about it. He contacted a lot of women on the site. "I sent her a message, so I guess I contacted her first. Why?" He waited through the silence. After what felt like forever, she looked away from her weapon and focused back on him.

"And you had no idea who she was?"

"No, I didn't even know her last name until you just said it." He began to pull on his wrists again. "Look, I'll tell you whatever you want to know. Can you just untie me?"

Cassandra looked amused but didn't respond.

"Seriously, this hurts. My hands are asleep."

"And I should care why?" Her gaze returned to her hands—and the object she held in them. "Did you know she is involved in planning the restoration project where that fire happened last year by Cascade Lake?"

Huh? "What does that have to do with anything?"

"Did you know?" she demanded.

Rick shook his head. "She asked about it but didn't say anything about ties to her job." Something twitched in the back of his mind, but he couldn't make out what it was.

"And what did you tell her?"

"I, well, I can't remember. I'd had a few drinks by then, and—"

Without any warning, Cassandra leaned forward and pierced his abdomen, pressing down just enough to cut the surface of the skin. He clenched his jaw as red lines formed on his stomach.

"I said no lying."

"I'm not." Or was he? He tried to focus on his alcohol-blurred memory of the evening. What did they talk about? Campfires. And . . . oh no.

"Rick, I think you just remembered something you'll want to share with me."

He couldn't believe this was really happening. Why *had* he told Rachel his suspicions? Then again, he never imagined how serious a slip it would be. None of this made any sense.

"How did you know I was on a date with her? Were you watching me?"

"Someone was. Now what did you tell her?"

Rick considered lying, but apparently she had a built-in lie-detector gene as she knew he wasn't telling the truth even before he knew. *Who was this woman?*

"I may have let it slip—remember, I'd been drinking—that I thought it was arson."

"And what else?" She stared at him, silently waiting.

He let out a long breath. "That I was told not to tell anyone about my suspicions." He watched with resignation as Cassandra reclined in the chair and peered at him.

"That's what a certain someone was afraid of." She exhaled loudly before abruptly shifting toward him. Pain radiated through his stomach from the inside out. It was like nothing he'd ever felt before. Had the drug done something to his insides? He noticed Cassandra was leaning over him, as if inspecting his abdomen. The ache was getting worse, much worse. He wasn't sure he could bear it. Tears filled his eyes, and he caught a blurry image of her hands reaching for him. He squeezed his eyes shut, then reopened them, the moisture running down his cheeks allowing his vision to clear. She wasn't reaching out for him. She was holding the knife in his gut. And twisting it.

The pain was unimaginable. Was this really how it was going to end? He looked up at her. "Why?" he mouthed, realizing he could no longer speak.

"I think you know." She withdrew the knife and wiped it on his sleeve as casually as a wife adjusting her husband's tie. "Just so you know, you've signed a death warrant for Rachel and anyone else she may have told."

Rick couldn't prevent his eyes from widening. He wasn't exactly the best or most honest guy in the world, but he'd never wish physical harm on people. Rachel had promised not to tell anyone, but would she? What would it matter? This woman, this murderer, aimed to kill her regardless.

"And one more thing." Cassandra stood and grabbed her coat. She placed the knife back inside the pocket and shrugged her arms into the sleeves. "You were going to die tonight either way."

He watched, helpless to do anything, as she unwound his wrists with her bloody gloves and tucked her scarf into the other pocket. Rick commanded his arms to reach up and grab her, but he was too weak. Once released from being bound, they simply flopped onto the bed. She reached over to his ankles. The pressure relaxed, and he noticed her tuck the shoestrings that must have bound his ankles to the corner posts in another pocket. A minute passed, and a hint of feeling returned to his extremities. He registered the sound of the front door closing. He had to do something. He recalled leaving a disposable phone in his bedside drawer last night after his dinner with Rachel; it was one he used with many women. *Focus.*

Rick summoned all of his strength and carefully turned his body to the side. With his arms still shaking and partially numb, he managed to slide one out and pry open the drawer with his fingertips. Blackness threatened to take him as he fixated all of his energy on his task. Finally, he felt the phone. By some miracle he managed to wrap his hand around it and pull it back. He pressed the power button and concentrated on not dropping the device. Once it was powered up, he carefully entered his code to unlock it and tapped on the call icon. It brought up the recent calls list, and he saw Rachel's number. First, he'd call 9-1-1, then he'd tell them to warn Rachel. His fingers slipped as he tried to press the keypad.

His vision blurred. He no longer had the strength to hold the phone up to view the screen. He let his arm drop to his chest, his hand still gripping the phone. He could hear Rachel's voice telling him to leave a message. But hadn't he called 9-1-1? *Shit!* When it beeped, he tried to speak but found he no longer could. He fell back on the only way he could think of to communicate. He began to tap his nails by the speaker as tears fell down his cheeks and regret filled his heart at all the mistakes he'd made.

~

"That's odd," Rachel said as she stared at her phone. With Jill in the midst of a heated text discussion with her son, she'd decided to play back the fresh voice message. Although the noise of the restaurant made it difficult to hear, she could swear all she heard were tapping sounds.

"What?" Jill asked as her attention remained partially focused on her cell. Rachel had observed that her female friends with children developed an amazing ability to focus on two conversations at once.

"Weird call," she mumbled, pressing the back key to get to the list of numbers, hoping a second look would bring recognition of who had called.

"Oh. My. God!" Jill announced, then slammed her phone down on the table, after which her face flushed and she looked around the room. Several nearby diners had stopped their conversations to gawk at her. "Sorry," she said and smiled apologetically. "Teenagers at home." Several onlookers nodded their heads with sympathetic expressions.

"What's wrong?" Rachel asked, slipping her phone back into her pocket. She could follow up with the strange caller later.

"Tanner, my dear, sweet son." The annoyed expression she wore contrasted with her sarcastic words. "He's upset I won't let him go to a senior party this weekend." She sighed. "He's fourteen! I'm not about to let him hang out with a bunch of eighteen-year-olds."

"Yikes." Rachel sipped her wine. "I'm curious, how did a fourteen-year-old get invited to said senior party?"

Jill snorted. "The girl he's interested in invited him. It's her older brother's party."

"Double yikes! Teenagers, booze, and hormones. Bad combo."

"Did you really just have to make a reference to hormonal teenagers? Because I wasn't already worried enough."

"Sorry. Okay, this may be a naive question, but did you already have 'the talk?'"

"He's fourteen!" Jill pleaded.

"And? You weren't thinking about the opposite sex at fourteen?"

"Well, of course I was . . . but I wasn't thinking of *having* sex with them."

Rachel stared at Jill. Waiting. Knowing what was coming.

"Damn. You're right; it's not like I haven't thought about the approaching Armageddon. Guess I just hoped I could put it off a bit longer. Like ten years. Not ready for my babies to grow up, ya know?" She reached for her glass. "But I always said I'd talk to my own kids more than my parents did. We had a brief sex-ed lesson in junior high that didn't explain much. Most of my early education on the subject came through reading steamy historical romances. Talk about being let down when I eventually did the deed," she laughed.

"Yes, I imagine there was some disappointment after those books raised your expectations." Rachel tore off another piece of bread.

"So back to a positive subject: how is Lorenzo's bedside manner?"

Jill grinned. "No disappointment. *At all.*"

"Cheers." Rachel lifted her glass.

~

"You need to go back and clean things up. I need more time before he's discovered," Monica instructed.

"Are you serious?" Cassandra griped into the receiver, unable to keep the annoyance out of her voice.

"What do you think?" The question was purely rhetorically.

Cassandra sighed. While she knew she could find somewhere to stash Rick's body easily enough, she hadn't anticipated hiding the victim would be required this time. She had just removed the wig and combed through her own blonde locks; at least she still had the cheek implants set in place. There had been no need to give Rick a fake name since he wasn't going to last through the night, but it was important bar patrons couldn't accurately describe the woman he'd picked up in a bar.

Cassandra exhaled, resigned. "Will a 'discovery' eventually be necessary? I need to know because it affects how I handle this."

"No. Do what you like. I'll expect a text from you when it's completed, then wait to hear from me." The call ended before Cassandra could even reply. She slowed, careful to follow all speed limits as she turned around and headed back to the firefighter's condo, not looking forward to the task in front of her, but knowing she had to do it.

When she let herself into his bedroom minutes later, she observed the still form on the bed, illuminated only by the dim hallway light she dared to turn on. A small black device near his hand caught her eye. Was that a phone? She scrambled to the bed and reached for it, pushing the power button with her gloved fingers. The display didn't turn on. Maybe, just maybe, she'd gotten lucky and it hadn't worked for him. She slipped the sleek phone into her pocket and placed her hands on her hips as she stared at the lifeless figure in front of her. It was too bad she'd had to kill him, especially given how good-looking he was. It would have been fun to have had the chance to play with him first.

After completing her mission and arriving home, Cassandra was pleased to discover her own cell charger was compatible with the firefighter's phone. Unfortunately, the feeling was short-lived when the device powered on and prompted her for a password.

She had to find out if he made a call after she'd left him to die. Looks like she was going to have to call in a favor from an old friend with a knack for getting around security.

Chapter Seven

Two days after her failed dinner with the firefighter, Rachel was surprised to find herself agreeing to another date. This time it was in person, not online. Seth, as he'd introduced himself, had struck up a conversation with Rachel as she waited for her rare treat from Alpina Coffee Café: a large white mocha with an extra shot of espresso. Ironically, she took down her online profile late last night after returning from dinner with Jill. She wasn't interested enough to go through all the effort; plus, she felt it wasn't fair to herself or her dates. Go figure she would meet someone interesting "the old-fashioned way" so soon afterward. And of course, *after* she'd decided to mentally reestablish her status of "not looking right now." She was enjoying their conversation, which had started while waiting in line and migrated to a nearby table once their coffees were ready. The conversation had moved to one of her favorite subjects, hiking.

"I just hiked up Stanislaus Peak yesterday. It's down by—"

"Sonora Pass! Yes, that's a good one. I took my pups up there earlier this summer. It was quite a scramble to the top." *Oh wow, did I really just cut him off like that? Not cool.* "Sorry for interrupting you. I can get a little overexcited when discussions involve bagging peaks."

"No problem. It's nice to meet someone as enthusiastic about it as I am." Seth sipped his beverage. "Say, Rachel, it's been great talking to you. Would you be interested in meeting up for dinner later this week?"

Caught up in her enthusiasm over the topic, Rachel agreed. Only later, as she drove home with the extra shot of espresso ramping up her nerves, did she question her decision. What was she doing? It was so clear she wasn't ready to date yet. Yet she should be, right? After all, it had been over a year since she and Luke had called it quits. Was there something else going on in her brain that she hadn't yet realized?

Chapter Eight

Leo hid in the trees and watched through a pair of binoculars. Waiting, just as he'd been doing for the past week since his return to the Lake Tahoe Basin after the incident with the hunters. *Assholes.* He brought his thoughts back to the present.

After walking around the old boarded-up house and freestanding chimney near the highway, Luke and his friend Ted, who Leo had been upset to learn the day before was actually a detective with the South Lake Tahoe Police Department, hiked upstream along what Google Maps identified as Silver Creek. The two momentarily paused by a downed log before continuing until they found boulders to cross the water. Once on the other side, they made their way uphill, meandering through the broken patches of brush and scattered pine trees for roughly a quarter of a mile until finding a large outcropping with a view.

They now sat against a half-rotted pine tree, sheltered from the afternoon's gusty winds and talking as they each sipped from amber bottles. Leo continued to peer through his binoculars at the pair. Finally, Luke tilted his head back, gulped the rest of his beer, and stuffed the bottle in his backpack. *Nice to know he isn't going to leave it behind.* Leo wouldn't pretend to be a good person, per se, but he did have a huge problem with two things: trashing the environment and harming wildlife.

"All right, let's hit the road." Although he was too far away to hear Luke, it was easy to make out what he said. Leo had grown up with a deaf cousin who'd taught him all about reading lips. Luke lifted his backpack over his shoulders. Ted repeated the motions.

Leo slowly stood up, preparing to follow the two men back down the hillside. This was another wasted trip. He'd been watching Luke for over a month now. After the bike "accident" last week, Leo had expected his instructions would involve something more actionable. He assumed there had to be a reason for all of this; he certainly hadn't been hired to simply watch the guy for weeks on end and scare him once or twice. Yet for now that was his primary job, as mundane as it was. At least it provided the extra perk of being close to the person he held responsible for ruining his previous career.

Leo had been instructed to intervene only if Mr. Reed were threatened by someone else. Why his boss anticipated such an occurrence had not been explained. A few times he figured Luke suspected someone was watching him, but so far nothing had come of it. Leo had taken greater efforts to keep himself hidden, including installing a few small cameras on the property around Luke's house and office where he could record comings and goings. If all he had to do was watch and listen, why did he need to be there in person? Installing the cameras under the cover of night had been easy.

But cameras only worked where they were located, so sometimes he had to do the job in person. Like now. He felt confident he could continue to avoid detection; he'd been shadowing Luke all afternoon and evening. It had become easier when the two men continued driving past the small town of Markleeville and toward Highway 4 into an area with greater tree cover. He'd been informed they were heading out this way, but the exact location hadn't been well described; he'd just been given reference to some kind of historic chimney.

Leo kept his distance as the two men returned down the steep mountainside they'd bushwhacked up earlier. While it seemed like a harmless walk in the forest, his boss's reference to a potential threat against the man had Leo remaining extra watchful, even in what seemed a benign location.

"I think I'm going to cross it this time." Luke was yelling, presumably to be heard over the wind and moving water.

"Not smart, bro. If you lose your balance . . ." Ted called out his reply as he stared at a large tree trunk spanning the creek. Ted was likely noticing the same threat Leo saw; the log was a dangerous bridge to anyone who dared cross it. Ted pointed down toward the streambed, perhaps twenty feet below. It was a blend of hard granitic rock intermixed with deep areas of quick-flowing water.

"I had one beer, Ted. I'm fine." Luke stepped on the upper end and carefully grasped the raised root system as he maneuvered around the base of the tree. "It's going to get dark soon; this will save some time."

"Have at it; I'm going the way we came." Ted waved in obvious annoyance.

"Suit yourself. I'll wait for you at the car."

Leo watched as Luke began stepping across the makeshift bridge. The fallen tree was two or three feet in diameter—not the narrowest of crossings, but nothing to shake a stick at either.

Leo was so focused on Luke that he almost missed it: on the other side of the creek, roughly ten meters from where Luke was crossing, a large movement caught his eye. He focused his binoculars on the area, wondering if a black bear or some other forest creature was making its way through yet also keeping in mind his boss's warning that someone may want to kill Luke. He saw nothing. Was it just a tree blowing in the wind? Leo continued to monitor the scene, an uneasy feeling gripping his insides. There was another movement. This time he could see the partial outline of someone. They were lining up the sight of their gun and aiming it toward Luke, who was now midway across the old pine.

Not good. If there was ever a time for the intervention his boss had mentioned, this was it. He slowly removed the pistol tucked into the waist of his jeans, thankful he'd brought his silencer. The last thing Leo needed was to give himself away. While it wouldn't eliminate all noise, it would suppress it enough that the wind and water would cover the remaining sound.

Leo fired at his target as the loud sound of a shot echoed through the forest—no silencer on that one. He watched as Luke's arm jerked and he stumbled backward, his foot slipping as he struggled with his balance. Leo heard Luke call out "Ted!" just before he fell to the side, one of his arms reaching toward the trunk to no avail. There was nothing to grip onto, and he plummeted down into the churning water below.

Leo looked back to where he'd seen the attacker. The only movement came from the trees blowing in the wind. Whoever it was must have fled while Leo viewed Luke's descent. His gaze returned to the fallen Mr. Reed. If not for the heavy thunderstorms over the previous few days, there might be nothing more than a minor trickle in the creek below—nothing to cushion a fall. But since a large volume of water was flowing, maybe he would survive.

"Luke!"

Leo saw, more than heard, Ted shout while crawling back up to the end of the downed tree presumably to keep cover from the shooter. From his angle, Leo could still see part of Ted's expression as the man looked down at the rushing creek, his features twisted in a mix of shock and horror. Instantly, like the practiced cop he was, Ted switched gears into rescue mode. He reached behind his back, his hand reappearing with a gun as he visually scanned the area around him, no doubt for the source of the gunshot he'd heard. Ted appeared to debate his next move. Leo could imagine the difficulty of the decision: help his friend at the risk of being shot at by the perpetrator he couldn't see or look for the shooter while his friend was in serious trouble. After one more intense look at the area around him, Ted frantically searched for a way down. The slope was steep and impossible to descend.

"Luke!" Leo barely heard Ted's voice, but he easily made out the frantic call. He watched as Ted examined the log his friend had just fallen from, then looked upstream in the direction they'd hiked.

Ted took off, running upstream along the route they'd come, opting for the safer crossing. Leo remained where he was, alternating between watching the forest where the shooter had been and looking upstream on the other side of the creek for Ted to appear. It was impossible to peer down into the water below without having to move out of his hiding place. *Damn, Luke Reed had better not die.* Although Leo had no idea who the other shooter was, his employer would be apt to take out his frustration on him. Just as he started to question if Ted would return, Ted appeared on the other side, scrambled down toward the streambed, and repeatedly called out to Luke.

Leo risked moving forward, keeping low to the ground as best he could, hoping to see a still-breathing version of Luke Reed below. Once he had a clear line of sight to the area beneath the log, he was dismayed to see no sign of the man. Downstream, multiple pools of water intermittently cascaded along the creek.

Ted half ran, half walked along the creek's edge as he continued calling out to his friend. Leo backed up and made his way in the same direction, Ted's continued shouts guiding him without the need to repeatedly look.

"Oh no, Luke!" Ted's voice, barely discernable, suggested he'd finally located his friend and whatever he'd found had scared him. Leo inched forward until he could view the scene below. The limp body of Mr. Luke Reed bobbed in one of the deeper pools.

Ted rushed into the creek, the water lapping up to his waist. It was typical of many rivers in the Sierra Nevada; water could be just a few inches or ten feet deep depending on where you stepped. Combined with the flowing water and continued gusts of wind, Leo struggled to hear what Ted was saying since his position made lipreading impossible. But the visuals were enough.

Leo watched anxiously as Ted lugged his friend to a flat dry area several feet above the water; Ted almost lost his footing twice as he struggled with the weight. He checked Luke's neck for a pulse and began to perform CPR. *It didn't look good for Luke.*

Ted's attempts at resuscitation grew more frantic as the minutes passed. *How long will he keep trying?* Leo's arms ached from merely watching the effort.

Ted continued an established rhythm of alternating chest compressions and trying to breathe life back into his friend. After several minutes had passed, maybe longer, Leo figured it was a lost cause. He pondered his options as he carefully retraced his steps, following the same route Ted had taken before Luke made the fateful decision to cross on the log. Leo couldn't do anything more for Mr. Reed, but maybe he could track down the person who'd shot at him. It might be the only thing that could save him from the wrath of his boss.

Twenty minutes later, Leo had to concede that the other shooter was long gone. He wondered whether the sniper had intended to kill both men. After all, how nuts would you have to be to try to take someone out in front of a cop, unless you planned to take the cop out as well? Certain the other person had left no trail to follow, Leo slowly walked back up to his tucked-away parking spot, removed his car keys, and slipped inside his pickup. With his target dead and the shooter gone, there was nothing left to do but report to his employer and deal with the consequences.

Chapter Nine

Rachel stared at the back-and-forth movement of the merlot swirling in her glass. Her mind drifted, and she began to imagine a wine tsunami. She had attended a science conference the week before where the presenter talked about the geology and history of the Lake Tahoe Basin. It was amazing to think that an earthquake along one of Tahoe's fault lines had actually generated a tsunami with waves upward of one hundred feet high in the past, and it could happen again someday.

"Rachel?"

Pause.

"Rachel, where did you go?"

A scratchy male voice disturbed her thoughts as abruptly as avalanche control guns blasting on a quiet winter morning. She looked up from her wineglass. Seth gazed at her expectantly and grinned as she felt the heat of embarrassment flush through her face.

"Sorry, Seth, I'm not sure what happened there. Um, what were you saying?" This time, she barely glanced at her glass before tipping it to her lips as she subtly examined the man across the table. Seth was good-looking, with a military-like hairstyle and caramel-colored eyes that were so intriguing she wondered if they were contacts. She'd never met a man who smiled so much; at least that was her impression after seeing him a few times over the past week. Tonight was date number three if you considered their meetup at the coffee shop date number one. And now Rachel was starting to ask herself why she had agreed to a third meetup. He seemed like a nice guy, and she enjoyed comparing notes on outdoor adventures, but at this point, if she wasn't feeling the ever-important physical chemistry with him, it certainly wasn't going to spontaneously develop overnight. Add to that his obvious self-interest in discussing his career as an attorney, which had begun to creep into all of their conversations. The few times he'd asked her about her own work, it hadn't taken long for him to find a way to change the subject back to his. So why did she say yes? It wasn't fair to either of them.

"You okay?" he asked, reaching out to touch the hand she had resting on the table.

"I'm fine. Long day. Just drifted off for a moment there, I guess." Rachel wasn't sure what else to say. She knew what happened. He'd started talking about his work again, and her mind had wandered. She couldn't bear to hear one more lengthy story about legal briefs and judges.

"You do look pretty tired. I know you had to get up early for a meeting in Truckee. Want to call it a night now? We can forget the movie," Seth offered.

"You're right. I'm beat," she sighed, deciding to act like a grown-up and be honest about her lack of interest in a relationship with him. "Seth, I just—" The vibration of the phone in her pocket couldn't have come at a worse time, or better time, depending on how she viewed it. "Damn, let me check this, just to make sure it's not CiCi with a dog issue or something."

It was a harmless little white lie. While the dogs were always fine with her neighbor and good friend CiCi, she'd left them home tonight. But Seth didn't know that. She was tired—that had been no lie—and the distraction would give her a few moments to think about how to let him down easily. She raised her phone and glanced at the display. It was Ted, his personal number, not the police station's line. He wasn't one to call to chat. "I should get this." She smiled apologetically at Seth, stood up, and made her way to the outside of the restaurant, not only for privacy, but also by habit. People who talked on cell phones in the middle of a restaurant were as irritating as a tourist driving twenty-five miles an hour in a fifty-mile-per-hour zone when it was barely raining.

"Ted, what's up?" She infused more perkiness into her voice than she felt. She'd left her coat inside, and the crisp late autumn air chilled her bare arms.

"Rachel, I have some bad news. Are you alone?" There was a somber tone in his voice that she'd never heard before.

"At the moment. What's wrong?" Rachel waited, her body tense.

Ted sighed, "Luke had an accident this afternoon. He . . . he didn't make it, Rachel."

"He what?" The world spun. Rachel had to catch herself before she crashed onto the hard ground. Instead, she leaned her back against the building's facade and slid down until she was sitting on the patio floor.

"He didn't survive. I'm so sorry to break it to you this way; I didn't want you to hear it from someone else."

"What? How?" she choked out as tears blurred her eyes. Rachel's body went numb as she listened to Ted recount the events of the afternoon. She wasn't sure she understood what happened but didn't belabor the details. Rachel asked Ted where he was with the intention of meeting him, but she wasn't sure why. She didn't want to see the body. Luke's body. *Hell no.*

"I'll be at the station in thirty. You can drop by there. Frankly, there's nothing to be done. Maybe you should see if Kris is home, grab your dogs, and go spend some time with her," he suggested.

Rachel thanked him and ended the call. Eventually she managed to stand and slowly make her way back inside. Her heart was barely beating as she stepped around other patrons to make her way to their table. Seth was sitting with his head down, looking at something on his phone. In a mental fog, she walked to her chair and reached for her coat.

"Seth, I'm sorry, but . . . I need to go. Something's happened." Was that really *her* voice?

Startled, he looked up at her. "Rachel, is everything okay?" He gently reached out to touch her arm.

"No, no it's not. I can't talk about it right now. I need to go." The walls were closing around her; she needed to get out of there immediately. She slipped her arms into the sleeves of her coat, bent over to grab her small purse, and retrieved her keys.

"Can I help?" he asked.

"No. I'm sorry. I just—I need to go. There's, uh, been an accident, and an old friend passed . . . away." It was all she could manage before turning and escaping out the front door. She had no idea where she planned to go.

Once behind the wheel, she sat and let the tears flow. After a few minutes of curses and a soaked handkerchief, she decided to drive straight home. Her two sweet dogs wouldn't let her mourn alone, nor would they expect her to talk. She managed to send a quick text off to Ted before placing the key in the ignition.

~

Ted's thoughts raced almost as much as his emotions as he drove the final stretch of State Route 89 over Luther Pass and descended into the Tahoe Basin, his SUV rounding the road's final curves before straightening out south of the small community of Meyers. Another ten minutes and he'd be back at his desk, yet the last thing he wanted to do right now was talk to his fellow officers. Not only would he have to do some talking, he was going to have to answer a barrage of questions about Luke. Several years had passed since Luke had been laid off by the department due to budget cuts, but he was still highly respected by those who knew him on the force.

The visual of Luke's limp body when he'd retrieved him from the water, so still and lifeless, replayed through his mind as a new round of thunderstorms roared overhead. He didn't want to think of that image. He had to concentrate on something else. Another flash lit up the sky. Ted counted the seconds until the boom caught up to see how close it was, just like when he was a kid. *One, one thousand; two, one thousand; three, one thousand; four.*

Boom.

The temporary distraction didn't last long enough, and his mind replayed the call to Rachel. It had been one of the most difficult things he'd ever had to do in his forty-four years of life. While Rachel and Luke had broken up quite a while ago, the look on either's face when the other was mentioned easily revealed how much they still loved each other. Seeing Rachel after hearing the devastation in her voice was not an experience he was looking forward to. It had been difficult enough to break the news. How had this happened?

His phone vibrated and startled him out of his reverie. A quick glance at the display told him Rachel would not be coming by the station after all. *Thank God for small favors.*

Chapter Ten

Seven days. Only seven days had passed since Rachel had received the horrible news. They had drawn on, with Rachel feeling like she was struggling to find her way through a dense fog. It had taken an enormous amount of effort to just get through each day, and she was exhausted every night, not that she was able to sleep. Friends and relatives had stopped by; some even tried to get her to go out, but she hadn't been able to do anything beyond walk her dogs.

She'd have no choice starting tomorrow. It was the "Celebration of Life" for Luke. It's what he had wanted according to his will. No funeral, just a big party. They'd never talked about stuff like that when they were together. As they both were in their early thirties, death had always seemed so far off. Hesitant at first, Rachel was glad Jill convinced her to come back to her home in Minden after the memorial gathering to spend some time with Jill and her kids. Although now in their preteen and teenage years, they still appreciated visits from "Aunt Rachel," and of course Bella and Avi. Plus, the Carson Valley location would get her out of the Tahoe Basin without being too far from home, and that was probably a good thing.

Rachel's cell phone chimed again. *Please, not another text from Seth.* She'd asked for some space in response to his first text the night she'd fled the restaurant, yet two unexpected visits—for both of which she had pretended not to be home—and multiple daily texts indicated he was not willing to provide it. She ignored the message as she pulled an old ice chest out of her closet, setting it in the kitchen for tomorrow when she packed for Jill's house.

Scuffling sounds and yelps of excitement emanated from the backyard. Rachel smiled. Her dogs were a lifeline, spreading joy around her when she needed it most. Dusk had set in, masking all but the swirl of the black and white figures doing their puppy dance. She stepped on the deck and looked out into her backyard to watch them play. She shivered as the cool night air penetrated her senses. Rachel glanced at her wood pile, figuring it was going to be cold enough tonight to warrant a fire in her woodstove. She went back inside to grab her favorite light sweatshirt but realized she'd already packed it in the bag for Jill's house. Instead, she wrapped herself in an old coat hanging on the wall, after recalling the leather gloves she wore to carry wood were out in her pickup.

Rachel slipped on her shoes and opened the front door. The remnant tendrils of light were enough to outline her path without turning on the porch light. She carefully stepped down and walked along her driveway. The night was still; the only sound came from the flowing waters of the Upper Truckee River nearby. As she reached out for her truck handle, there was an odd disturbance in the night air. Hair prickled on the back of her neck as a branch cracked nearby. Rachel opened her mouth to call out, assuming it was a raccoon, or maybe the bear that sometimes walked across her front yard on its way to the river. Usually a few loud words were enough to startle it away.

"Move along, oh furry one—" Searing pain cut off her words as something smashed against the back of her head. She felt her body crumple, and darkness closed in.

~

Jill watched in horror as the figure slammed something against the back of her friend's head. It all happened so fast. One minute Rachel was walking out the front door, unaware of Jill's approach in the distance, no doubt because she'd parked in the neighbor's vacant yard and sat in her car for ten minutes texting with her rebellious son. Then someone had jumped from the side and attacked Rachel.

Once her friend had dropped, the stranger—Jill was sure it was a man based on his height and physique—leaned over her and moved as if to pick her up. Jill's original plan to sneak up on the guy immediately shifted; what if he was carrying Rachel and Jill surprised him, causing him to drop her body? Jill couldn't risk her friend's head taking another beating.

"Hands in the air or I'll shoot first and ask questions later!" she bluffed, using the take-no-bullshit voice she'd perfected during two stints as an army doctor. He paused, clearly startled by her presence. The stranger let go of Rachel and bolted back in the direction he'd come from. *Damn!* If she chased him while Rachel needed medical help . . . *oh, damn!* Jill dropped down next to her friend. It was too dark to make out details. Important ones, like how much blood there was; head wounds could bleed substantially. The lack of any response from Rachel indicated she'd lost consciousness.

Jill reached into her back pocket for her phone. "Hang on, Rachel," she whispered as she swiped the screen, turned the flashlight feature on, and scanned the area around her to see if the perpetrator had returned before shining it down at Rachel. For the first time in a week, Rachel's face looked peaceful. Jill debated her next move. The most ideal choice would be to load Rachel in her car and rush her to the emergency room. But with what Ted had told her, and the attempt to abduct Rachel—or worse—that could prove dangerous. Instead she dialed Ted. He answered on the second ring.

"Jilly, what's up?"

"Teddy, we've got a situation. I'm at Rachel's. Someone just attacked her—"

"What?" Ted exclaimed.

"She's okay. I think so. I hope so. Look, just get over here ASAP."

Ted must have driven with his light flashing because Jill had only managed to get Rachel inside and laid out on her bed when he arrived.

"What happened?" Ted rushed through the front door and closed it behind him seconds before the two dogs greeted him. As if they knew their owner was injured, their tails wagged but without the usual fervor. Ted rubbed both of them while Jill relayed the story.

"We've got to get her out of here. Now," Jill stated as she began tossing items from Rachel's refrigerator into a large ice chest that had been placed nearby.

"I know. But what about her head? I mean, she only recently got past all that postconcussion crap. Could this cause more damage?"

Jill knew he wasn't just thinking out loud; she was a medical examiner, and Ted wanted her professional opinion. "I hope not. Trust me, I've gone back and forth on this, but we don't know who we can trust. And we know all too well how easily someone can access a patient in a medical facility. I say we take her somewhere safe, and if there are any signs of problems, we'll get her to the nearest facility with a fake name or something. I'd offer my house but the kids . . ."

"I know. It's not that hard to track down who-knows-who these days. Given how the Carson Valley and Tahoe medical facilities are fairly interconnected, we should stay away from there too." He glanced into the open doorway of Rachel's bedroom. "You know where we can take her; *no one* would look *there*." Ted glanced back in her direction, his weary eyes meeting hers. "I hate to ask, but can you stay down there with her tonight?"

Jill nodded. "I can ask my mom to watch the kids. She usually doesn't mind. There's the service for Luke tomorrow of course. I suppose it won't look suspicious if I'm unable to get back in time, but it will if you're missing." Jill closed the lid of the ice chest, confident she'd packed the basics. "But I'm scheduled to work the early shift the day after tomorrow."

"Let's cross that bridge when we get there. For now, I want to get her out of here as fast as possible. We don't know whether the attacker will return with reinforcements."

"Sounds good." Jill set the container down near the front door next to a large bag with "Bella and Avi" stitched elegantly in the side. "Luckily she listened when I suggested she pack today so she wouldn't have to deal with it tomorrow." Jill reached down to check the dog bag, making sure it contained kibble, treats, and other dog gear. "I've sure felt bad lying to her; *this* is going to be a whopper."

"I know, but what choice do we have?" Ted looked sorrowfully at the two canine figures as they walked into Rachel's bedroom, climbed up on the bed, and lay down next to her still form.

~

After putting several miles between himself and Rachel's home, Leo pulled off onto a desolate side road. He turned off the headlights and parked, reminding himself to calm down. It was not like him to have two failures in the span of a week. *Close your eyes, take a deep breath. Count to ten, and let the anger drift away.* He began to whisper, "One. Two. Three." He finished the remaining digits silently, then opened his eyes and stared into the black night.

Nothing was going according to plan; inevitably Murphy's Law always reared its ugly head. *What can go wrong will go wrong.* Leo had quickly contemplated whether to fight and attempt to subdue the approaching woman—a cop?—but the commotion may have alerted the neighbors. That, and he didn't want to risk getting shot. He didn't know the identity of Rachel's visitor, and he'd barely seen her face in the dim moonlight, but something about her suggested she meant business. He'd learned the hard way never to underestimate a woman. Better to go back and try again later. He may have to wait a day or two if the cops were brought into the situation, but he could work around that. Leo opened his glove box and retrieved one of the disposable cells he kept on hand. As he waited for the call to connect, he worked to calm his anxiety.

"What?" Mike's voice was abrupt as usual. Leo had hoped the call might go to voice mail. His boss wasn't always able to answer right away. Not all guards at the prison were on Mike's payroll, nor did he likely want other inmates to know he had a burner phone.

"The attempted retrieval tonight failed." Leo cringed as he listened to a string of curses that would make a sailor blush. Finally, it ended.

"When will this problem be remedied?" Mike demanded.

Leo shifted in his seat as though the man's eyes were bearing down on him through the phone line. "Give me a day or two."

"Okay, take care of it. And make sure she doesn't die like Mr. Reed." The phone call disconnected. Leo thought back to the previous week when he had to explain what happened to Luke. To say Mike had been upset was an understatement. It was just an unlucky turn of events that Mr. Reed drowned, yet why his employer was so angry about it was beyond his comprehension. But Leo wasn't being paid to care.

Chapter Eleven

Rachel heard a muffled voice in the distance. She felt like she was wading through the deep waters of Lake Tahoe, trying to reach the surface but never breaking through. As if the lake kept filling up with more and more water.

"Rachel? Please wake up."

A female voice. She knew that voice, but it was like the synapses firing in her brain couldn't connect. She had to climb her way out of the strange watery fog, and a part of her knew it was going to hurt like hell.

"Rachel, can you hear me?" She felt a soft touch on her hand, then realized someone was holding it. With her awareness still murky, she managed one successful communication: she squeezed.

"Oh, my friend!"

Rachel squeezed the hand again, willing her eyes to open at the same time. The voice was familiar. She tried to speak, but a moan came out instead. Her head throbbed. Maybe she didn't want awareness yet. Something wet touched her cheek. It was cold, yet also soft and familiar.

"Take your time, sweetie. I'm just glad you're coming back to us."

Again she felt something cold and moist touch her skin.

"As is Bella," the female voice laughed. Rachel felt another snout, this one nudging at her toes. "And Avi."

Her eyes obeyed her brain's command to open. "Jill?" she mumbled.

"Yes, it's me. The girls are with me too."

Rachel's vision began to clear as she studied the figure in front of her.

"What happened?" She looked around in confusion. While attempting to sit up, she asked, "Where am I?"

Jill gently touched her arm. "Don't try to get up. Just relax for now."

Rachel lay back, realizing she was sprawled out on a soft bed. Bella was sitting next to her with her tail swinging from side to side.

"Someone snuck up on you in your front yard. Whacked you pretty good too." She tried to keep her tone light, but Rachel could see the worry lines etched on her friend's face. "You've been out for hours."

"Great. Just when I got over that last concussion . . ." Rachel sighed as she reached up to feel the back of her head and winced as her fingertips brushed a large lump.

"Don't touch it. You'll just make it hurt more," Jill advised.

Rachel let her hand drop. "Where am I?"

"We brought you somewhere safe."

"We?"

"Sorry, Ted and I."

"Why? I don't understand?" Rachel closed her eyes again, as if shutting off her sight would make her head stop throbbing. It didn't, so she reopened them and looked at Jill. Something buzzed on a table nearby, and Jill glanced at it.

"It's probably my kids." She stood up and grabbed the cell phone, glancing at the display. "Yep." She paused, then looked back at Rachel with a bleak expression on her face. And something else. Guilt? "There are some very important things I need to tell you, but I have to take this call first." Jill turned to go. "Don't get up. Just relax. I'll be back in a few minutes. There's a glass of water for you next to the bed, and the suitcase you'd packed for my house is in that corner." She waved, smiled, and held the phone to her ear as she walked out.

Rachel certainly didn't want to move and would have been

happy to follow Jill's orders, except she really had to pee. She tried to wait, giving Jill some time to return. The sound of Jill's "angry mom voice" in the other room gave Rachel the impression the call wasn't going to be a fast one. It was red alert time; nature wasn't just calling, it was screaming. She gave the dogs a quick rub with each hand and pulled the covers off while she slowly raised herself. The pounding in her head didn't feel any better, but it also didn't feel any worse. She placed her feet on the floor and stood. Some mild dizziness and nausea; nothing too extreme. Gaining more awareness with each step, she slowly walked toward the door. The dogs shuffled next to her, their tails wagging. It seemed a high level of excitement for simply opening the door; she wondered what else had them so worked up.

"Sorry, girls, no hikes right now." She smiled at them, then peered out the door. A hallway extended in each direction. It opened into a larger room to the right where Jill's voice was coming from. She looked to the left and saw two doors. One of them had to be the cherished facility. After closing the door behind her to keep the dogs in the bedroom, Rachel tried the first knob and sagged with relief when it opened. A couple of minutes later she emerged, planning to go directly back to the bedroom. While she was curious about this place, she would rest and wait for Jill to return, as requested.

So focused on her mission, Rachel almost jumped when the other door opened. Assuming it could only be one other person, she spoke before seeing him. "Ted, hey," she greeted, then paused as the figure emerged from the doorway. Her heart stopped, and she found it difficult to breathe. She blinked, wondering if her head was worse off than she thought.

Standing in the open doorway with a sleepy confused expression on his face, a bandage on his arm, and nothing on but boxers was Luke.

~

Luke awakened from another round of fitful sleep; he was certain he'd heard a female voice somewhere in the small house. Had he left the TV on? Other than Ted and Jill, there had been no visitors, and Jill wouldn't have shown up without telling him. According to the digital clock next to his bed, it was barely five a.m. He was probably imagining it; who knew what this opiate withdrawal was doing to his brain? He'd gone cold turkey twenty hours ago, and from what he'd read online, he expected the full-body aches and accompanying twist in his gut would get worse before they got better. Falling asleep had taken longer than usual, which made him more annoyed to be awakened so early.

He rolled over and reached for the weapon stowed in the drawer next to the bed and stood up. Luke quietly walked to the door and listened. He still heard a voice but no other sounds or footsteps. Perhaps it was just the TV, but given someone had tried to kill him, he waited for a moment after opening the door before stepping into the hallway and making an easy target of himself.

Nothing happened, but he could more clearly hear the voice. It sounded a lot like Jill, but that made no sense. Luke stepped into the doorway and was startled to see another person coming out of the bathroom just a few feet away. He focused his sleepy eyes and was shocked upon recognizing the familiar figure.

Standing in front of him with a confused expression on her face was Rachel. Their eyes met; they both stood, aghast in silence. He wasn't sure how much time passed before she spoke.

"Luke?" she finally uttered, her eyes wide, those beautiful blues he could so easily get lost in.

"Rachel," he blurted out, uncertain of what to say or do. Why was she here? *How* was she here?

"But you're—"

He saw moisture fill her eyes before a tear began to slide down her cheek. "Not dead," he said, knowing what she was thinking. It had been killing him to let her think otherwise, but Ted had insisted it was important no one else knew. Ted told him the only reason Jill had been brought into the fold was because Ted needed someone with medical training that he could trust and with access to an ambulance.

Rachel moved another step closer. Luke remained in place. Deep down, he always hoped to see her face-to-face again one day. To hold her. But not like this. And not while he was finally on his way to ending the horrible addiction that he'd brought upon himself.

"I—" Rachel stepped closer until she was standing right in front of him. She reached out impulsively and cradled his cheek.

The touch of her fingers brought it all back. The sweet way he felt when she caressed his skin. And how much he loved this woman. She reached up with her other hand, grasping both sides of his face as she met his gaze head-on.

Rachel suddenly pulled him toward her and crushed her lips against his. *Oh my God. She felt so good. So sweet.* Luke's tongue gently nudged her lips open, and he returned her kiss with fervor. How he had dreamed of this. Just as he was about to wrap his arms around her, anxious to feel her entire body pressed to his, the kiss abruptly ended, and she backed away from him. He opened his eyes just in time to see her pull her arm back, swing it forward, and slap his cheek with surprising momentum. She recoiled in pain, fell back against the wall, and placed her head in her hands.

"I deserve that," he whispered as he rubbed his sore jaw. He waited for her to look back at him, but she stayed in place, still cradling her head.

"Rachel? Are you okay?" The female voice he'd heard moments ago was louder now. Jill came around the corner. She stopped when she noticed Luke.

"Aw, shit." She walked over to Rachel. "Here, come with me. Let's get you back to bed," she said, wrapping an arm around Rachel and turning her. Jill glanced at him pointedly as they walked away, her message clear: do not follow.

~

"Rachel, I'm so sorry," Jill said as soon as the bedroom door was closed. After greeting them at the door, the two dogs followed Rachel back to her bed where she now sat with her legs folded across each other and waited. The canines were seated at her feet like two stoic guards protecting their queen.

"I don't understand. *How? Why?*" Rachel's brow furrowed as her hands moved to pet the dogs.

"Damn Ted for creating this mess!" Jill said, looking around the room as though there were an escape hatch she could use to leave.

Ted should be doing the explaining. She shifted her gaze back at Rachel. "Let me start from the beginning." Jill realized she had begun pacing and stopped, opting to sit on the corner of the bed.

"Ted called me last week. What you heard—I mean, what he told you—about Luke slipping off a log into Silver Creek, that was true. But he didn't just fall. Someone shot him." Jill noticed Rachel's posture immediately stiffen. "Obviously, he's fine. The shot caught him in the arm. No major damage."

"That explains the bandage," Rachel muttered, obviously still grappling with the shock of seeing Luke alive and well.

"Yeah." Jill scooted farther back on the bed and turned her body so she faced Rachel directly. "Someone had attacked Luke at least once before. Ran him down on his bike. Luke also suspected he was being watched."

"For how long?" Rachel cut in.

"Several weeks or so." Jill paused, but Rachel didn't follow up. "Stubborn man that he is, hell, they *all* are, he didn't take it all that seriously. Thought the driver was drunk and that he was overthinking the rest. But he told Ted anyway. Luke said he'd be more cautious and, at most, let Ted have a patrol car drive by his house periodically. Nothing else happened for several days, so they both thought it was just a bad coincidence."

"A few days, that's all?" Rachel asked, shaking her head. "Not surprised."

Jill nodded, then continued. "Ted wanted to go check out that old house with the freestanding chimney off Highway 4; he'd just read a historical blog that mentioned it. So he invited Luke along, figuring they'd combine it with a bike ride up on Ebbetts Pass afterward. While they were browsing around the area, Luke decided to take a shortcut across the creek on an old log. While he was crossing, someone shot him. The impact startled him enough that he fell into the creek, got disoriented, and was carried downstream by the currents. When Ted finally got to him, Luke wasn't breathing. Ted had to perform CPR to bring him back."

"So he really *had* died, kind of." Rachel looked at the floor. Jill suspected she wasn't sure how to feel. This was a lot to take in.

"Yes, somehow he became trapped under the water before Ted

got to him. Considering the previous attempt on Luke's life, Ted decided the best way to protect Luke was to make the perpetrator think he'd succeeded. He called me, and I was able to contact an ambulance driver who owed me a favor. It was only for show in case the shooter was still watching. Once we made sure we weren't being tailed, we slipped off the highway and transferred Luke into Ted's SUV. Ted said he had a buddy with an empty house in Pioneer, and it all just fell into place—"

"That's where we are? Pioneer, the small town along Highway 88?" Rachel interrupted, looking out the window even though nothing could be seen in the early morning darkness.

"Yes," Jill affirmed, then struggled to resume her explanation in the strained silence of the room. "Ted figured I could monitor Luke from a medical standpoint, and if we needed to, we could drive him to the emergency room in Jackson and use a fake name. Taking him anywhere in Tahoe or Carson was too risky; someone might recognize him. You know how small our world can be up here," she chuckled. "Plus, they were already far out of town either way. Ted arranged to use this house, and we came straight here."

"How did you make this work, legally? I mean, there's a service being planned and everything."

"A lot of careful maneuvering and a fake cremation and urn. Some doctored paperwork on my part. Given Luke's self-imposed separation from his family so long ago, it's not like Luke's parents have been beating down doors to claim his body, but I assume Ted notified them to keep up the pretense."

"This whole situation is a big risk. For both you and Ted."

"Well, first, they hoped it wouldn't go this far and they'd have identified the suspect by now. Second, Ted's captain is in the loop, so it should eventually be made legit on paper."

Rachel moved her hand away from Bella to wipe her cheek, smearing wetness across her face. "And what is their plan now?"

"They hoped they could figure out who's behind the attempts while Luke remained in hiding." The room fell silent. Rachel remained still with a concentrated look on her face. Jill knew that expression; her friend's mind was racing to process the data dump. Jill remained quiet, letting her friend take it all in.

Rachel focused on Jill with accusation in her eyes. Jill had known the anger would surface as the shock wore off; she braced herself as Rachel spoke. "And none of you thought I could be trusted with this?"

"It's not that. We just didn't want you to have to try to pretend. Let me rephrase—*they* didn't want you to have to pretend. *I* wanted to tell you, but I admit they convinced me not to. It killed me. But in their defense, they expected to figure it out before it went this far. When they couldn't, they decided to schedule that damn 'Celebration of Life' to see if it could draw out the killer, and because some people were asking about services. It complicated things." Jill bit her lip as she waited for Rachel's next question. It was an annoying habit she'd been trying to quit for years.

"I can't believe all of this," Rachel finally sputtered and then looked up at Jill. "You're my friend, and I love you, but you let me think he was dead! And you comforted me! I'm so . . . just so pissed off right now." Rachel winced like the heated words caused her pain, and Jill suspected they likely did. She waited. Finally, Rachel spoke again. "I need to be alone right now."

Jill wasn't sure if she'd have preferred being yelled at to the quiet disposition and obvious disappointment in Rachel's expression. "Of course." Jill stood. "I'm really sorry, Rachel. I never meant to hurt you. Let me know if you need anything." Jill waited for a few seconds, but when no response came, she continued, "By the way, your truck is still at your house. We'll drive it to my place tomorrow to support the story that you're staying with me." After another brief moment of silence, she closed the bedroom door. Jill couldn't blame Rachel for being upset with her. She'd internally debated about the situation ever since the men devised their plan the week prior, then again this evening as she drove Rachel down after the attack, but Rachel hadn't regained consciousness during the trip.

She glared at Luke's closed door as if Luke could see her discomfort through it and feel guilt for his role in the lie. That Rachel and Luke had run into each other before Jill had the chance to explain made it that much worse.

Chapter Twelve

Monica sat up and watched her lover roll out of the bed. She admired his backside as the sheets fell down. He looked a lot younger than his sixty-two years. Gray hairs peppered the sides of his head, but for the most part he kept his dark hair. He worked out regularly, boasting a sculpted physique she'd rarely seen in the five and a half decades of her life. And he was a successful state senator. How had this man come to be with her? She certainly didn't consider herself beautiful. "Handsome" was a word more often used to describe women who looked like her, at least before she'd put on those extra pounds in recent years. Stupid menopause had screwed up her entire system, adding weight and redistributing it in the most unflattering ways. Realizing the room had grown silent, she pulled out of her frustrated thoughts to see he was looking at her expectantly with a big smirk on his face.

"You're doing it again."

"Doing what?" she said with a grin.

"Staring at my butt."

"Can you blame me?"

"No, I kind of like it." He grabbed their half-empty wineglasses from the nearby dresser and walked back, handing one to her as he leaned against the headboard. "So how is our little side project going?"

Monica took a long sip of her wine in an effort to keep the

disappointment from showing on her face. This was the last subject she wanted to discuss right now.

"I'm working on it. We've almost contained the leak."

"Almost?" His smile faded.

"There were some unforeseen circumstances, but my people are patching things up." Or so she hoped. At least Luke Reed had been taken care of, regardless of how it happened. She'd advised her contact that actions were best taken in Alpine County where her old "friends" in law enforcement could ensure that little fuss was made, or if it was, that any potential evidence would be lost. But out along a creek like that? Even though they knew exactly where the two men had been headed and how remote the location would be, it was still a dumb place to try something! Then again, it worked out in the end—and even better, his death had been officially declared an accident without need for any further intervention on her part. So far as she was aware, Ted Benson had never heard or seen the shooter Monica had hired; otherwise an investigation would have been started. Instead, Luke had conveniently drowned. Plain and simple. All told, she couldn't complain.

"You understand what happens to me if you fail, right? I mean, they already burned my cabin down!" At the harsh reprimand, Monica's attention turned back to the present. Her heart dropped. They could have been sitting in a cold, sterile boardroom at the office talking company finances for all of the intimacy he now displayed. It was like a light switch had been flipped.

"Of course I do." She heard the defensiveness in her tone and internally cringed at how whiny it sounded. Why was he turning so cold? She was, after all, doing this for him. Well, mostly. That she had her own motivations wasn't something he needed to know. "Look, I'm taking care of it."

"Have you spoken to Mike lately?"

Of course he'd ask about that. "It's been a week or two, but I'm keeping him updated."

"I still don't understand why he's tangled up in this."

"Neither do I." Monica wondered not only why Mike was involved, especially given his current residence courtesy of the legal system, but why he had seemed upset about Luke's death. *Upset!* It made no sense after he spent years blaming Luke and Rachel for his circumstances. She sighed and settled against the pillows. "Can we table this discussion for now? We were having so much fun." Monica slowly reached out and touched his chest, her fingers seductively swirling through the dark hairs.

He paused before speaking, then finally relaxed. "Sure, baby." He reached for her goblet with his free hand and set the two stemmed glasses on the bedside table. She could tell he was irritated, but she could fix that. She'd done it before.

~

Leo was perplexed. Where the hell was Rachel? After confirming she had not checked into the local emergency room—the only medical facility nearby that she could have been taken to in the middle of the night—he waited a few hours before driving back to Rachel's home, just in case the police were there. He had no idea how much damage he'd caused with just one hit; he'd aimed to knock her unconscious and take her, not kill her. Had she regained awareness and decided against seeking medical treatment for some reason? Her pickup was still parked in the same spot. All of the lights were out, although that was typical in the neighborhood.

He looked in all of her windows and even knocked on the front door; not that she'd answer, but he'd expect to hear stirring from inside if she were there, and he felt a slight thrill at the thought of confronting her again. But no dogs barked and no sounds arose from within. Had she gone to a friend's house?

Then it hit him; Luke Reed's memorial service was later today. Of course she'd be attending. His death was the reason she'd been so reclusive over the past week. All he had to do was be patient until the afternoon and she'd be easy to find; no need to waste time trying to track her down beforehand. Leo smiled. The crisp autumn air and clear skies would make for a nice relaxing morning lounging on the shores of Lake Tahoe as the sun rose.

~

Cassandra looked at the caller ID and smiled. About time! She answered with a quick "Yeah?"

"Cassie, I got the phone all opened up for ya."

"Finally!" she spat, then decided it would be a good idea to stay in this man's good graces. "Sorry, let me rephrase. You're awesome, and I appreciate it."

"That's better." His response was curt. Yes, she'd pissed him off.

"Did you start looking through it?" She hadn't asked him to, but she suspected he was curious enough to snoop on his own. She didn't care; it's not like he was going to tell anyone.

"I may have poked around a bit," he chuckled.

"I'll swing by and get it later, but did you happen to notice the last number he dialed?"

"I sure did. Looked it up; belongs to a Rachel Winters."

Talk about worst case scenario. What had Rick told the woman? She couldn't imagine he would have even been able to talk, given how she left him. But it was best to err on the side of caution and assume he had said something. Cassandra didn't realize she'd been silently mulling it over in her head until his next words penetrated.

"You know her?" he asked.

"Don't worry about it. Look, I've got to go. I'll text before I head over." She ended the call before he could respond, sure it would irritate him further but unable to care right now. It was time to pay Miss Winters a visit.

Chapter Thirteen

Luke wanted to simply go back to sleep and enjoy the bliss of unconsciousness instead of thinking about what had just transpired with Rachel. But his body had broken out in a sweat, and thoughts raced in his mind. She was here, just down the hall, after working so hard to avoid her for so long, telling himself that he'd still have a chance with her someday if only he could get himself straightened out first. And now here he was, facing the worst of the withdrawal with her just feet away.

Something else bothered him too. He hadn't realized it at first—how could he, with a kiss like that?—but she appeared to be in physical pain. At first he thought it was frustration with seeing him combined with the hour—Rachel's loathing of early mornings was well known.

Why had Jill brought her here? Of all places! Luke decided it had to be something serious for Jill to have done so, especially without giving him any notice. As if she'd been following his train of thought, he heard three small taps on his door and Jill quietly calling his name.

"Luke, it's me. Can I come in?"

Luke grabbed a tissue from a nearby Kleenex box and wiped it across his forehead, then stood up and walked across the room.

"Okay," he said, keeping his annoyance to a minimum as he opened the door and backed up. Jill silently stepped into the room.

He closed it behind her and waited. There was no need to verbalize his next question; Jill would know.

"We had nowhere else safe to take her."

"What do you mean *safe*? What happened?"

"Someone attacked her in front of her house last night. I was able to run him off, but I was too worried about Rachel to chase after the guy."

Luke sat down on his bed and reached up to touch his healing wound without thinking. "Do you think it's the same person who came at me?"

"Not sure, but it would be quite a coincidence otherwise, don't ya think?" she shot back testily while keeping her voice low and pacing across the room.

"Why are you getting snappy at me? I'm not the one who brought my ex-girlfriend to the same safe house that I'm using!" Luke returned her heated gaze. Like her, he kept his voice closer to a whisper.

"Sorry, I'm just . . . emotional. Frustrated. Scared for both of you. Plus full of guilt for not telling Rachel; as expected, she's pretty upset with me. And as if that's not enough, I'm also ticked off at my kids." Only then did Luke notice the dark circles under her eyes. His anger rescinded.

"Look, no worries. And I'm sorry for being upset. I know you wanted to tell her about our plan and we convinced you not to," he said. "This situation just really, really sucks!" He ran his hand through his hair, hoping Jill hadn't noticed the moisture on his scalp, yet, strangely, he was no longer warm. What, was he having hot flashes now? *Focus, Luke.*

"I know this isn't ideal, and we'd hoped to tell you both—separately—what was going on before you saw each other. But my son Tanner called, and, well . . ."

"Got it." Luke started to feel cold. He glanced over at the two windows; both were closed. "So now what?" he asked.

"Ted is busy dealing with your 'Celebration of Life' today." She smirked as she positioned a folding chair next to a small writing desk to face him.

"That sounds so weird."

"It sure does," she agreed. "Look, I need to get home to my kids so I can see them before I attend the service. I was going to stay if Rachel needed medical attention, but she seems fine enough, just dealing with a bad headache. Plus, you can keep an eye on her now too. But just in case, you know where the emergency room in Jackson is, right?"

Luke nodded. The chill penetrated deep into his bones, like the feeling he got after jumping into Lake Tahoe in the middle of winter on a drunken dare, only worse. The room was silent, and Luke looked up at Jill, unaware until that moment he'd been staring at the floor.

"Are *you* okay? You kind of zoned out."

"Sure, just got cold for some reason." He suspected the cause but wasn't about to tell her.

"You look a little pale."

"I'm fine. Just didn't sleep very well." That was an understatement. He reminded himself of her earlier question. "Yes, I can keep an eye on Rachel; I still remember what to look for after dealing with her previous concussion."

Jill stood, nodding. "I'm sorry. I know there's a huge emotional toll involved in this situation. But we couldn't risk that whoever is targeting you is now coming after her."

"Where will people think she is?"

"She was going to come stay with me tonight after your service. So the good news is she was all packed up and people weren't expecting to see her for a few days at least."

"But did the attacker see *you*? Won't he come after you? Your kids?"

"It was dark, so I don't think he saw enough to identify me. But it did occur to me on our drive down that it wouldn't take long for someone to figure it out if they started looking into Rachel's friends. The kids are at my mom's, and Ted made sure there would be regular police patrols going by her house. He also asked one of his law enforcement friends to come stay with them until I return. Then we'll figure it out from there. That's why Tanner called so early in the morning. He didn't like having to stay with his grandma, let alone with a stranger in the house, so like any teenager, he wanted me to suffer right along with him."

Luke smiled, thinking of stories he'd heard about Jill's headstrong son, although he'd only met him a couple of times. "Well then, go ahead. I'll watch Rachel. You need to get home. It's what, a couple of hours to your place in Minden?" He waved at the door.

"Give or take. But it occurred to me earlier that in the rush to get her out of there, we forgot to set Rachel's house alarm, so I'll swing by and do that if I have time. Otherwise, Ted can send someone."

"She's got a security system?"

"Yes, she gave in after that sicko attacked her last year. But she wasn't happy about it."

Luke was relieved. He also knew having to install a security system had to irritate Rachel. "I imagine not," he replied. "All right, get going so you can have breakfast with your kids." The strange chills were abating, but mild nausea had started to form in his gut. While he meant every word he said to Jill, he was also anxious to be alone.

"You sure you're okay?" she asked, hopping to her feet as though the idea of seeing her kids had given her a sudden energy boost. Luke figured it probably had.

"Yeah, think I ate something bad," he mumbled, glancing toward the bathroom.

"Don't have to ask me twice. Last thing I want to do is see you puking. One of the benefits of all of your 'patients' being dead is that they'll never throw up on you," she joked. "But seriously, I'll talk to Ted, and then we'll all just figure out what's next."

"It's tough to be stuck down here, watching from a distance as someone else works to figure out who's trying to kill me. And damn, maybe Rachel now too. I can't even call my usual contacts!"

"Give yourself some credit. You need to stay 'dead' for now, and I know you've been doing what you can online."

Luke nodded. "Still feel worthless."

Jill opened the door. "Take it easy, Luke. And be gentle with Rachel, got it?"

"Of course, and I'm sorry we didn't let you tell her I was alive.

Now go see your kids."

Jill made one last cursory glance his way, as if debating whether to say more about his health, but opted to keep quiet. Once she was gone and he had the room to himself again, he fell back on his bed, ready to dash to the attached bathroom any second. His stomach roiled, not a good sign of things to come.

Chapter Fourteen

Cassandra glanced around at the empty streets surrounding Rachel's house, which were barely lit by the early morning sunrise. It was still dark enough that had there been any neighbors watching, they wouldn't be able to see more than her outline. Just to be safe, she'd adorned one of her more subtle wigs, with a shoulder-length bob and a crocheted hat covering most of her head. Just another Tahoe local out strolling on a cool morning.

Cassandra, aiming for the gate to the backyard, walked past the dusty Tacoma parked in the driveway and along the side of the house. The gate was locked but easy enough to crawl over using the pile of stacked wood nearby as a step. She boosted herself up and dropped down into the backyard, half anticipating the woman's dogs to come running out at any minute, but they were apt to be sleeping inside. Two fresh bones were stowed in her pocket in the event a canine distraction was needed. Nothing happened. *Good.*

After rounding the corner, a large window facing the backyard came into view. She peeked inside and discerned the faint image of a large bed and dresser, lit by a dim night-light. Yet no one was in it. While this appeared to be the master bedroom, it was possible the woman slept in another room or maybe fell asleep on the couch.

The well-worn deck squeaked as Cassandra walked across. She waited, but as before, there was only silence from inside. A few more steps and she peered through the sliding glass door. Vertical blinds blocked most of her view, but a six-inch gap provided the opportunity to look inside. No Rachel, no dogs. She suspected there was only enough space for one more bedroom in this one-story house, so she stepped down from the deck and walked around the other side, seeing another window, this one smaller than the first. Repeating her careful glimpse inside, she saw office furniture.

Either Miss Winters hadn't slept at home last night, even though her truck was parked out front, or there was more to this house than appeared from her vantage points. Cassandra debated about breaking in. She questioned whether there was anything to gain from a search but decided it couldn't hurt. And if the woman was inside, so be it. After all, Cassandra had originally come with the intention of having "a conversation" with the woman.

With her mind made up, she reached into her pocket for her gloves as she walked back to the glass door. She began to inspect the sliding glass door with her fingers securely covered. It had a typical locking mechanism, nothing substantial. A small sticker in the lower left corner caught her eye. Leaning over, she saw the icon and phone number for a local alarm company.

"Damn!" Did this old cabin really have an alarm, or was it just a means to deter would-be burglars? Debating, Cassandra looked out behind the yard. Her vehicle was parked over a block away, tucked in with a group of cars overflowing on the streets from a nearby vacation rental. If she had to leave the house in a hurry, she could skirt the trees in the forest behind it and make her way back to her car.

Cassandra considered her entry point. The bedroom window would likely be easier and faster than dealing with the sliding glass door, depending on the locking mechanism. If she could find something to step on, she could reach it well enough to remove the screen and climb inside. Glancing around, she eyed a small ladder propped against the nearby wooden fence. *Perfect.* Her luck continued when she discovered the window's lever wasn't in the locked position. Within a matter of seconds she was crawling into what she'd considered the master bedroom; no sirens or alarms interrupted the serenity of the early morning. No phones rang. Perhaps it was merely a sticker placed as a deterrent.

A quick look through the dresser drawers and closet revealed nothing of interest, other than confirming the woman had poor taste in fashion as she appeared to live in jeans, shorts, and T-shirts. She browsed through the snowshoes and ski gear tucked into the corner. No hidden treasures there either. Cassandra walked out into the hallway and saw an open door leading into the office she'd observed from outside. There was an empty spot on the desk outlined by a light surface of dust, no doubt where a laptop would be placed. It was surrounded by several piles of documents. A quick look indicated a variety of environmental papers, large reports, and legal language.

She walked out into the family room, her eyes scanning in all directions as she walked across the floor. She glimpsed at a small paper or flyer of some type placed atop the end of the kitchen counter and picked it up; it was a funeral announcement for Luke Reed. *That's right!* The service was later today.

"Well, not as exciting as crashing a wedding, but it should be interesting," she muttered as she reached into her pocket, retrieved her phone, and snapped a picture of the flyer. She continued to browse, finding a stack of papers with a list of names and numbers on the top sheet by the phone. Did people really write down lists like that anymore?

She continued sorting through the various sticky notes and other items. One of the scrawled lists referenced dog beds and dishes, a laptop, extra shoes, and a hat. Cassandra looked around the house, realizing there were no water or food bowls anywhere in sight. She glanced inside the refrigerator and confirmed her suspicions. It was almost empty, other than basic condiments. No fresh fruits or vegetables, no open milk containers. All signs that Rachel had packed for an extended trip. Not a problem; Cassandra knew exactly where she'd be later that afternoon. Feeling even more secure in her opportunity to keep searching, she continued to look through the house but turned up nothing else worth noting.

When she was done, she placed the window screen back in place, put the ladder where she'd found it, and carefully made her way out of the yard.

Chapter Fifteen

Rachel's head throbbed, but it was more of a dull ache compared to the previous night. The clock on the bedside table displayed 12:03 in dark red letters. She assumed it was p.m. given the sunlight peeking in around the blinds. Where was she?

Before she could get her wits about her, Bella's bushy tail brushed against her face as the dog turned and rolled over, displaying her belly for her regular morning rub. Rachel automatically complied, her left hand massaging the dog's bared stomach while her right hand reached over and stroked Avi's stubbed ears. Although she rarely noticed the dog's mutilated ears, or "earlettes" as she'd labeled them to try to make light of a bad situation, Rachel recalled the events that led to her adopting the pup over a year ago after being rescued from an abusive owner.

Once the dogs were pacified with morning greetings, they jumped off the bed and began bouncing around the room. As she watched, hoping their energy would stimulate her own, the events of the night before began to replay through her mind, and it hit her all over again: Luke was alive! She wasn't sure if the butterflies swarming her stomach were from excitement or angst over their encounter earlier. After spending over a year trying to get over him, then the past week struggling to accept he was gone for good, her emotions ran in chaotic circles like a Disneyland rollercoaster. Of course, she had no idea what to say to him. Jill's confession that

Luke and Ted prevented her from telling Rachel his death was fake added anger to the swirl of feelings already running through her. That it was Ted's call, not Luke's, didn't do much to help alleviate her anger.

Would he be out in the kitchen? She wasn't ready to face him again, but the dogs needed to go outside and Rachel desperately coveted coffee. The house was quiet as she stepped into the hallway and carefully glanced to the left. The bedroom door where Luke slept was closed. Ignoring the mix of emotions she felt from his close proximity, she followed the dogs as they bounded to the right, leading her into a large family room containing an overstuffed sofa, two recliners, a long mahogany coffee table, and a large TV mounted to the wall. The room had a musty odor like an old mountain cabin that hadn't been lived in for a while. The kitchen was around the corner to the left. Between the family room and kitchen there was a door that she guessed opened to a backyard. She quietly turned the latch and looked out. The yard was enclosed by a tall chicken-wire fence. *Perfect.* She could let the dogs roam without watching them. Rachel stepped out, keeping the dogs inside as she examined the area for any potentially dangerous items. Confident it was safe, she opened the door and said, "Okay." The dogs anxiously ran past her and leapt outside.

Rachel left the door open, stepped back into the kitchen, and observed the counters. The blessed sight of a coffee maker brought a smile to her face, creating a welcome distraction from her aching head. She opened the refrigerator to find that Jill had packed up her food. That was Jill—always thinking of the details. Rachel was anxious to apologize to Jill for her bad reaction the night before; Jill had been placed in a tough spot. Lying to Rachel had no doubt been difficult.

Rachel reached for her creamer, then perused the cabinets, finding a container of coffee grounds on one of the shelves. The sound of the dogs' tags floated in as she prepared the machine for brewing. She was soon savoring the hot beverage like her life depended on it. Sometimes Rachel thought it had.

"Okay, Jill, where did you put the dog supplies?" she wondered aloud as her eyes searched the room. The familiar large blue bag with "Bella and Avi" stenciled on it in white, courtesy of her crafty mother, sat in the corner. As if knowing the exact moment her hands reached inside and retrieved the packed dog food, the two canines came rushing in and sat attentively at her side. "I'm getting the dishes. Just wait a minute," she said before filling the bowls. Once the girls were happily devouring breakfast, Rachel walked over and closed the back door.

"You two good out here while I shower?" Of course they wouldn't respond, but she still talked to them. They were her kids after all. Rachel went back into the bedroom she occupied, grabbed toiletry supplies and fresh clothes, and then trudged into the bathroom after pausing for a second to listen near Luke's door. The distant sound of running water suggested he was taking a shower. Rachel tried not to picture the water beading down his contoured chest, or the sexy way his hair stood on end when wet. *Too late.* She sighed inwardly and stepped away.

~

This is miserable. Utterly freaking miserable. Luke had never felt so bad in his life. Not even when he had walking pneumonia in his twenties. Maybe not even when he was shot through his chest a few years ago. Everything ached. His body altered between shivering with chills and sudden bouts of sweating. He felt the urge to throw up but couldn't. Gurgling sounds in his stomach foretold of extended time on the toilet in the near future.

This is what you get for letting yourself get addicted to those damn pills, he self-criticized as hot water beat against his neck. Steam rose and filled his nostrils. Luke sucked in deep breaths, replete with resolve. He wasn't going to give in. Hell, he *couldn't.* There hadn't exactly been time to run home and grab his stash of extra pills after the incident. With just a week's supply packed in the small go-bag he always kept in his car, he'd decided it was a sign that it was time to go cold turkey. Of course, he was supposed to be alone when this happened. And the last person he wanted to see him in this condition was currently just down the hall.

The only option was to play like he was sick. Rachel would gladly avoid being exposed to potential flu germs. She always said being sick and owning an energetic border collie were incongruous;

now she had two of them. Pulling the illness card was the easiest way he could think of to ensure she kept her distance. Hopefully he'd be through the worst of it within a few days and could then begin to "heal" from his flu bug.

The water instantly turned cold, and he jumped in surprise. It warmed again, reminiscent of his body's shifting temperature. He turned the spray off and stepped out to grab a towel, noticing the nearby sound of running water. Rachel must be showering in the other bathroom; Luke couldn't help but picture the curves of her body glistening as streams of water caressed her skin. One thing they had never struggled with was physical chemistry; it was off the charts. But there had been more between them than just sex. There still was. Presuming he could beat this narcotic addiction, would she even want him back?

His stomach twisted, reminding him he was now paying a hefty physical price for his addiction. He decided to write her a note about his "illness" before she finished cleaning up. It was an easy way to avoid face-to-face contact for the time being. After drying, he wrapped the towel around his waist, charged back into his room, and grabbed notepaper and a pen. He quickly scrawled a message and slipped out the door.

The dogs trotted up to greet him. Bella profusely wagged her tail as she rubbed against him while Avi observed cautiously from a few feet away, her tail moving hesitantly as if she were unsure about whether to be excited. The younger dog was still skittish around him. Luke swiftly walked into the kitchen and set the note on the countertop, the aroma of fresh coffee tormenting him. No way could his stomach handle it now. After retrieving several energy drinks and a few snacks he'd purchased several days ago at a nearby store, he returned to his room. Just as he slipped back inside his temporary self-imposed prison, the shower turned off. Luke closed the door, tossed the items on the bed, and dashed to the bathroom as nausea overwhelmed him.

Chapter Sixteen

The stench was like nothing she'd ever smelled before. It clogged her nostrils. *Is that burning human flesh? Is it mine?* Strangely, Lacey didn't feel any pain. Smoke irritated her eyes, already blurry from excessive rubbing. Another crackle, just feet away. Hadn't she escaped?

Lacey bolted upright, rousing so ferociously from the dream that she was instantly awake. Her eyes scanned the room, hoping to see she was lying in bed, comfortable and safe, at her grandfather's cabin by Cascade Lake. But as awareness set in, she knew it wasn't possible. The small cabin had been her getaway, her sanctuary over the years; now it was gone—consumed by the firestorm that had disguised her own abduction.

She gazed across the room that had been her prison for several months now, although it felt more like years. The only way she knew how much time had passed was by placing a mark on a sheet of paper from the sketchpad she'd been provided. It was her only entertainment in this fortress besides the old beat-up copies of "classic" books like *Moby Dick* and *Pride and Prejudice* she had no interest in reading. Until it had broken about a month ago, there was also an old DVD player with a handful of dated movies including the *Indiana Jones* series, *Dirty Dancing*, and the *Vacation* movies with Chevy Chase. It was as if they expected to abduct someone her mom's age. Tracking the passage of time hadn't occurred to her until a few days into her abduction because, at first, she anticipated someone would show up and rescue her. Only after some time passed and her nerves had unwound at the knowledge that, at least temporarily, they weren't going to kill her did she consider that her family probably didn't know where she was. Was it possible they thought she'd perished in the fire?

"Stop it," she whispered to herself. It would do no good to go down that road again. Lacey had to maintain hope her parents and grandfather were looking for her. Her job was to get through this alive. Better yet, to escape, though she had yet to figure out how. Unfortunately the one window in the space had bear-proof grills bolted on the outside. While she could open the window for air, it provided no opportunity for escape. Lacey had since spent countless hours looking out that window at the thick oak trees and bushes nearby.

In the first few days here, she'd screamed at the top of her lungs until her voice ran out. No one answered. One of her kidnappers eventually came to the other side of the door and laughed as he told her to yell all she wanted; no one would hear her. After several months, she hadn't seen nor heard anyone other than her captors.

Why am I here? A tear slid down her face and she chastised herself for acting like a baby. She was fifteen; she could do this. It had taken everything she had to keep her cool, but something told her she wasn't supposed to be here forever. The inexplicable instinct that this was temporary gave her hope; it helped her focus. She needed both to keep her mind from wandering a slow path into insanity.

Lacey only hoped her intuition was right.

~

Ted stared into the single bathroom's small mirror at his moisture-filled red eyes. When Jill suggested he slice onions before the service to make it look like he'd been crying, he almost laughed. But she'd been right. It was difficult enough to pretend to be mourning his friend; trying to add tears on his own would have been impossible.

It was time to get back out and focus on the crowd. Sometimes murderers liked to attend the funerals of their victims to relive the kill or some other kind of mental derangement. He also felt there was a chance that whoever was after Rachel—who could be the same person that shot at Luke—may expect to find her here. With Jill's help, he'd created a story to eventually explain Rachel's absence; for the time being they would pretend to expect her arrival at any time.

"Teddy?" Jill's voice barely registered above the small tapping against the door.

He opened the door and whispered, "How's it going out there?"

"As expected. Some people are asking about Luke's family. I just say they were estranged." She paused, then slipped inside and closed the door. "I feel so bad to be letting these people suffer. Bad enough to have let Rachel believe—"

"Look, I'm sorry. I know you weren't happy about that decision. But—"

"It's done. I'm not the one you need to apologize to at this point."

"Just so you know, it wasn't easy for me to withhold it either," he murmured.

"I know," Jill said. "Were you able to turn on Rachel's alarm?" In her rush to get home from Pioneer earlier that day, Jill had called Ted for help.

"No, ran out of time. But I got someone to drive her truck to your place about an hour ago and asked Kris to take care of the alarm."

"Good. I presume you told Kris the story we discussed?"

Ted gave her one of his "give me some credit" glares.

Jill grinned before her expression quickly turned serious. "So we're supposed to keep an eye out for anyone looking suspicious?"

"Yes, but I don't know all of Luke's friends or associates. I'm sure some of his clients are here. Although I'd prefer to catch our perpetrator today, we're getting video from several locations. It will take some time to get through it all later if we have to. Wish the guy would be kind enough to just announce himself."

"If only." Jill rubbed her eyes. Ted wasn't the only one who'd used the onion trick.

"Heard from our reunited couple?"

"Rachel texted earlier. Said Luke was sick and staying in his room."

"Think that's true or just an avoidance tactic?" Ted wondered as he reached for another tissue to rub his irritated eyes.

"He was looking pretty bad when I saw him. He thought he had food poisoning, but it sounds like it's more than that. Shoot, hope I don't get it now," she muttered.

"How are your kids doing?"

"Unhappy but alive. Thanks for having your buddy stay with them. We've got them all settled in that house you provided in Genoa. They were not thrilled to hear the news this morning and reiterated their displeasure when I got home with the loudest round of packing I've ever heard."

"Wonder where they get that stubborn streak?" he chuckled.

"At least when I'm stubborn, it's with good cause." Ted started to say something, but she cut him off. "Don't say it."

"Say what?" he played along. "But seriously, the more they get from you, the better. That worthless piece of crap they call dad doesn't realize just how awesome his kids are." He heard the muffled sound of music starting to play.

"Well, guess the show's about to start." Jill opened the door. "Let's go."

Ted nodded and followed her out into the hallway. They reentered the main room and looked around at the sixty or seventy attendees. Some stood or sat mournfully. Others laughed, sharing stories and savoring memories about Luke.

"Here we go," she whispered as she pointed toward a row of chairs up front. Like the rest of the people in the room, they somberly took their seats.

~

Cassandra scanned the room but saw no sign of Rachel. Was she running behind? The music started and everyone began to take their seats. She found an empty chair in the back row, positioning herself so she could see those who arrived late. Looking around the room, she recognized a few faces. Not surprising, as South Lake Tahoe could be a very small town, even with the 23,000 residents and millions of visitors each year. That was one reason Cassandra had taken extra care to disguise herself so that she was confident no one would recognize her. Stage makeup and face implants along with the right wig, clothes, and mannerisms allowed her to play many roles. She actually enjoyed it. *Maybe I should've been an actress*, she mused.

Cassandra's gaze fell on the face of a man at the opposite side of the room when he turned to look in her direction; even though disguised, it was a face she knew well. Hell, she'd helped him assemble that particular costume once before. What was Leo doing here? If there was anyone who might recognize her upon close inspection, it was her ex-lover. She slithered down farther in her seat and leaned over to retrieve a tissue from her small purse. Pretending to wipe tears from her eyes, she glanced his way. He was facing forward again, allowing her heart to stop racing. She needed to get out of there fast. Just as she knew his disguises, he knew hers. Several people were still finding their way to seats, so it shouldn't draw too much attention if a guest stood up. Before strolling out the back door, she peered into the room one last time; Leo was looking forward. There was no way to know if he'd turned to see her departing or not.

Keys in hand, she crossed the parking lot and opened the door to her rented car. Perhaps this was for the best. If she found Rachel out here before she went inside, there would be no one to see them. Cassandra sat back in her seat. As she settled in to wait, she considered Leo's attendance. Given the past history he'd confided to her years ago, she shouldn't be too surprised to find him involved in this situation. While she understood his desire for revenge, she couldn't fathom what his role was in all this. And what end game he had in mind.

Chapter Seventeen

Kris tucked loose hairs behind her ear as she turned from Highway 50 toward Rachel's house. A last-minute call from Ted as she was en route to Luke's service had changed her plans. Ted informed her that Rachel declined to attend the service. Given her brief conversations with her heartbroken friend over the past week, this didn't surprise her. According to Ted, Rachel packed up her luggage and the dogs and headed straight to Jill's house, contacting him when she realized she'd forgotten to set her house alarm.

Kris ached for her friend's suffering but had to admit she didn't mind missing the "Celebration of Life." When she turned the final corner and Rachel's small house came into view, Kris was surprised to see a strange SUV parked in the driveway. She slowed; danger tended to surround her friend like long-lost relatives of a lottery winner. As she cruised closer, the rental sticker on the bumper came into view. Kris stopped her car in the street and hoped no one would come driving up behind her.

She began to reach for her phone, prepared to dial 9-1-1, when she noticed movement. A man wearing a purple and gray ball cap and dark sunglasses breezed around the side of the house, stepping back up to the front porch. He knocked, waited, then stepped to the side, removed his sunglasses, and cupped his hands to peer into the front window. Kris debated, deciding it was better to be safe than sorry. She tapped the "9" key on her cell phone as he turned and looked in her direction. Her heart fluttered, just once, as recognition set in. Kris stepped on the gas and parked her car next to the rental. He stared at her, appearing just as surprised as she was. Kris took her time getting out of her car, not wanting to appear anxious in any way. Because she wasn't, right? As she walked up toward Rachel's porch, she called out.

"I see the prodigal brother has returned."

"Hey, Kris."

"Derek," she acknowledged. He hadn't changed much since she'd seen him over a year ago. His dark hair still hung loosely to the top of his ears, currently smashed down by the Colorado Rockies hat. His cocky grin was barely discernable through the otherwise flustered look on his face. Was it from seeing her, or because of his obvious expectation that his sister would be here?

"You're looking well. I like the colors," he said, briefly glancing at her hair before stepping down to face her and pulling her into a hug. "It's good to see you."

Kris didn't know what to say. This was the last thing she'd expected. But then again, she'd never reunited with someone she'd been held prisoner with. What was the proper greeting?

"You too." She stepped back, fingering her red, orange, and yellow-highlighted locks. "Celebrating autumn," she answered. "Did Rachel know you were coming?"

"No. I was able to get some time off at the last minute. Figured she could use some support after the service yesterday."

"You mean *today*, as in, right now." This was indeed the Derek Winters she'd heard about from Rachel for years, the one who tended to forget important details and sometimes dropped in unannounced, typically at inopportune moments. While she'd seen some of that side of his personality during their abduction, she'd also observed several positive traits, which had been both thrilling and dangerous.

Derek froze like a deer in headlights and then groaned, "Crap." He removed his cap, ran his fingers through his hair, and replaced it back on his head as he looked around the yard.

"Yep," she agreed as she walked around him, pulling the key for Rachel's house from her pocket. "She's not here anyway. Already went down to Jill's place. Ted said she was too upset to attend the service." She heard Derek's footsteps following behind as she opened the front door and walked inside. It felt strange to be greeted only by silence.

"Damn," he cursed from behind her. "I guess I'd hoped she would be handling it better. They broke up quite some time ago."

"You know as well as I do that those two had some kind of connection that doesn't break so easily. Not that I haven't tried to help her move on." Kris thought of the pressure she'd placed on Rachel to date again, feeling guilty for realizing too late that it wasn't helping. She just wanted to get her friend out of the rut she had fallen into. Heck, even if Rachel could just get laid a few times, it might help her move on.

"You're right." He walked over to the refrigerator.

"What are you doing?" Kris asked, surprised at his brazenness.

"Looking for a beer." He opened the door.

"Seriously? I just told you your sister is majorly grieving, and the first thing you do is look to steal a beer from her?"

"It's not stealing if it's family."

Kris rolled her eyes. "I'm not even going to dignify that with a response."

"This thing is empty anyway!"

"I assume she took food with her. And you know she doesn't drink beer."

"But she had some before—"

"She kept it for Luke," Kris cut in. "Look, I don't know what to tell you. She's not here and won't be for several days."

"Then why are *you* here?"

"To turn on the alarm. She overlooked it when she left earlier."

"Oh, that's right. I forgot she had that installed." He started opening cabinets and browsing through food items.

"So . . . what are you going to do then?"

"Not sure. Suppose I'll give her a call, see if she wants to come back and hang with her big bro."

"And if she doesn't?"

"Why wouldn't she?" He grabbed a can of mixed nuts and ripped the lid off.

"Where do I start?" Kris replied, pulling the can from his hand. "Have a little respect."

Derek looked confused. "Huh?"

Kris grabbed the lid from his other hand, placed it back on the can, and set it back up in the cabinet. "Not sure you'd comprehend it even if I explained," she muttered. "Okay, look. I'm sure she'd have no issues—well, major issues—with you staying here solo, so I'm going to leave you two to work it out. Do you know the alarm code so you don't set it off on accident?" Kris spoke as though she were talking to an obstinate child, which was fitting given the less desirable version of Derek standing before her. This wasn't the sensitive, caring guy she'd gotten to know locked away in that cabin.

"No, how about you give it to me? I'll get in touch with Rachel, and if she wants me to leave, I'll go. Scout's honor." He put up three fingers in the customary gesture of scouts.

"Were you ever a scout?"

"No," he said with the smile that could melt a girl's heart if she wasn't careful. But Kris knew how to be careful. She shook her head as she turned to reach for a notepad. After writing the number and instructions down, she turned to go.

"Think you can handle it?"

"What am I? Twelve? Yes, I can handle it."

"Famous last words," she said as she smirked and walked out. "See you later." She stepped down from the front porch and heard a distant chuckle as she walked to her car.

~

Leo scratched his forehead. The wig was too tight, but his disguise had to be believable among the crowd of mourners. He chose a seat in back that allowed him to watch the room and keep an eye out for Rachel. It would be tricky when it came time to approach her and find a way to spirit her away after the service ended.

Leo twisted in his chair and scanned the entire room. Still no sign of her. He paused at the sight of a petite woman sitting at the other end of his row. Her chin-length brown strands partially obscured her face, yet something about her was familiar. She was looking down to her side, reaching into a purse. Her hand came up with a tissue, and she blew her nose.

Leo was overthinking; time to focus on his primary mission. He faced forward again, his eyes following the movement of the cop alongside a tall athletic-looking woman with dark hair and an olive complexion. Leo stared at her as his mind connected the dots; it was the woman who'd fought him off Rachel the other night. He was sure of it. No way would she recognize him, even if it hadn't been dark the other night.

The few guests still standing began to sit, and conversation died down until the room was silent, barring a few sniffles from people in the crowd. The sound of a door closing in the back of the room interrupted the otherwise silent room. Leo turned and looked behind him, expecting to see Rachel. A stooped old man walked toward an empty seat in the back row.

He turned back around, beginning to sense that Rachel was not coming and he was, therefore, wasting his entire afternoon. Leo was tempted to leave, but the last thing he needed to do was draw attention to himself, even if no one could possibly recognize him.

After two hours that felt more like four, the formal aspect of the celebration was complete; numerous people had spoken with shaky voices, sharing stories about Luke in between occasional bouts of tears. Mourners were advised of food and beverages being provided in a large hall next door and asked to stay to take comfort with their friends and family. Leo saw his opportunity to quietly sneak out.

How could Rachel have missed this? Had she been more hurt by his attack than he'd thought? He considered the possibility that her friend had taken her to another medical facility, one he hadn't checked. The only way he could think of to find out now was to follow the friend. And a name would be a great way to start. He thought she'd introduced herself as Jill when she spoke about Luke. Perhaps she was listed in the funeral program he'd been handed when he walked in. He retrieved it from his pocket. Inside, it listed the names of those who had organized the service and were among the first to speak; toward the top was "Dr. Jillian Reynolds." Leo was going to have to do a little digging into Dr. Reynolds.

~

Cassandra watched Leo slowly walk out of the large building. His gait was casual, and his head was bowed like he was grieving. But she could see underlying tension in his body; he was on guard. He slipped sunglasses on, an obvious ploy to hide the fact that he was scanning the parking lot. Looking for her? Rachel? Or someone else? Or did he just happen to be acquainted with Luke in some way? She sunk down in her seat, hoping he wouldn't notice her outline as she chastised herself for not leaving sooner. Clearly Rachel Winters was not going to be here; why she had waited so long she didn't know. This entire project had morphed into a much larger headache than she originally anticipated. Cassandra was relieved when Leo turned, headed to her right, reached into his pocket, and retrieved his keys. She waited to see what his next move would be.

It was almost laughable when he climbed into a beige pickup and sat behind the wheel without starting the engine. If he was going to sit there and watch, she may be stuck as well. Leaving might draw his attention, at least until other people shuffled out and cars began to depart the lot. Curious, she continued to observe him as he sat up; it was a slight move but enough to indicate his interest in a couple walking out of the building. Cassandra recognized the pair: Luke's friend, Officer Ted Benson and . . . what was the woman's name? She'd heard it somewhere before but couldn't seem to recall it now.

After a brief conversation, Ted and the woman went their separate ways. Leo's gaze followed the woman from his post inside the old truck, giving Cassandra the answer to her question about who her ex-lover was so interested in.

Chapter Eighteen

Rachel wasn't sure how to feel as she glanced at Luke's door on her way to shower. Knowing Luke was just feet away, separated only by two inches of wood, stirred a mix of emotions. She'd been surprised by his note yesterday. Was he really sick or just avoiding her? While Jill confirmed Luke appeared to be coming down with something or had food poisoning right before she left them, the timing was still suspicious. But would he be so juvenile as to lie like that to get out of having to see her? She didn't think so. They'd briefly spoken through the door yesterday afternoon when Rachel informed him she was taking the dogs for a walk; he had sounded legitimately exhausted.

After a full twenty-four hours passed since he'd apparently fallen ill, she'd switched from questioning his motives to worrying about his health. That was it—if he hadn't emerged by the time she ate breakfast, she was going to demand to see him whether he liked it or not.

Fifteen minutes later, her brain finally beginning to wake up, she walked back into the kitchen. Bella and Avi were playing tug with one of the rope toys she'd packed in their travel bag. She decided to check her email and scan the Tahoe area news. Once her laptop was booted up, she sat down on a backless stool and opened the browser. An ad for phone service on the main page reminded her she hadn't checked the messages on her landline since before she'd been attacked. She looked around and saw a cordless receiver by the front door.

Since she had forwarded all landline calls to her cell starting the night before Luke's service, she need only check her cell's voice mail. Without the handy app on her cell phone, temporarily out of commission lest someone was tracking her, she had to think for a moment to remember the passcode.

The newest messages played first. A few acquaintances had called to offer their condolences after seeing news of Luke's service in the local paper. Two days ago it would have had her bursting into tears; now she felt an infusion of anger and relief. Guilt tried to work its way into the mix as well, yet she reminded herself she had nothing to feel bad about. She hadn't set this up, nor had she lied and let everyone think Luke was dead.

The next two messages were from Seth. Rachel bit the inside of her cheek as she listened. The most recent one played first; according to the verbal time and date stamp, it had arrived about twenty minutes ago.

"Hi, it's Seth. Just checking in. Sorry for another call. I'm just concerned. Please, shoot me a text or something. Thanks." She detected a hint of annoyance in his message. She couldn't blame him, but he was coming across as far too concerned for having just gone on a few dates with her.

The next call was stamped yesterday morning. "Hey, Rachel, it's Seth again. I'm sorry if I'm pestering you, and I know you are dealing with the loss of your friend, but I'm just . . . I'm worried about you. Can you please just call me back and let me know you're okay? Or even send a text? And if you need anything, let me know. Okay, well, I'll talk to you later. Bye."

Damn, Seth again. She didn't want to talk to him, though she also didn't want to be one of those women who just ghosted a man either. "I can't exactly text you since I can't use my cell," she mumbled. Calling anyone right now was out of the question; she couldn't deny that her acting skills left something to be desired.

Another message played. Her brother's deep voice left a simple message: "Hey, Sis, it's me. Please give me a ring as soon as you get this. It's important." His clipped voice softened before he added, "I hope you're doing okay after the service."

What did Derek want? She hated when he left messages with no indication of what his call was about. There were plenty of times when his "urgent" messages were related to coordinating gift purchases for their parents' birthdays or asking how snow conditions were out her way because he was debating where to ski. Rachel decided Derek would just have to sit tight and wait.

She was about to hang up when the playback continued with an older message she had previously saved. After the machine identified the caller's phone number, time, and date, she heard the strange tapping noises from the other night. The odd message had completely slipped her mind. Rachel listened as the taps went on and on for at least a minute. She replayed the recording. Once again the electronic voice stated the phone number. Something about it was familiar. Rachel contemplated where she'd seen the number before. The message replayed.

Click-click-click. *Tap*, pause, *tap*, pause, *tap,* pause. *Click-click-click.*

Both answers slammed into her consciousness at once. One, the phone number was Rick's, the firefighter she'd dated that one time. They'd only spoken and texted a couple of times, but she recalled the number because the last four digits were all sixes. And two, those sounds weren't random; they were Morse code. Not all of the clicks followed the same pattern, and the sounds alternated between the higher click of a fingernail and softer tap of a finger pad. She only knew one thing in Morse code: SOS.

~

"Kris, have you spoken to Rachel?" Derek demanded the minute the call was answered. He'd been lucky Rachel displayed a list of contact numbers by her phone.

"Good morning to you too, Derek." She sounded groggy.

"Look, have you heard from her or not?"

"Chill out," she complained. He heard shuffling noises. Was she still in bed? It was almost nine a.m. "Nothing on my cell. Let me check my landline . . ." He heard the sound of footsteps. Derek swallowed any snappy remarks for her to hurry up, despite the anxiety that coursed through his veins. It was not like Rachel to fail to even reply via text when she wasn't in the mood to chat.

"Nothing on my home phone either."

"Don't you think that's odd?"

"I suppose. However, when I texted her last night about, well, *you*, I didn't say she needed to get back to me." A quiet motor-like sound interrupted their conversation.

"Is that Nemo?" Derek asked, surprised at how loud the cat purred.

"Of course," she said, and then he heard her whisper, "Good boy."

"Did you just crawl back in bed or something?"

"Yes, not that it's any of your business."

"It is when Rachel's missing!" he snapped, gripping the phone.

"Derek, calm down. I'm sure she's just keeping a low profile. She didn't even attend the service; obviously she doesn't want to talk to anyone."

"But she usually texts, even if it's to tell me to 'screw off.'"

"Maybe her phone died and she forgot to recharge it. Or maybe the app isn't notifying her. Sometimes mine won't—"

"This is Rachel we're talking about. Saying trouble follows her is like saying you have a few tourists in town for the Fourth of July fireworks."

"Understatement, yes, I get your point," she sighed. Derek heard more shifting, and the purring disappeared. "Okay, I'm up. Look, did you call Jill?"

"Yep, got voice mail there too."

"Try anyone else?"

"Not yet. Who should I call next?" Derek skimmed the handwritten list of numbers. He recognized a few of the names as people she'd talked about over the years. He'd met a few but didn't otherwise know any of them very well.

"I'd go straight to Ted Benson. The officer from—"

"I know who he is. Think I'd forget that?" Derek pictured the serious visage of the detective who'd helped rescue them over a year ago.

"I'm just trying to help. Stop being such a dick."

That stopped Derek's racing thoughts. She was right. "I'm sorry. I'm just worried."

"It's fine. Look, you want me to call Ted? I know him well enough."

"No, I'll do it. How about you give Jill another try? Maybe she didn't recognize my number and let it go to voice mail. Like how Rachel refuses to answer unknown numbers." He scratched his stubble-covered chin as he looked out the glass door into Rachel's backyard.

"Sounds like a plan. I'll call if I learn anything; you do the same."

"Got it." He was about to hang up but thought better of it. "Thanks, Kris."

"Uh-huh," she acknowledged before the call ended.

~

After three long hours of watching videos of people crying, laughing, wiping their tears, and telling stories about Luke, acid threatened to burn a hole in Ted's esophagus, a byproduct of his guilt, no doubt. He hated what he had to put so many people through, but in the heat of the moment on the day Luke had been shot it had seemed the only option available to prevent his real funeral.

It had been frustrating to realize they'd lost an entire week focused primarily on who might be targeting Luke. Until the other night, there was no indication Rachel could be in any danger, so naturally Ted, as well as Luke and Captain Taylor, hadn't been considering motives which involved her too. That all changed two nights ago. On one hand, it narrowed down the options to situations that included both of them. On the other hand, it opened up more possibilities for Ted to investigate.

Ted reached for the hot tea in front of him and took several long sips. The raspberry-flavored liquid felt good as it warmed his throat, left sore from talking to so many of Luke's friends the day before. He replayed the last video clip again. Something caught his attention this time. *What was it?* He'd viewed the video over ten times now, following the movements of a different person with each playback. Just a few more people to go. This time, he focused on a shy-looking man who had sat in the back row. While the attendee occasionally stopped and chatted briefly with other people before and afterward, no encounter ever lasted for more than a minute, if even that.

Ted's interest was piqued. First, the man didn't seem to know any of the other attendees. This was not in itself suspicious; several people there didn't appear to know anyone else, but it was worth noting. Second, there was something odd about how he looked. It wasn't natural. Was his face lacking symmetry? Whether that could be just his physical shape, or maybe the man had an accident that plastic surgery hadn't been able to fully repair, his detective's instincts, built upon three generations of cops, told him something about this guy wasn't quite right.

After rewinding the clip to see when the curious man arrived, Ted switched to a different camera overlooking the entry where a large guest book was laid out on the table. The guest book provided the perfect excuse for him to obtain people's names—presuming they didn't make them up. It was more of an exclusionary tactic, but it couldn't hurt. He selected the approximate time the man arrived and let the clip play. Not all of the people stopped to sign in; some became engaged in conversations and passed by without noticing it. Others walked right past, some giving it a glance or two but not signing in for whatever reason. The man who currently held his attention fell in the latter group along with about half a dozen other people.

Ted planned ask some of the other attendees if they knew who the man was. If that didn't pan out, he could ask the police department's recently retired electronics guru to run facial recognition under the radar and see if the man popped up in any databases. But first things first. Ted froze the screen to capture a clear image and immediately texted the picture to Jill.

Chapter Nineteen

"Mom, *please find me,*" Lacey said as her eyes filled with tears. She thought about all the times she had argued with her parents over stupid things. Cleaning her room or dusting the house. Or when they'd extended her curfew an extra thirty minutes and she'd complained it wasn't an hour. She had been so horrible to her parents, especially her mom. *I'm so sorry. I wish I could take it all back.* Lacey wiped moisture from her cheek. While not raised in a religious household, Lacey felt there were things in this world no one could see or explain. Maybe if she reached her mind out enough, she could get a message to her mother. "If you can hear me, please come find me."

Yeah, right. You're fifteen, and you know better. Magic isn't real. Maybe she wasn't holding on to her sanity as well as she thought. Needing to move, Lacey jumped up and began pacing. The carpet's wear pattern reflected her path. Walking was one of the few things she could do to keep herself occupied and moving. She had also taken to doing jumping jacks and other exercises she had learned taking aerobics with her mother years ago. Why had they stopped going to those classes? She couldn't recall now.

After a good hour of movement, she was sweating. Time for a shower. The house she was being held in had a small bathroom that contained a scuffed bathtub. There was no storage around the sink inside; it was just a generic porcelain bowl design from probably twenty years ago. While there was a medicine cabinet above it, the door had been removed, making Lacey wonder if her keepers worried she might try to use the broken glass or mirror as some kind of weapon.

Not wanting to be in the bath when her lunch arrived, she glanced at the clock. Meals were served three times a day by one of her abductors opening the door and setting a tray on the narrow table just inside. She'd quickly learned that it was impossible to try to escape during one of these times. Attempting to do so had resulted in her food being promptly removed and withheld until the next day. It was too early for the next delivery; she had time.

As she grabbed a set of clean clothes from the small collection that had been provided to her the day after she arrived here, Lacey thought back to the day of the fire. She recalled bursting out of the front door and dodging the flames as she squinted her eyes to see through the intense smoke.

"Lacey!" a man had called out. The voice hadn't been familiar, nor could she see the features of his face through her watery eyes. But she could see he was smiling, and relief charged through her. Could it be one of the neighbors she'd met a while ago? Or one of her grandpa's coworkers? Sometimes his associates dropped by unannounced, often to the frustration of her grandpa.

"Lacey, I'm so glad you're okay. Please, come and let me get you somewhere safe!" The man had smiled, beckoning her forward. As soon as she was within arm's length of her "savior," his hand shot out and grabbed her wrist, twisting it to what felt like the breaking point. "Get in the car," he demanded, holding her arm in the painful position.

"N . . . no!" Lacey stuttered as she kicked out, her heel connecting to his shin. In movies and books, cops always warned people not to let a bad guy get you into a car. She had to fight.

"Lacey, listen to me," the man said calmly. Her eyes were clearing, allowing her to see him with more detail. He had short black hair and stood about a foot taller than her five feet six inches. His glasses reflected the orange-red flames of the burning cabin behind her, the image temporarily mesmerizing. "Lacey!" his stern voice broke her trance. She refocused to find a gun aimed right at her. "Get into the car!"

She froze.

The man paused, took a deep breath as if he were trying to control his emotions, and then continued in a low, chilling voice. "Look, I promise if you listen, I won't shoot you."

Like Lacey would trust the "promise" of someone in this situation. But what other choice did she have? If she didn't listen, would he really shoot her, just like that? No one else was around.

"Lacey, get in the—"

"Okay!" Hearing herself conceding like a snotty teenager but unable to stop it, she reached for the door handle.

"Good girl." He smirked as she climbed inside. "Now hold your hands in front of you."

Lacey obeyed with her palms turned downward. The man reached into his pocket with his free hand and removed handcuffs. She flinched as he smoothly clicked them around her wrists. "Scoot back," he said. Once she slid farther into the car, the door slammed behind her. Could she get out while he circled the car to the driver's side? It would be awkward, but she could still run. As though he read her thoughts, he paused and tapped the window with his gun, his eyebrow raised as if to say, "You really going to try anything?"

Lacey bowed her head and stared at her ash-smeared hands. Her body ached all over, and it felt like this was all happening to someone else. The man climbed into the front seat and held up the weapon. *Yeah, as if I can forget.*

"Don't try anything stupid," he said.

"Who are you? Where are you taking me?" she cried, trying to keep the fear from her voice.

"You can call me Buddy. How's that sound?" He laughed as he put the car into gear and sped away. Lacey turned and stared at the burning remnants of what had been her favorite getaway.

Never had she imagined she'd be held like this, let alone for several months. "Buddy" had been one of the regulars who brought her food and beverages, although he often disappeared for days or weeks at a time. There had been one other guy who'd popped in now and then too. He said his name was Phillip, but people called him Phil. She got the impression he had some kind of mental disorder. He never made eye contact and seemed socially awkward; at the same time, he acted like he wanted to be her friend. He even tried to get her to play card games, even though she always declined.

Lacey glanced out the window, peering outside as she'd done every day. "Mom, Dad, Grandpa, someone, please find me." She watched as a single gray-and-orange robin landed on a branch, its beady eyes staring right at her as though it sensed her distress.

After a few moments, she turned and walked into the bathroom, resigned to spending another day in her prison.

~

Valerie stared down at the picture of her beautiful daughter as tears slid down her cheeks. She could smell the musky scent of Lacey's favorite perfume clinging to the comforter on her bed.

"Oh, Lacey, where are you?" Since her daughter disappeared, her insides had been coiled so tight that she felt she'd just collapse inward, like one of those roll-up bugs Lacey played with in her younger years. The moments between hearing about the fire, learning Lacey had skipped school, and then receiving the news from a neighbor that someone appeared to have driven off with her daughter while the house burned had been the most terrifying of her life. Little did she know it could get worse; for over three and a half months she wondered whether her daughter was still alive and, if so, where she was. What was she going through?

Valerie's father continued to assure her with generic platitudes. "It'll all be okay. We'll find her." A pat on the shoulder here, a stiff, uncomfortable hug there. But his eyes never met hers. He knew something he wasn't telling her. He may think he could hide his deception from her, but after growing up watching her father move up the political ranks, she recognized when he was holding something back. The esteemed Senator Rand Mason may be able to fool others, but not Valerie.

"Valerie, dear, are you in here?" Her husband's voice penetrated her thoughts. She didn't answer as footsteps echoed down the hall. She suspected her father wasn't the only one keeping secrets from her. A moment later, he stood in the doorway. "Honey, I was calling for you."

"Sorry, Ian, I just, well . . ." She looked down at the picture in her hands. "I can't stand not knowing where she is. Is she okay? Is she being hurt? Or worse?" Ian quietly walked in and sat next to her on Lacey's bed.

"Your dad has the best investigators looking into this. He's very confident they'll find her." He reached up toward her and tucked loose hairs behind her ear as if comforting a child.

"Damn him and his *investigators!*" she spat out and leaped off the bed. "It's been almost four months since our daughter was kidnapped. *Kidnapped!* How the hell can you be so calm?"

"All signs indicate she's alive." Ian stood up and approached her. She backed up without even thinking about it, overwhelmed by a sudden need for space. Ian paused, and a hurt expression crossed his features. The room fell silent; the only sound was the high-pitched jingle of the blowing wind chime on the front porch below the window. Ian retreated and gently sat down again.

"I just don't understand how you can be so calm about this," she said, not hiding her exasperation. It wasn't the first time she'd accused him this way. She'd been frantic for months, unable to sleep, barely able to eat, and jumping at every ringing phone or text message, waiting for a ransom note or anything that would let her know her daughter was alive and well. Ian should have been feeling the same anxieties, but he wasn't. It was one reason she found herself avoiding him as much as possible.

"I just know it doesn't do any good to get upset."

"That's bullshit, and you know it! What aren't you telling me?!" she insisted. Over the years the close relationship between her father and husband had pleased her; now it created a wall between them that Valerie was constantly trying to climb while Ian just sat quietly on the other side.

He flinched as though her words physically struck him, but he didn't respond.

"Look, it's clear my father knows something he's not sharing. And I strongly suspect he's confided in you. He's my dad; that he'd lie to me doesn't surprise me, although knowing he'd do so about my daughter breaks my heart. But you, *you* are my husband. This is *our* daughter we're talking about. You need to tell me what's going on!" Valerie smacked her hand flat against the dresser, unable to hold in her anger and the intense fear that ate at her every waking moment.

"Just calm down, honey. Let's—"

"Are you seriously trying to placate me? Oh my God, now you're acting like him too? What happened to you, Ian?" Who was this stranger in front of her? She turned and rested her elbows on the dresser as she rubbed at her cheeks.

"I don't know what to say," he finally replied. His face was slack and his arms hung limply at his sides.

"How about the truth?" She ran her hands through her shoulder-length hair.

"I just . . . I can't. But I need you to trust me when I say that it will all be okay. We'll get her back."

"How can I trust you when you're withholding information about *our* missing daughter?" Valerie whipped her head around; her gaze seared into him like she could look inside his soul. She placed her hands on her hips, unsure of whether to confess her own secret to him, but some small part of her hoped sharing her plan might jar him into being the man she married again, the one who told her everything. "You know something? I hired a private investigator too."

"You what?" Ian was clearly surprised.

So I'd managed to keep it under wraps after all. Good, Valerie thought.

"What did your PI find?" Ian asked with a newfound hopefulness in his voice.

"I'm not quite sure. Because he died a week ago."

"Wait, what?"

"Yeah, how about that? Word is he slipped and fell while crossing a river or something. Got stuck and drowned before his friend could get to him."

"I think I heard about that somewhere." Ian looked at his feet as if the most mesmerizing thing he'd ever seen rested on his toes.

"I don't believe he just slipped. Something else went on, but no one's talking. So tell me, what should I think when the man I hired to look into my daughter's kidnapping dies under suspicious circumstances?" Valerie knew how the media worked; she'd been a journalist. The story about Luke Reed felt off; the fact that no one wanted to talk about it only fueled her convictions.

Now was the moment of truth; Ian would either drop his shield and confide in her, or he'd drive the wedge between them so deep it could never be repaired. Valerie remained still, waiting for his response as butterflies slammed around inside of her stomach.

~

Rachel considered calling Ted, but given that she wasn't sure she could withhold her anger at him for lying to her about Luke, she reasoned that she had a perfectly capable ex-cop-turned-private-investigator down the hall. Would he have learned Morse code in his police training? Rachel saved the message, placed the phone in the cradle, and walked down the hall. She stopped in front of Luke's door, took a deep breath, and lightly knocked.

"Luke?" No response. Rachel placed her ear against the door and listened. The lack of running water told her he wasn't in the shower. "Luke, you in there?" She knocked again, heavier this time.

The distant sound of a toilet flushing explained why he hadn't responded. She waited a few moments before speaking again. "Luke, I need your help." Rachel waited anxiously as the sound of footsteps finally approached from the other side of the closed door.

"What's wrong?" he croaked.

Rachel almost flinched at the scratchiness in his voice. "Are you okay?" she asked.

"Yeah, I'll be fine."

"If you are as sick as you sound, maybe we should get you to urgent care."

"No!"

Luke was as stubborn as any other man when it came to seeking out medical care, but this seemed a bit over the top. "Look, don't be an ass. If you're—"

"I'll be fine. What do you need help with?"

"First, be honest with me. How sick are you?"

"Not sick enough to need a doctor but sick enough to keep from exposing you to whatever this is."

Rachel knew that tone; his mind was made up.

"All right," she sighed. "Any chance you know Morse code?"

"Um, yeah."

At the sound of his confused response, she sensed her question surprised him. "I got this weird message from . . . an acquaintance, and I think he was tapping out something in Morse code." It was only when the words left her mouth that Rachel realized Luke may inevitably ask who this friend was. While she hadn't done anything wrong, her recent foray back into the dating world wasn't a discussion she wanted to have right now.

"Wait, you didn't put your cell back together and make a call, did you?"

"Give me some credit, Luke." While she knew he didn't think her to be stupid, the question still annoyed her. "I used the house's landline to check messages."

"Sorry, didn't mean to imply . . . just, sorry," he muttered, then spoke louder. "However, it might be best not to check your messages at all. Don't check email, Facebook, anything. If someone were trying to track you, they might be able to trace your IP address on your internet connection."

Rachel had known better than to call Rick's number directly, but she hadn't considered the full suite of communications she needed to avoid. Why would she? Being an environmental consultant didn't require tapping phones or hacking computers. Well, then again, as she thought about some of the nasty political antics she'd seen throughout her career, maybe it did for some. Just not her.

"Understood. But the damage is done, so how about I play you the message anyway, then I won't make any more calls."

"There's an extension phone in here. I'll just pick up the phone and listen to spare you any exposure."

Rachel was not going to argue with that; she certainly didn't want whatever illness he had. After dialing into her voice mail system and confirming he was listening from the receiver, she set the message to play. Seth's voice boomed through the connection. "Hey, Rachel, it's Seth again." *Oops.*

"Wrong message; hold on." Rachel pressed the number to advance to the next message. The tapping sounds began. She waited as the message played through its entirety. Once it ended, she asked, "Need me to replay it?"

"Yeah, probably a few more times." After several more repeats, Luke spoke. "You can go ahead and hang up now."

"What did it mean?" Rachel complied, waiting anxiously for his answer.

~

Ted reclined on his sofa after reading through the report submitted by Officer Peltier in Alpine County. The officer arrived at the scene soon after Ted had placed Luke into the ambulance and driven away. As far as Peltier would have known, Luke died en route to the hospital.

Ted recalled initially grappling with cooperating with the officer yet withholding the truth, but it turned out Peltier hadn't been overly curious from the start. While it made Ted's job easier, it also raised some red flags.

The report he'd just received confirmed his suspicions. Ted picked up his phone, scrolled through his contacts, and dialed. His captain's loud but friendly greeting burst in his ear.

"Officer Benson, how are things?"

The formality told him someone was nearby.

"Hey, Cap. Just checking in. Got a moment?"

"Yes, let me shut the door. It's loud in the station." He heard a click followed by the whooshing sound of air gushing from Captain Taylor's office chair as the man sank into it. Ted could easily visualize him leaning back and propping his feet on the corner of his desk. "All right, it's safe to talk. What's up?"

"I was just looking over this report you obtained from the officer in Alpine County."

"Pretty slim, wasn't it?"

"Took the words right out of my mouth. While I admit we don't want them looking too hard, at the same time, this seems strange. I was barely questioned, and although I withheld the information about the gunshot, still seems like they should have done some additional follow-up, especially given the victim 'died.' Either they simply just didn't care, or . . ."

"Are you thinking there's a bad seed over there?"

"I don't know. But there's still the unanswered question of why someone would have followed Luke, along with his *cop* friend, all the way out to Highway 4 and risked taking a shot at him. I mean, why not just go after him at his house or on one of his bike rides? It's one of the questions plaguing me."

"I've wondered that myself."

Ted heard the tapping of nervous fingers on a desktop coming through the phone. He continued brainstorming out loud. "This is a stretch, but given what we've seen in recent years, I'm trying to keep an open mind. Officer Peltier showed up rather quickly to the scene. In fact, I barely had Luke loaded into the ambulance before he drove up, yet I didn't call it in until just minutes before Jill's friend arrived with it. And now this half-assed report."

"I get what you're saying. I suppose having a friend in law enforcement could be one reason the shooter followed you out there. But how would they have known where you were going in advance?"

"I've thought about that. We'd planned it in advance over the phone. Probably a couple of phone calls at least."

"So you think someone was listening in?"

"Not on my line; I had it double-checked just in case. Luke's usually good about his own cell as well. But he's been distracted lately; I'm not sure by what. It's possible he hadn't kept up with regular scans of his phone. Or perhaps someone planted a bug in his house or office?"

"Do you have his phone?"

"It's with him." Ted added, "He's keeping the battery and SIM card separated. But I'll mention it to him. I was also planning to have his house swept for devices."

"Not a bad idea, but that's going to be tough to explain given his 'accidental death.' Do you have any friends that you could trust to check?"

"The fewer people we involve, the better. If I have access to the right equipment, I can do it myself. No one should think too hard if I'm over there. Someone's going to have to sort through Luke's stuff eventually, right?" Ted moved his head back and braced his feet on his coffee table.

"I think I can make that happen. Let me get back to you."

"Thanks, Cap." Ted tossed his phone on the table. He'd been

running ragged over the past week, doing not only his regular job, but the side investigation involving Luke and helping to plan the "Celebration of Life." Ted just wanted to celebrate some sleep time. Even a short nap would help, he thought, as he lay on his couch and closed his eyes. His phone jittered on the glass table and blared a generic ring tone. No rest for the weary, he thought as he reached to pick it up. He didn't recognize the number, but the 303 area code was from Colorado.

"Benson here," he answered crisply.

"Ted, its Derek Winters. Sorry to bother you, but I could use your help."

"Derek, hey! How are you doing?" Ted worked hard to infuse friendly enthusiasm into his voice. He had nothing against Derek; he was just bone tired and running on fumes.

"I've been trying to get in touch with Rachel, but I'm not hearing back from her. I also called Jill and—"

"I don't think she wants to talk to anyone. She's taking Luke's death pretty hard."

"I get that, but she hasn't even replied. Not even a text. I've been contacting her since yesterday."

Ted rubbed his hand across his face. He did not need this.

"Just give her some time. I'm sure she'll be in touch when she's feeling up to it."

"But what about Jill? I left her a message and also no response." It was clear from Derek's tone that the older sibling was losing patience.

"She's probably dealing with some kid issues. Look, how about I check in with her and see what she knows. It may be she doesn't recognize your number and let it go to voice mail. She'll do that when she's busy."

"Okay, sure." Derek's agreement lacked fervor, but Ted didn't know what else to say. Rachel would have to get in touch with Derek in some way before her brother could sound the alarm and blow this whole thing. Or could Jill's reply to him be enough? Ted heard a phone ringing through the line.

"Sounds like you have another call. I'll let you go and—"

"No worries. It's Rachel's landline; I'll let the machine get it."

Wait, Derek was at Rachel's house? Oh no, this situation just got a lot worse. Ted almost stuttered over his response. "Oh, so you're in town then?" Ted jumped up from his couch, anxious to make a move but not sure what.

"I thought I'd come keep her company after the service. Kris let me know I had the day wrong and mentioned that Rachel was planning some time at Jill's."

"Did she know you were coming?" Ted was sure he knew the answer. Derek wasn't one to ask in advance before dropping in unannounced.

"Well, no."

Ted waited for more elaboration. But the line remained silent, so he finally spoke up. "I'll see what I can find out and let you know."

"Appreciate it."

As soon as the call ended, Ted dialed Jill's number. *So much for a catnap.*

Chapter Twenty

"Cassandra, did you just say that you don't have Miss Winters yet?" Monica reminded herself to remain calm, not only to maintain her focus, but she also didn't want to upset Cassandra too much; the woman might just quit. It wouldn't be the first time.

"She didn't come to the funeral gig."

"Are you sure?" Now *that* surprised Monica. Even though the couple had broken up some time ago, word was they each still had a thing for each other.

"I stayed the entire time. No Rachel."

"Did you happen to learn *why* she didn't come? Or better yet, where she is?"

"Not yet."

Monica heard a hitch in Cassandra's voice. There was something she wasn't telling her.

"What is it?"

"What is what?"

"Don't be coy with me. There's something you're not saying." Monica fiddled with the beaded straps attached to her glasses. She heard Cassandra's heavy sign of resignation.

"My ex was there."

Monica didn't think she could be more surprised, but that did it. And the news could only mean one thing: trouble.

"Did he see you?"

"No, I don't think so. I was pretty well disguised, as was he. I slipped out once I noticed him and waited in the parking lot."

"And?" Monica knew there was more to this story. Her fingers twisted one of the beads and spun it around and around.

"Nothing. He eventually came out along with everyone else, got into his truck, and that was that. But I did notice him intently watching one of Luke's friends. A female. I'm going to put some time into figuring out who she is."

"Describe her."

"She was around five nine or five ten and trim but built. Brown hair just below her shoulders. Conservatively dressed."

"It's a funeral. Everyone is usually conservatively dressed," Monica quipped, then realized she was pushing too hard again. "Anything else you noticed?"

"No, she had a plain look about her. She was walking with that cop. Tom or Ted Benson, something like that."

"Would you say she's around forty?" Monica had a feeling she knew who the woman was.

"Sounds about right."

"Jillian Reynolds," Monica stated matter-of-factly. "She's a medical examiner down in the Carson Valley."

"Well, you just saved me some trouble."

"I'll text you her address as soon as I retrieve it. Shouldn't be too hard to find." Monica relaxed; she always walked a fine line with Cassandra, but the woman was usually very good at what she did. "Keep me updated." Monica ended the call and swiped at the pile of papers on her desk, knocking a handful onto the floor. This mess kept getting worse. *You'll figure it out. You always do.* It's one reason she wasn't in jail while some of her past associates were. She leaned back, instructing herself to inhale a long, deep breath and then exhale slowly. "You can still work this out," she spoke aloud, calming her own nerves.

Within minutes she'd located the woman's home address and texted it to Cassandra. Either Rachel would be at Jill Reynolds's house, or the woman would know where to locate her. Cassandra was great at retrieving information people didn't want to let go. Just as Monica set her phone down, it rang. Glancing at caller ID, she swore but knew it best to answer.

"Hello, Mike," she said.

"Monica, my friend, how are things going?"

Friend? Yeah right. "Moving along," she replied and tilted her head up as though he could see her show of confidence. The line remained silent, barring some distant voices in the background and more clanging metal. He was no doubt expecting more detail. *Let him wait.*

Finally, he spoke. "I'm going to need a little more information, Monica."

She begrudgingly responded, "I'm close to getting a handle on Miss Winters."

"Close. Meaning you don't have her yet?" She could easily visualize him at this moment: his jaws clamped together so tight he'd be grinding the enamel off his teeth and his fists clenched as he worked to hold back his temper, especially in light of his own current situation. In fact, Mike reminded her of her no-good father, a man who'd abandoned his family right before her tenth birthday.

"She hasn't been home. My contact attempted extraction at Mr. Reed's service, but she never showed."

"Son of a bitch!" He raised his voice and then quieted back down into a whisper. "What are you doing to find her?"

"Just located a friend of hers that we suspect knows where she is."

"Good. Make sure you find her," he commanded before the line went dead.

"Jerk," she muttered, then glanced again at her phone, second-guessing whether she ended the call before her utterance. Thankfully she had, and there was nothing to worry about. Well, nothing beyond making sure this whole plan worked out. Part of which involved withholding her true intentions from Mike as well.

Chapter Twenty-One

The Metallica ringtone on Jill's phone alerted her Ted was calling.

"Hey, Teddy, give me a few seconds. I'm just stepping out of an autopsy," she answered. She set the phone down before she removed her mask and gown. Placing her phone back up to her ear, she headed toward her office. "Okay, I'm back. What's up?"

"We have a problem. I mean, *another* problem."

Jill fell back into her seat, her head resting against the chair as she cursed under her breath. "Go on."

"Derek, Rachel's brother, decided to drop in for a visit. Naturally he's looking for her. Kris told him she was with you, but he's complaining that she hasn't responded to his messages or texts. Said he also called you and left a voice mail."

"You've got to be kidding me," she sighed.

"Wish I were, Jilly."

Jill smiled at his use of her nickname. They'd been friends for years; no one else was allowed to call her that. "Of all the times! From what I hear, this is so typical of that guy."

"We need to have Rachel get in touch with him somehow." He paused before speaking with renewed enthusiasm. "How about we text him from your phone, say it's Rachel, that she isn't up for talking, and she didn't use her phone because it's broken?"

"Could she just call him from her disposable?"

"Probably not a good idea. We have no idea who's after them

and what resources they have. Speaking of which, did you get a chance to look at that picture I texted?"

The subject change caught Jill off guard. "You sent a picture? I didn't see it. Let me check." She looked at the display on her phone; sure enough, there was a new text from Ted. "It's here. I guess I didn't hear the alert." She studied the image and tried to recall seeing the man at the service. "I think I may have seen him at some point yesterday, but I don't recognize him from anywhere."

"I think he's altered his appearance, and unfortunately he appears to be good at it. I want to get this picture to Rachel as well. Has she set up a dummy email account yet?"

"Not sure. I'll call her in a bit. I need to get back into the exam room before my assistant screws up something."

"Can you forward the image to her?"

"Will do."

"Don't forget to send Derek a text."

"What's the number again?" Jill scribbled it down as Ted replied, thanked him, and hung up. She composed a simple text to Derek, following the suggestion from Ted to say Rachel's phone was broken. Once sent, she focused on getting through the remainder of her work day.

~

"Rachel, tell me again who left you this message?" Luke didn't like what the translation suggested.

"Just tell me what it means," she pleaded.

He relented. "It's not the smoothest, but I can make out 'Danger. Coming for you. Cascade.'"

"Cascade? What the . . . oh."

"Rachel?" Luke asked, anxious for more information.

"I think it might be in reference to the fire by Cascade Lake a few months ago."

"How are you involved in that?" Luke wiped the sheen of sweat beading on his forehead as his stomach rumbled.

"I'm contracted to help with the postfire management, but I don't think he knew that."

Luke could almost hear the gears shifting in her brain. He waited, hoping he could hold out a few more minutes before having to dash to the bathroom.

"I wonder if this is related to how the fire started?" Her last comment was so quiet that he barely heard it.

"What do you mean?"

"My acquaintance is a firefighter, and he mentioned to me in confidence that he thought the fire was arson. You know, the fire that burned that senator's house down. Thankfully, the media reported his granddaughter escaped before being burned alive."

Luke had been on the verge of inquiring about Rachel's "acquaintance," as if it were any of his business, when something else clicked in his mind: Valerie Mason-Spears. "Rachel, I normally wouldn't share client details with you, but I think we need to compare notes."

"What do you mean?"

This was not a conversation to have through a closed door, but he didn't know what else to do. "Something is going on here. I need to know you'll keep what I'm about to tell you in strict confidence."

"Of course."

"The senator's granddaughter, Lacey, did get out, but then someone took her. She's been missing ever since." He heard Rachel's swift intake of breath.

"I don't understand; I haven't heard anything about it."

"Senator Mason has been keeping it under wraps. His daughter, Valerie—Lacey's mother—hired me to help find her about a week before my fake death."

"Why wouldn't he want the cops helping to locate her?"

"That's the million-dollar question."

"I can't believe he's kept this secret all this time! And the poor girl. I hope she's still alive."

"Let's hope so." Another intense wave of nausea hit Luke, and he bent over. "I need to go; be right back." He ran into the bathroom, wondering if there was anything left to empty from his gut. After a round of mostly dry heaving, he rinsed with mouthwash, spit it out, and walked back to the closed door. "You still there?"

"Yes, and I really think we should get you to a doctor, Luke."

"No!" he retorted, harsher than he'd intended. "Sorry," he said more calmly. "It just needs to run its course. That's all." There was a pause, and he sensed Rachel was internally debating whether to push the issue. She apparently decided to let it go.

"Fine. So back to the granddaughter. Her mother came to you? Why not her father? This just doesn't make any sense. And how have they kept the girl's disappearance under wraps?"

"All good questions. Valerie suspects her father knows more than he's saying. He's got her husband, Ian, convinced that Lacey is all right, and she thinks that her dear old dad has shared something with Ian that neither of them are telling her." Luke reached into his pocket for some ChapStick and applied the moisturizer to his dry lips. "I hate that I can't keep working the case for her. At least to any useful degree. One can only do so much online without contacting anyone, including the client."

For a moment, Luke was reminded of what it had been like between them in the past: sharing information, bouncing ideas around, working to figure things out together. A pang of sadness wrenched his heart before his gut quickly distracted him from the ride down memory lane.

"What do you know about Senator Mason?" she asked. "I imagine you've spent some time learning about him."

"Yes, I have, but nothing explains why he's hiding his granddaughter, if that's what's going on. That, or he knows who has her. I've put together some information. I can get you a copy of my notes. Have you set up a new email address I can forward them to?" She told him the address. "I'll send it right now."

"What can I do?"

"You're good at finding out things about people or situations that don't necessarily pop up in my searches, especially political undertones. I'd say do your thing with Senator Mason, see if anything jumps out." Another rumble in his stomach. Time was limited. "I'd suggest following up with your acquaintance, but that may be a bad idea." Luke wanted to know how well she knew this firefighter but wasn't going to ask. "Unless it's someone you can trust." He waited anxiously for her reply.

"No, I don't know him that well, so contacting him when I'm

supposed to be in hiding is off the table. Send me those notes, and I'll see what I can find out, but I'll probably just be repeating what you've already done."

"A fresh set of eyes can't hurt," he mused.

"Did you tell Ted?"

"No. Until you played this message for me, it never occurred to me that there could be a connection."

"What are you going to do?"

"Now that I have this arson perspective, I'm going to rethink my observations to date. I may hold off on bringing Ted into this. Asking him to keep information from his boss always bothers me."

"Understandable. And Luke, take care of yourself. I'm getting pretty worried about you."

That made him smile because it meant she still cared on some level. Before he could reply, she continued.

"Even if I'm pissed as hell that you let me believe you were dead. And that conversation is not over," she warned.

Luke heard the taps of her feet as she briskly walked away. The sting of her last words caused him to wince, but he'd have to deal with that later.

~

Rachel rested on the sofa in her temporary hideaway as Jill's voice boomed from the speaker on her cell.

"As much as I joke about wanting some time alone, this house is just way too quiet. But they are safe; that's all that matters." Jill had explained that she was keeping her distance from her family to prevent anyone from following her to their hidden location.

"I'm so sorry you are wrapped up in this, Jill, whatever 'this' is." A single white paw placed mild pressure on her stomach.

"It's not your fault. Plus, remember, I was involved before you were."

"Okay, but if it turns out to be related to something I did . . ."

"Don't go there, Rachel. Even if it does, I'm a big girl. My family is safe. I got involved in this to help my friends."

A second paw gently pressed down next to the first one. Rachel couldn't help but laugh. "Avi, are you in need of some attention?" she asked, rubbing the dog's ears before turning her attention back to Jill. "Just so you know, Jill, while my dog may have distracted me, I did hear what you said. Yes, you're a big girl and a badass to boot, but you can't stop me from worrying."

"Rachel, no one can stop you from worrying. About anything. You do it too much," Jill teased. It felt so good to be able to talk with Jill again this way; after learning of her friend's deception, well intentioned as it was, Rachel had needed some time to process how she felt. By the time they'd spoken again, Rachel had come to understand Jill's position and accept it, whether she liked it or not. She couldn't know if she would have made the same decision in Jill's shoes, but there was nothing to be gained by holding it against her now.

"You're right. I do."

"By the way, have you looked at your new email account recently? I forwarded you a picture Ted sent of someone he's looking into."

"No, let me check it out now." Rachel sat up, eyeing the computer resting on the kitchen counter. As Rachel retrieved it and booted the system, she debated whether to tell Jill what Luke had confided. It was ironic she was considering withholding information, just as Jill had done. But at the same time, it wasn't her place to reveal what he knew because of one of his clients, it was Luke's.

Rachel typed in the website for the email program, then glanced at her "cheat sheet" where the password was scrawled on a Post-it note. She missed the days of using familiar words and numbers like birthdays or old pet names; now the instructions for creating a password could fill a novel and drive the reader mad. She clicked to open the message and studied the attached picture of a man.

"He kind of looks familiar, but yet not. Like it's more that he has 'one of those faces,' but he's not someone I know," she said, disappointed. So much for a big break in the case. She continued to stare, hoping something would come to mind. Instead, the more she studied it, the more she thought it looked too perfect. Fake, even. "It almost seems like he's wearing makeup and maybe a wig?" she pondered.

"I was thinking the same thing. I'll let Ted know. By the way, how's Luke doing? Is he feeling better yet?"

"I think he's feeling worse actually." Rachel closed the lid of her laptop, walked back into the living room, and plopped down on the sofa. "I suspect he's puking up his lungs or spending a lot of time sitting on the john. I recommended we go to urgent care, but he refuses. Says it just needs to work through his system some more."

"That sounds miserable. Normally I'd advise pushing him to go see a doctor, but given he's legally dead and all, I know that would require some extra effort. Just make sure he's getting electrolytes—Gatorade or even something like PediaSure—and drinking tons of water."

"I'm trying."

"Also, if you can find a thermometer, get him to use it. If he does have a high fever that's not breaking, then definitely get him to an ER; use a fake name or something. He's a PI. I'm sure he can figure something out." She paused and then asked tentatively, "How are you two getting along?"

"Our conversations through his door have been civil enough, I suppose. It's still all so overwhelming. I'm not sure whether it would be easier if he weren't sick and we were talking face-to-face. It's not easy being here with him after tiptoeing around each other for over a year; maybe it's good to be forced to have some kind of conversation. If anything, we share the same friends, and it would be nice if we could avoid the awkwardness that's always there."

"I suppose that's a good way to look at it. So what are you going to do next?" Jill asked.

"Luke and I compared some notes, so I'm going to do some digging, see if I notice anything with a fresh eye."

"That's good. I know he's been struggling to help with Ted's investigation. Being 'dead' sure makes it more difficult to do so, I'm sure."

"I'm just thankful he's not really dead."

"I sure hated putting you through that," Jill said remorsefully.

"No more apologizing. I understand you were placed in a bad situation."

"So I have one more thing to tell you, then I'll let you get to it."

"Uh-oh, I'm not going to like this, am I?" Rachel had noticed the hesitation in Jill's voice. Did they really need more bad news? "Okay, just tell me."

"Your brother decided to drop in on you."

Rachel didn't have to ask which of her two brothers. Surprise visits were classic Derek Winters.

"Of course he did," she scoffed. "What happened?" Clearly there was more to this story.

"He showed up at your house and got all worried you weren't there. Kris told him you were visiting me; still, he's freaking out because you haven't responded to any calls or texts."

"Wonderful," Rachel replied sarcastically.

"Ted suggested I text Derek and tell him your phone isn't working and you aren't up to talking yet anyway."

"Did you hear back?"

"Not yet. Sent it a few hours ago."

"Where is he now?" The words came out of her mouth a second before Rachel answered her own question. "He's bunking at Casa de Rachel, isn't he?"

"Sure is."

"There goes all of my snack food," Rachel mumbled. "At least he hates wine and won't raid my stash."

"Sometimes I'm glad I don't have siblings," Jill joked.

"He might wait for me for a while. I swear sometimes I think I'm just a place to stay so he can play around Tahoe."

"You know that's not true; he loves you. Even if he's a pig with no manners."

"I know. He's got a good heart. I just wish he wouldn't bury it below all that macho I-don't-give-a-crap mentality," Rachel admitted. "This could pose a problem, couldn't it? If he sticks around waiting for me?"

"It's a concern I share with Ted."

"If there's a safe way I could call him, maybe I could encourage him to leave."

Jill verbalized what Rachel was already thinking. "He's probably not going to do that until he sees you."

"I know," Rachel acknowledged.

"Give it some thought. In the meantime, call me if anything else comes up; otherwise, I'll be in touch. And Rachel, check that email periodically. I'll communicate with you that way so we can limit phone use."

"Got it. Thanks." When the call ended, Rachel set her phone down and yawned. While anxious to follow up on the information she'd learned from Luke, it was late and her headache had started up again. She couldn't fathom staring at her computer without first getting some rest. After letting the dogs outside, she stopped by Luke's door before going into her room.

"Luke?"

"Here."

She could barely hear his scratchy voice. "I'm going to grab a nap before looking into the Masons. I'm wiped out. Just wanted to let you know and see if you need anything first?"

"No problem. I'm fine." His tone was clipped as if he were anxious to end the conversation. Given his repeat visits to the porcelain god, she couldn't blame him.

"By the way, Jill said we should take your temperature if we can find a thermometer."

"I don't have a fever. I'd know if I did," he snapped. Rachel stepped back.

"Okay. Understood. Just passing along *medical* advice from a qualified physician," she retorted. She turned to go, barely hearing his thanks as she walked down the hall.

~

Derek reread the text from the number with the 775 area code. The message said it was Rachel using Jill's phone; he checked the handwritten list of numbers Rachel kept by the phone, and it matched. It was frustrating that Rachel apparently didn't want to talk to him. He'd flown all the way out here from Colorado to help his sister, and she couldn't even have one conversation with him?

Derek reminded himself she'd just suffered a great loss. While he had reservations about Luke ever since learning of his narcotic addiction, which so far as he knew Rachel did not know about, he had to respect the guy's instinct to protect his sister. He'd seen it first hand when Luke and Rachel had searched for him and Kris after they were abducted. But he also could never understand how his sister, who had always been such an independent woman, had pined away for Luke for so long after they'd broken up. Sure, she said she was fine with it, but he could always hear a tinge of heartbreak in her voice when she talked about him. Which is why he'd taken time off work and hauled his ass out here to be with her after Luke had died.

He finally sent a quick "Got it, will be in touch" and set the phone down in order to raid her cabinets, looking for anything that wasn't healthy. The only foods that qualified were chocolate bars and mixed nuts. Well, the nuts were borderline, healthy but seasoned with Cajun spices. He retrieved the nuts can, grabbed the lone milk chocolate bar he'd found hidden among the stack of white chocolate, picked up his phone, and walked into the family room. He'd give her one more day. If she wouldn't talk to him, he'd just have to go and see her at Jill's. He knew Jill's phone number, last name, and that she lived in Minden; it shouldn't be too difficult to find an address.

Derek propped his feet on the coffee table and reached for the TV remote. The screen was so small he almost had to squint; his sister wasn't big on electronics. She'd only recently "upgraded" to a flat screen. Perhaps in another ten years she might even consider a smart TV.

"Tomorrow, dear Sister, we're going to talk," he proclaimed to the empty room as he stuffed a handful of nuts into his mouth. His eye briefly caught a photo collage framed up on her hearth. It included a picture of Rachel and Kris, huddled together during a hailstorm. They were tucked under a large granite overhang, laughing as white marble-sized balls stacked up nearby. Their hair was soaked, Kris's hatless head far more than his sister's. He couldn't help but think of the kiss he'd shared with Kris so long ago. He'd been with women since, but something about her soft lips and how they'd felt against his own had stuck with him. He shook his head as if he could shake off the memory. It didn't work.

Chapter Twenty-Two

Luke opened his eyes. The only light in the room was the red display on the clock: 5:46 a.m. For the first time in several nights, he'd managed to sleep continuously for more than a couple of hours. Insomnia was yet another fun result of the withdrawal. He waited for the now familiar wrenching pain in his gut to hit his awareness, but only a dull ache remained. No worse for wear, and thankfully no need to rush to the toilet. Maybe he was over the worst of it.

As he shifted, he felt something solid at the end of the bed. He lifted his head and noticed his laptop balanced precariously on the edge of the mattress. He sat up and swiftly grabbed it before it could topple off the side. Remaining under the covers, he tapped the power button to bring it out of hibernation. After typing his passcode, the screen opened to the last project he'd been working on. It was a Google search for Senator Mason. It wasn't the first time he'd performed this search; each time he'd try different terms and follow links within the various stories.

Luke decided to take a shower before diving back into his search. He craved coffee but hadn't dared touch it over the past several days with his entire GI system already out of whack. Caffeine pills helped take the edge off, but it wasn't even close to the alertness his morning java brought.

Ten minutes later he emerged from the bathroom refreshed and feeling slightly better than half-dead—an improvement over yesterday. Luke tried to remain quiet; while Rachel might not hear him through the walls, her dogs likely could, and their reactions might wake her. He could hear the exhaustion in her voice last night; she had been through a lot over the past couple of weeks. Regardless, he knew as soon as she awoke she'd be rearing to take action to investigate their circumstances. So for now, he let her sleep.

A quick beep pulled him from the thoughts of the beautiful woman sleeping just down the hall. He turned and looked for the burner phone he'd been using since taking up residence in his hideaway. It was tucked under his pillow. He retrieved it and noticed a text from Ted: "Call me when you're up." It was time-stamped seven minutes ago. He dialed.

"Morning," Ted answered after just two rings. Luke pictured his friend sitting at the round table in his small kitchen, enjoying a mug of hot tea and an "old-fashioned" newspaper. Probably the *San Francisco Chronicle*. The *Tahoe Daily Tribune* was no longer daily—the paper now only came out once a week. *Another victim of the rise of social media and online news.*

"What's up?" Luke asked, rubbing his eyes.

"Checking in. I assume Rachel told you we've moved Jill's family?"

"Uh, no, but I admit I wasn't the nicest person to talk with last night, and then we both crashed early."

"Well, you can be quite the asshole sometimes," Ted jeered.

"Can't deny that." Luke leaned against the dresser and ran his free hand through his wet hair. "So what's the deal with Jill?" Luke listened intently as Ted explained moving them to a safe house. "Sounds like a good call."

"It's driving me nuts that we can't figure out what's going on here. Until Rachel was attacked, I focused on the idea that the killer was solely after you. Now we have an entirely different avenue of inquiries. Do you have any new ideas?" Ted's frustration was evident in the anxious tone of his voice.

Luke considered what he'd learned through talking with Rachel last night. As much as he didn't want to put Ted in a position of withholding information from other law enforcement officers yet again, it was too important not to share the potential lead. "Rachel and I may have identified another possibility." He explained the message in Morse code, his efforts to try to locate the missing granddaughter of the senator, and what Valerie Mason-Spears had shared about her father's curious behavior.

"You have got to be kidding me," Ted chuckled. "You and Rachel . . . you just can't avoid getting yourselves involved with politicians, can you?"

"It's my favorite pastime." Luke reached for the half-empty bottle of Gatorade resting nearby. It was warm, but the flavor still hit the spot as he greedily emptied the container.

"I'm going to have to give some thought on how to handle this new information. Since the cap is working with us on this, I'll talk to him about it."

"Good, Taylor's been a good ally in all of this. Even if he isn't too fond of Rachel." Luke recalled hearing about Rachel's initial interaction with Captain Taylor years ago after she'd discovered a murder victim along a hiking trail, only to have the body disappear before she could return with law enforcement.

"Oh, he's over that. He figures he deserved her wrath given how he talked to her when she was reporting what he eventually learned to be the truth. He grudgingly admits, only to me, that she's earned his respect."

"His admission is safe with me." Luke set the empty container down.

"Good, because I wasn't supposed to tell anyone, but seriously, this is going to be difficult. I want to talk with Valerie, but how would I know about her daughter's disappearance if the only person she's told is dead?"

"That's a tough one."

"I suppose figuring it out is why I get paid the big bucks, right?" Ted grumbled. "Hey, can you send me the files from your investigation?"

"I'll email what I have here. I also left some notes in my office. They are in the safe behind the printer paper." Ted and Rachel were the only ones who knew the combination.

"Perfect. I'll run by and get those in a few."

"Another question . . . I haven't asked Rachel since she's still sleeping, but I'm wondering what happened to this guy who left her the coded message. She was going to look into it, but I think she zonked out before she could do much last night. She mentioned his name was Rick and he's a firefighter?"

"I have no idea who that might be. You'll have to ask her and let me know so I can try to look into it."

"Ted, was she dating this guy?" Luke wished he could take back the question as soon as he asked it.

"I have no idea, my man. But you two have been apart for a long time. If she was, it's none of your business."

"I know," he sighed. Knowing that after the breakup Ted always grew uncomfortable when the subject of Rachel came up, Luke let the topic go. Light tapping sounds filled the hallway. Rachel was awake, or at least her dogs were. "She's up. I'll give her some time to become human again, then see what more she can tell me. Thanks for letting me know about Jill's family."

"Sounds good." The call ended. Almost as if on cue, nausea returned, albeit it was milder than before. He also felt suddenly overheated and wondered if this is what menopausal women felt like with out-of-the-blue hot flashes. This would suck to have to deal with for years on end. He wiped his forehead with the back of his hand and noticed an oily smear on his skin when he pulled back. Luke flopped onto his bed, deciding to remain horizontal while waiting for Rachel. He'd learned right away that she was not a morning person, and attempts to communicate with her immediately upon waking were often unsuccessful; the memory made him smile. He didn't realize he'd drifted off until he heard knocking on his door. Glancing at the clock, he saw he'd been lying down for over half an hour.

"Luke, answer me. I'm worried about you," Rachel said, her fists pounding. How long had she been there?

"I'm fine," he called out as he sat up. He felt light-headed and paused, hoping the feeling would pass quickly.

"Are you still puking your guts out?"

"Seem to be better this morning." He inhaled a deep breath and waited for equilibrium to return.

"No fever?"

"No."

"Then open the door. We've got work to do."

Luke opened his mouth to decline, but Rachel continued.

"I don't care what you look like. No fever plus two days means you're past what I consider the contagious point of whatever you had, if it wasn't just food poisoning. I'm tired of talking with you through the goddamn door."

He knew better than to argue with her, especially given her logic was sound. If he didn't comply, she'd probably find a way to break in. "Okay, but I'll come out there. You don't need to come into this germ-infested room." In reality, he wanted to bleach the hell out of the bathroom before anyone else even got near it.

"Fine."

Luke stood and walked to the door with his nerves on edge. Why? He didn't know. He unlocked the handle and opened it. "See, I'm alive," he said, waving his hands out to his sides as if modeling his status as alive and well. Naturally, a massive cramp blasted through his stomach just as he took a step through the door. He bent over, holding his stomach as though that would stop the pain.

"Luke, what's wrong?" she asked with concern etched on her features. He felt Bella's muzzle gently nudge his cheek. Avi was still hanging back behind Rachel.

"Just a cramp, nothing to—"

"Screw this. It's been days. We're getting you to a doctor," she said, reaching out to gently grab his arm.

"No!" he demanded, wincing as he waited for the pain to subside.

"Yes! Stop being so stubborn. You're not a doctor; for all you know you're suffering from some kind of easily curable but deadly virus or something."

"I'm not."

"And you got your medical degree when?"

"Damn it, Rachel, I'm not sick. I'm in withdrawal!" The words flew out of his mouth without any thought. So there it was; the secret he'd been hiding for so long was out in the open. He straightened, his gut pain subsiding. Rachel's expression said it all. Shock. Concern.

"You're what?" she finally asked, her blue eyes staring at him in confusion.

~

Derek roared down the empty highway, the speedometer reading an accusatory ninety-three miles per hour. Wind poured through the open windows of the classic corvette and blowed hair into his eyes. He kept pushing the strands out of the way, refusing to close the windows and put the cover on because the openness was part of the experience. The radio blared one of his favorite AC/DC classics, and he tapped the wheel as he sang along.

"You shook me all night long . . ."

Thump. Thump. Thump. What was that? Did a tire blow? Yet there was no pull on the wheel.

Thump. Thump. Thump. He looked in the rearview mirror and saw only blackness. *Huh?* He focused on the road in front of him but instead saw the image of a bedroom window with shades framed on the sides by small slivers of sunlight. As he began to emerge from the dream, he recognized where he was: in the guest room at Rachel's.

Thump. Thump. Thump. As his sleep fog cleared, he realized someone was pounding on the front door. Derek jumped up, pulled on his jeans, and called out, "I'm coming" as he stumbled toward the entryway. Realizing he was in his sister's house—and said sister had a knack for dangerous people intruding upon her life—Derek looked around for some kind of weapon. He didn't need to be shot again. It had sucked enough the first time. Recalling one of Rachel's weapons of choice, he opened a small closet and retrieved the can of bear spray. Thankfully, she was a woman of habit. Before opening the door, he asked, "Who's out there?"

"My name's Seth. I'm a friend of Rachel's."

Who was Seth? The guy didn't sound very tough; in fact, his voice reminded him of Keanu Reeves's earlier years, way before *The Matrix.* He'd gotten such a kick out of *Bill & Ted's Excellent Adventure* growing up.

"Look, I just want to make sure she's okay," the man pleaded. Derek held the can tight, his finger resting on the trigger, as he unlocked the door and slowly pulled it open, keeping his arm out of sight. Seth was several inches shorter than Derek; he sported hair in a clipped military cut and a nervous smile.

"Who are you again?" Derek asked, squinting in the bright sunlight.

"Seth. Rachel and I are dating, but I haven't been able to get in touch with her." His cheeks blushed. Derek could not picture his sister with this guy. He'd have to ask Kris about it later.

"You're dating my . . . Rachel?" Derek decided to toy with the man, let him squirm a little. Something about this guy bothered him, but he couldn't figure out what.

"Uh, yes." The visitor cleared his throat.

"I see." Derek scratched his chin. This was too much fun. Derek waited quietly.

"And you are?" Seth finally asked, his tense body language revealing his anxiety; in fact, it was so palpable as to almost seem contrived. Well, regardless, it was time to put the poor guy out of his misery.

"I'm her brother." The man's body immediately relaxed.

"Oh, good. I mean, nice to meet you." Seth held out his hand. Derek stared at it for a few seconds and then complied.

"How long have you been seeing my sister?" Derek asked, curious as he hadn't heard a word about it.

"It's been a few weeks, I think."

"I see." *Yeah, "dating" might be an overstatement.*

"We were out when she got a call about an old friend passing away. I've been giving her some space but haven't heard back from her in several days. I've been a little worried."

"Welcome to the club," Derek mumbled.

"Huh?"

"Oh, nothing. Look, so far as I know she's staying with one of her friends down in the valley." While it had been years since Derek lived in Tahoe, he still referred to the Minden area as "the valley" like most locals. The man appeared to think about this for a moment.

"Jill?"

"Yeah, you know her?"

"I know of her. Rachel's mentioned her name once or twice."

"I see." Derek began to question whether he should be telling this stranger anything. A few dates didn't mean much, presuming that was actually the truth. He shouldn't be so open about his sister's whereabouts. He tried to backtrack the conversation. "Look, she's having some phone issues. I'm sure she'll be in touch once it's working." Anxious to end this conversation, he added, "I'll let her know you stopped by."

At first, Seth didn't move. He looked as if he was going to say more but apparently decided against it. "I'd appreciate that," he said hastily, and then he turned and walked down the front porch steps. Derek watched him until he grabbed the door handle on a small car. He wasn't sure, but it looked like a Prius. *Go figure.* Derek stepped back inside, closed the door, and peered out the window.

"A few dates," he muttered. Although he wasn't one to seek relationships, or even to "date" someone long term, showing up unannounced in the early morning hour seemed a bit over the top for just a few dates. And clearly the man didn't know Rachel very well; the last thing she'd want was a visitor dropping by without notice this early. "Speaking of which, dear Sis, you and I are going to have a face-to-face of our own today," he said, looking for his phone and hoping for a direct message from her. As expected, nothing. It was time to track down Jill's house. Sure, she wouldn't appreciate it, but too bad. He merely wanted to make sure she was okay. And yeah, he had to admit he was annoyed she hadn't been in touch directly. After all, Jill's phone obviously worked. It wouldn't kill Rachel to make a simple phone call.

After a quick shower, Derek grabbed his keys and anticipated a quick stop at the small coffee shop in Meyers before he headed out of the basin on State Route 89. It occurred to him he may see some nice aspen displays in Hope Valley along the way; the timing was about right when the trees' leaves burst into shades of yellow and orange before eventually dropping off for the winter. He'd never admit it to anyone, but he loved watching the changing colors during the years he'd lived in the area. It was hard not to stare in awe at a multicolored aspen grove, the leaves gently flickering in the wind.

Just as Derek turned the key in the ignition, he heard a motor approach from behind. A look in the rearview mirror told him a car had blocked him in. He jumped out of the driver's seat, ready to yell at the person to move, when he recognized who it was.

"What are you doing here?" he blurted.

"Where are you going?" Kris asked through her open window, ignoring his question.

"To see my sister."

"Good, I'm coming with you." She backed up her car and parked along the short fence lining the front yard.

"No, you're not," Derek called out, unsure why he cared so much either way. In fact, Kris had probably been to Jill's house before; a real live navigator would be better than GPS. She strode his way, her short hair blowing in the mild breeze.

"Yes, I am. In the oh-so-famous words of Rihanna, 'Shut up and drive.'"

Derek stood, his mouth agape, as Kris settled herself in his passenger seat. Finally, he turned and climbed back inside. "Who the hell is Rihanna?"

"Seriously? You need to get up to speed on your pop culture. Where have you been for the last twenty years or so?"

Derek rolled his eyes as he put the car into gear.

~

"Well this is interesting," Leo said as he held the binoculars in place, watching the exchange between Derek Winters and Rachel's friend, Kris. They hadn't appeared to be friends, but you never knew these days. Anyone could manipulate their body language to portray what they wanted. It wasn't that difficult once you understood how.

Leo couldn't make out everything they said from this distance, but he'd been able to discern from reading Derek's lips that he intended to go see Rachel. How convenient; these two were going to lead him straight to Rachel. His efforts to track down Jill Reynolds's address after the service yesterday had resulted in two properties under her ownership, one with a Minden address and another in Genoa. He had intended to check them both out and hoped Rachel would be at one of them. But following Rachel's brother, who presumably knew which one Rachel would be at, would save him the trouble. The downside was he'd have to wait out their visit, but he was a patient man.

Chapter Twenty-Three

Speechless, Rachel stared at Luke. Had she heard him right? She finally managed to sputter, "Did you just say you were in *withdrawal?*"

Luke stood up straight; there was pain underlying his expression. He looked directly at her before speaking. "Yes."

"From what? I don't understand." Rachel noticed the pale shade of his skin. His gaunt face was oily, and dark circles formed half-moons under his eyes.

"Let's talk somewhere else," he said, waving toward the hall. Rachel turned and followed him into the living room. She sat down, and Bella and Avi both placed themselves by her feet. Luke took a seat in the old recliner across from her. "Damn, this is hard," he said, glowering at the floor.

"Just tell me what's going on. Please." Upset as she still was at him for letting her believe him dead, Rachel could see this wasn't easy for him to admit. She put her anger aside and patiently waited for him to continue.

"You may remember that after I was shot in Wyoming I had a lot of shoulder pain. The doctor prescribed some painkillers."

Rachel's mind raced; he was referring to something that happened almost two years ago. Had he been taking narcotics this entire time? Realizing he was waiting for her to say something, she chimed in, "Go on."

"Well, long story short, the pain got worse, so the doctor increased my dose. I'm not sure at what point I became addicted to them, but I did. After a while, it wasn't helping as much, so I, uh, found a second source."

"Wait. Just . . . wait." Rachel put up her hands as if she could physically stop his words. "Are you saying you've been taking opiates this entire time? Like, even when we were together?"

"Yes."

"Whew," Rachel replied, overwhelmed to realize the gravity of what he'd been doing. "Okay," she said, gathering her thoughts. "I don't really know what to say." It was the truth. Rachel knew addiction was a disease. Luke's mother was an alcoholic; addiction ran in his family. But to think this entire time he'd been hiding this. Lying about it. That's the part she couldn't comprehend. "How could you not confide in me?" she finally asked.

"I was, I mean, I *am* embarrassed. At first, I thought it was temporary. My shoulder would heal, no more pain, no more pills. But that didn't happen. And it just got worse. And then I found I felt even more pain when I hadn't taken them. I kept thinking I'd quit, eventually, and confess everything to you. But then stuff kept happening; it was never the right time. I knew it was going to be rough when I stopped; I tried tapering twice, but it was too hard. So I just kept putting it off. Until last week."

"Let me guess; you ran out of pills," Rachel surmised. *How long would he have continued on this way if that hadn't happened?*

"I did. I have more at home and could have found a way to get them, but I decided it was time to stop. Cold turkey."

"And that's why you've pretended to be sick since I arrived?"

"Well, technically, I *have* been sick. I swear my insides have been cleared out from both ends," he responded with a grimace.

Rachel held up a hand. "Too much information."

"Too early to joke about it?"

"Just keep those details to yourself," Rachel instructed. "Look, you know me. I'm not going to judge you for suffering from addiction. But I'm having a hard time understanding how you hid this from me for so long . . . the whole time we were dating! You lied to me—*repeatedly.*"

"I know. I'm so sorry." Luke looked as if he would say more, but he suddenly jumped up and placed his hand over his mouth as he ran back toward his room.

Rachel stood and walked over to peek out the window to the backyard. The dogs briefly trailed behind her until Bella picked up a rope toy lying nearby and turned to play tug with Avi. Rachel didn't know how she felt. Anger at Luke for the lying. Sorrow and sympathy that he had been dealing with this alone. Or she assumed as much. Did Ted know? Did anyone know?

A small yellow-colored bird, a finch of some kind by her guess, hopped around the narrow branches of one of the tall bushes lining the backyard. The leaves rustled from its movement. Footsteps approached, and she felt Luke's hands touch her shoulders. Rachel tensed.

"I can't say this enough: I'm sorry." Luke's tone was soft. Resigned. Rachel smelled the pungent odor of mouthwash. She gently removed his hands and turned to face him.

"I know, but give me some time to process this."

He stepped backward and placed his hands in his pockets. "Fair enough."

Another thought occurred to Rachel. "This is why you were pulling away from me when we were together, isn't it?" Luke's gaze told her she'd guessed right. Their breakup had been mutual, but they had been struggling with an inexplicable distance before they ended the relationship.

"Yeah."

That was it. What else was there to say right now? "Okay. Look, like I said, I need to sit on this for a while. We must figure out who's after us and why, so can we just focus on that for now? Table this discussion until later?"

"Agreed."

"Will you stop with the one-word answers?" she quipped.

"Sorry," he said. "Oh, I mean, *I am sorry.* Let's get to work then."

Rachel smiled, nodded, and thought to ask, "How are you feeling right now?"

"Everything aches, I've barely slept, my insides are a wreck, but at least I'm not rushing to the bathroom every five minutes. Those first few days, man, they—"

"Got it," she said and forced another light smile to further minimize the tension in the room. "I nodded off last night before I could get a chance to look up info on Senator Mason or check out the file on your case."

"You needed the rest." Luke walked into the kitchen, opened the refrigerator, and withdrew another bottle.

"What's the deal with all the Gatorade?"

"I read the electrolytes could help during withdrawal, so I ran into that little store in Pioneer the first week I was here and stocked up."

"Does it?"

"Not sure; never been through this before."

"Good point." She got up, walked to the kitchen counter, and opened the laptop that sat on the hard surface. "Can you give me the short version of what you'd learned so far in your investigation into Lacey's disappearance?"

"Not much yet. I'd just started working on it before this all happened."

"She waited that long to hire you?" Rachel was astonished.

"Yeah, she was struggling with her father's assurances, her husband's acquiescence, and I suppose a desire to believe them both." He took another sip. Rachel noticed the blue liquid had darkened his lips. "I did figure out how the senator, or perhaps a few goons working for him, managed to hide her disappearance," he added.

"How?"

"They made it appear they'd whisked her into an ambulance and covered her so she wouldn't be exposed to media. Then they spread the rumor that she'd been taken to a private hospital facility, but no one was told where in order to maintain privacy."

"That had to take some crafty maneuvering. Of course, it always helps when you have the money to pay off people," she opined and then whispered, "Bastards." She heard a small chuckle from Luke. He was well aware of her feelings about wealthy people using their money to do questionable, if not illegal, things. "Anything else?

"A neighbor recalled seeing a large black SUV leaving around the time the fire engulfed the house, but being so focused on the fire itself, he didn't pay much attention to the car. Right before my accident, I contacted a friend of mine to look for any traffic cameras in the area, but I didn't expect that to pan out. The nearest cameras are too far away to allow for any narrowing of suspects. Of course, I haven't been able to follow up with him. Now that you have the rundown on what I know, what about the guy who left you that message? Can you track him down some way other than calling him?"

"That's the first thing I'm going to look into." The room grew silent, save for the quiet tapping of her keys. She paused and looked up at Luke. Watching her, he leaned back against the refrigerator door. "You're wondering who he is to me, aren't you?"

"It's that obvious?"

"While it's none of your business, yes, I had one date with the guy." Rachel pulled one of the wooden stools out from underneath the counter, sat on it, and reoriented herself toward her computer. "Not my type, but during the course of our dinner, the fire by Cascade Lake came up. He's a firefighter. He'd been drinking and let it slip that he thought it was arson. When I asked him for more details, he clammed up and said he shouldn't have mentioned it. In fact, he'd been specifically told not to say anything. Anyway, I haven't talked to him since."

"You have his number?" Luke walked around, stood next to her, and looked at her screen. Rachel turned and gazed up at him, waiting. It took all of five seconds for him to figure out why. "Dumb question. Of course you do; we listened to his message last night."

Rachel grinned and turned back to her computer. She typed in *Rick Bellamy, Tahoe City*. Along with several references to Tahoe City, various lists with "Rick" and "Bellamy" popped up in the search, but nothing with the names combined. "I'm pretty certain he was just looking to get laid, and I suspect he did so regularly. Put on quite a show actually. Almost humorous to watch. That said, it's possible he lied to me about his name." She saw Luke shift at the mention of "getting laid." "What if we called his number with my burner?" Rachel asked. "Would that be safe?"

"In this day and age, you never know. Someone with the right equipment and knowledge may be able to trace the location of the signal. But if Ted were to try, that's a different story."

"Good point. I wrote his number down when I first listened to my messages; let me find it." She began thumbing through a small stack of notes piled up next to the house phone. Luke hadn't noticed them before.

"I see you still rely on Post-its to make it through daily life."

Rachel stopped and stared at him, keeping her expression flat in fake annoyance. She noticed a new sheen of sweat across his forehead. "Go wipe off your forehead before you drip on my keyboard."

He nodded and walked away, apparently following her suggestion. Rachel let a small smile creep across her lips. She located the number on the third note in the stack and called out, "Did you tell Ted about Rick and the Morse code message yet?"

"Talked to him earlier," Luke called out as he returned from the hallway with tissue paper in one hand and a cell phone in the other. "I'll call him and let him know Rick's full name and number." Rachel handed Luke the paper before continuing to search with new variations on his name, location, and fire district names. The results remained disjointed, listing a lot of items but none with all of the terms together.

She heard Luke talking with Ted but wasn't paying full attention to the conversation. Her mind replayed her dinner with Rick, hoping something new would occur to her that could help them.

"Ted is going to look into it and get back to us." Luke's voice was so close it startled her.

"Don't sneak up on me like that."

"I wasn't trying to."

"You're right," she acknowledged. "I'm snappy. My apologies. On that note, how would you feel about pouring me a cup of coffee?" She noticed Luke hesitate. "No biggie. I can get it myself. I brewed some extra, and I'm feeling like the cup I had before I woke you up just wasn't enough."

"I can do it. I was just debating on whether to risk some for myself."

"Oh, I hadn't thought of that. Your gut has got to be hurting. How are you surviving without your beloved caffeine?"

"As best I can, but clearly it's not pretty. I'll admit to taking the Excedrin that has caffeine in it to help take the edge off." He left her side, speaking as if passing on coffee was breaking his heart. It probably was. Luke required three cups just to get through a day; no wonder he was dragging his feet. "I'll pour you some."

Rachel continued typing. As Luke set down the mug in front of her, his phone rang. They made eye contact, and Rachel mouthed, "Ted?"

Luke looked at the display and nodded.

"Yo, Ted. You're on speaker." He set the phone in front of them.

Rachel forced down her anger with Ted. She hadn't spoken with him yet since learning about his deception regarding Luke's death.

"All right, first, I called that phone number; it went straight to a generic voice mail, so no luck there. I also did some research, and there's no one by that name in Tahoe City or anywhere in this vicinity."

"Not surprised," Rachel muttered, then, recognizing the frisson of excitement that tinged Ted's voice, she asked, "But you found something, didn't you?"

"I sure did. There's a firefighter who's been missing from that area. Only his name isn't Rick Bellamy. It's Jake Richard Antone."

"What?" Rachel stammered, staring up at Luke. "That's Jill's ex-husband!"

Chapter Twenty-Four

Ted fumbled with his spare key ring as he walked to the front door of Luke's office with a gym bag slung over his shoulder. Other than his SUV, the parking lot was empty. There had been a few people out walking and riding bikes as he cruised through the streets of the Gardner Mountain neighborhood. It was a typical quiet autumn Sunday morning. Like most locals, Ted appreciated the "shoulder seasons" when the weather was still conducive to biking and hiking, but the Tahoe Basin wasn't crowded by the millions of visitors who came during July and August. Yes, tourists were Tahoe's bread and butter, and he liked that people could come enjoy the area, but he didn't like the associated crowded roads and overrun trails.

He slipped the key in the lock and opened the door. Luke kept his files well secured, shunning suggestions that he install an alarm system. There had been talk at the memorial service about "someone" needing to clean out Luke's office. Ted volunteered for the task in order to delay it indefinitely and prevent others from accessing Luke's office in the meantime. He had hoped Luke could return to the living sooner rather than later.

The musty smell associated with the first use of a natural gas heater after summer's end filled his senses. It was a comforting odor; that, and the changing colors of the trees created a pleasant feeling of anticipation for the upcoming winter. Ted scanned the office space. It was small but decorated with nice clean furniture:

straight edges, lots of glass, and leather chairs. That Rachel and Luke had ever paired up in the first place boggled his mind; they were such opposites in so many ways. He wondered if they were on their way back to each other by now.

Focusing on the task at hand, Ted decided to perform a sweep for listening devices before accessing the files in the safe. While it was possible someone could have broken in and retrieved one after Luke's "death," he'd been keeping an eye on the office and having patrols do regular drive-bys. It wasn't 24/7 coverage, but it was something. Ted removed the radio frequency detector from his bag. It was the easiest way to search, although he knew it may not pick up all devices since some used different frequencies. He walked around the office; no signals were detected. That would have been too easy anyway.

Ted began a physical search, looking for anything that appeared to be out of place. He checked the smoke and carbon monoxide detectors, light fixtures, furniture, and the few potted plants Luke kept around. Nothing. He ran his hands along the external surfaces of Luke's desk. Nothing. The green power light on Luke's printer caught his attention, and Ted began feeling around the outside; he then lifted it up and checked underneath. His fingertips felt a small round bump in the front corner. Ted knelt and positioned the printer on its side, peering at his find. Someone had indeed bugged Luke's office. The device must have been using a frequency not picked up by his detector. Well, that explained how someone knew about the drive they'd planned toward Ebbetts Pass the day Luke was shot. How long had it been there, and what else had been heard? Ted debated; should he leave it so the perps wouldn't realize it had been discovered, but then risk them retrieving it? After all, he couldn't have someone watching the office every single minute of every day. On the other hand, if he removed it, they would know right away it had been discovered and take efforts to cover their tracks.

Leaving it in place for now, Ted opened the safe and withdrew the papers. Perhaps he could get the department's audio/video expert to swing by and do his electronics magic to see what more could be gleaned. Just as he began walking away, he heard what sounded like a muffled sneeze. Ted jerked back around, his eyes examining the office. There were two closed doors: one to the bathroom and one to a closet. Ted set the papers down and reached for his gun.

"Police, show yourself," he said as his eyes darted from one door to the other. A scuffling noise came from inside the closet. *Bingo.* "Come out now," he demanded, taking slow steps toward the source. The door creaked open. "Show me your hands, nice and easy."

Two pairs of hands appeared about eye level. "Please don't shoot," came a man's timid voice. "We're not armed." A man and woman slowly emerged. Ted placed them in their midforties. The woman was petite, not even five feet tall, and had short blonde hair. The man stood a good foot above her, his eyes wide open and staring at the barrel of Ted's raised weapon.

"Who are you and what are you doing here?" Ted remained alert. They could be lying about not being armed.

"My name's Valerie Mason-Spear."

"You're Senator Mason's daughter?"

The woman nodded. "This is my husband, Ian."

"I'm Officer Benson." Ted was about to ask them to explain why they were here when he remembered the listening device he'd left in place. "I'm going to need you both to come with me. Keep your hands in the air, and walk in front of me. No sudden moves." The couple appeared confused but did exactly what he said. Once they were outside, Ted shut the door and motioned for them to walk down the porch steps. Granite boulders large enough to sit on lined one side of the parking lot. "Have a seat," Ted said as he pointed to the boulders. The couple quietly obeyed. Both wore nervous expressions, clearly not career criminals. "Okay, Mr. and Mrs. Spears, tell me why you're here." While Ted assumed this had something to do with their missing daughter, they didn't know *he* was aware of the situation.

"We, uh," Valerie responded and then looked at her husband as if she were uncertain about what to reveal.

Ted waited quietly. Ian gulped. Valerie again broke the silence. "I hired Mr. Reed to look into a . . . matter for me not long before he passed. I wanted to see if he had found anything."

"And you thought you'd just break into his office?" Ted almost felt bad for putting them through the wringer. But they *had* broken the law.

"We were desperate," Ian replied, standing taller and moving closer to his wife. Ted sighed and holstered his weapon, then glared at them. He waited.

Finally, Valerie choked out, "It's about our daughter. She's missing." She leaned into her husband, and he wrapped an arm around her.

"Have you reported it?" Ted knew they hadn't.

"No." Valerie shook her head.

"How long has she been missing?"

"Almost four months," Ian said, cringing like it physically hurt to answer. "Since the day of the fire. I mean, the fire that—"

"I remember hearing about the fire on the news, but I recall reports that your daughter had escaped unharmed. Tell me why you didn't contact the police?" Ted asked, exasperated.

"We couldn't." Ted waited for the woman to continue, but she just looked at her husband before staring down at their joined hands.

"I'm going to need you to tell me everything," Ted instructed.

~

"So, Kris, what do you know about this Seth character that Rachel's been dating?" Derek placed his arm across the seat with his hand behind Kris's headrest. She looked at his arm, then at him. Her point was lost, however, because he was concentrating on driving, which was not something she could complain about.

Kris gently reached up, grabbed his wrist, and slowly moved his arm away from behind her. "That's an odd question. Where did you hear of Seth?"

"He showed up this morning."

"He what?"

"Yeah, the twit woke me up, pounding the door as if his life depended on it. Claims he was worried about Rachel. Said they'd been dating, but the more I talked to him, the more clear it became that it wasn't serious."

"Your instincts are right," she said, pushing the button to open her window. The car was stuffy, and it smelled of grease and sweat underlying the chemical odor of a fruit-scented car freshener. Reminding herself she'd only partially answered his question, she confessed, "CiCi and I may have put some pressure on Rachel to get back into the dating pool."

"Really? And it worked?"

"It took several months of 'strong encouragement.' Looking back, we should have just let it be, but we hated seeing her still hung up on Luke."

"Understandable. I'm surprised she gave in."

"Me too. In any event, she's been on a few dates, pretty much all thumbs down on the first try. But then she meets someone at a coffee shop, and next thing we know, she's agreed to have dinner with him. Says he's a nice guy who's really into outdoorsy stuff like her." The wind felt good, but Kris's hair was blowing around and some strands flew into her mouth as she talked. She carefully removed them, tucking the hairs behind her ear before rolling the window a few inches higher.

"A nice guy, huh?"

"He seemed to be. But after a couple of dates, she knew she wasn't feeling 'it.' She thought she'd let him down easy on the last one. But then she got the call from Ted about Luke and left without talking to him about it, naturally. Ever since, he's been calling and texting; apparently he's added unsolicited visits to his repertoire. It's becoming rather stalker-like."

"I'd have to agree. What else do you know about him?"

"Not much. She hasn't even told me his last name; then again, I never asked." With her hair still blowing into her eyes and mouth, Kris gave up on her desire for fresh air and rolled up the window. She reached over and adjusted the vent, turning it up and setting it so the air flowed in from outside.

"Sounds like someone we need to keep an eye on," Derek said, observing the dashboard controls she'd just changed.

She expected him to switch them back, just for spite, but he let it go. *Wise choice,* she thought. "Slow down up here; the trees are changing, and a lot of cars have been stopping along the highway for a look," Kris warned as they began to descend from Luther Pass into Hope Valley.

"Thanks for the heads-up." They drove in silence, passing the myriad of vehicles parked alongside the road, swarmed with people holding cell phones or cameras, their mouths agape. The trees were bursting with yellow-orange colors reminiscent of flames.

"It's so gorgeous out here," Kris remarked, taking advantage of being a passenger and able to more attentively admire the scenery.

"I agree. I used to come out here just to take walks through the aspens when I lived here. Nature can be awesome."

Kris turned and stared at Derek. "That was an unexpectedly sensitive statement."

"They slip out sometimes, but it's pretty rare. If you breathe a word of it to anyone, I'll have to kill you."

"Ha ha," she laughed. "I'll keep your secret, so long as you stay in line."

"Ouch. You drive a hard bargain."

"Damn straight." Kris smiled inwardly. It was nice to see this other side of Derek again. In their previous time together, he'd been wounded, which had mitigated the robustness of his ego and made him far more tolerable, even enjoyable to be around. But until this car ride, she'd been subjected once again to the other persona of Derek Winters.

"Why did you come over this morning? And your timing . . . do you have ESP or something? I mean, seriously, I was literally backing out."

"Like you, I too expected to hear from Rachel by now. My call to Jill went unanswered. While I'm sure she's fine, I'd rather see for myself. I tried calling your cell, but I guess you were still asleep. Being the attentive friend that I am, I decided to come wake you up and suggest we do exactly what we're doing."

"Admit it, you just hoped to see me in my morning briefs."

Kris punched his shoulder.

"Ow, what was that for?"

"Do you really have to ask?" she retorted. "And by the way, I've seen you in your skivvies; nothing worth making a special trip over." Kris remembered how anxious she'd felt tending to Derek's bullet wound on his upper thigh. So much blood, and she hadn't known if she could stop it.

"Now that, Ms. Drew, was a low blow."

"Just had to bring you down a notch, Mr. Winters." Kris turned her head, admiring the picture-perfect display of the aspens surrounding Sorensen's Resort. She'd always wanted to stay in one of their cabins, but it was hard to justify the expense when she lived barely twenty minutes away.

"I might deserve that, just a little though," he admitted.

"Back to our ultimate goal here, have you thought about how to approach Rachel? She's probably going to be annoyed that we just invited ourselves down. Well, actually, she'll probably be annoyed that *you* invited *yourself* down. I anticipate getting the friend pass."

"Not one clue; just living by the seat of my pants. On that note—"

"Do not even go there," Kris cut in before Derek could make another lame sexist joke.

"You're no fun."

"Oh, I'm *lots* of fun—with the right people."

Chapter Twenty-Five

Mike waited for the metal doors to slide closed, locking him in for the night. He turned and sat on his small bed.

It had been two long years behind bars. The first year had been spent plotting revenge on Luke and Rachel for messing up his property deal and landing him in prison. Then last year, without warning, his daughter, Lori, came to visit him. He could still visualize the pleading look on her beautiful pale white face. In her early twenties, she reminded him of her mother at that age.

Mike recalled the feeling of sitting in the visitor's room and looking up to see who had been escorted into the room. At first he thought it was a hallucination. Lori hadn't attended his trial or attempted to contact him before.

"Lori?" he uttered, moving to stand; a warning look from the correctional officer caused him to remain seated.

"Hello, *Mike*." Her voice was strong yet feminine. He couldn't recall the last time she'd called him Dad.

"You sure you don't want me to stay in here?" the guard interrupted.

"We'll be fine," Lori replied. The man nodded, left the room, and stood just outside of the doorway.

"Good to see you," Mike said, realizing his hand was shaking. It shocked him. Nothing scared him. Ever. How could a visit from his daughter throw him off this much?

Lori nodded, but her expression gave away nothing. She carefully sat in the chair across from him. At least they could talk face-to-face; he had been a model prisoner from day one, and as a result of his good behavior, plus his "friends" both in and outside of the facility, he received certain benefits. One being that he could see visitors in a separate room like this, not through a glass panel or other type of separation.

"You're probably wondering why I'm here," she said. A quick stutter was the only indication she was just as nervous as he.

"Yes, but I'm just glad you are."

"Just to be clear up front, I'm not here for a lengthy father-daughter visit."

Mike's heart sank, even though her statement shouldn't surprise him. He'd never been a part of her life, and their first encounter as adults had been after he was arrested, with one of the charges being that he'd murdered her boyfriend. "I'm just glad you're here. I never thought—"

"Let me cut to the chase. I'm here to ask you to let go of your vengeance against Luke Reed and Rachel Winters."

The topic was so unexpected that Mike was left speechless. Why would she care about two people whom she'd never met?

"I hear things," she said. Mike noticed her spinning a thin silver ring on her left middle finger. "You aren't the only one with connections. I know you're planning something against them."

"I, uh, I don't know what you're talking about. I've found God, realized the error of my ways."

"I wasn't born yesterday, Mike." As if it had all been an act for his benefit, her nervous fidgeting and barely perceptible stuttering ceased. "Yes, you've been a great prisoner. Followed all the rules. Said your *pleases* and *thank yous*. You may have some of the guards here fooled, but not all of them. And don't think there aren't other prisoners who are happy to share information when they get something out of it."

Mike was completely blindsided—by her visit, her accusation, and her boldness. In fact, a small swell of pride ran through him at the realization there was more to his daughter than met the eye.

"Okay, yeah, I've been complaining. That's all it is. What could I possibly do from inside here?" He waved his hands around him.

Lori leaned forward and began to whisper. "I'm not stupid. Don't pretend that you don't have friends in here helping you. That we're sitting in this room freely is confirmation enough. Let me guess, you probably have a cell phone all to yourself?"

"Shhh . . ." He looked up to see if the guard outside the door had shown any indication of hearing what she said.

"Exactly." She smirked and leaned back.

Once he composed himself, he continued, keeping his voice quiet. "What made you come here today to ask me this?" He was curious. He didn't have his plan for Luke and Rachel worked out yet; there were plenty of years to execute his revenge.

"I understand you have been saying some things." She paused and looked him square in the eye. "You broke the law. You murdered people; whether you did it yourself or had one of your minions do it, you're responsible. You deserved to get caught. When I learned what your scheme had put those two through, I felt guilty. That I am related to someone who would do that . . . I couldn't understand it. So I made a point to learn more about them. I wanted to make sure they were doing okay."

"And are they?"

"As if you don't know," she scoffed. "I decided to do some checking; I have friends of my own, you know. You've hurt them enough; don't add to it. Please, just let it go." Moisture filled her eyes, but she looked away and calmed herself.

Mike was at a loss of what to do. He was not a good man, but he'd dreamed of having a relationship with Lori someday. How could he deny the only thing she'd asked of him in her adult life? "Okay," he finally said, exhaling a deep breath.

"Really? Just like that?" She stared in disbelief.

"Just like that. You're my daughter. I'll give you anything you want."

"I wanted Spencer," she snapped back as a tear ran down her cheek.

Mike looked down at the table, for the first time feeling remorse that he'd had the boy killed. "I'm sorry."

"Save it. Just do this one thing for me. That's all I came here to ask." She wiped under her eyes.

"As I said, I'll do what you ask." The idea of not retaliating was a difficult pill to swallow; it's one of the key things that had kept his mind occupied during his monotonous days in prison. But he'd do it. *For her.*

"Thank you." Lori slid her chair back, then stood to leave.

"Lori," he said, causing her to look back at him and wait. "If you ever change your mind about having a relationship with me . . ." He let the words drop off. Her expression reflected a mixture of sorrow and anger. She didn't respond and, after a moment's hesitation, turned and walked out the door. Mike remained seated in his chair, his mind racing. Could he really keep this promise? After all he'd been planning? He had no choice.

Meanwhile, a year had passed since that visit; Mike had kept his word. Yet his not exacting revenge didn't mean he couldn't keep an eye on the couple and take advantage of any unexpected opportunities that arose. Nonlethal opportunities, of course, because he'd made a promise to the one person who mattered. Word "on the street" was Rachel and Luke weren't a couple anymore. *So much for the two lovebirds living happily ever after.*

When one of his outside acquaintances reported hearing about some people who seemed far too interested in the couple, Mike ordered a more in-depth investigation. It had led him straight back to his former associate, Monica Jameson. He'd been even more surprised to learn she was banging Senator Mason, an amazing coincidence given Mike's recent interactions with the man.

After hearing of Luke's death from a supposed hiking accident, Mike suspected Monica had something to do with it. Coincidentally, this was around the same time he'd learned of the connection between Rachel Winters and the other project he was involved with. That's when his instructions to Leo had been modified.

~

Monica turned and stared at Rand; he sat no more than a foot away on the plush sofa. While a healthy dose of skepticism was necessary for any successful state senator, she couldn't believe he was questioning *her* loyalty. After all she had been doing for him. Well, *mostly* for him.

"What do you mean, am I really on board with helping you? What do you think I have been doing all this time?" She reached up and touched her fingers to the jeweled chain holding her glasses. While his question left her shocked and angry, a part of her worried about pushing back too much. She couldn't handle losing this man.

"I'm sorry," he said, relaxing his muscles and reaching his arm across her shoulders. "I suppose I'm just frustrated with the situation and worried about Lacey. Yeah, she's alive, being fed and taken care of somewhere. But she has to be so scared and confused. And I don't like lying to her mother."

"I understand." Monica rested her cheek against his arm.

"I'm doing exactly what they instructed me to do, but there are no guarantees. What if it goes badly and they take it out on Lacey?" He bent his head back and stared at the ceiling. "I may not have been the best grandfather. Hell, I wasn't the best father to Valerie. I justified the late nights and weekends away as necessary for my job." He closed his eyes. "What if I screw up again?"

"You won't. You're an esteemed state senator. People listen to you. You're going to pull this off." She reached over and placed her hand on his lap. He didn't seem to notice.

"That's what I thought until that damn firefighter went blabbing to one of the most vocal and least intimidated people I know."

"And that's why I'm helping you with—" A ring interrupted her. She withdrew her cell from her side pocket and looked at the caller ID. "I need to take this. Give me just a minute." She stood and walked down the nearby hallway. "Cassandra? Where are you?"

"I'm hopefully on my way to see Rachel."

Monica wanted to feel relieved, but that wasn't going to happen until Rachel was shut up, for good.

"Hopefully?"

"I'm driving to Dr. Reynolds's house. Funny thing: I placed a tracker on both vehicles parked at Leo's place the night after Luke's service. He's currently headed in the same direction as I am."

"Well don't let him get to Rachel first!" Monica snapped, exasperated, before lowering her voice. "I can't figure out why Mike hired someone to keep her alive. Does he think he can *talk her* into keeping quiet?"

"I understand. I'll keep you updated." The call ended. Monica turned and was shocked to find Rand standing just a foot away.

"What, exactly, are you planning to do to Rachel Winters?" he asked with a horrified expression on his face.

Chapter Twenty-Six

"I can't believe I went on a date with Jill's ex," Rachel said.

"You'd never met him before?"

Rachel stared at Luke.

"Right, another dumb question." He gulped more Gatorade, and a renewed layer of blue coated his lips, giving him a youthful look.

"Jill took down all of the pictures of him long before I met her. I know the kids had pictures in their bedrooms; Jill complained about having to see his 'lying, cheating face,' but she couldn't say much because she didn't want to make it hard for them to still love their dad. I guess I never noticed him in any pictures the few times I was in their rooms." Rachel wiped her hands against her shirt as though she could wipe off the odd feeling the knowledge had created. "It's sad. He was an ass and a womanizer, but those kids . . . I hope he's found alive and well. Based on that Morse code message, though, I'm not holding my breath."

"Yeah, I don't envy Ted having to break the news of his disappearance to her," Luke replied somberly. "So while Ted talks to Jill and tracks down more information about Rick, or Jake, whatever his name is, I say we focus on learning more about how Senator Mason may fit into all of this."

"I agree," she said and began typing. Luke didn't say anything, nor did he move. She finally looked his way. "You going to help out or—" She stopped short because of the expression on his face:

pain. Only then did she notice how tired he looked. And how pale. "Why don't you go lie down, grab a quick nap."

"No, it's fine. I can—"

"Seriously. You look pretty bad. Plus, you won't be much good if you're half-ready to keel over."

"All right, thirty minutes tops."

"Take an hour. I don't need your help to type," Rachel quipped. She was trying to be understanding about his situation, but the anger of being lied to about *two* major things was reinserting itself in the forefront of her mind. She needed to focus on the task in front of them.

Luke nodded before slowly making his way down the hall.

~

Derek glanced in the rearview mirror. "I think we're being followed." He'd noticed the same small car several times, but it had seemed benign. A lot of people went to the Carson Valley this way. He only became suspicious after it followed them off the main route and onto Centerville Lane.

"Are you kidding?" Kris turned to look behind them.

"It's that green car."

"I think you're being paranoid." She shifted back and faced forward again.

"Maybe so, but when it involves my sister, can you blame me?"

"Good point," she agreed. "It just seems so unlikely. Oh, turn left here," she suddenly directed.

"I'm not sure we should go by Jill's place just yet." Instead, Derek turned right and accelerated, keeping an eye on the rearview mirror. The car followed.

"He's still coming this way." Kris turned and looked at Derek. "Now what?"

He glanced at her. "Okay, let's go up toward Kingsbury Grade. If he's still following us, then we'll make a plan B."

After passing through the intersection at the base of Kingsbury Grade, Derek noticed a large paved park-and-ride area just up the road. He turned and pulled off as if he were making a U-turn, but he stopped once they were facing the road. The interior of the car remained silent as they watched to see what the green car would do.

~

Ted glanced at his cell display and wondered who was calling. It took a second to recognize the number, but once he did, he felt mildly annoyed. What did Rachel's brother want now? He debated about whether to let it go to voice mail but decided to get it over with.

"Hello, Derek. What can I do for you?" Ted hoped his voice didn't give away his irritation.

"Ted, so glad I caught you. We were going down to Jill's place when—"

"You were going to Jill's?" Ted sat up straight, unable to believe what he was hearing. There was no way to cover his frustration now.

"Yes, just let me finish!"

Ted remained quiet as his grip tightened on the phone.

"Kris and I think we're being followed."

Anxious to hear what was going on and how Kris was involved in this, Ted waited for more information, but Derek didn't elaborate. "Why do you think you're being followed?" he finally asked.

"The same green car has been behind us since Meyers. At least that's when I first noticed it. He followed when we turned onto Centerville, so I went up to Kingsbury and stopped in the park-and-ride area. He just drove by and started up the hill, but it looks like he's slowing."

"He's turning around," Kris's voice called out nervously in the background.

"Okay, are there other cars and people around?" Ted asked as his mind worked to consider what his next move should be.

"Yes, quite a few."

"Chances are this guy, *if* he's following you, wouldn't do something out in the open. Stay put. I'm going to contact one of my buddies down that way to come meet you."

"Could he be following us to Jill's? Looking for Rachel?"

"It's possible, yet in this day and age, it wouldn't be hard to find her address directly. Someone wouldn't necessarily need to follow you."

"Ted, there's more going on here than you're telling us, isn't there?"

Ted rubbed his face. This was the last thing he needed. Silence hung in the air.

Derek must have given up on expecting an answer. "Just be honest. Is my sister okay?"

"She's fine. Look, stay put. I mean it. I'll call you back in a few." Ted hung up before Derek could question him further. He dialed the number for one of the officers he knew in Minden, explained the bare bones of the situation, and had his friend's assurance that he'd go meet Kris and Derek. Next, Ted dialed Jill. He hadn't had the chance to notify her about her ex-husband's disappearance yet. He had hoped to have more information for that conversation. But the call couldn't be put off now; Jill needed to be warned.

Chapter Twenty-Seven

Monica was unable to speak. Rand stared at her and waited for a response. Her phone rang again. *Saved by the bell.*

"Let it go to voice mail," he demanded.

"It's related to helping *you*!" she exclaimed as she glanced at the display, expecting that Cassandra had called her back. But it wasn't Cassandra's number. She turned from his angry stare and answered the phone. "What?"

"Hi to you too, Monica," the man chuckled.

"It's not a good time. Has something come up?"

"Actually, yes. I was alerted to a conversation picked up by our listening device. Seems Valerie and her hubby broke into Luke Reed's office."

"They *what?*" Monica screeched, feeling blood rush to her cheeks.

"Earlier today. They were talking about finding some kind of file. A cop showed up, and they hid. He found them." Monica knew they had to be looking for files related to Luke's investigation into Lacey's disappearance; problem was, she hadn't told Rand about what his daughter had been up to, hoping it would be buried along with Luke Reed.

"What is it?" Rand asked from behind her. She raised a finger, signaling him to wait.

"And?" she asked into the phone.

"I don't think they found our listening device. I'm waiting to hear back on whether they were arrested."

"Monica!" Rand yelled.

She placed her hand over the receiver and snapped at him, "Give me a minute!"

Monica had to think fast. Could Rand hear the other end of her conversation? She didn't think so. Before hanging up, she had to confirm her suspicions. "What was the name of the officer?"

"Benson."

"Just what I expected," she said, her mind racing. "All right. Can you get his cell information? Who he called, when, that sort of thing?"

"Child's play," he snorted. "I'll get right on that and get back to you as soon as I have something. I may be limited as it's a Sunday, though, and some associates of mine won't be available. It is the Lord's day after all."

"Great, thanks." Monica ended the call and turned to Rand. She had never seen him so angry. His normally smooth, relaxed cheeks were sunken in the way a kid's face imitates a fish. His posture was erect, and his hands rested on his hips.

"What's going on, Monica?"

~

Mike carefully glanced at the display on his hidden phone and saw he had a message from his informant. He slipped into a janitor's closet using a key provided last year by one of the guards on his payroll. He didn't need to advertise his possession of the cell phone to the other prisoners. He returned the call.

"Do you have something for me?" he asked without preamble.

"When I skimmed through the officer's phone calls, there's one number he's communicated with several times over the past couple of weeks, and more so the last few days. It's a prepaid phone, but the location can still be tracked. Possibly only to cell towers, but we'll see."

"Excellent. Does our mutual friend know yet?" Mike asked as he smiled. Monica had no idea her technical guru was working for them both. Of course, it had required Mike to compensate the man at a much higher rate than Monica, but it was worth it. Not only did he get the same information, but he also had the opportunity to influence what data she received.

"I promised to look into the numbers but haven't followed up on what what I've found; someone was yelling in the background, so I have a good reason to wait and tell her more later. I may not have anything until tomorrow, but I'll let you know."

"Perfect. I'll check in around ten a.m., but as soon as you know more about the location of that prepaid caller, I need you to call another contact of mine and relay the details." Mike gave him Leo's number and then quickly hung up. This entire situation had gotten out of control, he thought, but if anyone could reclaim it and keep a lid on everything until the election, it was Leo.

~

Leo hadn't thought Rachel's brother would pay that much attention, but as soon as he saw the guy park in the carpool lot, he suspected he'd been spotted. Not a problem—he'd come this far, so now he just needed to spend a minute or two on his phone to pull up the location of Dr. Reynolds's properties again. One of them couldn't be too far from here, and Leo doubted the couple would drive there now; they wouldn't want to lead whoever they suspected to be following them straight to her, which gave him the perfect chance to get there first. Leo slowed and pulled into a dirt driveway and turned around the car. As he cruised back down the hill, he glanced at their car across the highway. Leo retraced his route and turned right at the intersection. He recalled a parking area for a popular trailhead on the way in.

Leo almost missed the sign for the Jobs Peak Ranch Trailhead. Glad no one was behind him, he whipped his car into the lot at the last minute. About half a dozen vehicles sat in the lot; no hikers or equestrians were around. He parked where he could keep an eye on the street and began typing on his phone. Within less than a minute, he had the street address for Jill's nearest home mapped out on his GPS system. He assumed they would have contacted someone for help or even called the cops to go check out Jill's place. He'd have to act fast. Leo threw the car into gear and spun out of the lot.

Leo knew about Monica's involvement, which begged the question about whether she'd enlisted Cassandra to do her dirty work. He had once been fond of Cassie but hadn't been interested in anything serious, nor could a relationship with anyone succeed given his current employment situation. Plus, the woman had some serious crazy moments, even though she always achieved what she set out to do. In fact, it had occurred to him too late to keep an eye out for her at the funeral. Either way, Leo needed to get to Rachel before someone else did, as Mike suspected was the case.

He followed the GPS's route to a modest-sized ranch-style home sitting on about five acres. A white fence with peeling paint stretched across the front of the property at its border with the road; the sides were lined with what looked like barbless wire fencing. A heavily landscaped area blocked most of the garage from view by passersby. Luckily, the gate at the entryway was open, so he could drive right up to the house. As Leo cruised up the length of her dirt driveway, the rest of the home came into view, along with a dirty blue Tacoma parked on the side. *Bingo.*

After walking up the front steps, Leo pushed the doorbell button and plastered a sincere, neighborly smile on his face; it always felt awkward with the cheek implants he used for this disguise. He waited, but there was no response. He rang it again. Another minute passed with no sound. Leo knocked and called out, "Hello?" Nothing.

He walked around to the side of the house, glancing toward the thick patch of trees and bushes, confident they hid him from view by people living in adjacent residences. A wooden fence enclosed a well-sized backyard. The side gate was closed but not locked. He easily reached over the top and opened the latch, then thought twice. *What about Rachel's dogs? Does Jill Reynolds have dogs too?* He called out but again was met with silence. He suspected with all of his knocking and walking around that if they were there, they'd have been barking by now. Either way, he'd have to risk it.

Once in the yard, he closed the gate and walked toward the house. A large weathered deck stretched out beyond a sliding glass door. It took him less than five seconds to maneuver around the lock. As the door opened, hot air rushed outside like the house had been waiting to exhale. He quietly stepped inside. No dogs.

He checked all of the rooms and found no one sleeping, nor any signs typical of a guest, like a suitcase or other items. No extra dog beds. *Where's Rachel?* Something was amiss. Leo needed to locate her, and his only link appeared to be Jillian Reynolds. He glanced around, noting the house's interior. It all looked comfortable: the furniture was worn but not too worn. A long narrow table lined with pictures stood against the back of the sofa. He eyed them more closely. There were pictures of a woman around his age and a boy and a girl who looked to be in their teens. In one of the larger photos, the boy, clearly the older of the two, wore a colorful sports uniform with a high school logo lining the sleeves. His dark hair was frosted on the tips with platinum blond coloring. The girl was pretty with long blonde hair and a crooked smile. Leo snapped pictures of the images and then glanced at the time. He'd been here long enough. Leo retraced his steps back out to his vehicle. It was going to take more time, but he'd track Rachel Winters down, one way or another.

~

Cassandra parked down the road from the driveway to Jill Reynolds's house. She retrieved the binoculars stowed in her glove box and watched as Leo climbed out of the small car and walked up the front steps. It hadn't been possible to get in front of him without drawing undue attention. At this point, she'd decided to let him do the work; if he located Rachel, she'd take action. If he got caught, she could simply leave with no one the wiser.

After his knocks went unanswered, he walked out of sight around the side of the house. She deliberated but decided to wait and see what he did. Or whether Rachel appeared. Just over five minutes had passed without any commotion by humans, dogs, or otherwise when Leo reemerged and dashed to his vehicle. He didn't appear to be carrying anything other than an anxious look on his well-disguised face. She remained where she was as he drove back up the driveway and turned onto the road, heading in the opposite direction. No doubt Rachel hadn't been there; no one was. Monica was not going to be happy about this.

She contemplated briefly about retracing Leo's footsteps but noticed a vehicle approaching from behind with the distinct outline of a bar of lights across the top. She quickly held her phone to her

162

ear, pretending to have pulled off the road to take a phone call in the event the officer thought her suspicious. The patrol car drove past her, slowed, and made a right turn into Jill's driveway. Cassandra tossed her phone on the passenger seat, put her car into gear, and headed back toward South Lake Tahoe.

Chapter Twenty-Eight

Rachel hadn't found anything unexpected online with regard to Senator Mason. He generally voted along party lines and never wavered in his long-held views regardless of changing facts or circumstances. Rachel looked through her contacts and placed a call, hoping her friend would answer since she wasn't calling from her normal phone.

"Hello?" the woman asked on the second ring with hesitation in her voice.

"Elaine, hey, it's Rachel."

"Rachel, how ya doin'?" As always, Elaine was perky and chronically enthusiastic, just as she'd been when they both attended school at the University of Nevada, Reno. She often wished the woman's seemingly endless energy would rub off on her, especially in the morning.

"Doing okay. How about you?" There was no need to launch into any long "life updates," as they connected periodically but didn't regularly follow every detail of each other's lives. Rachel doubted Elaine would even be aware of Luke's "death."

"Hanging in there. My kids are keeping me busy for sure."

Rachel smiled. Elaine's "kids" were her political science students at California State University, Sacramento. The two had met in Reno through their graduate studies in environmental science; however, as they learned more about environmental policy and how political pressure continued to affect the world, Elaine switched her major. For the past several years, she'd divided her time between teaching at the college and working at the state capitol in Sacramento.

"I bet. Look, sorry to bother you on a weekend, but I have a question, and I think you might be able to provide some insight."

"No problem. What's up?"

"This is on the QT, but I was wondering if you could tell me whether Senator Rand Mason has done or said anything lately that seemed off. Or are there any new policies he's been pushing extra hard on lately?" Rachel heard a door squeak on its hinges a second before both dogs jumped up and dashed toward the hallway.

"Hmm, let me think," Elaine said. Rachel could easily envision her friend tapping her fingertips on whatever nearby surface was available. It had driven Rachel nuts back in the day, so much so that she tried to be on the other side of a classroom during exams. Elaine was the kind of person who laughed it off, never offended by Rachel's test-day proximity avoidance tactics. "You know what? Now that you mention it . . . there is something strange. I heard he was working hard to get his supporters to vote in favor of Proposition Forty-Three."

Rachel knew exactly which bill that was. The federal administration had been talking about passing a new bill that would exempt industrial operations, like mining, from having to meet the protective environmental review requirements. In response, California officials had proposed Proposition 43, a ballot measure that would ensure environmental protections remain in place in the event the federal government tried to repeal them.

"Mason *supports* it? What's the catch?" Rachel couldn't imagine why the state senator would be supportive of such a bill given his track record on environmental legislation.

"Nothing sinister is buried in the measure, but it stands out to me for the same reason you're surprised—because he supports it."

"That's definitely out of character." Rachel scrawled a few notes as she spoke. "Has no one else wondered about it?"

"He's been questioned about it many times. His explanation is that he believes it would create unfair competition for the existing mining companies who have had to pay the higher costs associated with meeting environmental requirements."

"Hmm, that's an interesting spin," Rachel mused. While she could believe Senator Mason would base his view on the financial implications to large mining companies, it just didn't sit right with her. Yet she recognized that her feelings were apt to be biased due her awareness that there was more to the story. "Have you heard the most recent numbers from the polls? Has he had any influence?" Rachel watched as Bella dashed down the hallway, her tail wagging, and Avi tentatively followed. Luke must be awake.

"Last I heard it's likely to pass with bipartisan support."

"While that's certainly good news, I have to wonder, what's in it for him personally?" Rachel looked up at Luke as he strode into the kitchen with both dogs following at his heels.

"Good question," Elaine replied. "I'm sorry, but I need to get going. Feel free to call me if you have more questions. I'm meeting up with some friends tonight, but we shouldn't be out too late."

"No problem. Thanks, Elaine. You've been a huge help!" Too worked up to sit, Rachel slid off the barstool. There was something here. She knew it.

"Aren't I always?" Elaine laughed before ending the call.

"What's got you giddy like a school girl?" Luke angled himself against the countertop with his arms crossed and a grin on his face.

"I may have something." Rachel recounted what she'd learned from Elaine.

"Are you thinking what I'm thinking?" he asked.

"If you're thinking his granddaughter's kidnapping could have something to do with his unlikely support for this ballot measure, then yes." Rachel quickly opened the back door, and both dogs dashed outside. She sat back down, her hands reaching for the keyboard. "Let's look at the details." Her fingers typed quickly as Luke came and stood next to her. His breath tickled her ear when he leaned in to view the monitor. Hairs rose on the back of her neck as her awareness of his nearness increased. Her mind began imagining the feel of his lips touching that one sweet spot on her neck, right where he knew it drove her wild.

"Rachel?" Luke interrupted. "You okay?" She blushed, hoping

he hadn't noticed. Apparently she'd stopped typing.

"Uh, yeah. My mind is just racing; that's all," she stuttered as she hit *enter*. The search results popped up on her screen, and she selected the first link. After reading it, she reclined. "Proposition Forty-Three is exactly what it appears to be; it will keep existing requirements in place for any new or expanded operations as well as retain the authority of local governments to regulate it. I can't imagine Senator Mason supporting this for anything other than personal gain of some kind."

"Why not just bribe him? Don't they all cave to that eventually?"

Rachel turned and looked at Luke. It was a big mistake as his face was just a foot away. Although his nap hadn't gone much beyond an hour, he appeared refreshed. *Damn, he's easy on the eyes.* She reminded herself to stick to the subject at hand. "I've really tarnished your view of politicians, haven't I?" When she had first met Luke, he occasionally paid attention to politics but hadn't been very involved. Seeing firsthand the level of planning and dealmaking that could go on behind closed doors had been an education for him. "In this case, I don't know that a bribe would work. As much as I disagree with Senator Mason on, well, just about everything, word is that he is not one to take bribes."

"There's a first time for everything."

"True, but here's what I'm thinking. What if his granddaughter was taken in order to force him to build up support for the ballot measure? Instead of ransom, the kidnappers could be using Lacey for leverage. That would explain why he's confident that she won't be harmed, according to what Lacey's mother told you. The elections are coming up soon; presumably she'd be returned once the voters pass it." Rachel felt excitement building. She loved putting the puzzle pieces together on stuff like this.

"Why wouldn't he have involved the police?" Luke took a step back as if the closeness was as difficult for him as it was for her.

"I suppose for fear the kidnappers would harm his granddaughter?" Rachel guessed. "Same reason people don't always contact the police when someone is kidnapped for ransom."

"I think you're on to something, *mountaingirl*," Luke said as he rubbed his chin.

At his use of the nickname he'd assigned her years ago, Rachel's insides jumped. How could she be reacting this way after all that had happened? All the lies he'd told? Rachel's mind shifted as she noticed callouses on Luke's fingers. Two fingernails were also partly darkened as though they were bruised. She recognized the injury; she'd grown up on a ranch and was all too familiar with what happened when fingers were slammed into doors or accidently hit while hammering a nail. "What happened to your hand?" she asked, reaching out without meaning to. Her fingertips brushed his knuckles. He dropped his hand and looked at it.

"Oh, I took up a new hobby: woodworking."

Rachel was shocked. She couldn't picture Luke in a woodshop, hammering away. "You did what?"

"I'm taking a class at the college. It's been a steep learning curve, but I've actually managed to build some decent furniture. After several practice items of course."

Rachel wasn't usually so cliché, but damn if she didn't start imagining him with a hammer in hand, pounding nails into wood as sweat beaded down his face and his arm muscles flexed. "That's great," she stammered and looked back up at his face.

Their eyes met. Everything around them fell away.

~

Jill answered Ted's call on the first ring.

"Teddy, hey," she said, sounding out of breath.

He heard pounding footsteps in the background. "Jilly, catch you at a bad time?" Ted adjusted the volume on his car speaker. He didn't like talking while driving, regardless of his hands-free setup, but time was of the essence.

"No, just out for a run, but I can talk. What's going on?"

Ted deliberated. He'd prefer to tell her about her ex face-to-face and with more information. He elected to start with Derek and Kris.

"First, Derek and Kris decided to pay Rachel a surprise visit at your house this morning."

"They *what?*" Jill asked with exasperation in her voice. The footsteps stopped.

Ted explained what he knew. "My friend told them to go back

to Rachel's and with the message that I would come talk to them this evening. Not looking forward to that," he mumbled.

"How much are you going to share?"

"I'll narrow it to the attack on Rachel and explain that she's somewhere safe. But nothing about Luke."

"Sounds reasonable." Jill's breathing was slowly returning to normal. "What a bad time for Derek to be the supportive big brother."

Ted nodded and then realized she couldn't see him. "Yeah, that's for sure."

"What else? You said 'first.'"

Ted sighed. "It's about Jake."

"What's he done now?"

Ted knew Jill had good reason to expect bad news when it came to Jake. "He's missing."

"What do you mean?"

Ted began explaining Jake's use of the fictitious name and his connection to Rachel. Before he could mention the Morse code message, Jill cut in.

"Oh my God, Rachel has to be freaking out."

"She was not pleased." Jill's apparent lack of concern over her missing ex-husband didn't surprise Ted. He'd gone missing often enough in the past, including while they were still married. "Jill, this all came up because of a message he left Rachel—in Morse code—before he disappeared: *Danger. Coming for you. Cascade.*" The line went silent. "Jill?"

"Still here. Just taking it all in. That message sounds . . . morbid, doesn't it? And why Morse code?"

"We don't know—"

"Teddy, it's me. Don't give me any BS platitudes. While I despise that man, I certainly don't wish him dead. And my kids . . ." She paused. Ted didn't know what to say. She was right. "So back to what led up to this. He was using a fake name, fake story, and trying to seduce women?"

"According to Rachel's assessment, yes."

"That doesn't surprise me," she scoffed.

Ted could visualize Jill rolling her eyes. She was used to Jake's exploits by now. "I've got people looking through his house in Truckee. I'll let you know if we find anything. I'm also looking into whether he had any other properties or rentals under another name." A beep interrupted the call. "Hold on. I've got a text." Ted glanced at his phone. It was one of his fellow officers with an update about their search for Rick, aka Jake. "Speak of the devil," he muttered. "Jill, they've found a rental under Rick's alias in Tahoe City. They're going there now."

"I can't believe this. What do I tell the kids?"

"That's up to you, but it might be a good idea to hold off until we have some news." He didn't like to give parenting advice to anyone, even when asked, yet Jill consistently sought his opinions over the years.

"You're right. I'll wait. Plus, I wouldn't want to tell them something this important over the phone. And as you suggested, I'm staying away from the safe house so no one can follow me. It's not easy. I want to see my kids!"

"I know. Just remember it's temporary. Given that someone was following Derek and Kris to your house, I really don't think you should go back there alone. I wish someone had been available to keep an eye on your house, but I've called in all the favors I can."

"Teddy, I can handle myself."

"I know you can. I'd advise anyone the same thing in this situation, even a fellow officer."

"All right, I'm still near my office. Went jogging on my lunch break. I'd like to go home this evening though."

"Good. That gives me some time to find someone to meet you there."

"You know I don't like someone babysitting me."

"I know, Jilly, I know."

Ten minutes later Ted's phone rang. It was the officer who had previously texted him about the apartment rented by "Rick."

"What's up?"

"Ted, we're standing inside Rick's apartment right now. No one's here, but there's a huge bloodstain in the bedroom."

"How bad?"

"It's hard to imagine anyone could survive that much blood loss."

Ted thought of Jill's kids, Tanner and his younger sister, Nikki. Although Tanner had come to recognize his father's faults in recent years, his sister had no idea what Jake was really like. Jill had put significant efforts toward preserving her kids' positive views of their dad for as long as possible. Then again, there was no body. No guarantee it was Rick's blood.

"Get the techs there, and type that blood. See if it matches our guy. It won't be a positive ID, but it would be something. DNA could take weeks."

"On it."

~

Luke couldn't tear his gaze from Rachel. Her blue eyes sparkled in the sunlight, and her face bore the youthful appearance that usually meant something had her juices flowing. She was clearly excited over the new discovery about the senator. He attempted to look away, but his focus moved to her lips. As always, they were lined with a shiny yet subtle lip gloss. She was staring back at him with the same expression of lust as he was feeling. He moved in closer. Time froze. Disappointment settled over him when Rachel suddenly turned away.

"We'd better get this information to Ted ASAP." She stepped toward the kitchen.

Luke was instantly reminded of where they were and what they were facing. Disappointed as he was at the lost closeness, it was for the best. Even if she could forgive him and reconsider a relationship, they had a lot to work through first. Not that it would keep him from kissing her soft lips if given the chance.

"Luke, you want to call him or should I?" Rachel's raised voice and penetrating stare suggested this hadn't been the first time she'd asked this question.

"Uh, I'll do it. Keep doing what you're doing." He reached for the phone stowed in his back pocket, reminding himself he needed to call Ted. It was not the appropriate time to be fantasizing about what he wanted to be doing with Rachel.

Chapter Twenty-Nine

Monica had to think fast, which wasn't easy in light of the angry glare Rand was giving her. Besides her pounding heart, the only other sound was the ticking of the old clock hanging on the wall. Eight clicks echoed before she answered; she conceded she'd have to give at least a partial truth and hope it would also distract Rand from following up on his earlier question about her intentions for Rachel.

"It appears that Valerie hired Luke Reed to locate Lacey." She purposefully omitted the details of how long ago she'd found out.

Rand's face turned white. "Valerie did what?"

She didn't answer; it was clearly a rhetorical question.

"How did this come about?" He ran his fingers through his hair as he collapsed into a nearby chair.

"I have a contact within the police department," she began. That was technically true, yet that contact wasn't the reason she knew, but revealing the listening device would also mean telling him she'd known Valerie's plans for weeks. "She and Ian were caught breaking into Luke Reed's office."

"No! We can't bring the police into this!" He looked around the room as though he could find the solution in a piece of furniture.

"It's under control for now. There's no official report, and the officer doesn't appear to have told anyone else, assuming she was honest about why they were there. Given the lack of any report, it's possible they didn't tell him about Lacey."

"Then how did your contact find out?"

Monica removed a handkerchief from her pocket and blew her nose, stalling for time while she thought of a believable reply. "I don't know and didn't think to ask." It was the first outright lie she'd had to tell him in this conversation, but it seemed to appease his curiosity.

"I can't believe this. That husband of hers was supposed to keep her in line, not join her!"

Monica walked over to him and placed her hand on his shoulder. "It may still be okay. As I said, the officer hasn't filed a report. Apparently he let them go from the scene without calling it into the office. With Luke gone, the investigation is over. I'll keep in touch with my contact to see what the officer does next."

"This can't be happening. My sweet Lacey. Oh, they can't hurt her. They just can't." Monica reached up to caress his chin, and he leaned into her palm.

"They won't," she said and then moved until she was kneeling in front of him. "Look, they need to keep you 'incentivized' to follow through until after the election. That's just another week or so. It would make no sense to harm her now."

"She's not an incentive; she's my granddaughter."

"You know what I meant." Monica realized he was being combative because of his frustration.

"I don't understand how all of this is happening. Someone puts the pressure on Mike to put the pressure on me. Apparently that's not good enough because next thing I know, someone has burned down my cabin and taken my sweet granddaughter, holding her all this time. Now one of the people tasked with finding her is killed?" He lamented. "Frankly, I find Mr. Reed's 'accident' too much of a coincidence."

Monica had hoped he wouldn't raise the last issue again; although since the paperwork concluded it was an accident, she shouldn't have to worry too much. "I'm doing my best to try to help."

"I know," he said, reaching for her hand. "I'm sorry. My emotions are all over the board right now." He looked into her eyes. "I'm not sure I thanked you for doing whatever you did to get Rachel to keep her mouth shut."

Monica winced internally. She hadn't confided that Rachel had been MIA for the past few days. Cassandra would find her, and Rand never needed to know about the lapse. "Thanks. Like I said, I want to help you get Lacey back home safely." And that much was true. "Are you going to tell Valerie what's really going on?"

"I think I have no choice. She's persistent. I doubt she'll let this go. For all we know she's already hired another PI."

Monica wasn't sure how she felt about bringing Rand's daughter into the fold; the more people who knew, the greater the chance of someone talking. She had too much on the line to allow word to get out.

Chapter Thirty

Rachel could hear the water running from Luke's shower as she stepped into the hall. They had stayed up late the night before, talking about the case before straying to more personal topics. Somehow she'd managed to bury the ache of being lied to, at least for the night. After preparing her coffee, she walked back down the hallway and reached out to knock on Luke's door when she heard his voice through the hollow door.

"Yeah, I'll chat with Rachel and get back to you." Pause. "We're doing fine." Pause. "Seriously. We've talked a few things out." Pause. "You know you have your own reckoning coming for letting her believe I was dead, right?" Pause. "No, I'll let you two work it out directly. I've got my own penance to pay. I'll be in touch."

Rachel turned and retraced her steps. She heard his door open just as she turned the corner back into the kitchen. Luke's footsteps neared.

"Good morning," he said.

"Morning." Rachel leaned against the counter. "I need to take the girls for a walk and figured I'd head out in a few minutes. I don't suppose you're up for going along?"

"No, you go ahead," he said as he opened the refrigerator. She stared at him as he grabbed a small carton of chicken broth and drank straight from the carton. When he was done, he caught her eye and grinned. "What?"

"Cold broth?"

"It actually tastes pretty good. And it is safe for the GI." He patted his stomach.

Rachel shook her head. "At least heat it."

"Why waste the effort?" he laughed. "By the way, Ted just called. He met up with Jill last night when she went home after work. The only thing irregular they found was the sliding glass door was unlocked. Jill said it's possible one of her kids failed to lock it in their haste to leave, but Ted is wary. Especially after that guy followed your brother."

"Speaking of which, has Ted had a talk with Derek yet?"

"He went by and spoke to him late last night. He confided that someone had attacked you, so they'd placed you in a safe location until they could figure out who and why."

"Did he believe that? I mean, if that were the only thing that happened, would cops really whisk me off to a safe house so quickly?"

"Ted's feeling was that Derek suspected more was going on, but he didn't push it, not that he didn't initially try."

"So he's still hanging at my house then?"

"Yes. I'm sure your next satellite bill will be interesting," he chuckled.

Rachel rolled her eyes. "I don't even want to think about it." With her coffee mug almost empty, she stood up and looked around, trying to recall where she'd left the dogs' leashes. After spotting them in the corner, she grabbed her coat, stuffed her arms through the sleeves, slung a small backpack over her shoulders, and picked up the leashes. "Bella, Avi, let's go for a walk!" she called out into the yard where the dogs had been playing. Both canines bounded into the house. Upon seeing Luke, Bella ran past her and began brushing against his legs.

"Traitor," Rachel snickered. Avi stood partway between them with uncertainty in her posture.

"Which way are you going?"

Rachel looked back up at him. "I don't know; figured I'd just go out to that main road and follow it for a while like we did yesterday."

"Don't get lost."

"Ha ha."

"And keep an eye out. I can't imagine how anyone could know about this place, but it doesn't hurt to be careful."

"Got it." She placed the empty mug in the sink before turning to attach their leashes. "I'm not used to using leashes; they listen so well after some intense training last year. But I don't know this area." Why was she explaining herself to Luke?

He nodded, smirking. It wasn't the first time she'd rambled in his presence.

Rachel reached for the front door and, as if it were an afterthought, grabbed her disposable cell phone and tried to slip it into her pocket, forgetting the pockets were too small on her shorts. "Okay, see you in about an hour," she called as she placed it into her backpack and walked out.

Chapter Thirty-One

Leo parked down the street from the boy's high school. An internet search had revealed his name to be Tanner Reynolds. Getting the kid would be difficult, but attempting to nab the daughter would have been even worse. She was still in junior high and would no doubt be watched more closely. He'd hoped they would have returned home the previous night, but after driving by the house this morning, it was clear the kids hadn't returned. He adjusted his collar, glimpsing at himself in the rearview mirror. This was one of his best disguises yet—perfect for an innocent father looking for his son.

Leo slipped on gloves and stashed a small container of liquid in his pocket, his mind focusing on how he would approach Tanner. As he rose from his vehicle, he noticed movement near one of the buildings. He quietly sat back down and retrieved the image he'd stowed in his pocket, then looked back up. "You've got to be kidding me!" Leo began to quietly laugh. *Of all things*. Not fifty feet away, the very person he was looking for was sneaking alongside a building looking guilty as sin. It was as if the boy had been gift wrapped and delivered straight to him. Leo watched with amusement as the juvenile delinquent exited from the school's campus alongside a long row of thick landscaped bushes, crossed the street, and headed toward a side street to Leo's right. Once his target was almost out of sight, Leo started the engine.

After scanning to make sure no one was around, Leo parked near the other end of the block, engaged the trunk release, doused the rag, jumped out, and hid behind the corner. The boy came walking past, bobbing his head to the tunes playing in his earbuds. Tanner clearly felt he was safely off campus. That was good; his guard was down. Approaching from behind, Leo pressed the cloth over the kid's mouth with one hand and wrapped his other arm around his ribs. After a few attempts to buck him off, the boy's body relaxed and turned to dead weight in his arms. Leo walked backward to his car, dragging the unconscious teen along with him. Within less than a minute, he had bound his hands and feet, placed duct tape over his mouth, and dropped him in the trunk. Leo pulled the SIM card and battery from the kid's phone so he couldn't be tracked; he'd toss it the next time he stopped for gas. They were on the road ten seconds later.

Leo turned on the stereo, and the audiobook he'd been listening to resumed. James Patterson would make the upcoming drive much easier. Five chapters later, the phone rang.

"What?" Leo asked as he pressed the answer button on his console.

"Mike told me to call you."

Leo paused. That was odd. Mike didn't want anyone else to know they were associated. "Mike who?"

"We both know damn well which Mike. Don't play games with me."

"You could be anyone."

"Look, Leo, or whatever the hell your name is. Mike told me to call you when I had narrowed down a cell signal. I don't know who it's for, nor do I care. I am merely doing what he asked, so do me a favor and just listen."

Leo didn't respond. He wasn't expected to.

"The subject of interest is down near Pioneer, California. I was able to narrow down the cell towers to locate the general vicinity of the prepaid but can't get more specific than that. I'll continue working on it, but Mike wanted me to relay this to you in the meantime. I'm going to text general coordinates to you."

Leo couldn't believe it. Had Mike somehow located Rachel?

And what was she doing down in Pioneer? *Of all the locations.* The irony didn't escape him; grabbing the Reynolds boy to encourage his mother to tell them where Rachel was had been unnecessary. *Too late to change that one.*

"Got it. Anything else?"

"No, I'll contact you if and when I can narrow it down further." The line went dead. Leo's phone beeped, indicating the incoming text.

"I feel like it's my birthday," he said aloud, glancing at the coordinates on the phone. As the audiobook resumed, Leo relaxed in his seat and smiled.

Chapter Thirty-Two

The road had one narrow lane going in each direction. Normally Rachel would never walk the dogs on paved roads like this, always opting for the forest or foothills instead, but in addition to the fact that most land was privately owned out here, the last thing she needed was to get lost in the array of rural roads meandering through the forest. At least it was lightly traveled. In fact, not one car had passed the entire time they'd been walking.

Rachel inhaled the musky scent in the air; it stirred distant memories of childhood trips to a nearby Christmas tree farm. Her reminiscing was interrupted by the rumble of an engine approaching from behind. She'd been walking along the opposite lane and positioned herself and the dogs over toward the farthest side to turn and watch the vehicle pass.

A small nondescript green car slowed. Rachel put both leashes in one hand and waved at the driver with the other, indicating for him or her to continue past. The driver didn't seem to catch on, and she watched in annoyance as the window rolled down.

"Excuse me, ma'am, but I think I'm lost," the man stuttered. Rachel could barely hear him but didn't move any closer.

"I don't live here; afraid I can't help you." The dogs sat patiently at her side. Rachel had the odd sense that she'd seen this man before. But how could that be?

"Oh, shoot," he sighed dramatically. "My GPS isn't working, cell phone has no signal." He held up a cell phone as if putting it on display.

"That's too bad. Perhaps if you go back out to the highway, you'll find a signal," she said with a smile. She turned to continue walking as an uneasy feeling settled over her. "Heel," she instructed to the dogs. After glancing at the driver one more time, the reason for the familiarity hit her—it was the image Jill had emailed her, passed on from Ted. The driver didn't look exactly like the man in the picture, but it was close enough to spook her. She picked up her pace as her fingers reached into her pocket for her phone before remembering she'd tossed it in the backpack.

"Miss Winters."

Rachel abruptly stopped and turned as her heart raced. The man produced a gun and aimed it at her chest. She froze.

"That's right. I've been looking for you since our last encounter. You haven't made it easy," he said as he sneered.

Their last encounter? Rachel felt the dogs growing anxious. They both remained in their sitting positions, but the slight rise in their haunches indicated they were ready to bolt, likely picking up on her nervous energy. Worried any threatening action on their part, even growling, could get them shot, she calmly said, "Shhh, it's okay, girls."

"Get in the car," he commanded.

Rachel looked up the road in both directions. Why couldn't someone else come driving along now? She looked back at the man. After her first encounter with a gun years ago, she'd taken a self-defense class. One thing they'd hammered home was to never get into someone's vehicle. The risk was far greater once they had you. Yet the dogs . . . what if she tried to run and he shot at her girls? But what would happen to them if she did get in the car? Plus, if this was the same person Ted had identified at Luke's service, this wasn't just a friendly chat.

Rachel barely recognized her own voice. "No."

The man loudly exhaled, parking off to the side of the road, all the while keeping the weapon aimed in her direction. Rachel considered her chances of dashing into the nearby forest. With her luck, she'd run into someone's fence.

"You're going to change your mind in about ten seconds," he said as he reached for something under the dashboard. The trunk clicked open, and he emerged from the vehicle. The man was tall and eerily familiar. The scene from the night in front of her house flashed through her memory, and she knew this was the same guy. Now she understood how they had "met" before.

"Why are you after me?" Rachel choked out, hoping against hope that someone would come driving around the corner. He walked to the back of the car.

"Look inside."

"Hell no." Getting closer couldn't be any safer. What should she do?

"Now," he said, waving the weapon. Rachel's feet moved before she realized what was going on. One step. Two. Three. The open trunk came into view. Rachel stared in horror as she realized there was a person in the trunk. One more step, and recognition dawned.

"Tanner!" she cried, looking for signs of life.

As if reading her mind, he chuckled and nudged the teen's ribs. Rachel heard a small moan. "See, alive and kicking."

"Who are you?" *Stall for time.* It's all she could think to do. Eventually someone would come along, right?

"Get in the damn car. I don't have time for this shit."

Rachel's eyes moved to the side.

"No one's coming. Crazy thing, there's some unexpected roadwork going on. They have the road blocked off from the main connector to the highway," he said as he smirked. "So easy to find those orange cones this time of year, I tell ya. Now dump that backpack and get your ass into the car."

"Why, so you can kill us both?" she shot back as she removed the pack and tossed it into the bushes lining the road. *There goes the prepaid cell phone.*

"Lady, if I wanted you dead, I'd have already shot you."

Keep stalling. "My dogs . . ."

"Will live. Someone will find them."

Rachel was sick at the prospect of letting her girls roam out here, but she also couldn't let this man do Lord knows what to Tanner. She had to think. *Fast.*

"Okay, please, just let me take off their leashes so they don't get caught on something." She leaned over before he could tell her no. Oddly, he didn't say a word. Rachel tried to position her body so he couldn't see her hands as she reached under Bella's collar and grabbed the small device clipped to it.

"Hurry it up, woman," he said. Rachel slipped the item into her bra, hoping the loose-fitting T-shirt under her light coat would hide it, before turning and unsnapping Avi's leash. She stood, the two leashes dangling in her hands as she faced him. "Toss those over there," he said, indicating the side of the road. She pitched them as instructed. "Now get in the car. Back seat." Rachel nodded and swiftly bent down to pet the dogs. Hoping the breeze overhead was loud enough to drown out her words, she commanded Bella to "Find Luke," then stood and pointed to the side of the hill. "Go," she said, wanting to get them off the road. She couldn't think about the possibility of someone speeding along and hitting them with a car. They always stayed away from moving vehicles but never had their training been tested while on their own. Yet what else could she do? She was confident Bella would find her way back to Luke so long as nothing got in the way. The dog's training to seek him out had been the unintended consequence of a joke when they were dating. Let them find their way back to Luke, and then, please, let Luke figure out what she'd taken and know how to act on the knowledge.

Although Bella and Avi appeared confused, they eventually listened and trotted to the side of the road. Rachel rounded the vehicle and saw, the entire time, the barrel of the gun follow her in her peripheral vision. She turned and watched her girls continue in the other direction as the car began to move.

~

Cassandra watched from her hiding place around the corner. Two hours had passed since Monica's call, explaining she had learned of the location of the phone they'd tracked through Officer Ted Benson's calls. No doubt it was Rachel Winters, hiding out.

Cassandra had been viewing Leo's location via the GPS tracking app on her phone, her mind pondering Leo's early morning foray to Minden. While it was curious, she had to take advantage of the opportunity to find Rachel and eliminate her for good. However, she couldn't help but periodically check Leo's location as she drove out of South Lake Tahoe.

Leo was driving south on State Route 88 near Woodfords. Cassandra wondered whether she'd pass him on the highway as he drove back into the basin. But he'd continued on the highway, passing through Hope Valley and up Carson Pass—in the same direction she was headed. They were separated by roughly five miles by the time she reached Highway 88. The thought that he'd learned of Rachel's location occurred to her, but how could he?

Her suspicions were confirmed when he turned off the highway onto a side road near Pioneer, just forty-five minutes west of Kirkwood—exactly the same area she'd been headed. Unfortunately Monica hadn't called back with additional information to help narrow down the woman's location. If their technical expert couldn't provide more details, she couldn't exactly go searching door-to-door.

She followed Leo's route, noticing the bright orange utility work warning sign on the side of the road. The small icon on her phone's app indicated he drove another mile before stopping. After a brief stop, his car began moving again. What was he doing?

She put her car back into gear and slowly drove in his direction. Around the first corner she saw a utility truck tucked off to the side. As she cruised past, she looked into the cab. The driver inside appeared to be sleeping. One more curve and she encountered three bright orange cones across the road. Another square sign advised a temporary road closure. *What are you up to, Leo?*

Within several hundred yards of Leo's vehicle, Cassandra stopped on the road and hid her car in an open space between trees. She began walking up the road, her ears intently listening for any sounds as she kept an eye on the small icon on her phone; Leo hadn't moved. As she neared, she heard voices. With a few more steps she saw a woman, two dogs, and Leo's car sitting in the right lane with the trunk wide open. She couldn't see what was inside from her vantage point. Cassandra hid behind pine trees as she made her way closer to the odd scene, periodically peering around the trunks to see what they were doing. As she closed the distance, she recognized the woman: Rachel Winters. She reached for the weapon in her waistband and debated; if she shot her now, she'd have to contend with Leo. And she couldn't exactly make a clean getaway; her car was down the road.

Cassandra watched the strange scene play out, with Rachel detaching her dog's leashes and encouraging them to cross the road before getting into Leo's back seat. Leo leaned inside, his arms shuffling. It took a moment comprehend that he was placing plastic ties around Rachel's wrists and ankles. He pulled something dark over the woman's head and cinched it snug around her neck. After closing the door, he walked around to the back of the car and slammed the trunk.

Thankful she had rented a car he wouldn't recognize, she crawled farther back into the trees, hiding herself as he turned and drove past her. She noticed the two dogs run up the bank along the side of the road. Once Leo had cleared the corner, she jumped out from her hiding place and ran back to her car.

~

Luke glanced at the clock. Rachel should have returned by now or, at a minimum, texted to say she was running late. Given their circumstances, he was confident she wouldn't stay out longer without letting him know. He dialed her phone and got no answer. He sent a text—no response. He slipped on his boots, grabbed his coat, and opened the front door, planning to drive around nearby streets. He'd barely taken ten steps when he heard a clinking sound in the distance. Luke froze, and his ears piqued. It took him a moment to recognize what it was: a bear bell.

Luke let out a huge sigh. Rachel was back. He waited as the chiming sound approached. Bella came trotting down the short driveway with Avi following at her heels. Bella's body language reflected a mixture of anxiety and a "happy to see you" vibe. The dog rubbed against his legs but didn't drop her front paws and encourage him to rub her back, one of her customary moves.

"Bella, what's wrong, girl?" he asked, rubbing her as his eyes scanned the area for Rachel. Avi stood nearby as though she were contemplating whether to join in. Something was wrong. "Rachel?" he called out. No response. Yelling louder with each repeat of her name, Luke began to walk up the driveway. "Rachel!" Nothing. He turned and examined the dogs. Neither appeared injured. He called out again and was met with only the distant sound of an airplane overhead. The dogs weren't moving either. He recalled Rachel, concerned about the strange location, had put them both on leashes this morning. There were no leashes now. He kneeled. "Bella, come here, girl." He waved and she immediately leaned into him. He wanted to see whether the leashes had been detached or torn off; if the latter, the clasp would still be hanging off her collar. No clasp. Why would she let them go like this?

"Avi, I know we aren't quite friends yet, but will you come to me?" He beckoned the shy dog his way. "Come on. Come here, girl," he continued, sitting on the ground and reaching out to her. She tentatively approached. As soon as she was within reach, he rubbed her nose. One more step and he could touch her ears. One hand gently massaged her ears as the other reached around to her collar where there was also no clasp. Something tapped at his brain. He tried to focus on it and retrieve the partially obscured thought. *Relax.* He closed his eyes. What was it?

Finally, it dawned on him. The collars. There was something on Avi's collar that was lacking from Bella's. It was one of those expensive GPS tracking devices Rachel had mentioned at a barbecue party at Ted's last summer. He could recall overhearing her answer to Ted's inquiry about the "little boxes on the dog's collars."

"Yeah, they weren't cheap, but since I've encountered some people lately who seem to have no problem hurting or kidnapping these wonderful animals, I decided it was worth it."

"What's the range?" Ted had asked.

Rachel had withdrawn her cell phone and opened the display as she responded. "Actually, these can be tracked and mapped from anywhere. See here?" She had tapped her phone several times and handed the device over to Ted.

"That's awesome!" Ted had exclaimed. "Shoot, this technology is probably more advanced than some of the department's own equipment," he laughed.

"Here, let me show you," she had said, then looked around until she spotted a fallen branch. Luke had watched from the corner of his eye as Rachel picked it up and called out to Bella as she threw it. "Bella, get the stick!"

"Wow, that's sensitive," Ted had said, staring at the display as Bella retrieved the branch. "How long does it last?"

"One charge can last about two weeks. I have to pay a monthly fee to maintain the full tracking feature, but these girls are worth it."

Ted then handed her the phone back. "And those pricey little boxes don't fall off the collars?"

"No," Luke recalled her saying. "They are extremely secure. I made sure of that. I have to pull pretty hard to get them off."

Luke refocused his mind on the present and slowly stood up.

"Okay, let's hope I can figure out that damn app," he mumbled. Tracking it would require putting the SIM card and battery back into her phone. It was a risk, but he didn't appear to have any other options. Luke dashed into the house, and the dogs following behind him. Luke's hands shook as he retrieved her phone and assembled the parts.

The cell seemed to take forever to boot up. His heart sank when it asked for a password. He tried the first and only one that came to mind, hoping she hadn't changed it. The display opened, revealing a picture of Rachel and the dogs with Lake Tahoe's famous blue water in the background. It was a picture taken on Mount Tallac, one of the few peaks he'd hiked with her when they were dating. He needed to focus. What was the name of the app? He scrolled through her app list, looking for something with "GPS" in the name. Finally he found an icon with a cartoon sketch of a dog's head and a shining tag on the collar blended with a drawing of a satellite. He tapped the key, and a map opened. He waited, his heart pounding, as the device searched for a GPS signal. After what seemed like forever, two small blue dots appeared on the screen. One remained stationary—the one on Avi's collar—while the other was currently moving southwest on Highway 88 at a high rate of speed. She was in a moving vehicle. What the hell had happened?

There was no time to ponder; he had to get moving. Deciding it was best to leave the dogs since he had no idea where his trip would take him, he topped off their water bowl and placed food in their dishes as he called Ted and left a long, detailed message, ending with "Call me as soon as you get this. I'm going after her. Oh, and I'm leaving the dogs in the house." After hanging up, he opened the door of the rental car Ted had secured for him. He missed his Subaru, but dead men don't drive their vehicles.

As he slid into his car, Luke checked the battery power left in Rachel's phone: 76 percent. He plugged it into the charger dangling from his console and noticed an option to select *History*. When he clicked it, a different map pulled up, showing the last hour's movements. The lines weaved along the main road and then stopped just around the corner. One line abruptly changed direction, following the road back out to the highway, while the other meandered back to the house they were staying in. Luke drove until he reached the location where she'd changed course. There was nothing strange about it at first glance. He parked off to the side and began walking along the stretch, his eyes scanning the roadside. Finally, he came upon something black tucked under a manzanita bush. Luke reached down and retrieved Rachel's backpack and leashes, his insides turning at the additional confirmation that something bad had gone down. He opened it up and found her burner phone and various dog supplies inside.

Luke turned to leave, dashing back to his SUV and setting out to catch up with the little blue circle that represented the one woman he couldn't live without.

~

Jill glanced at her phone, intending to ignore the call until she finished her report, but she recognized the number of Tanner's school. She quickly hit *Save* and grabbed the device.

"Hello?"

"Ms. Reynolds?"

"This is her," Jill said as she worked to control her nerves. Something was wrong; she could tell by the tone of this woman's voice. Tanner had been doing some acting out lately but nothing so serious as to require a call from his school.

"This is Marney Sheenan. I'm calling from Tanner's school."

Jill waited for the woman to continue, but apparently she needed some kind of acknowledgement. "Hello, Ms. Sheenan."

"I wanted to let you know your son has missed his last four classes. It appears he may have left the campus around ten this morning."

Tanner, skipping school? Jill didn't pretend to be one of those parents who assumed their kid did no wrong. But given her family was currently in protective custody in a freaking safe house, and her ex-husband was missing, she thought her fears were justified. "Appears?"

"The last time he was seen was in his third period class. We've spoken with his closest friends; none of them have seen him since. But one said they had plans to meet up for lunch and attend the grand opening of a new pizza place in town. He never showed. They tried calling him, but it went straight to voice mail."

Jill looked up at the clock on her office wall; it read 1:16 p.m. Her son had been missing for over three hours. Her insides knotted. Her kids were supposed to be safe within their schools' walls. Bodyguards escorted them to and from campus, but they had not felt it necessary to follow them throughout the day.

"Have you called the police?"

"No, ma'am, it's only been a few hours. We realize kids do things like this; we try not to involve the police, especially before checking with the parents."

Jill wanted to yell at this woman and accuse her of something, but what? She also knew it was just her own anxiety trying to find an outlet. She took a deep breath; as she exhaled, she reminded herself to stay calm. "I contacted your principal's office first thing this morning to advise them of a potential safety concern with my son. They promised me they'd keep an eye on him."

"I . . . I haven't been made aware of that information," the woman stuttered.

"Thank you for the call. I'm going to contact the police. Expect to receive a visit." Jill ended the call before the woman could respond. She quickly pulled up the Find My Phone app to search for Tanner's cell, but there was no signal. Jill immediately dialed her daughter's school. After explaining that someone may be coming for her daughter and they were to release her to no one other than Jill, she hung up and dialed Ted's number. When he answered, he sounded out of breath.

"Hey, Jilly. What—"

"Tanner's missing!" she blurted as she jumped up, reaching for her coat. She had to see her daughter immediately, to assure herself she was okay.

"Wait, what?"

"I just got a call from his school." She explained what the woman had told her, continuing her struggle to remain calm. It wasn't easy.

"All right, I'll contact the PD down your way. How about you go pick up Nikki, then check back in with me?"

"Keys are in my hand," she said as she grabbed her purse.

"I, uh, hate to have to give you more bad news, but you need to know."

Jill's heart dropped. Why couldn't she deal with just one crisis at a time? "What is it?"

"I just got a message from Luke, but it was left some time ago. Damn cell service in here is crap," he bemoaned. Jill knew the officers at Ted's police station had long complained about intermittent service inside the building.

"What's going on?" She urged him back to the point as she ran through the hallway of her office building.

"Rachel took the dogs for a walk this morning and never came back." Jill tried to process this as she pushed open the front door and headed toward her car. Ted explained Luke's message regarding "something about" the dogs and a GPS tracker. "He's following the tracking device as we speak on some kind of smartphone app. It looks like she's in a moving vehicle. I've tried to call Luke for more details, but I can't get through. Cell service down there isn't much better than up here. At least the GPS system still connects."

"Could this be related to where my son is?" It made no sense, yet she had to ask.

"We don't know yet. But hang tight. Not to mitigate the urgency, but there is still the strong possibility that Tanner cut class of his own volition. Teenagers do that sort of thing."

"He wouldn't flake on his friends like that. It's why I know he didn't leave voluntarily. Or maybe he did leave but intended to return. I don't know." Jill hit the alarm button to unlock her vehicle before wrenching the door open and sliding inside. "He's been acting out lately, I think in part because he's started to see what his father is really like." That was another problem. Where was Jake? "Speaking of which, any word on Jake?" Jill turned the keys and the phone call transferred to her speaker system.

"Not yet."

Something about Ted's response gave her pause, like he wasn't telling her everything. But right now, her kids were all that mattered. She knew Ted would be doing everything in his power to help locate Rachel as well.

"Okay, keep me updated. I'll call once I have Nikki." Jill sped down the roadway, figuring if a cop tried to pull her over, she'd be leading them on one hell of a chase straight to her daughter's middle school campus.

Chapter Thirty-Three

Rachel knew it would be best to stay calm. But when her abductor pulled her arms back and placed plastic ties on her wrists and ankles, then pulled the sack over her head, she felt an overwhelming claustrophobia. In her bound condition, her body rolled limply back and forth across the seat as the car took corner after corner. She tried to focus on the acceleration and direction, gleaning that they had gone back to Highway 88 and turned right. After that, she'd lost track.

Rachel thought of Tanner, hoping he remained sedated so he wouldn't wake up in a dark trunk. If she felt claustrophobic, a fourteen-year-old waking up in a small, dark space, tied up with duct tape over his mouth, would feel ten times worse.

Rachel hoped the dogs had found their way back to Luke, and he would figure out what she'd done. While fairly confident of the former given Bella's inadvertent training and her consistent ability to backtrack anywhere they'd hike, she couldn't recall if she'd ever mentioned the GPS tags to Luke.

Attempts to ask her kidnapper who he was and where they were going went unanswered. After she repeated her question several times, he turned on what sounded like an audiobook. Rachel tried to block the sound out and think about what her options were, but it took all of her effort to prevent herself from falling into the footwell. The shaking went on for what seemed like hours but probably was only minutes. Finally, the radio went silent, followed by the engine shutting off. She did her best to listen over the intense beating of her own heart.

Rachel heard the trunk open. Shifting sounds indicated a brief struggle.

Oh God, is he hurting Tanner?

A moan was followed by the slamming of the trunk lid. Heavy footsteps walked past the car and then diminished until she heard nothing. Rachel wiggled onto her side and debated about how to rise up. If she could get the lower half of her body in the foot space while keeping the upper half on the seat, she could prop herself up and reach behind her for the door. She carefully slid her hips and legs until they felt space underneath. As she dropped her lower half, she twisted so she'd end up facedown on the seat.

Of course, if you get the door opened, then what are you going to do? You can't run, can't reach your feet, can't pull this hood off your head. Rachel's mind filled with images of female actors pulling their bound wrists down and around their feet so their hands were in front of them. Did that really work? Maybe she could drop on the ground and give it a try once she was out of the car.

Just as Rachel raised her upper body and reached for the door handle, the footsteps returned.

"I see you've managed to get yourself moved around some," the man said as he wrenched the door open. She felt arms reach under her ribs and yank her out of the car, propping her on unsteady feet. Before she could react, she felt him reach under her arms and knees, lifting her as if she weighed no more than a small bag of dog food.

"Why are you doing this?" she asked as he carried her. She assumed squirming might result in an abrupt drop to the ground, so she remained limp.

"My job right now is to keep you alive. And you're welcome."

Huh? None of this made sense. "And how does kidnapping me and my friend's son play into 'your job?'"

He didn't respond.

"Answer me!" she cried.

"Lady, shut up. Conversation's over." He paused, and she felt him stop and reach for something in front of them, taking her legs with him. She heard the loud sound of a door handle in dire need of WD-40, then felt him resume walking at a much slower pace. The smells changed. Before, she'd been surrounded by the musky outdoor smell typical of the western slope of this part of the Sierra Nevada; now, she smelled dust and underlying tones of mildew and lemon.

Without warning, he dropped her. She had no time to react before her body landed on a semisoft surface. *A couch?*

"Lacey, untie these two once I'm outside. No funny business."

Lacey? The senator's granddaughter?

"Yes, sir," came a timid voice from somewhere nearby. The man stomped out and banged the door shut. Various clicks followed as though he were locking multiple mechanisms.

"Lacey Mason-Spears?" Rachel asked as she heard the shifting of clothes.

"You know who I am?" The girl was right in front of her now. Rachel felt hands reaching for the tie around her neck. She sucked in a deep breath as the bag was removed from her head. The thin, pale figure in front of her barely matched the bright, shiny girl she'd seen in pictures following the fire.

"Yes, but please go help Tanner first," Rachel said, her eyes darting as she looked around the room. She saw him lying on a large area rug nearby, moaning. Lacey nodded and turned, rushing to Tanner's side.

"How can I get these twist ties off? They haven't given me scissors or knives."

"Got fingernail clippers?"

"Yes!" Lacey walked across the room and opened a narrow door in the corner. Seconds later she returned with small metal clippers. She bent over and snapped the plastic ties from Tanner's ankles and wrists. Tanner still appeared to be half-conscious, but he instinctively reached for the duct tape on his mouth and attempted to rip it off. "Here," Lacey said. She grabbed the small section he'd peeled and yanked back. A yell escaped him, and he began rubbing at his mouth. "Sorry," she said.

Lacey returned, removed Rachel's ties, and then dropped onto a small twin bed pushed against the wall. She looked between Rachel and Tanner, her confusion obvious. Tanner looked around as if memorizing the scene. When his eyes fell on Rachel, he perked up.

"Rachel?"

"Yep, it's me, buddy." She jumped up and stumbled over to him, hugging him fiercely. "Are you hurt? Other than around your mouth." She lightly touched the reddened skin.

"Who are you two? And why are you here?" Lacey's voice was soft, but Rachel wouldn't call her shy or timid. She had an air of toughness about her. The girl would no doubt have to if she'd really been cooped up here for the past several months.

"I can tell you who we are, but I have no idea why we're here. But first, are you hurt?"

Lacey shook her head.

"Okay, good. I'm Rachel, and this is Tanner. I suspect the three of us have some stories to share." She did her best to smile, wanting to put the two teens at ease. Perhaps herself too, because inside she was shaking.

~

Mike couldn't believe what he was hearing.

"Let me get this straight, Leo. You nabbed the son of Rachel's friend Jill as a means to get said friend to cough up where Rachel was?"

"Yeah, obviously it was before I knew that her location had been tracked through that officer's phone calls. By then, I already had the kid."

"Well, if this isn't just one big snafu!" Mike looked down at his prison-issued shoes.

"They're all secured now. We won't need to keep them much longer."

"Will you be staying on-site then?"

"Of course."

"You've got an adult in there now, and she's got brains. You need to keep a very close eye on them."

"I'm aware. Phillip is assisting me with supplies, and we've got two guys protecting the perimeter."

"There will also be a major search for the boy."

"I was careful. I'm ditching this vehicle as soon as we hang up. Plus, you know how well I can disguise myself. Even if I were captured on any cameras, they can't possibly link it to me."

"And you weren't followed?" While they had multiple resources protecting their location, Mike was still worried something would go wrong. And if that happened, he couldn't bear to think what would happen to his own daughter, Lori. They all just needed to get through the election at this point.

"No."

Mike had to trust that Leo had kept a careful eye out for any tailing vehicles. What else could he do anyway? He was stuck in this damn prison, at least for now. The same people who were threatening violence against his daughter to get him to do their dirty work had also promised they'd get him out if his efforts were successful. Not that he fully trusted them to follow through. He'd do this either way to protect Lori, and they had to know that. In the years before he was sent to prison, he'd been partners on several deals with those very same people.

"Keep me updated," he said to Leo. Mike silently cursed as he ended the call. *How did this all get so out of control?*

~

Cassandra slowly passed by the narrow driveway where, according to the tracking device she'd placed on his vehicle, Leo had taken Rachel.

Chances were the senator's granddaughter was being held there too, which meant Cassandra would have to put some thought into how to gain access to Rachel. Leo wouldn't be patrolling this place alone. Nor could she go in guns blazing; that could inadvertently place Lacey in the crosshairs. Monica would never forgive Cassandra if something happened to her lover's granddaughter.

This would require scoping and preparation. She needed to learn about this property first. No house or other structure was within view of the road, and the driveway was blocked by an old barbwire fence. It appeared like any other forested land crossed by various old dirt roads. Down the road to either side there were no fences. That would make approaching it easier. Cassandra turned and retraced her route until she was back on Highway 49, heading into the town of Jackson, where she aimed to find a coffee shop to sit at and look up property records on her tablet.

~

Monica looked at the caller ID. It was her computer specialist. Anxiously, she hit the answer button.

"Hello."

"Monica, your girl's phone is on the move."

Monica perked up fast. "You mean Rachel?"

"Yep, the signal started up a couple of hours ago, give or take."

"And you're just now calling me?"

"I can't be available twenty-four seven; I called you as soon as I saw the alert," he snapped.

Monica was tempted to yell at him and remind him she was paying him a large sum of money. A lot could happen in two unchecked hours. But pissing him off wouldn't help the situation now. She held her tongue. "All right. Where?" She reached across her desk and grabbed some notepaper and a pencil.

"The signal began down by Pioneer. You know where that is?"

"Yes." She paused, waiting for more details. The location didn't surprise her; he'd already determined Rachel's general location earlier this morning through pinging cell towers on what was presumably a disposable phone in contact with Ted Benson. But Cassandra hadn't reported locating the woman yet.

"Then she went through Jackson and headed east on Highway 49. Turned north on some rural road and meandered up a ways. The signal stopped moving about five minutes ago, but it's still broadcasting. I'll send you the coordinates."

"Perfect," she said, waiting for the beep that would confirm receipt of a new message. It didn't take long. "Got 'em. Keep me updated." She ended the call before he could reply, anxious to give Cassandra the information. Monica dialed and waited through three rings before it was answered.

"Monica." It was a statement more than a greeting.

"I just learned Rachel's phone is back on. I need you to follow it. I have coordinates to send." Cassandra didn't respond right away. Monica heard the sounds of quiet chatter in the background. "Cass?" she asked.

"I'm here. Where is she?"

This was turning into an awkward conversation. "East of Jackson. I'd guess twenty or thirty minutes from where she was last time I called you."

"That's odd."

"What do you mean?"

"I'm in Jackson right now. Leo nabbed Rachel from the area you sent me to earlier before I could get there and then brought her to a remote property down here. I came into town to see what I could learn about the place before I went back out there."

Monica wondered how both of her "helpers" had failed to keep her updated in a timely manner. But more importantly, she wondered why Leo had taken Rachel. "Why would Leo grab her? Where did he take her?"

"Like I said, I'm trying to figure that out. I don't want to rush onto the property unprepared."

"Why would Leo take her and let her keep her phone?" Monica wondered aloud.

"Beats me. He's usually smarter than that."

Was that admiration in Cassandra's voice? Monica worried about the woman's feelings toward Leo. She wasn't privy to the details, but she sensed Cassandra still harbored a spark for her old flame.

Monica changed the subject. "Have you found what you needed about the property?"

"Still working on it. The owner's name appears to be buried in a shell corporation: no operations, no employees. You know the type. I'm trying to go deeper, find a layout of any structures and such on the property, but it's taking some time. The internet is slow."

"Don't take too long. Her phone is idle right now, but what if Leo moves her again? We can't afford to lose track of her."

"I'm working as fast as I can."

"Work faster," Monica barked and then ended the call. She wanted to toss the phone across the room. Just to throw something. *Anything.* She picked up her glass of water and tossed it against the wall, feeling instant satisfaction when it shattered.

This was all unraveling so quickly. She couldn't trust Cassandra anymore. Something about that man threw the stupid woman off center. "If you want something done right . . . ," she mumbled as she grabbed her keys and rushed out the door.

Chapter Thirty-Four

The trees flew by in a blur as Ted headed west on Highway 88 with the circling beacon placed on top of his SUV. While he had no police authority this way, he had the go-ahead from his captain to pursue the matter. Captain Taylor was the only other police officer who knew what was going on; even better, he was sitting in the passenger seat. As they passed Kirkwood Meadows where cell service was strong, Ted reached to dial Luke again but noticed a text from Jill. He glanced at it: *Got Nikki. Going to safe house.*

Good. It was bad enough Tanner was in danger; Ted couldn't have handled it if something happened to Nikki too. He dialed Luke's number. It went straight to voice mail.

"Luke, it's Ted again. I need you to call me and tell me where you are. I'm headed your way now. Just passing Kirkwood." Ted ended the call.

As his vehicle flew by the wide expanse of Silver Lake, where the late season water levels were so low that Treasure Island was now a peninsula, he began recounting the facts he knew with his captain.

"Okay, so someone wanted Luke dead. They bugged Luke's office, learned of our plans to go out to Silver Creek that day, and followed us there. Looks possible this person, or people, may have chosen that opportunity because they have a friend in law enforcement in Alpine County ready to do some cleanup of the report if need be. But Luke was officially declared dead by accidental causes, and as I never followed up with anyone regarding the gunshot, from someone else's perspective that threat went away. Next, Rachel is attacked outside of her house a week later. What's not clear is whether the perp intended to hurt her, kill her, or take her. We get Rachel into hiding. And now someone has taken Jill's son. Why?"

"Didn't you say Rachel's brother and some friend of hers were followed on their way to Jill's place yesterday?" Taylor reached up and smoothed his moustache, a gesture Ted knew meant he was concentrating.

"Yeah, but it's also possible someone figured out the connection between Rachel and Jill. It wouldn't be that difficult to locate her address once they had a name. So while our well-meaning dynamic duo may have made it easier to find Jill, it could have happened some other way regardless."

"How about Tanner's school? Any thoughts on that connection?"

"It's possible there was information online somewhere. Jill doesn't let the kids do Facebook or anything, but you know teenagers. They probably found a way unbeknownst to Jill." Ted glanced at the icon displaying the level of cell service: zero bars. "Another possibility is that they broke into Jill's house. I don't think I mentioned that we found her door unlocked yesterday. She blamed the kids, but I'm not so sure now. Someone could have seen their pictures around her house. She's adorned that entire place with ribbons and trophies too. It would be obvious where they each go to school."

"All right, no matter the method, we know they tracked Tanner and took him. So the question is why?" Taylor began sketching out some kind of flow chart. Ted appreciated the man's attention to detail. He was a very skilled detective, able to put clues together that others might miss.

"Is it possible someone thought Jill would know where Rachel was? Then took Tanner as leverage?" Ted brainstormed.

"Yeah, but why do that if they had a line on Rachel's location?"

"Good question." Ted glanced over at the paper and saw Taylor tracing over a large question mark between two boxes. "That begs another question. How did they locate Rachel?

Nothing associated with the house traces back to any of us."

"You said it belongs to an acquaintance who had been renting it through VRBO and was happy to rent it for cash, right?"

Ted nodded before realizing Taylor was still focused on the notepad. "Yes, and I don't think we were followed there. I check for tracking devices daily, and the only time Jill went there in her own vehicle was the night Rachel was attacked. But it was dark. She told me she kept an eye out for followers. Never saw any headlights behind her that looked suspicious. She even pulled off a couple of times and hid, watching just in case."

"Smart woman."

"That she is," Ted said as he smiled.

"And both Rachel and Luke are using disposable phones?"

"Affirmative."

"You know, I think this is much larger than one or two people who have an axe to grind with Rachel and Luke. For them to manage to pull all of this off . . . there's got to be some extensive resources at play here. Could they have more advanced tracking devices that aren't picked up by your sweeper?"

"It's possible. Our equipment didn't register the device in Luke's office." Ted glanced at the cell icon again. One bar was blinking in and out. Another option hit him. "If these people have connections up high, maybe they got a hold of my phone records and saw the number I was calling, then assumed it was Rachel? Our tech guy once explained to me how they can ping the cell towers and determine a general area, but it wouldn't lead them to the specific house." Ted bounced his palm off the steering wheel, frustrated he may have overlooked that possibility. But he hadn't been able to tell the department's main technical guru about any of this. When they first started investigating, nothing indicated this went beyond one person attacking Luke.

As if picking up on Ted's thought, Taylor added, "That wouldn't get them the exact location, but you said Rachel was out walking her dogs along a connector road, right?"

Ted saw where his captain was going with this. "It would be

quite a coincidence if our kidnapper just happened to be cruising in the right place when Rachel took the dogs out."

"But it's possible. I looked at the street map. There's one main road to access countless miles of properties back in where they were staying. It would be natural for someone to take that road if they were searching the vicinity identified by the tower pinging deal, or whatever you call it."

"I see your point. I guess the bigger issue now is, where are they taking her? And can we get to Luke in time to prevent him from doing something stupid?" Ted knew Luke to be an excellent detective, but even the best man could be distracted when intense emotions were involved.

"Luke's smart. Yes, his emotions may be clouded, but he's also extremely resourceful. It was a shame to lose him back when we had to cut so many positions from the force," Taylor mused.

"I agree, but I'd feel a lot better if we could actually talk to him," he said, glancing at the icon again. Two bars. That meant if Luke called, they'd be able to answer. "It's also occurred to me that if we don't hear from him by the time we get down to Pioneer, we aren't going to know which direction to go."

There was silence for several minutes as each man contemplated the information. Ted almost shook when the phone finally rang.

~

Luke parked the vehicle. During his drive through Jackson, several text messages had popped up on Rachel's phone. At first he decided against reading them, but as he continued driving toward her GPS tracker, he started to wonder whether they could provide any clues into who took her or why. Quickly, he scrolled through the unread messages. There were eight from someone named Seth, three from Derek, two from Kris, one from her parents, and a few from other friends. Everyone wanted to know if she was doing "okay."

Who is this Seth guy? His texts seemed progressively creepier, at least in Luke's opinion. The first one was time-stamped on Friday night. Second one, Saturday morning. Third one, Sunday night. The remaining six were basically repeats of the first three.

Rachel, it's Seth again. Just want 2 make sure u r OK. Plz get back to me.

Seth here. Look, I'm getting worried. Please call.

Me again. I know u r mourning a friend. But please give me a quick call.

There were no messages from today. Rachel would never be interested in someone so persistent. "Clingy" is probably how she'd describe him. In fact, the word "stalker" came to mind. Either way, a twinge of jealousy shot through his body before his brain could shut it down. Now was not the time to be having these thoughts. He had to be objective. What could it mean? If the guy hadn't texted again today, was it because he was getting a clue she wasn't interested—at least that's what Luke was going to tell himself for now—or because Seth had nabbed Rachel and thus had no need to text her again? Luke brought the tracking program back up on the display and set her phone on the seat beside him. He picked up his own, hoping the one bar of cell service would be enough as he dialed Ted's number.

"Luke?"

"Ted, it's me. Did you get my message?"

"Yes, I have Captain Taylor with me. We're on our way. Where are you?" Ted answered in haste.

"East of Jackson. I'll send you my coordinates. Hang on." Luke focused on his phone and sent the message off.

"Got 'em," Ted said. "We're about half an hour from downtown. What's going on?"

"The tracker has been stationary for the last forty minutes at a residential area out in the boonies. I just pulled up about five minutes ago. I'm parked about a quarter mile away. I drove by earlier; there's a dirt driveway with a dated wire fence and not much else. I can't see any structures from the road, but that's the case with a lot of places out here."

"What's your plan?"

"I'm going to go check it out. See what I'm up against."

"Luke, just listen. As you have no idea what you're 'up against,' I suggest you wait for us to get there. It will be much safer if—"

"No. Who knows what someone is doing to her? It'll be almost an hour until you arrive. Too much can happen in an hour."

"If something happens to you, it's not going to help Rachel."

"I have to take that chance." Luke watched another vehicle drive by; it was the only one he'd seen since leaving Highway 49. Fear caused him to again check the tracking program on his display; the blue dot hadn't moved.

"Okay, just keep your phone on and text me updates." Ted sounded tired.

"I'll try, but the service is spotty. I'm surprised we haven't been disconnected." Luke rubbed his chin. "I'm going to switch my phone to silent mode; I'll check it periodically. As to my plan, I'm going to head in on foot about three hundred feet west of the driveway. I'll attempt to follow the driveway at that distance as far as it goes. Then, well, we'll see." Luke checked his weapon and reached for the door handle.

"Luke, this is Captain Taylor." The gruff voice caught Luke by surprise. He'd completely forgotten Taylor was with Ted.

"Hey, Cap." Luke paused. Even though he hadn't worked for the department in years, Luke had never stopped calling him the nickname used by other officers.

"I realize you aren't going to wait for us, even though you should. Just . . . keep your wits about you. Act on your training, not your emotion."

"Got it. I'm going in now." Luke stood, engaged the locks, and pushed the door closed with his foot. "Thank you both for all you've done. By the way, Ted, as I mentioned in my message, I left the dogs back in Pioneer. Hopefully it won't come to this, but worst case, Jill may need to get down there tonight if none of us can."

"About Jill—"

The call dropped. Either Luke or Ted lost the signal. He had no time to ponder it. Listening intently for the distant sound of motors, Luke started out walking along the road. The wind was picking up, and occasional gusts whistled through the trees—not good since he was relying on sound to warn him. If a car approached, he'd have to find somewhere to hide, but if he didn't hear it before seeing it, he risked being seen himself. The mix of large oak trees and intermittent pine trees didn't provide the most consistent cover.

Luckily, no vehicles passed before he turned from the road and headed onto the land. The dusk-colored skies created illusive shadows throughout the forest. Multiple *No Trespassing* signs were posted along the property line with the road; it would be impossible to pretend to be a lost hiker if he were discovered. *Then just don't get discovered*, Luke thought.

The uneven ground required Luke to study the surface before taking each step. He periodically glanced around, checking the entire area while maintaining a route parallel to the long driveway. Manzanita bushes scraped against his bare legs. It hadn't occurred to him to change into long pants before taking off after Rachel. The skies dimmed as he continued. Good for his cover, but bad for finding his way around. *How far in does this damn driveway go?*

Finally, Luke saw a bright light in the distance. He guessed it to be a quarter of a mile away or more. *What is this place?* Luke checked his phone; the illumination appeared to be in the same area where Rachel's GPS tracker had been idle for the past few hours. Focused on the light, he began to follow, his determination to get to her overcoming the fatigue and cramping in his gut. He couldn't let his withdrawal symptoms slow him down. He had to push through it.

Increasing wind gusts rattled the trees overhead. Luke heard several crackling sounds nearby. Was that the wind? An animal? Or a human? He stopped and crouched low to the ground, his eyes and ears focused on the source. *Crack.* There it was again. Coming from perhaps twenty feet to his right. Luke reached for the handgun in his shoulder holster as he knelt, facing the direction of the sound.

Crack. Crack. It was now too consistent to be the wind. Luke's body tensed, ready to act.

~

Kris leaned back on her old sofa, her cat Nemo resting comfortably on her lap. She gently massaged his ears and worked her fingers down his back. It took less than a minute for Nemo's motor to start running. He purred louder than any other cat she'd ever known.

She was worried about Rachel. Ted explained to Derek and her the day before that Rachel was involved in a situation that required she remain off the grid. They'd pressed him for more details, but he said he couldn't reveal anything more yet. Over twenty-four hours later and still not one word. Derek had to be out of his mind; he was not a patient man. Then again, he might be sitting with a bowl of butter-lathered popcorn, his feet kicked up on Rachel's coffee table, watching porn. A ringing phone interrupted her thoughts. She reached over to the arm of the couch where her cell phone was propped. Nemo simply went along for the ride, his purring continuing uninterrupted as she shifted. She glanced at the display. *Finally!*

"Ted, what's going on?" she asked in lieu of a greeting.

"I need you to do something for me, although I can't tell you why just yet."

How frustrating, she thought, but she wasn't going to refuse. "What can I do?"

"I need some property information. I know you're good with computers, and isn't Derek some kind of computer tech?"

"I guess he's pretty up to date on software programs and stuff for his job."

"Perhaps the two of you can work on this together. I suspect more digging will be involved beyond just the basics you find on the assessor's data. I need owner, any specs on the property size, land use, buildings, if there are any—hell, just about anything."

Kris carefully picked up Nemo and gently set him at her side before jumping off the couch. "No problem. I'll get Derek on board and see what we can find."

"I'll text you the property location. And Kris?"

"Yeah?"

"You need to keep this between you and Derek. Period. No other officers, no one. Okay?"

That sounded ominous. "Got it," she agreed as she slid her feet into her shoes.

"Thanks. Please call me as soon as you have info. If I don't answer, just leave a detailed message. Service here is spotty."

"Where are you?" Kris looked around for her coat before remembering she'd tossed it on her bed earlier that morning. There was a pause. Ted was apparently debating whether to tell her. *Why so much secrecy?*

Finally, he replied, "Down near Jackson."

Odd, she hadn't expected that. As she packed up her laptop, she asked, "Ted, can you just tell me if Rachel's okay?"

"Yes, she's fine."

"Please don't let anything happen to her." As if Ted ever would. Not only was he a good cop, but he was also like a big brother to Rachel. "Are the girls okay?" She thought of Rachel's two sweet dogs.

"They are with . . . a friend. Look, I gotta go. Call me back. And Kris, thanks."

Kris struggled with not knowing what was going on, but she understood. For now, she had a job to do, and she'd better get to it. Kris dialed Derek's number as she flew down her front steps with her keys in hand. It went straight to voice mail.

Ten minutes later Kris was reminding herself of the forty mile-per-hour speed limit through Meyers. Her eyes darted between the road and her speedometer. Now would be a bad time to get pulled over. She cruised by The Divided Sky, a bar popular with locals, and noticed the various illuminated signs and shaded outlines of patrons on the second-story deck. It was getting dark so early now. Was Rachel out there somewhere at this moment with danger surrounding her as the darkness of night set in?

~

Cassandra was growing impatient. The coffee bar's Wi-Fi was slow and sporadic. She'd managed to pull up the assessor's data on the land and browse the owner's name, property details, and dates associated with annual taxes and ownership changes. Ten years ago, a nondescript company, called ML Investments, purchased the land. Cassandra clicked on the file to learn more when her connection crashed again.

"Damn it!" she yelled, banging her fist on the table. Conversation nearby suddenly ceased, and half a dozen pairs of eyes stared her way. "The internet service here sucks." She smiled bashfully, putting just a touch of apology into her tone.

"Agree with you on that, ma'am," a twenty-something hipster said before turning back to his companion.

Ma'am? Like I'm that much older than that little twit! She'd like nothing more than to run over to the kid and slam his straw up his nose; however, that might be viewed poorly by the other patrons and was apt to result in a call to 9-1-1. Instead, she closed the display on her tablet and tucked it into her purse before sliding out of the seat. She hated going in without more information, but she couldn't let Rachel slip through her hands yet again, and time was of the essence. Cassandra threw the front door open and ran toward her car.

~

Rachel did her best not to flinch as Lacey explained the events of the preceding months.

"I thought the person calling out would get me away from the fire. I didn't care who it was. Figured it was one of my grandpa's friends or neighbors. But then he kept driving, and driving, and told me if I tried to get out he'd hunt me down and shoot me."

Rachel pictured the scene. How scared the poor girl must have already been from the fire, only to be kidnapped and put through that. She's probably wondered every day for almost four months whether she'd live to see another one.

"I'm so sorry, Lacey."

"I don't understand why no one came for me. Weren't they looking?" Moisture began to form in the girl's eyes. Rachel pretended not to notice; Lacey's obvious efforts to maintain a brave face meant she probably wouldn't want her tears acknowledged. Rachel debated how to answer the question because doing so would implicate the girl's own grandfather.

"I'm not sure of the details. Your family worked hard to keep you out of the media. I had no idea you'd been missing this entire time until my friend told me."

"Then how did your friend know?"

Smart girl, Rachel thought. "He's a private investigator. Your mom hired him to look for you."

"My mom?" Lacey picked a stray hair off her shoulder. "But what about the police?"

"I'm not sure what the police are doing. Sometimes they keep things under wraps so they don't give away something important. But I know your parents are working hard to find you." She heard a shuffling noise and noticed Tanner sitting on the carpet nearby with his legs crossed. He had listened without interruption, occasionally reaching up to rub his face. It had to hurt, but hopefully the ointment they'd found in a small first aid kit under the sink had helped in some way.

Finally, Tanner spoke. "Rachel, I don't understand why there's been no Amber Alert or anything? She's been missing for months!"

Oh, how Rachel wished he hadn't said that. She'd wanted to steer the conversation away from the lack of police attention.

"That's right! I've heard of those. How can they not be trying to find me? My grandpa is a senator. Has lots of friends. I'm sure he's been pushing them!" The girl crossed her arms.

"Look, I'm sorry I can't tell you the details. For now, we need to focus on figuring out how to get us out of here. But first, Tanner, tell us what happened to you."

"What's the point?" he seemed to mutter to himself. "I was sneaking off campus while classes were in session," he said hastily, then continued as if he expected Rachel, the only adult in the room, might object. "I knew something was going on, and I wanted to keep an eye on my sister at her school. Someone pulled up and nabbed me, and here I am." He dropped his arms to his sides.

"Are you hurt? Other than your mouth?"

"No, my head hurts a little, but it's not too bad. I feel kind of weird, like maybe he drugged me?" He rubbed his eyes.

"Is it wearing off?" Rachel hoped that whatever it was would be out of his system as soon as possible.

"Yeah, it was pretty bad there for a while. Now I just feel like I took a Benadryl, tired and kind of foggy in my brain."

Rachel looked around and noticed a used plastic cup sitting next to the sink. She turned to Lacey. "Is the water potable?"

The girl nodded and followed Rachel's gaze. "There are some glasses in the cabinet to the right."

Rachel stood up and filled a glass for Tanner. "Drink up to help flush out whatever he gave you." She walked over and handed it to him, then went back to pour one for herself. "Lacey, need anything?"

"I can get it," Lacey snapped, her reaction surprising Rachel before she reminded herself of how she was at that age—fifteen—an age filled with hormonal fluctuations and mood swings. Add being held captive for months and the girl could react however she wanted. Rachel nodded and reached up for another glass.

"I imagine you've looked around this place for ways to get out?" Rachel queried as the water poured.

"I've checked everything I can think of to check. Locks on the front door are impossible. Windows are too small or barred. No other doors. No hidden ways in or out, like under the carpet or anything. I knocked on all the walls and didn't hear anything other than you'd expect. Checked behind the few pictures hanging around. Nothing."

Dang, this teenager was smart *and* thorough. "Good job. Mind if we look over it? A second and third pair of eyes and all?" Rachel waited, gulping half of the water in her glass and hoping the girl wouldn't think Rachel was accusing her of missing something.

Lacey shrugged her shoulders. "Help yourselves," she said and waved her hand.

As both she and Tanner began snooping around, Rachel asked, "Have you been stuck inside this place the entire time? I mean, do they let you outside at all?"

"Phil does. But I have to wear a blindfold, and he just walks me around slowly for a while. Jokes that I need my vitamin D."

"Who's this Phil? Is that the guy who took you? Took us?" Rachel walked up to the front door and examined the multiple locks. She knocked. The deep sound confirmed the door was solid.

"No, I think he works for the man who brought you in here. 'Buddy' is what he said to call him. The guy who took me, I mean. I think Phil is disabled or something, like in his brain. He's nice to me, and I get the impression he doesn't quite realize what's going on."

"Are those the only two men you've seen?" Rachel asked as she carefully inspected the wall, searching for a crevice, dent, or any variation of a bad paint job. Not that she had a clue what she was looking for. Just something that was off.

"There was one other guy. Kind of reminded me of that old

actor. Gosh, what's his name? He was in *The Notebook*. My mom made me watch that with her *so* many times." Lacey rolled her eyes.

"Ryan Gosling?" Rachel forced herself not to react to the "old" comment. She didn't think the actor was much older than she, and, in her opinion, he was pretty easy on the eyes.

"That's it!" Lacey responded excitedly. "Like him but beefier."

Bang. Both women looked toward the kitchen.

"Sorry." Tanner blushed. "Didn't mean to slam the cabinet." He continued perusing through the kitchen. "No knives or anything, I take it?" He looked at Lacey.

"Just a butter knife."

"Lacey, did you ever hear anything notable from anyone? Personal details or weird comments? Stuff that stood out?" Rachel prodded as her fingers continued their work. Lacey scrunched up her face as if she were deep in thought.

"Not really."

Rachel stopped what she was doing and focused all of her attention on Lacey. "Did you ever see any cars?"

"No, I only heard them sometimes."

"And his brother . . . did this Phil ever mention him by name? Is he on-site somewhere?"

"He never said anything else about him." The girl perked up and looked back at Rachel. When she smiled, her whole face lit up. It was the first time she'd seen an expression other than fear and worry since her arrival. Lacey continued, "Do you think this is important?"

"I don't know," Rachel answered honestly. She shifted and the GPS tracker slipped farther down into her bra. Should she tell the kids about it? What if someone came to check on them and the teens inadvertently gave it away? No, she'd wait, much as it bothered her to keep it from them. Besides, while she told herself the dogs had to have made it back to their temporary house because she couldn't imagine something happening to them, that wouldn't mean Luke would have determined what she'd done. If he did, though, he'd have tried to log on to her cell phone. For once, her procrastination at changing the passcode could work in her favor.

While she retained hope that Luke would figure it out, at the same time she had to assume they were on their own. And their options were looking bleak.

Chapter Thirty-Five

Luke kept his body pressed to the ground as the footsteps neared. All he could see in the failing light was the outline of someone drawing near.

The figure walked slowly. Luke noticed a small red circle move from face height downward like it was held in someone's moving hand, and he realized the person was smoking. Didn't this jerk know they were still in fire season?

With his eyes now adjusted to the darkness, Luke could discern more details. The man appeared to be about Luke's height. His chest was broad, and his body was stocky. The guy had at least twenty pounds on Luke, but Luke had surprise on his side.

When the person closed in with two more footsteps, Luke's muscles tensed. Not knowing who this was, he didn't want to shoot first and ask questions later, nor risk drawing the attention of anyone else on the premises. But if this guy had a gun, all bets were off. He watched as the man took another drag on his cigarette; he then reached into his pocket and retrieved something.

"Yeah?" As he spoke into the cell phone, he turned and began walking back the way he came. "On my way back now." The man continued talking, the space between them growing with each word.

Once he was beyond Luke's line of sight, Luke stood and began to follow him from a distance. He did his best to keep quiet and was aided by the wind masking the noise his shoes made with each careful step. It was easier to move without fear of being heard but conversely more difficult to hear potential threats. After what he guessed to be twenty or thirty feet, Luke emerged from the trees into a large clearing, catching a brief glimpse of the man still heading in the other direction. Worried he could still be spotted if the figure turned around, or if someone else were around, he jumped back into the trees. Luke looked down at his attire; he was far from dressed for a reconnaissance mission. Thankfully, he preferred dark T-shirts and jean shorts, but his shoes were white. He began to dig his feet into the dirt, making sure to coat all of the sides until he could barely see them. There wasn't much he could do about his white legs other than smear them with soil as well.

Once he had camouflaged himself, he stood back up and examined the clearing. Although his sight was limited by the night's darkness, the opening appeared to be large, save a couple of oak trees near the middle that wouldn't be sufficient to hide behind. He looked to either side; it was impossible to tell how far the clearing went. Dare he follow now and risk being seen or continue along in the trees searching for a way around the clearing? Fearing that time was of the essence, he opted for plan A. Once he could no longer see the man, he dashed toward the double-tree island of oaks. No guns blasted, no security lights flashed, and no men came roaring into the clearing with their weapons blazing. Hoping the other side wouldn't be too far away, Luke let out the breath he didn't know he was holding, jumped up, and ran past the trees.

It wasn't far. All too soon he was back into the forest with manzanita bushes assaulting his bare shins as he continued following the man.

~

Cassandra searched for a good spot to pull off within a quarter of a mile from the driveway. *Should have paid more attention this afternoon when there was daylight.* Twice she'd noticed what looked like dirt roads branching off the main road, only to discover wide shoulders. Another open area came into view on her left. She slowed and scanned it as she passed; it looked like an old logging road. She put her car in reverse and turned onto the dirt road, which ended after a couple of hundred feet. Another vehicle, well hidden from the main road, was parked on the right. Given the pathway ended and she saw no homes or landscaping, she didn't think it was someone's driveway.

As she inched up next to the parked car, she could see it was empty. Strange, but sometimes people would backpack in the oddest of places. Cassandra tucked into the small space next to the other vehicle; together, the two cars effectively took up half of the circular turnaround. She grabbed the flashlight stowed behind her seat and jumped out, aiming the beam into the empty vehicle. There was nothing to provide any insights into the driver; no letters were tossed on a seat, no food wrappers, no dice or jewelry hanging from the rearview mirror. She walked around to look into the other side when her eyes caught a small bumper sticker on the lower left side. With closer observation, she was able to discern the Enterprise emblem, which was curious, but nothing to get worked up over. It was time to get to business, and she didn't have time to find somewhere else to park. She planned to walk along the road with her flashlight off, unless someone drove by; then the only option was to literally dive for cover. While the increasing wind would hinder her from hearing oncoming motors, the headlights would be sign enough.

Within a few minutes she neared the entryway she'd seen earlier. Should she dare walk up the driveway? It would be the easiest way and didn't appear to be illuminated. While intermittent slivers of moonlight passed through the trees, there was no way could she travel through the forest without her flashlight, but that would be equivalent to putting a target on her back. She opted to walk along the driveway.

Her luck held, and she soon noticed faint light in the distance. It grew brighter as she approached; eventually she recognized it as the porch light on a moderately sized home. Cassandra continued following the driveway as it curved around behind the house. She came upon a small structure at the end that looked like a typical guesthouse: one story and small enough to be more of a studio with a bathroom and kitchen. Unlike the main house, this one had lights coming from inside the closed windows. *Could it really be this easy?*

Suddenly, a flashlight appeared from the side of the small house. Cassandra jumped to her side, placing a tree between her and the light, then peered around its edge. The person holding it walked casually; nothing indicated alarm on his or her part, so Cassandra didn't think she'd been spotted. More light appeared in front of her. It took a second for her to realize a car had come up the driveway. Its headlights were aimed at the small house and lit up the man walking next to it: *Leo!*

Although the illumination didn't come close to exposing her, she still moved farther back into the copse of trees to watch. A dark SUV pulled up in front of Leo and stopped. He put his hand up to block the light from his eyes.

"Leo?" a man's voice called out.

"Turn off those damn lights!" Leo yelled, squinting. Once again the night was dark, broken only by Leo's small flashlight and the dim light coming through the gaps along the windows. The vehicle's door opened, and a man hefted himself out. Leo said something, but it wasn't loud enough to hear over the gusts. He strode over to the new arrival with his hand out in front of him. They shook, then patted each other's backs; it was clearly someone he knew well. , Uncertain of what to do other than wait them out, Cassandra remained in place. Eventually they'd have to go indoors; who would stand out in this wind for a chat?

She'd been standing there, watching them, for what felt like five or ten minutes when she saw movement along the back of the guesthouse. Was it an associate of Leo's coming to see who arrived? Or could Rachel be escaping, assuming she was being held inside? The second option prompted her to move. She had to know. Cassandra crept farther into the forest and carefully made her way along the outer edges. Her pace was slow as it was difficult to discern what was in front of her, but she wasn't about to use her flashlight. She carefully lifted her legs high with each step in case a bush or small tree blocked her path. Finally, she arrived at the area where she'd seen the movement. Someone was tucked against the small structure, his or her body crouched low as if he or she were hiding. But who?

~

Kris walked up Rachel's front steps with her laptop in hand. She hadn't called Derek on the way over, figuring if he wasn't here for some reason, so be it. She could get started on her own. However, his rental car was parked in the driveway.

Raising her fist to knock, Kris pondered the odd silence. The dogs usually knew she was there before she'd even left her car, so Rachel often greeted her at the door serenaded by a chorus of happy yelps. Prior to installing the house alarm, Kris used to just walk in, knowing the dogs would have alerted Rachel of her arrival. She banged against the door.

"Derek, it's Kris," she yelled and then waited. No response. Another few seconds passed, and she knocked harder. Still nothing. She pressed her ear to the door even though it was doubtful she would hear anything with the wind blowing through the trees overhead. She wrapped her knuckles against the door and called out again, "Derek! Hello?" Silence. "Okay, we'll play it your way," she said. Suspecting Derek may not be using the alarm while he was here, she reached and turned the knob. It turned easily in her hand. *Typical male.*

The door opened, and she stepped inside, calling out, "Derek?" The living area was empty. Light from the TV illuminated the otherwise dark room. A program had been paused on the screen. She stared for a moment, recognizing Ellen DeGeneres. *Derek watches* The Ellen DeGeneres Show? Kris grinned as she switched on a light behind the sofa. Soon after, she heard shuffling sounds coming from the short hallway. Kris set the computer down and turned. "Sorry, I tried knocking several—" Her next words halted in her throat. Fresh from showering, Derek emerged from the bathroom with nothing but a towel wrapped low around his waist. Moisture dripped from his wavy hair and beaded down his oh-so-sculpted chest. He looked as surprised as she was.

"Kris? What are . . . what are you doing here?" He appeared to recover quickly as a smirk immediately replaced the astonished look on his face. One corner of his mouth tilted upward.

"I, uh, Ted called," she stammered. "He asked if we could help research information on a property for him."

"Did he say why?" He walked toward her, swapping his grin for a concerned expression. "How's Rachel?"

"He said he couldn't tell us details but did say Rachel was fine."

"I hate being out of the loop on this!" He ran his fingers through his hair, much to Kris's delight because it made his biceps bulge. *Dear hormones: inappropriate timing.*

"Ted said she's okay, and I believe him." Kris turned back around and retrieved her laptop before walking to the front of the couch and plopping herself down. "I can get started, but if I recall, you're a computer whiz or something like that, right?"

Derek smiled cockily. "That's computer *genius.*"

"You just can't turn it off, can you?"

Derek walked over and sat next to her. Kris winced at the strong disinfectant smell coming off his skin.

"What did you wash with? Formula 409?" She pushed the power button and waited for the screen to light up.

"You don't like it?" he teased.

Kris looked at him with her face as void of expression as her answer.

"Sorry, just something I picked up at CVS earlier. I couldn't handle smelling like Vanilla Bean or Creamy Coconut for another day."

"You don't like Rachel's Body Shoppe shower gels?" Kris entered her password and the main screen appeared.

"I prefer Strawberry Medley or Peaches and Cream."

"Good one," Kris chuckled as she pulled up her browser. Derek scooted closer to get a better view of the screen. It caused the towel to loosen and begin to slide down his hips. *Damn.* "Why don't you get dressed while I get this started?"

Derek looked down as if only now he realized he was still wrapped in a towel. He grabbed the edges as he stood. "I'll go do that." Kris nodded and began typing in search terms from the information in Ted's text. She hit enter and turned to watch Derek walk down the hall toward the guest room. It was a great view.

"Stop staring at my ass," he called out without turning around.

"Funny how men never like it when the tables are turned," she mumbled.

"Say what?"

"Nothing. Go put some clothes on!" Kris turned back around and scanned the list generated by the search engine. First, she'd start with the easiest route—the public assessor's database. After a few more clicks, she finally encountered the screen asking for the assessor's parcel number, or APN. She typed in the number from Ted and selected *Search*. The property information displayed the basics: lot size, owner, zoning, school district, tax rolls, and several other details. "ML Investments?" she recited aloud. Kris pondered the ownership information, so she opened a separate tab and started another search. Footsteps stomped back into the room.

"Got it all figured out yet?"

She heard the refrigerator door open briefly. After it closed, a drawer opened, and then she heard the sound of a bottle top being popped off.

"Want a beer?"

"I'm fine, thanks." Part of her was surprised he even asked. It was so out of character for him. Finally he rounded the furniture and sat down next to her. His plain black T-shirt and blue sweatpants made it much easier for her to concentrate. Kris explained what she had started doing and the results so far. "This is what I just pulled up on that company." She waved at the screen.

"Looks like a shell corporation."

"Exactly. Is that something you could check out while I check into some other things?" Kris looked around. "Got a tablet or iPad?"

"Right here." He leaned to the side and reached out to an end table. She hadn't noticed the device before. She watched as he quickly glanced at the TV and then back at her. He casually picked up the remote on the coffee table and turned it off before starting up his tablet.

"So . . . *Ellen*, huh?"

"I just had it on for noise."

"Uh-huh." She snickered, then looked back at her laptop and began checking other search results. Derek didn't respond, his attention focused on his own work. Kris scrolled through the files, but the various links provided limited information. "This property is hundreds of acres. Looks like it's bordered by public land on one side and private forestland owned by a timber company on the other. According to this, there's a house, barn, and mother-in-law unit. It used to be a farm back in the day, but it doesn't look like it's been anything more than a residence for some time. That's it. Some serious privacy for sure."

"Where is it exactly?" he asked as his fingers continued tapping.

"Several miles northeast of Jackson as the crow flies."

"Do you think Rachel is there?"

"Maybe," she acknowledged. "Anything yet?" She nodded her chin toward his device.

"Still digging. Information about this corporation is buried deep."

"That's not a good sign," Kris muttered as she began clicking on permitting files associated with the property. There were minor permits for things like a new storage shed, a deeper water well, and other small projects. There was nothing suspicious or strange that she could see so far, but there were several links to go.

"I've got something!" Derek exclaimed. "It traces back to a company in Nevada."

"Okay." Kris waited, knowing there was more to come.

"A mining company out near Elko."

"That's odd. It's owned by a company, not just one of the owners or something?"

"Let me try one thing here . . ."

Kris was astonished at how fast the man could type. Although she knew he was intelligent and his job required extensive computer skills, she had no idea how versed he really was. It was hard to fit this studious version of Derek with the egotistical moocher who loved helping himself to other people's things.

"And I've got it. It actually belongs to one of the partners who own the company. A Drake Fischer."

"Was that information the public could find? I mean, without hacking?"

"What makes you think I'm hacking?" he scoffed. Kris just stared and waited. He smiled. "No, it was not public information."

"I wouldn't think much if someone in Nevada owned a property out here. Some people like their getaways. But why hide it?"

"Good question," Derek agreed.

Chapter Thirty-Six

Luke tried to hear what the two men were saying as they stood next to the newly arrived vehicle, but the distance and gusting winds made it impossible. He also continued to look in the direction the smoker had gone. When the man had disappeared into the shadows on the other side of the guesthouse, there had been no way to follow and remain out of sight of the headlights beaming down the driveway. As the two men by the SUV smacked each other's backs in greeting, Luke kept his back pressed against the wall. Was Rachel in there? A dim light from inside shined around the edges of heavy curtains. Luke kept himself positioned below any streams of light seeping outside. He slid carefully along the building and moved another foot closer to the talking men. Then another.

Finally, he was able to pick up snippets of their conversation: "she's inside too," "third one, a kid," "just a week," "Mason had better," and "head inside." After these last words, the men turned and walked up to what appeared to be the back door to the main house. He hoped "she's inside" was in reference to the structure he was now leaning against. Once he was certain he was alone, Luke slowly rose, peering through the small opening at the edge of the window. There were bars on the outside, which were common enough in higher crime urban areas, but out here in the middle of nowhere?

He rose higher until he could see through a wider section of the gap on the side of the curtain. A young girl, in profile, was facing toward the front door and talking to someone. Based on pictures he'd seen, Luke was certain this was Lacey. Could she be talking to Rachel? And what about this "third kid" that one of the guys mentioned? Was someone else in there guarding them? Someone he couldn't see with his limited view? He dropped down, aiming to investigate the other side. As he carefully inched back around the corner, he was hit with the strong odor of smoke. This was not from a cigarette; it smelled like burning wood. He saw no flames in the distance. He hoped it was simply a woodstove or fireplace in the house.

Luke rounded the second corner and found another window identical to the one on the other side. More light trickled out. Luke paused and gazed around for any movement, yet even with his eyes adjusted to the dark it would still be hard to see anyone. Luke stood again and peered inside. This view allowed him to see a broader area of the room. Lacey was in full view. A lamp blocked his field of vision to her left, but he saw enough to know that Rachel was indeed with the girl. Just as he was about to drop back down and contemplate his next move, something behind Lacey shifted. Luke stood up on to his toes, trying to improve his line of sight over the couch where they sat. A boy in his early to midteens sat on the floor with his back against the other wall. He looked familiar, but Luke couldn't figure out why. *What is going on here?* Luke crouched back on the ground, pulled his cell phone from his pocket, and cradled it in his hands so that the screen's illumination would not give him away. He dimmed the display and typed, uncertain the message would go through but needing to try anyway: *On property next 2 small house behind main house. Rachel, Lacey, unknown teen boy inside. 3 men on premises so far w 2 in main house, 1 MIA.* Another whiff of smoke penetrated his nostrils. He added: *Smelling smoke, getting stronger.* Luke hit send, his eyes staring at the one signal bar fading in and out. The device was still searching for enough electronic juice to send the message when Luke turned off the display and put it back in his pocket.

Something told him he didn't have much time to linger. He swept the area around him one more time, rose to his full height, and turned back toward the window. Luke reached through the bars and tapped on the glass.

Inside, all three people were startled and shot wary gazes in his direction. He waved. Could they see his hand? No one moved. Luke knocked again and then thought of a signal to Rachel. He began rapping the Morse code for SOS—the one line of code she knew. He saw her mouth move, her lips forming what was clearly his name with a questioning look in her eyes. She stood and carefully approached. He tapped the three-letter code again. Rachel came over and pushed the curtain to the side. She squinted. He saw the moment her eyes made him out. Her anxious features relaxed.

Although he couldn't hear it, she said his name excitedly. He watched her pry open the window with some effort.

Rachel beamed. "Luke, you're here!" she quietly exclaimed. "Is Ted with you?" She looked to his side, likely forgetting she couldn't see anything in the dark.

"On the way," he whispered, aware that any of the men, let alone other people he may not have yet seen, could return. "Who's in there with you?"

"Lacey and Tanner."

"Wait, Tanner?" Something familiar scratched at the back of his mind.

"Jill's son."

And there it was, the reason for his recognition. He had met the teen a couple of times, but once he and Rachel had called it quits, he rarely saw Jill, and even less so, her kids. "How? Why?" he blurted, then shook his head as though he were clearing the fog. "Okay, that's not important right now. Is anyone hurt? Are you okay?"

"I'm fine. Kids are too, for the most part." Rachel looked back into the room and then turned his way again. "Are my dogs okay?"

"Yes. Clever, by the way," he said as he grinned, and then he grew serious once again. "What do you know about this place?"

"There's no way out. We've checked everything. The front door is bolted. Lacey has told me about at least five people. The one who took her, a guard, his brother Phil—who Lacey thinks is mentally disabled and unaware of what's going on—plus another guy I haven't seen yet, and someone who periodically shows up in a loud vehicle like we heard about ten minutes ago."

"Okay," he said as he nodded, then asked, "Any chance there's a fireplace or woodstove burning inside there?"

At his question, Rachel looked confused. "No, there's a fireplace, but it's not in use. Why?"

"I'm smelling smoke. I followed a man, perhaps one of those guards, who kept lighting up cigarettes, and it's sure windy." He looked around, scouring the area for approaching guards.

Rachel knew where his mind was taking him. "We've got to get out of here quickly, don't we?"

"I wanted to wait for Ted and Cap to get here. While the smoke could be coming from far away or someone's chimney, something tells me we shouldn't delay."

"How far away are they?"

"Not sure." Realizing the phone was still in his hand, he pushed the button to light the display. It was still trying to send out his text message. *Damn.*

"Okay, then what do we do?"

Luke pondered this. "I'll be right back," he said, and then he crept around to the front door. He saw that the lock relied on a passcode rather than a key; he debated on whether he could shoot it open. Of course, if that was his only option, they'd have to flee into the darkness quickly because someone would no doubt hear the shot, even over the wind. But there was no guarantee a gunshot would be enough to break it open. He walked back to the window. Rachel appeared relieved to see him. The two other inhabitants were standing next to her.

"Wait, aren't you dead or something?" Tanner asked abruptly.

"Or something. Long story," Rachel said before Luke could respond. "Now what?"

"Yeah, I'm wondering the same question." A deep, throaty voice emerged from the darkness nearby. Luke turned around. There was just enough light coming through the slit in the window to illuminate the shadow of the man Luke had been following earlier.

~

"I may have figured out why this Drake person went to such lengths to keep the property files under wraps." Derek leaned over toward Kris and examined her screen while quietly inhaling the sweet lavender scent wafting from her body. It had been driving him mad since she'd first arrived.

"Oh yeah?" she asked excitedly. She turned toward him and was visibly surprised when she saw how close he was. He moved backward.

"From what I've been reading it looks like he may be one of those survivalist types. They believe that the world will eventually sink into anarchy, so they stock up on hidden properties so they can 'survive' when our social systems fail. Food and supplies, off-the-grid houses, weapons, you name it."

"I've heard of that. I think they're also called 'preppers.'"

"Sounds right." Derek swiped at a nonexistent gnat by his face. He hadn't been prepared for how it would feel being so close to this woman again. The car ride the other day had been tough, but for some reason this was worse.

"Are you thinking he may have had the place Ted asked about set up as one of his home bases?"

"It's possible. I'm running a search now for other properties he owns, but if they are disguised in shell companies like this one was, it won't be easy to find. It's one thing to have the property address and work our way backward; it's another to try to start from his name and go forward." He typed several more commands, initiating a new search from a different browser tab.

"I don't suppose property records would reflect any weapon stashes?" she muttered, clearly a rhetorical question.

"I'm trying very hard not to be worried, but I don't like Rachel being caught up with this."

"I agree, but we have to trust Ted. It's all we can do."

"Wasn't Ted with Luke when he had the fatal accident? I mean, I realize Ted is your friend and all, but he's not exactly Superman." The room grew silent, and he looked back at Kris. Her face had grown somber. "I'm sorry. That probably sounds insensitive. You knew Luke better than I did."

"It's okay. And yes, Ted is good at what he does, but no one can control everything one hundred percent of the time."

Derek watched as Kris unconsciously tucked her hair behind her ear. The silky red-orange strands caught the light from the nearby lamp so that the colors almost glowed. *What am I—a chick? Where are these thoughts coming from?* Perhaps his mind was simply attempting to mitigate his fear for his sister by creating distracting thoughts. That had to be it.

"Speaking of Ted, let's call him again and give him this update." Kris picked up her cell phone.

"Sounds good," Derek said, forcing his eyes back to his screen as Kris waited for the call to connect.

~

As soon as the phone rang, Ted pulled off to the side of the road, wanting to stay still so the call wouldn't get dropped. Taylor remained quiet as they listened to Kris relay what she and Derek had found. Once the call was over, Ted cruised forward until they arrived at the entrance to the property.

"It's surprising a prepper wouldn't line his property with something more than a few *No Trespassing* signs," Ted commented as he, anxious for word from Luke, glanced at the display on his phone. "Aren't they pretty anal about stuff like that?" Just then a text popped up, and he skimmed the message. "Luke's there. So are the kids. He has seen three guards, but Lacey mentioned at least five."

"I would expect tight security, especially when they are holding people there against their will. What about a security system?" Taylor wondered.

"Good question. But if Luke's gotten that close, there have to be gaps." Ted looked at the sliver of moon overhead and deliberated for a moment. "I'm concerned about his reference to smelling smoke. It could be nothing, or it could be something. It wasn't long ago a huge fire roared through an area not far from here."

"I don't think driving in with guns blazing is such a great idea."

"Not suggesting that. But I also don't think we should assume we have the time to tiptoe around the property either, or to go in the way Luke did. I'm thinking"—he paused and shut the headlights off—"that there's enough light to navigate slowly down the driveway. We could try that, unless you think there is some way to drive up and knock on the door without the risk of being shot. I've heard these survivalist types may shoot first and ask questions later when someone's on their property uninvited."

"Got your vest on?" Taylor eyed Ted with his brow raised.

"Not yet." Ted retrieved his bulletproof vest from the back seat and slid it on. He knew from the extra bulk that Taylor was already wearing his. "All right, let's go." As the vehicle accelerated, Ted rolled the windows down, even though the wind would likely cover most sound. The faint odor of smoke drifted into the vehicle.

They traveled a quarter mile when the first gunshot echoed through the trees. Ted turned toward Taylor, yet he couldn't see much other than a faint shadowed image of the man's face.

"Let's go!" Taylor said. A second shot rang out; Ted flipped his headlights on and slammed his foot down on the accelerator.

~

"Everyone, get down!" Luke's shout was almost immediately followed by the cracking sound Rachel knew all too well. Whoever was out there had a gun and was using it.

"Drop to the floor!" she instructed to the two teens, waving her arm. Tanner was still sitting in the corner. Fear and panic flashed across his features as he dropped all the way down and then snapped up his head to look at Lacey. She slid off the sofa and lay below it against the floor. "Get behind something sturdy." Rachel hoped her voice was calmer than she felt. Another shot rang out, sending Rachel's already hammering heart into overdrive. As she bent down, keeping her body below the window frame, her desire to peer out and catch a glimpse of what was going on was overruled by her desire to not get shot in the head. Had Luke been hit? Had he injured the other man? Images of Luke lying on the ground years ago, bleeding from a bullet wound in his shoulder, flashed through her mind. *Please, not again.* Seconds passed with the only sound coming from the blowing leaves and pine needles outside.

Rachel waited. *One. Two. Three. Four. Five.* She heard someone grunt, followed by scuffling sounds. Another shot rang out. She remained where she was, frozen. Then she smelled it—the familiar odor seeping in through the small gap in the open window. This was no prescribed burn, not on a windy day like this. In addition, trapped smoke inside these closed quarters wouldn't do them any good; then again, burning up in a structure fire wouldn't either. Rachel carefully reached up and kept her finger to the bottom of the frame as she slid the window closed. When she dropped back down into her hiding place, she tried not to imagine Luke getting shot or killed just feet away.

~

Leo's ears buzzed at the sound of a gunshot. Drake jumped up, tore the curtain aside, and peered into the yard.

"What the hell was that?" Drake asked, alarmed.

"I'll go check it out." Leo pulled his gun out of his belt and grabbed the handle to the back door.

"I thought you said we were secure," Drake accused as he ran his fingers through his thinning gray hair.

"You're the one who always wants the alarm turned off before your arrival. I get that you are para . . . *concerned* that the electronic signals may affect your brain, but turning off the alarm brings its own kind of risk, you know," Leo responded, then added hastily, "I need to go check."

Drake shook his head and chuckled. "I can't believe *you* used to work for Rand Mason. Being a respectable job and all."

Leo stiffened at the senator's name, the rage that always accompanied hearing it briefly distracting him. Before he could respond, they heard a second shot. Leo wrenched the door open and dropped to the ground, waiting for his eyes to adjust to the lack of light as he listened for more shots. Once he could discern dim images, he began to move, keeping himself close to ground level while shuffling toward the guesthouse.

As he neared, he saw the outlines of two men fighting. A third shot rang out just as bark flew off a tree several feet above Leo's head. *That was close.* Leo stepped back and tucked himself behind the tree before looking around it to continue watching the battle. In the dim light coming from the guesthouse's porch, he could make out

231

enough to see one of the guys was a guard, Kip; but who was the other man and why was he here? *How* was he here? Leo waited until his eyes fully adjusted to the near darkness. He watched the scene, wishing the area had been illuminated by more direct lighting, but Drake liked to keep lights to a minimum.

The figures suddenly stopped moving, and Leo was able to see the two men standing, facing each other, about six feet apart. Each had an arm raised and weapon aimed at the other. It was a standoff. Leo crept closer, sure the blowing trees would cover any sounds he made. As he approached their location, he was able to better identify the features of Kip's opponent. The man looked just like Luke Reed. *But how is that possible?*

Regardless, Leo had to stop this fight before either man pulled the trigger. "Drop your weapons!" he commanded, stepping toward them with his own weapon in position, carefully aiming from one man to the other and back. Kip didn't move but called out.

"Leo, I caught this guy trying to help the hostages escape." Neither man moved.

"I said drop your weapons, *both* of you." If this really was Luke Reed, then Leo had to keep him alive. If he didn't, and if Mike ever found out, that wouldn't be good for Leo.

"But Leo—"

"Now!" Leo hissed. Both men slowly lowered their arms. "Put them on the ground. Slow and steady." The two did as instructed, and Kip, obviously confused, glanced at Leo. Leo stepped forward, kicked both guns off to the side, and stared at Kip's counterpart. "Luke Reed?"

The man paused, but the close-up view had already confirmed his identification to Leo.

"I thought you died two weeks ago?"

"Why aren't you killing him?" Kip interrupted.

"Because those aren't my orders," Leo responded calmly. Luke looked down, presumably to see where his weapon was. Leo raised his hand. "Doesn't mean I can't hurt you, though, Mr. Reed." Luke looked back up. Leo could see his eyes were searching the area, probably for an idea of how to get out of this situation.

"What orders? From Mike?" Kip inquired. Leo was now almost

ready to shoot his hired hand himself. They never used names in front of others. *Never.*

Leo warned Kip with one glare. Kip remained silent, clearly frustrated.

"Where's your brother?" Leo demanded. The last thing they needed was Phillip stumbling into this mess right now; who knows what he'd do. He had the mind of a twelve-year-old.

"Down in unit one playing video games."

"Good. Now, let's—"

Luke abruptly leapt to the side and disappeared around the corner of the house. Leo saw Kip bend down and search the ground for his abandoned weapon. His head rose to Leo's as headlights penetrated the darkness moments before he heard the sound of a vehicle skidding to a stop nearby.

"Let's go," Leo said, motioning for Kip to retreat toward the main house.

Chapter Thirty-Seven

As her eyes adjusted to the dim light, Cassandra watched the scene unfold from her hiding spot near the corner of the guesthouse. The entire situation was downright entertaining. She still didn't know who the man was who'd snuck up and started talking to someone through the window—after a brief glimpse, she was sure the latter was Rachel—nor the second guy who had caught him. By his body language and demeanor, she assumed man number two was some kind of guard.

If Rachel was inside, was Lacey there too? Cassandra's hate for Rachel after she'd ruined her family's plans years ago had become so strong that she had fantasized about the different ways she could kill the woman. As boring as it was, a bullet would do just fine. First, she had to know who else was in there; Lacey had to be kept alive, even though it could limit her options with Rachel. She was debating her next move when a large white SUV roared around the corner and came to a sudden stop several feet from the guesthouse. The headlights were blinding to her night-attuned eyes. The doors flew open, and two men jumped out and immediately ducked, one on either side. The driver circled around and headed straight for her, although it was obvious he hadn't seen her yet. He waved his arm in what appeared to be an instruction to the passenger, who was older and heavier. The second man nodded, backed up to the small structure, and inched along it sideways.

A small glowing ember fell to the ground a few feet away between her and the house. It stopped the driver in his tracks, a blessing since the only way to avoid being spotted by him at that point was to run the other way—where she'd risk being seen by others. The driver turned and looked toward the tree line. Another ember floated by. Cassandra had been smelling smoke off and on, but she hadn't registered what it could mean until that moment. She peered in the same direction as the driver. An orange glow was visible in the distance. While the fire wasn't next to them—yet—the embers were being blown their way by the heavy winds.

The man who'd been talking to Rachel earlier came whipping around the corner and then stopped in his tracks when he noticed the other man. "Ted?"

"Luke?" the driver asked. *Wait, Luke? As in, Luke Reed?* Cassandra scrutinized the man, trying to see his face, but the moonlight wasn't bright enough to distinguish details from this distance. The man, presumably Luke Reed, quickly pushed himself back against the wall of the house, bumping into the side of "Ted," man number two.

"Luke, it's Taylor," said a third scratchy voice.

"Cap," Luke said, and then he spoke louder. "There're two men, both armed."

"And you?"

"Lost mine."

"Here, take my spare," Ted said, reaching down and pulling up his jeans. He retrieved a small gun from an ankle holster.

Once he handed it to Luke, they both checked around the side of the structure, and then Luke said, "Rachel's inside along with—"

"We've got another problem," Ted shouted, looking back at the glow in the distance.

"Crap!" Luke replied as he saw more embers starting to fall around them.

Cassandra watched several of them land on the roof of the guesthouse. Small flames began to flicker upward where the red hot ash had fallen moments before. *Must be an old wood roof to ignite like that.* Ted moved to join Luke and the man named Taylor. Cassandra was relieved to remain undiscovered. She could take one or two men out easy enough, especially with surprise on her side, but three armed men—that could be a bit much.

"We've got to get them out of there. The lock requires a security code." Luke sounded nervous.

Them? So Rachel and Lacey *were* both inside. That made things more difficult. She wondered if there was a way to take out Rachel without being detected, then slip away and let these three men "rescue" Lacey.

As she weighed her options, Cassandra noticed movement across the small yard. The two men who had retreated toward the larger home when the SUV pulled up were now positioned to her left. Someone new approached them. The three figures huddled, but she couldn't hear what was being said.

Finally, the trio separated. They fanned outward as they crept through the trees, one heading right in her direction. She slid backward, hoping the commotion of the situation would keep anyone from looking too closely. As she moved, she angled to her side, making a wide semicircle around them until she was closer to the guesthouse. Cassandra couldn't imagine the windows on an old structure like this were bulletproof. She had an advantage right now; there were lights on inside, but the exterior remained mostly dark on this side of the guesthouse. All she had to do was aim her weapon through the window until Rachel appeared and then shoot. Lacey would be fine. *Easy enough.*

She meandered, undiscovered. As if on cue, Rachel Winters moved into her line of sight. Adrenaline coursed through her veins, and her heartbeat quickened. Multiple shots rang out from somewhere near the front of the house just as she aimed and fired, but Rachel had disappeared from view. Glass shattered.

~

Rachel couldn't handle the silence any longer. She risked reopening the window to listen. Just as she leaned toward the glass, she heard gunfire. Rachel immediately dropped to the floor. A biting pain registered in her left bicep, and she heard a small cry. It took her a moment to realize it was coming from her own throat. *What happened?*

"Someone just shot out the window!" Lacey cried from her hiding place in the kitchen.

"Rachel, are you okay?" Tanner screamed. Rachel noticed he had crawled along the floor to a point where the couch didn't block his view of her. His eyes widened. "Were you hit?"

"I don't see how." She did her best to breathe through the pain as she held her arm, blood smearing the fingers of her right hand. She tried to examine the wound but the blood and angle made it impossible. Rachel inhaled deeply. *Focus.* Her eyes examined the slivers of glass around her as she tried to assess the situation. Had a piece of glass caught her? Adrenaline shot through her, numbing the pain.

"You two stay down!" she instructed. She had to tie something around her arm to stop the bleeding, but if she moved and whoever had fired that shot looked in the window, they'd no doubt see her. She had no choice but to stay hidden below the windowpane. Rachel eyed her clothes and considered whether she could use her teeth to tear off a strip from her shirt.

"Here," Lacey shouted as a balled-up dishcloth landed nearby. Rachel stretched out her leg, grabbed it with her heel, and slid it across the floor. It created a small path through the broken glass. She quickly let go of her arm, grabbed the cloth, and shook it hard to clear any shards picked up on the way. After a few extra shakes, she began to twirl it the way she used to do when they were kids, coiling it up like a twisted snake before lashing out to smack one of her brothers. Once it was rolled up, she stuck one end in her mouth, holding it with her teeth, while she double-wrapped the wound with her right hand. She managed to double-knot it, pulling as hard as she dared. She still wasn't sure if she'd been hit by glass or a bullet. Were the kids in danger? She glanced around the room, realizing a bullet could have ricocheted off the masonry around the fireplace or dislodged a piece of it.

"Lacey, Tanner, you two go take shelter in the bathroom." It was the only place she could think of that could provide cover from any angle.

"But it's like an airplane bathroom," Lacey replied. "Maybe if one of us stood in the shower."

"You go first, Lacey," Tanner called out.

"But—"

"He's right," Rachel said, although everything inside of her feared for the vulnerability of her friend's son. But he was bigger.

"Okay," Lacey agreed, and she began to move along the kitchen wall, keeping low to the ground, until she reached a small door on the left side of the room and slipped inside.

"Rachel?" Tanner asked nervously.

"Uh-huh," she answered, doing her best to keep her voice calm as she watched him crawl toward the safety of the bathroom.

"I think there's a fire outside," he said. "I can see embers through the window." Tanner, like Rachel, was clearly doing his best not to freak out. Jill had definitely raised a strong son. Rachel hoped she'd have the chance to tell her friend that as she looked up at the ceiling, wondering what kind of roof material was above them. Her sense from the nicked-up hollow walls, orange and green carpets, and olive and brown kitchen was the home had been constructed decades ago. It didn't come close to meeting current fire codes.

"Did you say there's a fire?" Lacey asked with a voice so high-pitched she sounded half her age.

~

Leo watched Luke Reed and the newly arrived men skirt around the back of the white SUV. He recognized one of them; it was the cop, Ted. Leo glanced up into the sky.

"We need to act quickly and get out of here," he warned his two cohorts. Suddenly, more shots rang out. Leo heard glass shatter, and he saw a hole in the vehicle's window. Two more followed. Someone was shooting from the front of the house. It had to be Drake.

Leo thought quickly. "Kip, get around the front of the vehicle. When I shout, aim for the one closest to you. I'm going to slip around the back."

Kip nodded and stayed low to the ground as he dashed from their hiding place and ran. The lack of gunfire suggested the three men hadn't seen him. Leo turned and moved farther away from the commotion. He circled around so he'd come out where Luke and his buddies were hiding behind the vehicle. Suddenly, he heard windows break as the SUV shook; bullet after bullet reigned. Drake was an antigovernment survivalist; of course he had an automatic rifle in his stash of weapons. It was a stupid move; there were too many variables, and Leo or the other guards could easily be hit. As it was, Leo couldn't follow through with his own plan since he could get hit by a stray bullet if he moved any closer.

When Leo peered at the backside of the SUV, he was perplexed to only see two men; both took turns aiming over the hood of the vehicle and shooting in Drake's direction. Ted yelled out "police," but either Drake didn't hear him or didn't care. Leo realized Luke was gone. How had he slipped away? Should he continue with his plan and risk Luke being in a position to shoot back from somewhere nearby? If only he knew Drake's intentions. Drake hadn't appeared, so Leo assumed he was keeping cover by the front of the house.

Something singed his right hand, and he realized an ember had landed on his skin. He shook it off, glancing up toward the forest beyond. The fire was closer now, and the blowing embers lit trees in front of their path. He glanced back at the guesthouse. Small fires burned on the roof. Leo knew the old place still had wooden shingles; it was a matchbox ripe to burst into flames. He needed to get the woman and kids out as soon as possible, especially Lacey. As much as he wanted Rand to pay for what he did to him, Leo wasn't about to let an innocent girl burn alive, no matter how much Rand deserved to suffer.

~

"There has to be at least three of them," Ted said as they leaned against his SUV. He faced Luke and Taylor. "I saw a third one join the other two before we ran over here."

"We don't have a lot of time," Luke responded, unable to help himself from glancing in the direction of the approaching fire. His eyes were starting to itch from the smoke.

"Agreed," Ted replied.

"We're sitting ducks if we stay here," Captain Taylor added.

"The trees closest to us aren't burning yet." Luke pointed toward the forest; it required crossing about ten feet of exposed driveway to get to it. "If we can get over there, we can hide behind those trees and make our way around to the other side while staying out of view. The two I encountered earlier could be anywhere."

"Someone needs to stay here and provide cover," Taylor said.

"That's suicide," Ted replied.

"Give me some credit. I was fighting criminals while you were waiting for the tooth fairy. Ted, you go first. Luke and I will cover you. Then—"

His words were cut off when a barrage of gunfire erupted. Glass shattered, and Ted's vehicle shook. Someone was shooting an automatic rifle from the front of the main house. Taylor and Ted both jumped up and fired back in the direction of the unknown shooter.

"Luke, go!" Ted shouted.

Luke bolted, anticipating searing pain would tear through him at any moment, but he made it into the cover of the trees unscathed. He swiveled back around and watched Ted and Taylor take turns returning fire. Taylor yelled something. Ted turned in Luke's direction, preparing to run, when Luke spotted the outline of a man standing next to a tree. Luke motioned, but thankfully Ted had seen him too and dropped back toward the SUV. Ted aimed and began to announce himself as a police officer, but the figure immediately backed up and began firing. After several quiet clicks, he stopped, turned, and ran away. Luke guessed the man's weapon had run out of ammo and that Ted must have figured the same; he took off in the guy's direction. Both disappeared into the darkness. Luke focused his attention back to Captain Taylor, who remained stranded next to the SUV.

Luke aimed his gun, expecting to begin shooting to provide cover for Taylor while he ran to the relative safety of the forest. But Taylor surprised him by dashing to the driver's door, wrenching it open, and jumping inside. Within moments the vehicle accelerated backward, limping along on tires that had been shot out on one side. Angled diagonally across the driveway, the SUV headed straight for the trees that lined the path. The door flew open, and Taylor burst out and rolled on the ground. Then he jumped up and ran into the trees not ten feet away as the car crashed. Metal twisted, and more glass shattered.

"Luke?" Taylor called out.

"Over here, double-oh-seven."

Taylor arrived next to him, his fast breathing the only sign of the crazy maneuver he'd just pulled off. "Where's Ted?"

"Someone was coming around behind you. Ted ran after him."

"I feel like someone who brought a knife to a gunfight with that damn AR going off," Taylor exclaimed as he dusted off his legs.

"I hear ya."

"All right, this is what we know. We've got three guys with handguns and a fourth with an automatic rifle. Number four is by the main house. Let's call the one Ted is chasing number three. Which way did they go?"

Luke pointed.

Taylor nodded. "Got it. Numbers one and two, where are they?"

"Last I saw, over by the corner of the house. But it's been several minutes now."

"We need help. Got your phone?"

"Yes, but the signal is spotty," Luke said.

"Okay then—" Taylor paused to clear his throat. "We can't wait with this fire coming. Let's head back toward that guesthouse."

Luke nodded, realizing there were no great options. They began to make their way along the edge of the forest, watching through the trees as best as they could. Luke tried not to consider that there could be more guards surrounding them. Who knew how many?

"Kip?" Luke heard a man's voice call out from somewhere in front of them. They both stopped. In the faint fire's glow, Luke watched a tall, lanky man walk straight across the driveway where bullets had been flying just moments before. "Kip?" he called out again. The smoking man Luke had fought earlier suddenly emerged.

"Phil, get down!" the man, Kip, yelled as he slammed into Phil. Both tumbled to the ground as automatic gunfire started again. "Dad, stop!" Kip yelled. "It's—" His voice cut off as his body jerked. *Dad? Is this guy's father the one shooting the rifle?*

"Kip!" Phil cried out.

Luke turned to Taylor. "Phil . . . Rachel mentioned him. Lacey said he was developmentally challenged in some way and had been nice to her." He rubbed his cheek. "Looks like Kip is down for the count," Luke remarked as he watched Phil cradle his brother in his arms, rocking back and forth.

"Okay, let's try to track down shooter number two," Taylor suggested. "Looks like we may not have to worry about number three, aka Kip."

They continued forward. The gunfire had finally ceased.

~

Ted followed as the man ran across a wide-open area toward a large barn in the distance. He felt mild burning in his lungs; no doubt the smoke was thickening as the fire approached. Ted pushed forward as the man slipped inside and the door slammed shut. When Ted reached it, he stood to the side and grasped the handle. To his surprise, it turned. Fearing that the perpetrator was lying in wait, Ted quickly yanked the door open and then remained off to the side and crouched low to the ground. While the guy had run out of ammo, there could always be more weapons inside, but no shots rang out. Nor did the man burst out to attack him.

The inside of the old structure was well lit by fluorescent lights. Keeping his head at floor level, Ted peered around the corner of the doorframe. Nothing moved inside that he could see, although his line of sight didn't include the entire barn. After making out an old tractor and several tools hanging on the walls, Ted pulled his head back and waited. Nothing happened, but the wind was so loud that he was unlikely to hear anything. Ted rose in a bended position and quickly dashed to the other side of the door. He waited, counting to thirty, and carefully looked inside, where he was now able to see the other half of the interior. More tools leaned against the walls, and tarps covered something that was about twenty feet long. In his peripheral vision, Ted saw movement in the back of the barn. His eyes focused on a back door. Had the guy just slipped out the back, or was he setting up a trap?

Contemplating his next move, Ted retrieved his cell phone from his pocket and tossed it inside. The phone bounced on the floor with the thick case protecting the device. Nothing happened. No shots rang out.

"Police! We're coming inside. Drop your weapon!" If the runner was still inside, maybe he could believe Ted's partner had come along. There was no response. Ted shouted out again, also keeping an eye on the sides of the barn in case his target had gone out the back and was now creeping his way toward Ted. With his gun held steady, he entered the barn, his eyes scanning every detail. The only place someone could hide from this angle would be behind the tractor. After closing the door, Ted quietly snuck around the side. With his weapon ready, he inspected the area around the corner. No one was there. He wasn't about to let his guard down yet, but chances were the man had gone out the back door. Still, it was possible he was hiding under the large blue tarp that Ted had observed earlier. He softly walked toward the covered object and quickly yanked the tarp with his weapon prepared to fire. There was no one underneath. In fact, what he saw scared him more than any gun-wielding criminal could.

About a dozen old gas storage cans were lined up. He stepped closer and noticed how several of them bulged, which suggested there was gasoline inside. He lifted one; it was full. The next, same thing. Of the handful of containers, about half were worn and dated. They clearly lacked the special devices now required by the state of California to prevent fumes from easily entering the atmosphere. He moved closer and observed how the seams on several of the older ones appeared to be under pressure from the inside. Ted thought of the fast-advancing wildfire.

Prompted by fears of an explosion, Ted surged out the front door and retraced his steps, taking the risk of keeping on his cell phone flashlight to guide his path as his eyes readjusted to the dark night. While he could make himself an easy target, he had to take the chance. Based on what was in that barn, time was truly of the essence.

Chapter Thirty-Eight

Leo intended to hide in the barn and attack the cop as he entered. Knowing he'd hear when the door opened again, Leo had felt safe turning on his flashlight to search for a good place to lie in wait. But with the ability to see came the horrible realization that Drake had been storing a lot of gasoline inside the barn, and the fire was fast approaching outside. He cursed and dashed out the back door just as he heard the squeaking hinges of the front door opening. With the cop inside searching for him, Leo rounded the building and ran back toward the guesthouse. As he neared the building, he heard the sound of someone crying out.

"Kip, wake up!" He recognized the voice. It was Phil, Kip's younger brother and Drake's impaired son. A moment later, he heard Drake's voice.

"No! No! What have I done?"

It didn't sound good, but he couldn't help them now. Drake was the one who'd been crazy enough to shoot off an automatic rifle; let him deal with the consequences. Leo had to get the woman and kids out before the fire burned the place down; Luke would just need to be dealt with later. As he ran toward the front steps of the guesthouse, he heard a woman's voice call his name. It was familiar but so out of context he couldn't place it.

"Leo?" she hollered again. A shadow emerged from nearby.

"Cass? What the . . . what are you doing here?" He couldn't believe his eyes. How in God's name was she here?

"Doesn't matter. Look, I need to—"

"I can't talk right now. This place is about to blow, and I need to get them out of here!" He raced toward the front door. Just as he tapped the first number on the keypad, a set of headlights emerged in the driveway. Leo remained focused on his task. He had to get the code in first.

"But—"

"You can help me, or you can leave. Your choice." The light stopped moving as the car stopped. Leo didn't look back as he pressed the fourth of six numbers.

A pain tore through his chest like nothing he'd ever felt before, and he collapsed, the world going dark.

~

"Leo!" Cassandra cried as his body crumpled to the ground. For a moment she was so shocked she couldn't think. A red spot quickly spread on his chest. Dropping down next to him, she cried as her hands felt his around the wound. "Leo?" Her fingers were already coated with his blood. "No, no, no!" she chanted, looking around as though a medic would suddenly appear out of the darkness.

"I knew you couldn't handle it." Monica's voice broke her concentration. Cassandra looked up frantically and stared into the cold, hard eyes she knew all too well.

"Mother, you shot him!"

"Ironic that this is what it takes for you to call me Mother again," Monica chuckled. "Now tell me what the hell is going on!"

"You fucking shot him," Cassandra screamed as anger overtook her sorrow.

"I think we've established that. Now where is Miss Winters?" Monica stopped two feet away and looked around. "Is she in there?" She pointed toward the front door.

"How could you?" Cassandra shrieked, then jumped up and tackled Monica, knocking her against the front wall. Monica was caught off guard by her daughter's reaction and didn't initially defend herself. After a few moments she reached out and tried to push Cassandra away.

"Cassie, calm down!"

Cassandra was so full of rage she couldn't even speak.

"Look, let's get Rachel and get the hell out of here. I don't know what's going on, but that fire is coming. I could see it from the road."

"You bitch!" Cassandra shouted at Monica's indifference to Leo lying on the ground in front of her, bleeding out and possibly already dead.

"Yell at me later. We've got to get going and fast." Monica grasped both of Cassandra's arms and held her back.

"You stupid, stupid woman. Leo was about to let them out! Now he can't!" She dropped back down, her hands feeling for a pulse. She didn't feel one, but maybe her fingers were just too slippery with blood.

"Get the keys!" Monica ordered with her hands braced on her hips.

"It requires a passcode, you moron!"

"Okay, so Rachel burns up. Not a problem."

"She's not the only one in there," Cassandra retorted. "Rand's granddaughter, Lacey, is in there too."

Monica's arms dropped to her sides. "What?"

"That's right. You just shot down the one person who could get them out!"

Monica took a step back like she had been physically slapped. "You mean no one else knows the code?"

"I don't know." Cassandra added, "You know what? Let Lacey burn! Dear Granddad Rand deserves to suffer after what he did to Leo!"

"What the hell are you talking about?" Monica hollered. When Cassandra didn't immediately reply, she took a deep breath and reminded herself to calm down before speaking again. "Never mind that for now. Are you here alone?" Monica looked around, searching for other people. "There are two other cars, yet one looks beat up."

"There are some other guards, but they ran off after that officer and two other men." Cassandra looked at Leo with tears streaming down her face. She'd never cared for anyone before Leo. She hadn't realized just how much until the prospect of his dying became real.

"We have to get Lacey out!" Monica had entered full panic mode.

"Good luck," Cassandra said, having no intention of leaving Leo's side. She felt Monica's fingers grab her arm and pull her up.

"You're going to help me! I'm not leaving here without you or Lacey." Her mother looked directly into her eyes. Cassandra gathered up her saliva and spit in Monica's face. "Real mature, Cassie. Now let's go!" She tugged. Cassandra tried to drop back down by Leo. "He's gone. Let's get Lacey and leave before we die with him!" As if she were in a trance, Cassandra complied, following Monica as she stomped around the corner toward voices she hadn't noticed before Leo was shot.

"Drake?" Monica uttered.

Who was Drake? Feeling like she was watching a scene play out from a distance, Cassandra followed along, numb inside. As they rounded the corner she saw an older man kneeling next to a prone figure sprawled out on the driveway. A third man held the injured one as he bellowed with agony like a child. The older man turned at the sound of Monica's voice.

"Drake, what are you doing here?" Monica choked. The older man didn't respond; he just turned back to the injured man. Monica dragged Cassandra along as she approached the three figures. The one lying on the ground was covered in blood, much like Leo. The younger one sat and cradled the prone man's head in his lap. Drake appeared to be in shock. Cassandra noticed an automatic rifle resting on the ground nearby.

"He shot my brother!" the younger man cried.

"Phil, I'm sorry. I didn't mean to. I thought—"

"You shot Kip!" he accused.

"Son, I didn't realize . . . I—"

"Drake, I'm sorry to interrupt, but we need to get out of here. Let's load him up and get to the ER," Monica interjected, then waved her arm around. "This place is going to burn."

"I . . . this wasn't supposed to happen." Tears fell from Drake's eyes.

"Do you have the code for the guesthouse?" Monica questioned, her tone calm but firm.

"I . . ." Drake looked at the other man. "Phil?"

"I do," the younger man answered.

"We need to get Lacey out of there," Monica said.

"Lacey. She's nice to me. I want to play cards with her, but she doesn't want to," he said as he pouted.

Cassandra was slowly emerging from her shock-induced stupor. "Yes, Lacey's in there," she said, working to keep her voice calm. Leo may be dead, but Cassandra would still have Rachel to take out. It's all she had left.

"Then let's help get her out of there before the fire burns her, okay, Phil?" Monica encouraged.

He nodded and then looked at Drake. "Can you hold him, Dad?"

"Of course, Son," Drake replied somberly. Focusing her rage inwardly toward Rachel, Cassandra watched anxiously as Phil stood up, wiping blood on his pants.

"You can just tell us the code, Phil," Monica said calmly.

"No, I can't tell anyone. I have to do it myself." The man spoke mechanically, intent on his new mission. Cassandra suspected he wasn't normal in the head. "Follow me."

Monica maintained her grip on Cassandra's arm as they walked toward the front of the guesthouse. At first they trailed behind, but Monica remembered Leo's body was splayed across the front step and realized it could cause a scene with the childlike man they were following. She leaned over to Cassandra. "Keep him here for a minute," she whispered.

"What?" Cassandra responded, her mind still not fully present.

"Just stall him!" Monica yelled.

Without thinking about why her mother was asking or whether she wanted to obey, Cassandra mumbled, "Okay." As Monica let go of her arm, Cassandra pretended to trip and fall, crying out as she landed on the ground.

Phil turned and walked back to her. "I'll help," he said, reaching out. Cassandra did her best to retain her focus on the young man while Monica dashed around the corner of the house.

"Thank you." She painted her most gracious smile across her face and slowly rose. Only then did Cassandra realize Monica was probably doing something with Leo. Panic struck, and she shook off Phil's hand. "Let's go!" she barked at him. He appeared momentarily taken aback and then began running next to her. Seconds later they rounded the corner; as she'd suspected, Leo was no longer in sight. Cassandra's heart sank, and something deep down finally broke inside of her. She couldn't think. A strange mix of sorrow and rage filled her from head to toe. Her body tensed. Monica appeared from behind thick brush, her gaze catching Cassandra's. She shook her head with a pleading look on her face.

"Lacey," she mouthed.

Cassandra stood, motionless, unable to respond as Phil stepped up to the front door, thankfully oblivious to the red stain on the step. She stepped back so a small tree blocked her from view of Monica and raised her weapon, ready to shoot whoever came out first, unless it was Lacey; then she'd just take out the second person to emerge. Call it her own version of Russian roulette.

~

Hiding around the corner, Luke fought the urge to cough and give himself away too soon. The smoke was thickening, and embers had started to rain down. He couldn't see the two women well enough to make out their faces yet, nor could he hear what they were saying. But they were approaching the front door of the guesthouse with the younger man.

As Luke debated whether to make a move, one of the women tripped. The man next to her turned and reached out his hand. The older woman dashed toward the front door and bent over, seemingly struggling with something heavy. A manzanita bush blocked Luke's view of anything below waist height. She backed up and briefly disappeared behind the corner. The other two perpetrators came around the bend just as the older woman stood up straight.

What would they do to the abductees inside? Luke couldn't risk it; they had to act now. He turned around to Taylor, who stood a foot behind him, and said, "You go approach from the other side." Taylor nodded, turned, and walked away. After he disappeared,

Luke jumped out with his gun raised.

"Open the door," Luke demanded, startling the young man whose fingers were reaching for the locking mechanism.

"I'm putting in the code!" the man replied as if exasperated. This must be Phil, the one Rachel said had been friendly to Lacey, Luke realized. "Was it four or six?" he murmured to himself. Realizing he shouldn't startle the man any further, Luke watched the two women standing off to the side. The older female looked familiar, but he couldn't place where he'd seen her. As she turned and stared back at him, recognition dawned in her eyes.

"You're supposed to be dead!" she exclaimed, pushing the younger woman to the side and stepping toward him with her weapon raised.

"Monica, is that Luke Reed?" the younger woman asked.

Monica? Her identity clicked into place in the back of Luke's mind, and he remembered. This was Monica Jameson, one of the women involved in the scheme that had Rachel and him running for their lives a couple of years ago. She had avoided legal charges even though Ted had pushed the district attorney as hard as he could. The only consequence she'd suffered was the loss of her job with Alpine County.

Monica glared at him, her eyes feral.

"Ms. Jameson, step back," Ted's voice asserted from behind Luke. Ted breathed hard as though he'd just run a marathon.

"You okay?" Luke asked over his shoulder.

"Yeah, but we've got to move. There are over a dozen old gas containers in a barn not far from here and a few look ready to burst." Ted stood next to him with his weapon aimed at Monica. She appeared to consider her options and then lowered her arm.

Luke froze, letting the information about the gasoline sink in, and turned to the young man who remained intent on the locking mechanism. "Please, get that code entered so we can all get the hell out of here!" He stepped back and glanced around the side of the house, a wall of flames now visible in the forest not too far away. No doubt embers had already landed throughout the property, including on the barn Ted had mentioned. In his periphery, he observed Monica place her weapon on the ground and slowly stand back up with both of her hands extended above her head.

Luke watched Phil's shaky fingertips punch in a six-digit code, and a small green light flickered across the lock pad. The door was pulled inward, and the young girl rushed out first, her eyes searching frantically around her. Phil stumbled back.

Taylor appeared from around the corner across from Luke. "Lacey, my name is Captain Taylor with the South Lake Tahoe Police Department. Please, come over here, and we'll get your friends out." His voice was calm and reassuring as he reached out his hand and beckoned her over. The girl looked shaken, but she complied. Once she was safely behind him, Taylor looked up at Luke. "I confiscated the guy's rifle," he said, holding up what looked like an AR-15.

Luke nodded and turned back toward the open door. No one else came through. "Tanner? Rachel?" he shouted as he stepped through the doorway. A wall of heat slammed into him. Light from the headlights bounced off the columns of smoke swirling inside the room.

"Over here!" The teenage voice was shaky and broken by a fit of coughing. Luke followed the sounds, his watery eyes struggling to see details. He could make out Tanner, bent over and apparently struggling with Rachel. She was folded across herself, coughing and heaving while she tried to crawl toward the front door, holding one of her arms close to her chest.

"I'll get her, kid. You get outside."

"But—"

"Go!" Luke insisted as he kneeled down next to Rachel. He reached out to touch her arm, and she flinched. Something moist coated his fingers. *No. Please, no.*

He saw Tanner finally move back, turn, and quickly run out the front door.

"I've got you," Luke said, carefully wrapping his arm around her back and underneath her armpits, hoping he wasn't making whatever her wound was worse as he moved her. The blood appeared to be thickest on her arm, but he wasn't certain.

"It's just my bicep, nothing major," she said as they advanced. Time slowed as the heat and flames billowed around them.

~

Ted kicked the gun Monica had placed on the ground; it slid about ten feet away. He glanced over at the older man holding his dying son. He didn't look like he was paying them any attention, but one never knew. Movement in the doorway caught Ted's attention, and Tanner stumbled out. Ted's heart lifted with relief. "Tanner!" he hollered. Just as the kid looked his way, Ted noticed movement to his other side. His brain comprehended that the younger woman with the curly blonde hair was aiming a weapon straight at Tanner. Ted jumped in front of the teenager a split second before something pounded into his chest. More pain exploded in his neck. He fell back, knocking the boy down to the ground. He heard Taylor yelling from somewhere nearby, but he couldn't focus. The pain was so intense. Ted gasped for air. Tanner squirmed underneath him, but it was as if Ted had no control over his body anymore. He couldn't move. He just lay there trying to fill his lungs while staring up into the smoke-filled sky.

"Ted!" the boy shrieked from below him. Finally, the teen managed to wrangle himself free. His head appeared in Ted's line of sight, fear tightening the otherwise soft skin on the boy's face. "Your neck!" Tanner cried. Ted heard coughing nearby, followed by Luke's voice.

"Ted?" Luke's visage appeared overhead, just shy of touching Tanner's forehead. "Oh shit! Tanner, help loosen his vest," Luke shouted as he ripped his shirt off and pressed it against Ted's bleeding neck. "Stay with me, buddy," Luke croaked. Ted wanted to listen, but his vision was growing dark. Noises merged in the background, and he drifted, the pain fading as his awareness floated away.

Chapter Thirty-Nine

Luke tried to keep his wits about him as he pressed his shirt into Ted's neck. The blood wasn't spraying out as would be expected if a carotid artery had been hit. But neck wounds were serious business more often than not. Sounds whirled around him, the gusting wind blowing against the trees and the ripping of Velcro straps as Tanner undid the bulletproof vest, as Luke tried to keep pressure on Ted's wound. Then a shot rang out a second after Taylor roared, "Put it down!" Another man, Luke thought it was Phil, bawled out something about Kip. Nearby, Rachel's coughing fits were slowing, and he suddenly felt the warmth of her next to him.

"Ted? No . . . ," she cried, her voice hoarse.

"He's still alive," Luke assured her.

Luke heard her choke back sobs before she asked, "What can I do?"

Before he could answer, Tanner spoke distantly, as if he didn't realize he was saying it out loud. "There's a bullet stuck in the vest. Right over his chest."

"We need to get him to a hospital!" Luke yelled to no one in particular.

"He saved me. Oh my God, he saved me," Tanner recited. All of Luke's focus remained on keeping his friend alive.

~

After stumbling over a body on the side of the house, Taylor made it back to the front just as Lacey ran out. As he tucked Lacey behind him, Ted kicked the older woman's gun to the side. Taylor glimpsed the younger woman, but the shadows from the headlights dancing in the smoke-infused air blurred her image. There was no time to stop her when she raised her arm and fired; it happened so fast. He heard two shots; both Ted and Tanner went down. Taylor instructed Lacey to drop to the ground as he fired back at the younger woman. She moved just as he pulled the trigger, and the bullet hit her wrist rather than her chest as he'd intended. She yelped, and her weapon dropped to the ground. She clutched the arm of the older woman with her uninjured hand, and the two dashed behind the vehicle.

Taylor couldn't chase her without leaving Lacey wide open, so he let them go and tuned in to the commotion next to him, his heart deflating as he saw that Ted wasn't getting up. The fear in Luke's voice told him it wasn't good.

"What's going on, Luke?" Taylor asked as he kept his eyes on the retreating women. For a moment, no one answered.

"Ted's been shot. His neck," Rachel sputtered over her shoulder.

"He's alive?" Taylor was afraid of the answer.

"Yes, it's not the carotid," Luke said matter-of-factly. Taylor let out the breath he hadn't realized he'd been holding. They had to get Ted to a hospital immediately. He glanced at the father holding his bleeding son nearby; neither had moved. He didn't like leaving them here, but Ted's situation was priority.

"Lacey, stay down," he shouted as he jumped forward and retrieved the two weapons nearby. He dashed back to the girl, his mind reeling. Where had the car in front of them come from? Were the keys inside? He began to creep behind the vehicle, intending to come around where the two women were hiding. Just as he passed the trunk, Taylor saw them both sprint toward the back of the yard. *Son of a bitch.* He had to let them go. Ted didn't have much time. He swung the driver's door open and reached inside. Keys dangled from the ignition, just as he'd hoped.

"Lacey, get inside on the back seat," he said as he opened the door and motioned her inside. He climbed into the front seat and started the engine.

~

Monica ducked next to her daughter, and both women used her car as a temporary shield.

"What the hell is going on here, Cassie?" Not that she expected an answer. But how was Luke alive? "I thought you said Luke died?" It wasn't the appropriate time or place for the conversation, but everything had become so out of hand that Monica didn't know what else to do.

To her surprise, Cassandra replied as if her trance had finally broken. "He did. I stayed there watching for a while afterward. That other guy, who I didn't know was a cop at the time—by the way, thanks for sending me out without that little tidbit—did CPR for a long time. My view of Luke was blocked by bushes, but Ted looked frantic." Cassandra sucked in a breath.

"You really screwed up this time! And now you go and shoot a cop? Do you have a death wish?" Monica spewed out questions, so angry at seeing Luke and Rachel, both still alive, that she needed to yell at someone. Cassandra and her screwups made the perfect target.

"Save it. We need to move now!" Cassandra gripped Monica's arm and pulled her along. Both women ran toward the direction where they'd last seen Drake and his sons, knowing the back of the guesthouse would block them from the view of others. Flames engulfed the entire corner of the structure. The heat was too intense, forcing them to keep their distance. Monica glanced back toward the front and then looked at her daughter.

"We can't let Rachel get away. *I* can't." Without thinking, Monica started to run back toward Rachel's direction. She didn't worry about what the others would do. Blind rage coursed through her veins. *That bitch wasn't walking away this time. Hell no!*

"Let it go, Monica." Drake's authoritative voice broke through the commotion surrounding her.

She stopped and turned around. Between the light from her vehicle's headlights and the flames of the burning building, she could easily see his expression. Drake, sitting on the ground and embracing his son's head, looked like a man who'd given up on life.

"It's over. You're daughter's been shot. I suggest you help her." His regard moved from her eyes to somewhere in the distance behind her. Conflicting emotions flickered on his face like the swaying flames nearby.

"Where?" she asked, looking at Cassandra, realizing her daughter was holding her hand close to her stomach. Something dark glistened in the amber-colored light. Her hand or her gut? Given Cassandra was still standing, she assumed the former and less life-threatening location. Cassandra looked her way, a mixture of anger and pain on her face.

Drake's voice diverted her attention. "Where's Leo?"

"She shot him!" Cassandra accused.

"You what?" Drake looked at Monica as though he saw her for the first time.

"You should be thanking me after how he dumped you! You ungrateful little slut!" Monica screamed, wanting to scratch her nails down her daughter's face and remove the condemning look. She felt pulled in different directions, unable to concentrate on what to do next. She needed to move—to do *something*. She tried to push past Drake, but his solid body stopped her momentum.

Anger flowed from him in waves, yet he seemed to swallow it down and speak calmly. "We need to go." He turned, looked somewhere in the distance, and then redirected back her way. "Now, help me get my sons."

Monica debated and eyed his empty hands.

"I'm a lot faster than you, woman," he warned. She raised her eyes and looked straight at him. Monica believed him. "Good. I'm going to get my SUV. You go over there and help Phillip with Kip," he instructed, almost choking at Kip's name, and then he took off toward the main house. She turned back around, resigned.

~

Cassandra's wrist burned. As Monica and Drake argued, she frantically considered what she could wrap around it to stop the bleeding. After Drake ran off toward his vehicle, Monica approached Cassandra and kneeled.

"How is it?" she asked, but Cassandra could hear the fake concern in her words. A level of contempt Cassandra had never felt before boiled through her, so she jumped up and pushed Monica with such intensity that the woman stumbled backward. Her body crashed into the burning edge of the guesthouse, and the flames enveloped her.

Cassandra remained still, frozen in place, watching as Monica struggled.

"Help me!" she screamed. Her hair caught fire. All Monica had to do was push against the structure and propel herself away from it. Yet she seemed too far gone to focus. Cassandra watched, transfixed, as Monica fell backward amidst collapsing wood. It was as if the burning house were eating her up. A disturbing odor she assumed to be burnt flesh tinged her nostrils, momentarily overtaking the smell of wildfire smoke. Cassandra breathed through her mouth to minimize the odor as her shoulders relaxed.

Years of her mother's tortured demands and constant badgering raced through her mind like a collection of video clips on fast-forward. Orange and blue flames danced in front of her where her mother had been standing moments before. She thought she saw arms reaching out, but it could have just been her mind playing tricks on her.

Barely penetrating the screams coming from her mother, tires squealed from behind Cassandra. She turned as the car stopped; Drake jumped out and paused as he regarded the direction from which Monica's fading shrieks were emanating. Horror flashed across his features before he looked back at Cassandra with renewed determination. He jumped into action again, rushing around to her side and opening the back door.

"Let's slide Kip in here," he said to no one in particular. "Phillip, help this woman move your brother, then sit in the back with him." The younger man who'd been holding the body began moving.

"I'll get under his arms. You grab his legs," Drake said. It took a moment for Cassandra to realize he was talking to her. Her wrist throbbed, but the no-nonsense voice was a welcome distraction; it gave her something to focus on other than the pain. After a brief glimpse in the direction she suspected Monica had placed Leo's body, she nodded and stood. They got Kip loaded in the car. Cassandra didn't see what good it would do. The man was already dead by the looks of his pale face and sightless eyes. Just like Leo's. The younger man Drake had called Phillip held up the legs and sat underneath them before shutting the door.

Cassandra dove at the handle for the front passenger side, realizing Monica's screams from behind her had stopped. She wrenched the door open and slid in, worried any delay might mean she'd lose her ride and be stuck here. They began to move just as she picked up her foot and closed the door. Drake turned the car around so quickly she flashed back to childhood days spent at Disneyland on the teacup ride that swung her in circles at high velocities. Nausea formed in her stomach. She looked up just as they whizzed by an older vehicle parked in front of the main house. She saw the outlines of several people inside. Drake didn't even flinch as they passed by.

"Are you taking him to the ER?" she asked, even though it would be futile. He was dead. She'd be too if she didn't stop her own bleeding wound. Cassandra tore at her sleeve with her good hand, getting just enough material to wrap around her wrist. Unable to tie it, she simply pressed it firmly against her wound. The car skidded to the right as they turned onto the main road.

Cassandra dared another question. "My car's just up the road. Can you drop me off?" She waited. No response. She saw the dirt path ahead on the right. "It's right up here," she pointed. The car suddenly jerked to a stop.

"Out!" Drake commanded. She opened the door and jumped, the back tire barely missing her feet as he sped away.

~

Kneeling, Rachel sobbed as she watched Luke frantically try to save Ted. Her own pain felt distant now, and she was dimly aware of Taylor and Lacey leaving. She reached into her pocket to retrieve her cell so she could provide more light for Luke but realized she didn't have it. Needing something to do other than stare at Luke's efforts, she turned and looked at the situation around them. The fire seemed to be everywhere. They would already be engulfed if not for the wide driveway and parking area where there was nothing for the falling embers to ignite. A new set of headlights appeared, and she froze until she realized the vehicle was passing by.

From somewhere else a car door slammed, drawing her attention away from the destruction around her.

"Let's get him loaded," Taylor instructed as he kneeled next to Luke. "Tanner, you get his feet. I'll lift his back. Luke, keep whatever you have pressed there in place. On three: one, two, three." Rachel scrambled to her feet as they followed Taylor's plan and carefully lifted Ted. Luke crawled into the middle section of the sedan as the other two carefully positioned Ted across the seat. Tanner jumped in next to him. Lacey remained on the other side, leaving the front passenger seat unoccupied.

"Rachel, let's go!" Taylor's shout penetrated the fog that had filled her mind while watching the grim scene. She reacted instantly, dashing into the vehicle.

Just as she was going to close the door, Taylor slammed on the accelerator. The momentum caused the door to swing shut on its own. She looked out the window and was mesmerized by the scene now slowly receding behind them. The fire was spreading fast like a starving creature devouring its much-desired meal. A large red-orange cloud sprayed up into the air a second before a large boom shook the car. Her heart beat erratically as she twisted around to look in the back seat. She noticed Tanner was also gazing out the back window, his eyes wide and reflecting the firestorm behind them.

"Tanner, are you okay?" she asked, injecting more calm into her voice than she felt. He stared a moment longer, turned, and locked gazes with her. "I'm not hurt, if that's what you mean."

"That's good enough for now," she said. When their distance from the fire increased, light grew faint in the car. Rachel began to feel the throb of her shoulder as the adrenaline surge waned.

"We need some light in here," Luke said.

She heard Taylor speak to Lacey. A second later, the overhead light came on.

"Rachel, your arm!" Tanner exclaimed.

"I'm fine." It pounded, but she was alive. They were all

alive—for now. She had to stay strong; Ted needed attention more than she did.

"You'd better be," Luke said as he glanced up at her with a somber expression on his face. She nodded.

"So had Ted," she said, her eyes filling with tears.

The car grew silent until Taylor talked to Lacey again, but his voice faded as Rachel leaned back in the seat and rested her head against the side window. The pain in her shoulder intensified. She felt weak. The strong odor of smoke and sweat penetrated the car. She closed her eyes, letting herself drift away as they sped down the road. The sound of oncoming sirens briefly awakened her. She opened her eyes and saw flashing red lights speed by them in the opposite direction. She couldn't bear to think of the devastation the growing fire might bring. She drifted off again, wishing it was all just a bad dream. At one point she thought she heard Luke calling out to her, but her mind refused to answer.

Chapter Forty

Barely able to stand, Rachel climbed out of the police cruiser. Exhaustion and pain were taking their toll. The sun beamed overhead, but Rachel barely noticed. Tanner slid out from next to her and grabbed her free arm. She leaned into him and turned back around.

"Thanks for the ride," she said to the officer.

"Sure, Miss Winters," the woman responded. "I'll stay out here and keep an eye on the place for now." The officer had been friendly, but she also hadn't pushed when Rachel didn't want to hold a conversation on the drive back from the emergency room.

Tanner closed the car's door, and they began to walk up the driveway of the hideaway she'd shared with Luke. Rachel squinted at the sky. While it was partially blocked by pine trees, she could see the dense plume of smoke in the distance and smell the smoke in the air. The fire had grown to over twenty thousand acres overnight; however, the firefighters expressed optimism at slowing the spread given the current lack of wind. Even so, it had no doubt already done a lot of damage.

The front door burst open, and Jill came rushing out.

"Tanner!" she shrieked, rushing to her son. He let go of Rachel as if anticipating the wave of maternal energy that was about to overwhelm him. Rachel smiled as Jill wrapped her arms around her boy and held on tight.

"Mom, I can't breathe," he finally whispered. Jill relaxed and stepped back, her hands reaching up to his face.

"I'm sorry. I was just so worried." Jill's fingertips paused when they touched the greasy ointment the nurse had applied around his mouth. "What's this?" She looked closer. "Tanner, what happened?"

"The guy who took me put duct tape over my mouth."

Jill examined him more closely as she bit her lip. "Does it hurt?"

"Not right now. They put some goop on it at the hospital," he said.

Rachel suspected he was holding back for Jill's sake because from what she'd seen it had hurt.

"Is Nikki here? And Grandma?"

"No, they didn't come. But they are safe. I promise," Jill said. She glanced one more time at his face before turning to Rachel. Her eyes swept over the sling holding Rachel's left arm in place. "And you're okay? I'd hug you, but . . ."

"I'm fine." Rachel smiled through the lie. The local anesthetic was wearing off. Rachel refused anything stronger than ibuprofen, but part of her began questioning that decision on the ride home. "Did Taylor tell you what happened?" Rachel asked, wondering why Jill hadn't been warned of their physical conditions.

"He just said everyone was getting checked out at the ER and to hold tight here. That Tanner was fine, you were injured but going to be okay. Luke was waiting with Ted. Taylor mentioned Ted was shot, but he had his vest on?"

Rachel sighed. Apparently she was going to have to be the one to tell Jill about Ted. They had known each other since childhood; this was going to be hard. "Let's go inside, and we'll explain everything." She began to walk. The other two followed. "Are the pups inside?" she asked, noting the front door was wide open but no canines had greeted her.

"Yes. When I saw you drive up, I put them in your room and closed the door, thinking the officers might come inside and the greetings would be too much chaos." Jill walked behind them as Tanner helped Rachel inside. The door closed, and Jill maneuvered by them, quickly hugging Tanner again before passing by.

"Mom!" he complained, and Rachel couldn't help but smile at the interaction.

"Ready for your girls?" Jill asked as she bounced down the hall.

"Yes," Rachel said, feeling their positive energy even before Jill opened the door and Bella and Avi surged out. A quick glimpse at Jill, a sniff of their snouts, and they turned, heading straight for Rachel.

"Hold on, you two. Don't knock her down!" Tanner laughed as he lowered. He caught Avi but was unable to keep Bella from slipping by and running to Rachel. Thankfully, Bella was not one to run directly into people no matter how excited she was; that was more of an Avi trait. Rachel kneeled and wrapped her free arm around Bella, propping her head against the dog's neck as her fingers massaged Bella's ears.

"It's okay, Tanner. You can let her go," she said, looking at Avi. He complied, and Avi dashed into place next to her sister. After several moments of excited hugs, the energy calmed. Rachel sat fully on the floor, her good hand flying between rubbing one dog, then the other, then back again. Tanner bent over and joined the reunion.

"Okay, looks like the greeting ceremony has died down. Now tell me what's going on? How's Ted? Luke?" Jill stood, staring at Rachel from where she leaned against the kitchen countertop.

Rachel didn't want to tell her the sad news while sitting on the floor, so she used her free arm to boost herself up. "Let's sit down," she instructed. She walked around and sat on a stuffed chair that faced the sofa. Jill looked tense as she came around and positioned herself across from Rachel. Tanner flopped down next to his mother. The two dogs followed Rachel and perched at her heels.

"Rachel, you're scaring me," Jill said, her voice shaking.

"Ted's hurt pretty bad," Rachel finally said. Jill's expression changed, her smile immediately erased.

"But he's alive?"

"Yes, for now." Rachel leaned back.

"He s . . . saved my life, Mom," Tanner stuttered.

"Oh, Tanner," Jill said, reaching out and placing her arm across her son's shoulders. "That sounds like something he'd do." She looked back at Rachel. "How bad?"

"He was shot twice. His vest caught one bullet, but the other went through his neck."

"His neck?" Jill abruptly sat up, rigid.

"It missed the carotid. I'll let the doctors explain the details, but they said if he had to get shot in the neck, it was the best place for it to happen." Bella rested her muzzle on Rachel's leg. Rachel reached out to pet her. "He lost a lot of blood, Jill." Rachel held back tears. "He's still in surgery. Luke's going to call as soon as there's any word. But we need to be prepared . . ." She let the words trail off.

Jill raised her hand to her mouth, and tears flooded her eyes. "No. He can't. Not Teddy," she cried.

"I'm sorry, Mom. They'd just opened the doors, and it was so hot and smoky inside. I was coughing. Luke was helping Rachel. I ran out without thinking and—"

"Oh, honey, none of this is your fault. You hear me?" She squeezed him closer and tipped her head against his. "None of this!" she reiterated with vehemence. Rachel watched as Tanner nodded. Jill turned to Rachel. "Did they catch whoever was involved?"

"I think the owner of the house and his sons, one dead, are still missing. Did Taylor mention anything about Monica Jameson or her daughter, Cassandra?"

"Yeah, but he didn't say what happened to them."

"Cassandra got away, but she was intercepted by the officers who'd just set up a roadblock minutes before; they didn't know the details at that time. Apparently she tried to pretend to be a resident in the area, but the odor of smoke on her was strong, and the officer also noticed smeared ash on her cheeks. When questioned about it, she threw her car into gear and tried to ram through the barrier. She was arrested on the scene. When Taylor later asked her where Monica was, she said her mother had burned in the fire."

"Cassandra was that woman's daughter?"

"Yeah, and every bit as messed up as Monica. Even worse, I'd say. Turns out she's the one who tried to kill Luke that day out along Silver Creek." Rachel stood up. "I don't know the full story and don't think anyone does yet. I had all but forgotten about the woman's existence after she was wrapped up in that deal with Mike Roe."

"That's right. She lost her job, but they didn't have enough to arrest her, if I recall?"

"Yes. Apparently she's harbored some strong feelings toward Luke and me all these years." Rachel stepped around the two dogs. "And now Ted's paying the price," she added.

"Can I get you something?" Jill asked.

"No, just need to use the restroom. I'll come back and give you the full rundown on what else I know."

"Is there anything we can do?"

"Just wait," Rachel said, then walked down the hall. As she emerged from the restroom a minute later, she detoured into her bedroom. The pain was immense now. Rachel tossed back two ibuprofen. The hospital had wanted to keep her there longer, but she'd refused. At that point Tanner had been checked out and was ready to go, and Taylor told her Jill was waiting for them back at the house in Pioneer. Luke hadn't been pleased to see her go, yet he eventually conceded and promised to call with any news of Ted.

"So is there any reason to think this guy with the two sons will come after you now? Either of you?" Jill asked, looking from Rachel to her son.

"No, they had several chances to take us out, but they didn't. Taylor also thinks he saw one of them stopping Monica from coming toward us with a gun in her hand. But they're still posting an officer outside."

"Okay, good." Jill jumped up. "I need to go to the hospital; I need to see Teddy."

"He's still in surgery."

"I don't care. He can't die," she cried. "He saved my son!"

Rachel nodded, understanding she couldn't stop her friend.

"Tanner, will you be okay going back with me?" Jill asked.

"Can't I stay here with Rachel?" Tanner whined.

"I need you next to me, so I know you're okay," Jill stammered as she looked around the room. For what, Rachel couldn't determine.

Tanner looked at Rachel; she nodded encouragingly. The boy visibly sagged but complied. "Okay, but can I grab something to eat first?"

"Of course," Jill exclaimed, and she reached out for him again. Another hug. The boy winced, but Rachel didn't think it was from pain this time.

"Mom . . ."

"Oh, sorry." She backed away, dropping her arms.

Tanner raided the kitchen, grabbing several snack foods and making a quick sandwich. He threw it all into a small bag and grabbed one of Luke's Gatorades. "Okay, I'm ready."

Once they left, Rachel dropped onto the sofa and stared at the ceiling. She still hadn't yet processed all that had happened. Nor could she accept that Ted might not pull through. She closed her eyes, but the image of his pale face and blood-smeared neck wouldn't leave her mind. Two furry figures cuddled up next to her. Exhaustion gripped Rachel; all she wanted to do was sleep. But she had a call to make first.

~

Derek looked at the unknown number displayed on his phone. Normally he would let it go to voice mail, but not tonight. Not when he was waiting to hear from his sister, knowing she was in danger but not knowing why or how.

"Hello?"

"Hey, Big Brother," Rachel said with a cracked and tired voice.

Derek smiled, feeling the tension he hadn't even known was there begin to leave his body. "Rachel, it's so good to hear your voice." Derek saw Kris look up from her laptop with an anxious expression on her face.

"Put her on speaker!" she said as she patted the sofa next to her, clearly wanting him to move closer. Derek obeyed on both accounts.

"Is that Kris?" Rachel asked.

"I'm here, girl," Kris responded instantly.

"You are spending time with my brother again *on purpose*?" Rachel joked.

"All for you, my friend. It's a worthy sacrifice." At her response,

Derek playfully nudged her rib. Kris rolled her eyes. "Are you okay? Ted hasn't told us much."

There was hesitation before Rachel spoke again. Derek wondered why she paused but didn't say anything.

"It's a long story. But just know that I'm okay. Dogs are good too." The soft chiming of dog tags could be heard in the background.

"Are you down by Jackson somewhere?" Derek asked. "Ted asked us to look up a property down that way."

"I'm back in Pioneer now. Luke's still—"

"Luke?" Derek and Kris interrupted in unison.

"Oh, that's right," Rachel laughed nervously. "It turns out he's alive; the whole death thing was meant to protect him from someone who wanted to make it happen for real." Derek didn't know what to say.

After a brief pause, Kris began peppering Rachel with questions. "And no one told you? Who knew? How long?"

"Like I said, long story. I'll tell you both when I get home."

"Which will be . . . ?" Derek let the question hang.

"I expect in the next day or two."

Derek looked at Kris. She looked just as confused as he felt.

"Why not now?" he asked. Rachel sighed. Derek had learned there were three kinds of sighs from his sister: one, the "you're-an-idiot" sigh; two, the "I'm-really-tired-can-we-talk-later" sigh; and three, the "bad-news" sigh. The latter was what he heard now.

"Ted was shot. It's bad. He was brought to the ER in Jackson. He's in surgery now. That's where Luke is."

Derek saw Kris slump at this news as her eyes widened. A small pang of jealously ran through him, and he chastised himself for it. Ted was a good guy who had helped his sister out a lot. And the guy was cool to hang out with from time to time. How could he even be feeling something as petty as jealousy when Ted was apparently fighting for his life? Derek needed to comfort Kris, not be a grade A asshole. He reached over and gently grasped her hand. It wasn't something he ever did with women, but he sensed she could use the touch.

"How bad, Rachel?" Kris finally asked.

"It went through his neck. Missed the carotid thankfully. He's in surgery now."

"Should we come down there? Is there something we can do to help?" Kris said as she squeezed Derek's hand, shooting him an appreciative glance.

"No, nothing you can do other than send good thoughts his way."

"You'll let us know when there's news?" Kris said as tears began to fill her eyes.

"Definitely, and I'm sorry for not explaining this all now. I've been up all night, and I'm beat. And this shoulder pain—"

"Wait, what?" Derek snapped.

"Oh, sorry. Nothing to worry about. Just got a little nick of something in my arm. That's all."

Derek looked at Kris, unable to hide his exasperation with his sister. "Just how did you end up involved in this situation, whatever it is?"

"I'll tell you more later, but there seems to be a tie with someone I went on a date with recently. Kris, you remember the firefighter?"

"Huh? Oh, yeah." Kris paused and then reacted as if suddenly recalling a bad memory. "I encouraged you to go on that date, didn't I?"

"No need to start guilt-tripping yourself, and remember I'm a big girl. You didn't force me to go; I went of my own free will. Anyway, he told me something he wasn't supposed to and it led to some unfortunate consequences. Still learning all the details."

"You've got a lot of explaining to do when you get home, Sis," Derek said, still hung up on the "little nick" in her arm but decided to let the other topic go for now.

"I know, and I will. Thank you both for helping out . . . Ted." Rachel stumbled over his name.

When the call ended, Kris quietly set the phone on the coffee table and reclined into the sofa. Derek continued to stare at the phone for a few seconds longer.

"Shit," he finally said, brushing his hand through his hair.

"Yeah, that's about right," Kris replied. Their hands remained locked together.

Derek wasn't sure if she even noticed it anymore, but then she turned and their eyes met. "Thanks for, I don't know, being here? Although I'm the one who invited myself over." A sad smile pursed her lips.

"You can invite yourself over to wherever I'm at anytime." And he actually meant it, even though he couldn't recall ever saying that to a woman before. He reached up with his free hand and swiped at a tear falling across her cheek. "Anything I can do to help?" Derek hadn't meant it in any way other than as a friendly gesture.

She closed her eyes and let her face drop against his palm. "Just let me stay around for a little while so I can process all of this," she responded.

He nodded, loving the feel of her soft skin against his fingertips.

Kris continued, "Ted has to be okay. He has to be. He's like that friend that you never worry about; they always get through any situation. I've always thought of him as invincible."

"Sounds like a strong guy who has a good chance of pulling through."

Kris nodded, but when she started to cry, he pulled her against him. To his surprise, she didn't resist and nestled her head against his chest.

"You know what's ironic? My first thought when we knew something was wrong was that Rachel got herself mixed up in something again. And here it turns out to have started with a date I encouraged. How messed up is that?"

"Not messed up at all. I had the same thought," he said as he grinned, even though she couldn't see it.

"Sometimes, Derek Winters, you can be an okay guy," she chuckled, then sniffled.

"Yeah, just don't tell anyone, okay? It will ruin all the intrigue."

~

"How is he?" Rachel asked Luke by way of answering his call. She sounded groggy.

"He made it through surgery," Luke replied, and he heard Rachel exhale.

She finally spoke again. "What's the prognosis?"

"It missed the major stuff, as you know, but he still lost a lot of blood. I think that has them worried the most at this point."

"So now what?"

Luke rubbed his forehead and reached for the can of Red Bull he'd bought from a vending machine; it was his third today. "We wait. They don't expect him to wake up for a while. In fact, they told me to go get some rest, but I can't leave him alone. I just can't."

"Jill's on her way."

"She is? What about Tanner?" Luke figured that poor boy had to be exhausted.

"He's with her. I think Jill was afraid to be separated from him."

"Can't blame her." Luke rested his head against the wall. He had tried lying on the seats in the waiting room somewhere around two or three in the morning to no avail. His body was now spent, but his mind kept racing. Worrying. Just as he closed his eyes, his aim to concentrate only on the sound of Rachel's voice, he heard commotion from across the room. Wondering what the fuss was, he opened his eyes.

An awkward-looking man roughly Luke's age had burst into the ER and ran up to the counter. "Where is my mother? And sister?" he blurted. The nurse behind the desk looked confused and annoyed.

"What are their names, sir?"

"Monica Jameson and Cassandra O'Conner."

Luke perked up, barely hearing Rachel's voice as she asked a question. "Hold on a sec," he said, following the unfolding conversation in front of him.

"And you are?" The nurse tipped her chin and observed the man over the top of her bifocals.

"Seth. Seth O'Conner. My mom went back to her maiden name when—"

"I don't have a Monica here, but there is a Cassandra O'Conner."

"Where is she?" The man tapped the counter.

The nurse sidestepped the question. "Let me have someone come speak with you."

"Just tell me which room!"

"Mr. O'Conner. Your sister is under arrest and currently being guarded by several of our officers. You're going to have to take a seat and wait until someone can come speak with you." The nurse waved her hand toward the almost empty waiting room. The man sank as she spoke. The woman had clearly perfected her calm but direct schoolteacher voice.

Luke focused back on the phone call. "Rachel, do you know a Seth O'Conner?" He waited for her response, picturing the texts he'd read earlier. The phone line went silent. He watched the dejected man turn away from the counter and take a seat across the room from Luke.

"Why do you ask?"

"Because he just walked in here," he whispered, after which he heard Rachel gasp. "Who is he?"

"Someone I went on a few dates with recently. Nothing serious," she added. "What do you mean he's *there*?" Luke could hear the utter confusion in her voice.

"He just stormed into the ER asking for his mother and sister."

"Odd, but what does that have to do with—"

"Monica and Cassandra," he explained. Her rapid intake of breath revealed her shock.

"Are you kidding me?" she finally said. "That son of a bitch!" And the rant began. She could be cute when she was stringing insults together. Finally, she got it out of her system, going silent before adding, "Sorry."

"No problem. But I have to ask, what did you see in this guy?" Luke couldn't help but wonder as he sized up the man. Plus the banter was a nice distraction.

"You really asking me that? Now?"

"Okay, it's maybe a little too early for that."

"What's that supposed to mean?"

Uh-oh. Luke needed to stop digging his hole deeper. He had no idea where things would go with Rachel, but he hoped somewhere. "Nothing. Bad joke in a lame attempt to lighten the mood," he mumbled. Movement outside of the doors caught his attention and he looked up just as Jill erupted through them with Tanner following close behind. She spotted him and swiftly changed direction.

"Luke, is he . . . ?"

"He made it through surgery," Luke said to Jill, then spoke back into the phone. "Let me call you back. Jill and Tanner just arrived."

After explaining what the doctors had said about Ted's condition, Luke yawned. He knew one could not continue to survive on energy drinks alone.

Jill must have noticed. "Luke, why don't you go back to the house and get some rest. We'll be here if Teddy wakes up." Jill grabbed his hand. "Seriously, you look like you need to sleep for about three days." She paused and then leaned toward him. "Did you get over your, er, food poisoning?"

The way she said it made him wonder if she knew what he was really doing. He doubted Rachel would have told her. Maybe she assumed he'd just been avoiding Rachel?

"It's better. Thanks," he said.

"You look like the walking dead. Go!" she instructed with what he concluded was her "mother voice."

Tanner looked at Luke as if warning him to listen.

Luke stood. "By the way, that guy over there?" He pointed where only she could see his gesture. "That's Seth. Some guy Rachel's been dating. Anyway, he just came in asking for his mother and sister. None other than Monica and Cassandra."

"You have got to be kidding me!" Jill exclaimed in a hushed tone, trying not to peer over at the man. "And they aren't dating, by the way. Went out a few times, but it never went anywhere. She was going to end it the night you 'died' but didn't get the chance." Jill lingered for a moment as though she were concentrating on something, and then anger flashed across her face. "That asshole lied to her about who he was, didn't he?"

"He has a different last name from Monica. But I don't believe for a second he just happened to encounter the very woman his mother was obsessed with for two years. In fact," Luke said as he glanced in the man's direction, "I'm going to have a talk with the jerk on my way out."

"Luke, don't start something. We've got enough to worry about," Jill cautioned. "And you know what? I think you should leave that to Rachel."

Luke considered her advice, finally admitting to himself that she was right. Rachel would want the chance to confront him herself. He respected her for that mentality, but it also drove him nuts sometimes. "You're right. I'll bite my tongue for now."

"Good. Now go get some sleep. Doctor's orders," she said as she smirked.

"Your patients are all dead."

"That's because they didn't listen to their doctor."

"Touché." Luke smiled at Tanner as he walked by. "How you holding up?"

"I'll be okay. Just worried about Uncle Ted."

"He's a fighter. Hold on to that." He gently patted Tanner's shoulder. "You did great tonight; we couldn't have gotten him out of there that quickly without your help."

Tanner nodded and bent his head down as wetness filled his eyes. Luke turned to walk out. He noticed Seth raise his head and look in his direction but saw no recognition in his demeanor.

Chapter Forty-One

Luke was thankful one of the officers had retrieved his car. He dropped into the driver's seat and reached over to the glove box to grab another high-caffeine energy packet. He hesitated and changed his mind. He could manage the twenty-minute drive. He needed sleep, and if he consumed another one now, that would be impossible. He banged the door shut and started the ignition. Although the air outside was cool and heavy with smoke from the wildfire, Luke kept the windows open as he drove north on Highway 88. He was considering slapping himself to stay awake when he came to the street that would take him to the safe house where he'd been staying. Rachel was there, likely sleeping.

He encountered the patrol car just down from the driveway and rolled down his window. The female officer recognized him and waved him by. He pulled the car forward, parked, and quietly made his way up to the front of the house. He hoped the dogs wouldn't get excited at his arrival and wake Rachel. He used the key to unlock the door and slipped inside. Two wet noses pressed against his bare legs as tails swished.

"Shhh . . ." He tried to keep them quiet.

"It's okay. I'm awake," Rachel's tired voice called out from the sofa.

"It's just me," he said. "Sorry to wake you."

"You didn't. I was just dozing anyway." She sat up and reached to rub her eyes but flinched when she tried to lift her wounded arm.

"How's your shoulder?" It was probably a dumb question, but he couldn't help but ask.

"Painful and annoying, but I'll live," she said and then winced. Not from pain, he imagined, but from her words.

"Ted is strong. If anyone can pull through, he can," Luke said as he rounded the corner and sat down next to her.

"I know. I just . . . damn, why does this have to happen?" Anger flashed in her eyes. "What makes a person so messed up that they hold a grudge for years and then try to kill us?" He knew she was talking about Monica and, by extension, Cassandra.

"People suck." He repeated the phrase he'd heard Rachel say sometimes when they were dating, especially after hearing a story about someone harming or neglecting an animal.

As usual, she responded, "And that's why we have dogs." A small smile tugged the edges of her mouth. As though they understood her words, the two canines began nudging her hand. "I can only manage one of you," she said with a laugh. Luke reached over to Avi, who was closest to him, and was pleasantly surprised when she turned and pushed against him.

"I think she's warming up to me," he said as he rubbed the dog's back. "Look, I know we have a lot to discuss, but I suggest we both get some rest and save it for later, if that's okay with you."

"Not a problem at all." Rachel stood up. "Not sure I can sleep, but I'm willing to give it a try."

Luke rose. Rachel moved but tripped over one of the dogs. He caught her, and she corrected her balance. Then she turned up to stare at him.

"My God, you're beautiful," he said without thinking. She didn't respond. Her blue eyes merely gazed into his. The dogs weaved around their legs, but when neither human made any further moves to pet them, they apparently grew tired and trotted off somewhere. "I'm so sorry for all of the hurt I caused you," he said, feeling the warmth of her skin against his arms.

"Later, remember?" she gently admonished.

"Later," he agreed. Without thinking, he leaned down and gently touched his lips to hers. He heard her intake of breath, but she didn't pull back. She didn't move. For a moment, neither did he, just treasuring the closeness. The scent of her skin was tinged with a dash of vanilla.

"We should wait," she whispered, the edge of her lips moving against his. "Talk first, right?"

"Definitely," he replied, but when she didn't move, he reached around and placed his hand against her neck, drawing her closer. Her lips pressed against his, and it was like instant warmth coated his insides. Damn, he had missed this. He'd missed *her*.

Rachel leaned deeper into the kiss, wrapping her free arm around him and pulling his body against hers. He held nothing back, tasting every part of her mouth with his. He trailed kisses across her cheek, making his way to her neck and shoulders. She tilted her head and moaned. Her response encouraged him to keep going. He licked her skin, savoring the sweet taste of her. When his breath caused goose bumps to break out across her flesh, it took all his strength to stop.

"We shouldn't be doing this," he said with his lips paused just above her skin.

"No, we shouldn't," she responded, breathless. But he could tell that she needed the comfort just as much as he did.

"Do you want me to stop?"

"No," she whispered.

The exhaustion he'd felt when he'd arrived just moments before had dissipated into a cloud of longing, love, and memory. He carefully placed his hands underneath her backside and picked her up, holding her against him. She wrapped her legs around his waist and held him tightly with her good arm. Luke gently carried her into her bedroom and placed her on the bed. She looked up at him, her eyes radiant with desire.

"I want to feel what's good in the world. Please," she spoke softly.

"One thing," Luke said as he bounced up and closed the door. "Love your girls but don't want them thinking it's playtime." He grinned, returned, and gently lay on top of her, his fingers skimming the sensitive flesh along her sides as he carefully removed her shirt, taking special care to protect her wounded arm. She rested her head back with an expression of pure bliss on her face as he began kissing every inch of her exposed flesh.

Chapter Forty-Two

When her house first came into view, Rachel yearned for nothing more than her own bed. While she had managed to sleep yesterday afternoon with Luke lying next to her, the subsequent night had been filled with another visit to the hospital to see Ted and more questions from the police. When she'd finally returned to the small house in Pioneer, racing thoughts had kept her awake. Ted hadn't woken up yet, and the doctors were concerned. Jill, Taylor, and Luke had taken turns sitting with him. She'd wanted to but had been instructed by the doctors to rest and take care of her own wound. Today, Ted was being transported to the UC Davis Medical Center for further observation and testing. It had been time for her to return home to Tahoe.

The rental parked in front of her house reminded Rachel that she owed Derek a lengthy explanation.

"You up to seeing my brother?" she asked Luke as he removed the keys from the ignition.

"Probably not, but let's get it out of the way."

Earlier she'd sent Derek a text about her return. He must have been watching because the front door flew open before she'd even approached the first step.

"Rachel!" he called out, running to her and wrapping his arms around her.

"Watch out," she warned as he pressed too hard against her sling.

"Oops, sorry." He backed away and looked her up and down. "You look like crap," he said. Yep, that was Derek. Always ready to kick you when you were down, although she knew he was just teasing her. That's how he expressed his love. Rachel realized Luke had let the dogs out of the vehicle when she felt two muzzles pressing against her legs.

"Nice way to greet your sister," Luke called out from behind her. Derek looked up, the surprised expression on his face revealing he hadn't expected Luke. He'd probably assumed a patrol officer would drive her pickup home. Perhaps she should have given him a heads-up. The two men had gotten along when they'd met over a year ago, yet Rachel sensed Derek had been happy to see them split; however, he'd claimed otherwise when she pressed him about it.

"She's used to it," Derek said, holding his hand out. Luke took it, but Rachel could sense the underlying tension between the two men. "Glad you're not dead," he added. Derek turned back to her. "Need help with anything?"

"I've got it," Luke said, nodding his chin toward the bag slung over his shoulder. "You can grab the dog beds out of the car."

"Sure thing." Derek headed toward the vehicle as Rachel walked into her house and immediately collapsed on the sofa. The dogs burst out the dog door and began playing in the backyard. "I think I need about forty-eight hours of sleep," she sighed as Luke set several bags down in the hall. Derek came in behind them and tossed the beds on the floor.

"I saw another suitcase; I'll go get it," he offered and went back out the door. Rachel looked up at Luke with her brow raised.

"Guess I need to get kidnapped and injured for him to show some manners, eh?" she said as she smiled, although it was a weak one. Her emotions were all over the place. She was worried about Ted and also still trying to process all that had happened. Then there was Luke. She wanted to be with him, but there was so much between them that had to be worked out. It wouldn't be easy.

"Okay, think I got everything." Derek popped back inside and shut the front door. "Need something to drink or eat?" he asked

Rachel, seemingly ignoring Luke.

Rachel answered, "Glass of ice water would be great." She couldn't recall the last time Derek was so intent on helping her like this. It was shocking.

As Derek went into the kitchen, Luke came and sat next to Rachel. He put his hand on her knee and smiled her way.

Derek returned and held out a glass. "Here ya go, Sis," he said, then sat across from them. "Okay, up for telling me what's going on?"

Luke began, starting with the man, Leo, who had been spying on him and playing some sort of watch-wait-scare game until Cassandra had tried to shoot Luke that day he was with Ted out by Silver Creek.

"Wait, who is Leo?" Derek interrupted.

"A hired gunman, but he was actually working to keep us alive. Anyway, it turns out he used to work for Senator Rand Mason. Had a huge beef with the senator after he was apparently forced to take the fall for something the senator had done. Lost his job and his career. All of this is according to Cassandra, so take it with a grain of salt. But I'll get to that more in a minute."

"Got it," Derek responded. "So, this Cassandra—why wouldn't she have just tried to kill you at your house? Why go through all that trouble?"

Luke replied, "According to Captain Taylor, they didn't want local cops involved. It was a lucky coincidence for Monica and Cassandra that Ted and I had plans in Alpine County, where Monica still had connections. Apparently, Cassandra and Monica hadn't realized my plans were with my *cop* friend. She was going to kill us both, but then Leo intervened and probably spared me a gunshot to the head. Ted's fast thinking not only saved me from drowning but got me out of there and hidden well enough that she wouldn't try again."

"Monica's old friend in the county sheriff's office was prepared to doctor the reports," Rachel added.

"Okay, so I get how this started with Luke. How did you get involved, Sis?"

Rachel explained everything she knew, starting with the fire by Cascade Lake and Lacey's kidnapping, Luke being hired to find Lacey, and then the additional information Cassandra had recently revealed to Captain Taylor.

"Cassandra is telling them everything," Rachel explained. "They suspect she has a mental disorder; I think she's setting herself up for an insanity plea. Maybe both, but she's a psychopath. Like seriously messed up. I think she's in a mental ward or something, pending trial. And it turns out Monica was in this up to her eyeballs. She was dating Senator Mason while working in cahoots with Mike Roe."

"Wait, isn't that the guy who came after you before? I thought he was in prison?" Derek leaned forward, confused.

"He is, but he's managed to have a lot of freedoms he shouldn't have. He has some friends in the right places," Luke answered. "It was Mike who hired Leo to keep an eye on us. Strangely, he also directed him to keep us alive. At least that's what Cassandra thinks. Mike isn't admitting to anything, and Leo isn't alive to explain. Captain Taylor has also been talking to Senator Mason, hoping to put the pieces together. Mason says an old mining friend of Mike's approached him about this voting situation—"

"What voting situation?" Derek cut in.

"I'll get there!" Rachel held up her hand. "Senator Mason claims Mike hadn't wanted to get involved, but the old mining 'friend' threatened to harm Mike's daughter if he didn't. So Mike ends up being the one to communicate with the senator, who happened to be having an affair with Monica. The senator asks Monica for help, leading the three to work together, in a sense, yet they each kept their own secrets from the others. The senator also claims he didn't know Monica had a beef with us from the past, nor that Leo, aka Jonathan Lorenson—his ex-chief of staff—was involved."

"This is all so convoluted," Derek said. "What is this big deal that brought all of these jerks together?"

"It's almost ironic," Rachel laughed sardonically. "Prop Forty-Three is on the ballot in the upcoming election. Let me step back. As you know, our current federal administration has been tearing down environmental protections right and left. So California legislators have been proposing bills and other measures to protect our resources in the event the federal government lifts protections. In this case, there was talk that the feds may allow for more destructive mining practices that have been prohibited in certain areas of California for decades due to the extensive environmental damage they cause. Prop Forty-Three would maintain current protections under state law in the event the feds rescind the regulations."

"Okay, I'm following, kind of." Derek waved for her to continue.

"Drake Fischer is the CEO of a major mining company in Nevada. He also owned the property where all of this went down near Jackson. It's right along the Mother Lode, a geological zone known for producing gold, among other precious metals. It seems he didn't want the competition from California."

"All this was about a hypothetical situation like that?"

"That's what we thought at first. But it turns out this Drake guy is a prepper. Do you know what that is?"

"Yeah, saw it on CSI or something," Derek mumbled

"His land was passed down through generations, and his grandfather and father were also preppers. But Granddad had constructed a huge facility underneath the ground."

"Barracks, living rooms, supplies like you wouldn't believe. It was a survivalist's dream," Luke commented.

"He was so worried about it being discovered that he wanted to ensure no one could ever find it," Rachel continued. "His land borders publicly owned lands where intense mining could potentially be allowed if the environmental protections were lifted. That posed the threat that someone could happen upon his underground kingdom. Which as you can imagine, has no permit and therefore isn't listed in any record, anywhere. It's also why we figure he didn't keep Lacey hidden in the bunker. Since he did intend to release her after the election, he didn't want her to be able to tell anyone about it."

"This is unbelievable," Derek scoffed. "What does this have to do with Senator Mason?"

"Mason never supports measures to protect the environment. He's another one of those egotistical, rape-and-pillage-the-land-for-profit bastards who—"

Luke interrupted, "What this boils down to is that Drake needed Mason to use his political influence to rally his supporters to vote yes on Prop Forty-Three."

"Thanks." Rachel smiled at Luke, fully aware that sometimes her political rants needed to be shut down.

"So he had the granddaughter, Lacey, kidnapped to make Senator Mason do all that?"

"Yep. Crazy, isn't it?" Rachel replied. "Set the Cascade fire to facilitate the kidnapping so they could get leverage on the senator, plus reiterate how serious they were. They were going to hold her until after it passed and then supposedly return her. The senator was so worried about what they'd do to Lacey if word got out that he didn't even tell his daughter—the girl's own mother—anything about it. Hence the mother hired Luke. Monica found out and, given her pre-existing hate for Luke, had her daughter, Cassandra, set to kill him. Once they learned I'd been told the Cascade fire had been started by arson, I guess it elevated her desire to see me gone too."

"What's happening to the senator?" Derek asked.

"Not sure yet. But since they can't turn the clock back on the political momentum to support the proposition, it will probably pass," she said, then added, "At least something positive comes from all of this."

"And Monica died in the fire at Drake's place?"

"According to Cassandra. Even if the crazy woman is lying, I don't think there was any way Monica could have gotten out of there on foot before everything blew to hell." Rachel didn't want to think about the destruction the fire had caused so far. Even though it had burned into a mostly undeveloped area, several homes were lost that first night. While firefighters had managed to create some good containment lines in the last twenty-four hours, if winds were to pick up again, it could flare up and advance toward several rural communities in the area.

"Where's this Drake Fischer you mentioned?" Derek asked.

"No one knows. Cassandra said one of his sons was dead by Drake's own gun. He and his other son loaded the body up and left. The cops have been trying to locate them, but so far the trail is cold."

"Will they come after you again?" Derek said as he tensed.

"Doubtful," Rachel commented, and then she explained the reasoning, just as she'd shared with Jill.

"This is too much." Derek's gaze bounced between Rachel and Luke, and then he spoke quietly. "I'm sorry about Ted. He's a good guy. I hope he pulls through this." It was one of the most sincere statements she'd ever heard her brother make.

"Thank you," Rachel said as tears threatened. She wiped her eyes and felt Luke's arm wrap around her. "At least Lacey is back with her parents now."

Derek, typically uncomfortable with any emotional display, changed the subject. "So are you two back together or something?"

"Or something," she said.

"You clean?" Derek, never one to mince words, asked Luke. It took a moment for the meaning of his question to sink into Rachel's mind.

"Yes, but I'll admit only recently."

Rachel looked from her brother back to Luke and then back to Derek. "Wait, Derek, you knew?"

"Aw, crap," Derek said, realizing too late what he'd just given away.

"You knew," Rachel said, this time as a statement. She turned to Luke. "Why didn't you tell me my brother knew?"

"It wasn't for me to say," he responded, although the deer-in-the-headlights look suggested he hadn't wanted to broach the topic at all. Rachel took a deep breath in and exhaled.

"Add it to the list for 'talk later,'" she said to Luke and then turned to her brother. "Same for you." He looked confused but didn't argue. She was about to say more, but the chorus of a Luke Bryan song broke the temporary quiet. Rachel blushed. "Nice to have my original cell phone back, but I forgot to silence it," she muttered, reaching into her pocket. Rachel had to look at the display to see who was calling. As the number registered, Rachel debated about answering, eventually deciding to get this conversation over with. "It's Seth," she said to the men as she stood and walked toward her bedroom for privacy. Luke began to rise, but she shook her head and mouthed, "I'll deal with this."

Rachel closed the door behind her and pressed the button to answer the call.

"Hello, Seth," she said, her voice devoid of any emotion.

"Rachel! I'm so glad you answered! How are you doing? Where are you?"

"First, I'm truly sorry you have to endure the loss of your mother," she said. While Rachel wasn't sorry the woman who had been trying to kill them both was dead, she was sorry for the pain he was no doubt feeling over his mother's death. Even if Seth was a manipulative jerk. She was about to continue when he spoke, his words so fast they almost blended together.

"Yeah . . . I guess it's been in the papers. Thanks. Look, I'd like to see you again. Can we—"

"Are you kidding me?" Rachel exclaimed in astonishment. "We have nothing to talk about. I only answered to tell you to stop calling me. Don't text me. Don't drop by. If you see me around town, walk the other way. I'm serious."

"I'm sorry. I just—"

"Tell me this. Did your mom or sister ask you to keep an eye on me?" Rachel was sure she already knew the answer but wanted to hear him say it. Silent seconds passed as she waited.

Finally, he answered, "My mom did. But I swear, I didn't know what she was up to. She just said to keep an eye on you, learn about your work, that sort of thing. Then I ended up really liking you. Still do."

Rachel found that she believed him, and her anger faded into pity. "Seth, it's not going to happen. Period. This is the last time we'll ever speak." Rachel ended the call and collapsed onto her bed. The tension in her muscles waned and she relaxed, letting out a deep breath. She should feel foolish for falling for his act, but she was simply too tired to care. She heard a light knock on her door.

"Rachel, you okay?" Luke asked.

"Yeah, come on in," she called out. Just as Luke came and sat down next to her, a Garth Brooks song erupted. This time, Jill was calling. Was there news on Ted?

~

"Hi, Rachel, it's me," Jill said as she stared at Ted's pale visage. The hospital room smelled of disinfectant, and the harsh lights augmented the stale atmosphere. Jill spent so much time examining dead people she was used to the scent of decay and the Vicks VapoRub that visitors to the morgue coated their upper lips with. But she wasn't used to these odors. Or the sounds of a heart monitor in the background.

"Hey, girl, where are you?"

"They just got Ted settled in a room at UC Davis. I sent Tanner out to grab something from the vending machine."

"How's he doing?" Rachel asked with a somber tone in her voice. It made Jill want to cry all over again. But no, she had to keep it together, for her son as well as for Ted.

"Same," Jill said. Her voice shook as she continued, "I just needed to hear your voice. I need someone to tell me he's going to be okay." Choking the words out, Jill gave in to her sorrow.

"He's a fighter, Jill. You know that more than anyone," Rachel encouraged.

"I just . . . I've always said he's like a brother to me. And he is. But he's also my best friend. Even though I hold back sometimes, he's there when I need him. I've told him things I haven't told anyone else. I just can't imagine . . ." Her words drifted off as she reached out and touched his cold cheek.

"Don't count him out of the game, Jill. He's already beat the odds and made it this far."

Jill knew Rachel was trying to be positive, but in her mind, beating the odds so far didn't help. In fact, people were likely only given so much luck in this world and maybe, just maybe, her best friend had used his up. "I don't know what to do. I need to get home, see my daughter, hold my kids and my mom close. Damn, Rachel, I haven't even told them about their father yet."

"One thing at a time, Jill."

Jill turned to make sure her son wasn't standing in the doorway before she spoke and then whispered, "That psycho Cassandra said she killed him and hid the body. Can you believe it? It's just so surreal. I hated the jerk but never wished for a second that something like this would happen to him."

"Yeah, Captain Taylor told Luke about that. I'm so sorry."

Jill straightened as if changing her posture would help stem the flow of tears. She wiped at her eyes before glancing behind her again. Tanner had just stepped into the room. With her voice back to a normal volume, she continued, "I wanted to let you know we're going to drive up the mountain tonight so my family can be together. I'll be driving back down here in the next few days, but Captain Taylor is going to stay with Ted for now." Although she was trying to stay strong for her son, she knew she'd failed when Tanner reached over to a side table, picked up the box of Kleenex, and handed it to her. She knew she had raised a fine young man. "Tanner's back now. I'll text you when we're home safe and sound." Jill wiped her cheeks. Once the call ended, she blew her nose and folded her son into her arms. "I love you so much, Tanner. I'm so proud of how you handled all of this."

"It's okay, Mom. I love you too," he said, once again letting her hold him like he used to when he was younger. "Uncle Ted's going to be fine, right?"

Jill released him and stood back. Then she gently caressed his shoulders while she looked him straight in the eyes. "Yes." She hoped she hadn't just told her son the biggest lie of her life.

Chapter Forty-Three

"About time your bro left," Luke teased.

"He only went to the store. He'll be back," Rachel warned. The call from Jill broke her heart all over again. As soon as it ended, the guys had bounced insults and half jokes back and forth, acting as though they were in a competition to elevate the mood in the house. Although there was still tension between them, it was starting to dwindle. Finally, Derek offered to run to the store to pick up dinner items and, as he put it, "some decent beer," and Luke and Rachel gladly agreed.

Luke pulled Rachel against him. "Damn, I missed this," he said, running his fingertips across her arm. Her skin tingled.

"So did I." The warmth of his embrace helped ease some of her anxiety.

"I didn't think I'd get a second chance," he admitted. Rachel sat up and looked at him. His expression was sorrowful, shameful. She decided to lighten the mood.

"What makes you think you're getting a second chance?" she quipped. He stopped rubbing her arm and the blood drained from his face. Rachel hadn't meant to sound serious, so she quickly let a smile warm her lips.

He grabbed her and squeezed her against him. "Honestly, though, I'm not sure I deserve one."

"Look, we all make mistakes. I'm not saying I'm over everything, and we definitely have some work to do, but I'm game to try."

"That's all I can ask," he said as he nuzzled his face against her neck, the touch of his skin against hers an instant turn-on. She shifted and looked at him. Before she could speak, she noticed in her peripheral vision a white paw appear on Luke's leg. So focused on their conversation, Rachel hadn't realized the dogs had come back inside. They both looked down to see Avi staring up at them. The look on her face suggested feigned innocence, and Rachel pictured the dog thinking, "What?"

A second paw appeared next to the first.

"Yep, it's official. She's beginning to warm to me." Luke laughed and patted her head. Bella immediately jumped up on the other side of Rachel and leaned into her.

"Jealous, huh, girl?" She laughed, then spoke to Luke again. "In this household, if you pet one, you've got to pet the other. This one-arm thing is going to be tough," she mused.

"I'll help," Luke said as he looked back at Rachel. "In any way you need me to." The raise of his brow was suggestive.

"You mean like the stack-the-two-cords-of-almond-wood-I-just-had-delivered-last-week kind of help?"

His face dropped. "Well, uh, sure . . ."

"Or did you mean like help-me-in-the-shower kind of help?"

Luke perked up. "Honestly, both, but the second sounds far more enjoyable. What do you say we get started now?"

"You mean stacking the wood?" She played along.

Luke tilted his head, and one side of his mouth lifted in a cocky grin. That look did it every time. "Well, if that's what you want to do right now . . ." He stood up. Avi stared at him like she was offended by the removal of his hand.

Rachel moved to get up, but Bella pushed against her, causing Rachel to bump against Luke's broad chest. He gently steadied her on her two feet, placed his hand behind her neck, and pulled her lips to his. A shock startled them both. Luke looked surprised as he touched his fingers to his lips.

"What the?"

"Static electricity. Bella picks it up from the carpets, blankets, you name it. Sometimes it rubs off."

"No, I think it's just us," he said, pulling her tight against him again and crushing his lips to hers. Rachel reveled in the sweet cinnamon taste of his mouth and the warmth that flooded her body at his touch. For just this moment, here with Luke and her two beloved dogs nearby, she could truly believe that everything would be okay after all.

If you enjoyed this book and have a minute to spare, a short review on the website where you bought the book is greatly appreciated. Not only does it help promote the *Mountaingirl Mysteries* series, but it also helps guide the future adventures of Rachel, Bella, and Avi.

For updates, newsletters, previews, and other information, visit www.mountaingirlmysteries.com and the *Mountaingirl Mysteries* Facebook page. And don't forget to sign up for our newsletter (via the website)!

ACKNOWLEDGMENTS

I am deeply thankful to the following people, without whom I would not have been able to write this book:

My parents, Carol and Terry, who instilled a love of nature in me from early on, not only from the beautiful ranch they built for us to grow up on, but also by introducing me to Lake Tahoe when I was six months old. I think a part of me has remained in Tahoe ever since. (Honestly, I can't leave; I tried a couple of times, but I always come back.) And as always, they reviewed the first draft of the manuscript and gave the go-ahead, along with several suggestions; any faults with the book are probably due to the ones I didn't heed.

My sister, Shelley Whittaker, who has been one of my most supportive fans as well as unofficial Northern California book promoter. And she still always makes sure to have a bottle of Bonterra when we get together.

My aunt Linda, who once again took the time to review the first draft of this manuscript and contribute valuable insights, including sage advice to tone down certain, er, political aspects.

Jared Manninen, a great friend and an amazing artist, author, hiker, and cross-country skier extraordinaire, who reviewed yet another *MgM* manuscript and who is always happy to help with lessons in "Social Media 101."

The talented authors of the Tahoe Writers Works for their support, wisdom, feedback, and patience with my "binge submissions" every year or two.

Mary Cook, who performed yet another round of excellent copyediting and proofreading, and who always goes above and beyond to fit me in.

My friends, who have stood by me through life's ups and downs, who make my world so much better, and who don't hold my reclusive phases (i.e. writing, editing, and publishing) against me.

My readers. Thank you for reading my books and encouraging me to keep writing. It takes a while to make it all happen (especially given the whole "day job" thing), and I appreciate your patience and understanding.

And last but never least, Bella and Avi, avid hikers, peak baggers, snow lovers, unofficial therapy dogs, and constant sources of love and positive energy.

AUTHOR'S NOTES

The first draft of *Sierra Nevada Burning Revenge* was written prior to the fall of 2018. Some of the plotlines may not stray far from actual events that have since occurred. When those are good things, I'm happy to take credit; otherwise, consider it a reflection of current trends in our world events. Most of all, I hope this book was fun to read, but I certainly won't mind if it also helps to raise awareness about some important environmental and social issues we are now facing. I thank everyone who continues to fight the good fight.

On a lighter note, I think it's time to call out the elephant in the room: yes, grammatically speaking, "mountaingirl" should be two words. This has created some confusion over the years, so to set the record straight, it's not a failure of editing or adherence to proper grammar. I take all the blame; I chose to combine the words because mountaingirl is the nickname Luke gave Rachel in the first book in the series, *Sierra Nevada Trail of Murder,* and for some reason, I liked it that way. Call me a rebel.

Finally, I leave you with my usual message about our beloved four-legged friends. For those who are looking for the amazing companionship a dog can provide, I encourage you to do some research into breed characteristics with your lifestyle in mind. After that, if you decide to add a dog to your family, first consider adoption/rescue. It won't be long before you find yourself asking exactly who rescued whom.

ABOUT THE AUTHOR

Jennifer holds a master's degree in environmental science and health and has spent over twenty years advocating for scientifically supported policy making to protect Lake Tahoe's environment and rural communities. She also makes a point to spend regular time hiking with her dogs, Bella and Avi, refreshed by the beauty of the Sierra Nevada and the joy of being outdoors.

Jennifer's creative side emerged when she adopted Bella and became inspired by the dog's antics. The *Mountaingirl Mysteries* series is a result of regular time outdoors; years of hard work in environmental science, planning, and politics; and two dogs named Bella and Avi.

Raised on a small ranch in Northern California, Jennifer's childhood revolved around an outdoor lifestyle with weekends and summers spent in the mountains. Jennifer loves all that the Sierra Nevada has to offer, although she is most fond of hiking, snowshoeing, and downhill skiing, and is typically accompanied by Bella and Avi—the true stars of her books.

www.ingramcontent.com/pod-product-compliance
Lightning Source LLC
Chambersburg PA
CBHW060950120726
47910CB00002B/569